RAVEN'S
RISK

ROBERT F. LACKEY

Heron Oaks, Murrells Inlet, SC

Copyright © 2017 Robert F. Lackey

ISBN: 0692831320

ISBN-13:978-0692831328

Other Pulaski Saga books by Robert F. Lackey:

Pulaski's Canal

Blood on the Chesapeake

Kingdoms in the Marsh

Brazen Deceit

Serpent's Compromise

Despot's Heel

DEDICATION

This book is dedicated to the amazing
Perry Baldwin Stewart,
horse master and house master,
the real life descendant of Mamie Stewart,
and who served as the spirit for that character.

-   *Robert F. Lackey*

ACKNOWLEDGEMENTS

No book can make its way to print without the hard work of many people.

I wish to acknowledge the valuable assistance of stalwart beta readers and thank each of them for their contributions.

Judee Cooper of Edgewood, Maryland

Angela Corrieri of Columbia, Maryland

Linda Cross of Avenue Maryland

Lori English of Las Cruces, New Mexico,

Lorie Joy of Chaptico, Maryland

Sandi Lackey of Murrells Inlet, South Carolina

Diane Bassette Nelson of Interlaken, New York

Peggy O'Donnell of Port Republic, Maryland

Gordon Plugge of Yulee, Florida

Buddy Quade of Columbia, Maryland

Marian Stokel of Leonardtown, Maryland

Nancy Testerman of Havre de Grace, Maryland

Mike Webb of Newport News, Virginia,

who aided significantly in finalizing this manuscript.

FURTHER ACKNOWLEDGEMENTS

I offer my appreciation and recognition for the wonderful generosity of

The Susquehanna Museum at the Lock House, Havre de Grace, Maryland

The Havre de Grace Maritime Museum, Havre de Grace, Maryland

The Chesapeake Bay Maritime Museum and the St. Michaels Museum, St. Michaels, Maryland

Captain Jordan Smith and the crew of the Pride of Baltimore II, Baltimore, Maryland for sail and Atlantic Ocean sailing advice.

Mr. Robert McAlister, Director of the South Carolina Maritime Museum, Georgetown, South Carolina for historical information regarding shipping and harbor protocols in 19th century Georgetown, SC, and sailing conditions in an around Winyah Bay.

Mr. John M. Barber, Famed Chesapeake Bay artist for his generosity in permitting his painting "Winter in Annapolis" to be used as the foundation for this book's cover art.

And that exquisite gem at the head of the Chesapeake Bay:

Havre de Grace

ROBERT F. LACKEY

1

August 10th, 1843. Spesutie Island , Maryland

Ben Pulaski fingered away cascading sweat from his brow as he stood up, examining the area of deck he had been scrubbing on his hands and knees. He flexed the ache in his shoulders, twisting from side to side under an angry sun. His weathered face peeked from behind his beard, at odds with his pale chest and upper arms. A meandering scar ran down on his lower back, still stiff and ugly after three years, still fighting against his movements.

The oppressive air at the peak of summer lay heavy and humid, sporadically pushed aside by timid Chesapeake Bay breezes. Even the muskrats in the marsh would raise their noses into the brief respite from the heat. The unrelenting chorus from the cicadas among the nearby trees pierced the air like something perpetually dying, but without relief. The schooner *Raven* lingered in Spesutie Narrows, five miles south of Havre de Grace. The location had been chosen by a madman as a hiding place for the *Raven*, while her holds were filled with kidnapped men and women of color, fresh property to be devoured by plantations of the deep south.

The surviving pirates were arrested after a bloody confrontation with deputized men. The victims were released, but with the captain dead, ownership of the *Raven* was lost in a rabbit warren of false and missing documents. It was complicated further by Ben's claim of salvage, still under tedious review by the Maritime Board in Annapolis.

Who did I kill here? he asked himself.

In the weeks since the fight to take the schooner, he had forced himself to learn the names of the men he had murdered in that pre-dawn fog, before the deputies attacked. It was his penitence for killing again, even after his promise to God that he would not. They had stood ready to hack him down, expecting him to arrive at daylight to claim his captive wife, Sonja, held by a man rabid with hatred for Ben.

Ben smiled at her now in the sunshine as she emptied a wash bucket over the other side of the ship. Her hair cascaded golden yellow curls in the vaporous air and her face was apple-flushed with life in the heat of the upper Bay. Her eyes crinkled at the corners as she smiled, but the once soft blue had been tainted with the touches of steel that warriors carry. She returned to the stairway and down toward the captain's cabin. She stopped with her head still above the deck.

"Aaron should come today, if there is wind," she said, then continued her steps.

"Yes," Ben said to the top of her head. "If there is wind."

Then he returned his gaze to the stains on the deck.

Johnson? No, I killed him below in the cabin. Frenchie? Yes, the one they called Frenchie fell here.

Ben looked farther along the deck, between the tandem wheels, where two other large stains merged together. Other pools of blood from bodies sliced open in the darkness, like fresh pigs.

"Ya can't get it all, Benjamin," Adam Tuttle said, placing a wrinkled hand on Ben's shoulder. "Ya can't scrub it from these decks, or your mind, or your memory."

Ben rested his hands on his hips. "If we get salvage rights to this ship, I may well spend years on her decks. I want to have more to look at than marks where I killed men."

"All you're doin is making the rest of the wood pristine, and makin those stains standout even more."

2

Adam lifted his cap above the wreath of bushy white hair to scratch his bald head and then spit tobacco juice onto the freshly cleaned wood. He received a fierce glare from Ben, but chuckled at him in spite of the stare.

"Let nature do its job, Benjamin. Let this deck become sprinkled with fish guts, and tar and seagull shit, like God intended. No self-respecting work boat is going to stay perfectly clean. It ain't natural."

Ben continued to glare into Adam's face, looking for a hint of weakness that he might pressure, but there was none to be found. Adam gave him a broad smile that dissolved Ben's anger at this old man he had known since childhood. Ben sighed and shook his head in surrender, returning Adam's smile and slapping him gently on his arm.

"Let's stretch sails over the cabin and the crew quarters. It'll give us shady places to sit, and keep enough sun off the deck to hold away some of the heat from our sleeping quarters."

-----<>-----

August 15th. Oyster Street, Havre de Grace, Maryland.

Sam Briscoe's face came close, his nose almost touching, his sneer proud.

Herbert Binterfield, President and owner of The Tidewater Bank and Trust Company, stood up straight. "How dare you..."

Briscoe shoved the blade into him with all his strength. He reached his left arm around Binterfield and pulled his body into the blade. Binterfield's eyes widened as their chests pressed against one another. Briscoe could smell the brassy fear in his breath. The knife blade, sharpened for hours on the smooth stone in Briscoe's rented room, slid easily through the fabric of the coat, vest, and cotton shirt. The blade tip ran through the skin and fat. It dove through and beyond the stomach, opening the aorta and then sinking its tip into Binterfield's spine. Binterfield tried to scream. Briscoe leaned him over like a ballet dancer laying out his partner, and placed him gently on top of Binterfield's desk. He cupped his left hand around

3

Binterfield's throat, squeezing it shut, not enough to kill, just enough to stop the scream.

Binterfield tried to speak. His eyes twisted frantically as he grabbed for the center desk drawer under him. He clawed at the drawer handle, angry fingers curling in a frenzy to open it, to save himself. He was still unaware that his wound was fatal. The reworked corner of the drawer was empty, the derringer gone from its place.

Briscoe laughed in a whisper. He angled the blade tip higher up within Binterfield's abdomen. He sliced in and out, cutting his way toward the chest within the torrent of warm blood. "It's in my pocket," he said. "I've wanted to do this since the first day I started working for you."

Binterfield lay helpless on the desk, his eyes wide open, paralyzed by the pain, but still alive. Briscoe straightened and twisted his shoulders to ease the muscle tension in his back. He drew in a deep breath.

He yanked open the vest and shirt of the dying man, loosened and pulled down the trousers just enough to present his canvas. He continued his bloody carving up the abdomen to the lower edge of the sternum, steering the blade back and forth through the surface skin. The lightning bolt design was the best he had ever done. He had much better light to work under, and a good tabletop surface. No need to kneel in the mud, glancing over his shoulder and rush through the work. He could take his time and do it right.

"Practice makes perfect," he whispered.

When he was satisfied with his design, he smiled and patted Binterfield's cheek with bloody fingers. He wanted to see that Binterfield was still alive, watching him. Then he jammed Ben Pulaski's knife into Binterfield's heart.

"Here's a conundrum for you, Pulaski," he mumbled to himself.

Outside, he washed his hands in the horse trough behind the bank and casually walked to his boarding house, humming to himself.

The next morning, Deputy Lyle Mattingly stood beside the big mahogany desk examining Binterfield's body.

Morning sunshine streamed in through the large front windows overlooking the boardwalk along Oyster Street. The distraught bank clerk had returned to his stall at the front of the bank. He looked over ledgers that no one would ask for today, doing whatever he could to remain away from the back office. Dark blood pooled on the plank floor around the desk, crusting over in the shadows, but still sloughed off the edge of the desktop in elongated tears. Mattingly took keen interest in the scrimshaw knife handle standing up from the blade impaled in the body.

"I know that knife," he said to himself.

Later that day, he rowed out to Spesutie Island, once again retracing his five-mile route from Havre de Grace across the tepid Susquehanna flats.

He thought as he rowed. *How many more times will I have to row to that damned schooner? Ben Pulaski and his wife, still holding vigil on that...slave ship. Damned Pulaskis. Hoping* the *Maritime Board will let* them *call it salvage. Been months now.*

He stood in his usual spot on marshland, looking across the short span of dark water to the stern of the *Raven* above him. She was still nestled in the rare deep channel behind the trees of the island, perfect for hiding. In the humid August air, the scent of the slave schooner wrinkled his nose. He called out for Ben Pulaski, then told him that Herbert Binterfield had been murdered.

"Can't say I'm either surprised or disappointed, Lyle," Ben said.

"Didn't expect it to be otherwise. Ben, you got proof you were on board all last night?"

Sonja and Adam came to the stern, so Mattingly could see them on deck.

"We were here together all night," Ben said.

"Can you tell me where your ivory handled knife is?" *The same one I took from you a year ago? When you stood in front of his bank and threatened to kill Binterfield?*

"I think I lost it during the fight with Hoagg's people, when we took this ship. I can remember handing it to Sam Briscoe, to cut himself loose when I found him tied to a

5

post in the hold, but then Hoagg made Sonja scream up on deck...I...I don't know what happened to it, Lyle. Honestly, I haven't given it a thought until you just mentioned it."

Mattingly exhaled, pulled out a small notebook and pencil. "It's an awfully pretty knife, Ben. Looked expensive, and you just forgot about it?"

Ben looked toward Sonja. "I had other things to worry about."

Sonja smiled at Ben and placed her hand on his.

"Did you find it, Lyle?" Ben asked.

"Yep. Shoved into Herbert Binterfield's heart," Lyle said without looking up.

"Well, I didn't put it there, Lyle."

"What about your black, Simon? You seen him since the fight, Ben?"

Ben shook his head no.

Mattingly made another brief entry in his note book.

"He still needs to hang for killing Hoagg. You understand that, don't you?"

"Hoagg was already dying, Lyle. All of us were trying to kill him when we attacked this ship, including you!"

"We didn't attack this ship, so you could claim it, Pulaski! Hoagg and his crew had kidnapped free people – including your wife! You forget that?"

"No Lyle. It couldn't have been done without you and the other deputies. But, Simon only finished a man that was dying anyway..."

"He was dying 'cause your boy already cut his hand off!" Mattingly put his hands on his hips. "Then he chopped the man's head off right there in front of half the white men from Havre de Grace! Can't have a slave killing a white man, Ben."

"Simon isn't a slave, Lyle. He's got papers. He worked with me for pay and you know that!"

"Don't make no difference, Ben. Hoagg was a white man."

Mattingly blew the air out of his chest and made another scribble in his notebook. Then he walked away, waving over his shoulder with one finger as he left.

"Good riddance to Binterfield and Hoagg," Sonja said toward Mattingly's back, watching him go. "Both were pirates, just Binterfield plied his thievery from his bank."

---<>---

August 18th.

Lydia Binterfield sat in the front pew listening to the pastor drone on about Herbert's immortal soul and his place in heaven with the Lord.

If Herbert had a soul, it is in Hell serving his master.

She had waited in the side alcove fifteen minutes, delaying the service, waiting for the church to gather more mourners, but still some pews were noticeably empty. She gave the pastor a curt nod as she moved to the front row. Sam Briscoe sat close in the second row, but not too close. She would not look at him now.

His cow eyes adore me, but I won't allow that display today. Won't recognize it. Not yet. Let him lay alone in his rented room a few more weeks. This damned veil feels like flies on my face. I can't wait to be shed of it!

"...Amen." The pastor nodded to Lydia to lead the funeral procession out to the waiting surreys. Alone, she walked slowly toward the door, giving the people behind her time to bunch up a little; to look more like a little crowd. She stopped on the second step coming out, forcing them to file around her, nodding royally at each one with a tilted glance.

"Thank you...you're so sweet...he would be glad you were here...Yes, he thought fondly of you as well...thank you...thank you..."

All the people who owed him money, kissing his ass, and beaming in his presence. What does my husband get now? No, what do I get? The dregs of the church and the debtors who still believe he had a shred of decency.

A last set of pitiful eyes presented in front of her face. Nadja Lister, wife of the undertaker, curtsied low mumbling condolences. Lydia ignored her and turned away.

At the grave site, another traditional ceremony. Black wool baking sweating bodies under a hateful August sun, wrapped in oppressive Maryland humidity that made breathing like inhaling water. More handkerchiefs floated across beaded brows than teary eyes. It was all an obligation. The Pastor called those in attendance, "Herbert's friends"

Lydia closed her eyes.

The closest Herbert ever had to a friend was Sam Briscoe, his business manager that he verbally abused, the man who bedded me when Herbert was distracted and the man who killed him.

Lydia brought her silk handkerchief up to her mouth to hide her smile, enjoying the memory of Sam laying with her in bed, telling her what he did. She had pushed him for all the gory details, while straddling him in a sweaty frenzy.

"...Amen," at last uttered. Meaningless hugs and fleeting butterfly kisses, the mourners had fulfilled their duty and escaped to their carriages. The pastor barely touched her hand as he shook it and wished her well.

Herbert held your mortgage, Pastor. You wouldn't dare do anything else. I need a God damned drink.

Sam Briscoe acquired her attention, took a step in her direction. She turned her back and quickly stepped to her enclosed carriage, ordering the driver to trot.

As soon as Lydia entered the mansion, she summoned her house slaves.

"Junie, I want you and Sissy to go upstairs right this minute and remove everything from Mr. Binterfield's room."

"Ever'thing, Miz Binterfield?"

"Everything but the damn furniture – and that new chamber pot, keep that up there too. Everything else comes down. Three piles in the drawing room: Clothes, bedclothes, and personal items" She paused and put her hands on her hips. "And take the guns to my room as soon as you find them. I'll have that damned boot pistol he coveted, even if I keep it at the bottom of my chamber pot!"

Lydia stormed into the music room, unlocked the

liquor cabinet and threw open the doors. Herbert had a unique etched whiskey glass, displaying the intertwined initials 'HB'. She yanked down the monogrammed glass and a decanter of his favorite brandy, then splashed some of the liquor into the bottom of Herbert's glass. She stood before the ornate fireplace and gulped down the brandy. She examined the glass in her hand for a brief moment, letting the split prism colors sweep across her violet eyes, then smashed it into the firebricks.

"You need me back down there, Miz Binterfield," Junie yelled, her voice echoing in the oval main staircase.

"Do what I told you, God damn it," Lydia yelled.

She picked up another glass. One of a dozen she had bought in Philadelphia.

You always complained that these were far too expensive.

She chuckled as she filled the glass with brandy, then carried it to the staircase, walking the fingers of her other hand daintily along the crest of the mahogany railing as she ascended the steps.

That's why I bought them!

Alone in her room at the far end of the second floor, she removed her heavy black dress and dropped it in the middle of the floor. She removed everything.

"Keep that chamber pot in there," she yelled through the door. She ignored the muffled responses. Knew they heard her at the other end of the hall.

That chamber pot replaced the one that woman smashed the day she quit. One of many results from Herbert having Sonja Pulaski in this house, so he could drool over her. The widow Pulaski, so valiantly paying her debts.

She examined her body in the full length mirror.

"We never needed another maid! I hope you managed to visit her thighs, Herbert. You sure as hell abandoned mine," she said to her reflection.

She pressed her fingertips softly into the fist size bruises covering her abdomen and breasts. The most recent were still sickly yellow borders with centers almost black, like grotesque Black-eyed Susans. Others, were fading with time.

"What did you do to him that day at the bank, Sonja? What did you do to turn my mouse into a monster? He never raised a hand to me before that. He never stopped afterwards. What did you do?"

She sighed and slipped a bright red silk shift over her body, then took another deep drink of brandy. She placed the glass next to her wig mannequins and sat down at her dressing table, removing her wig in front of the mirror. The hair of the wig was still shiny black and soft, like it had been on the Chinese child who had her head shaved so her family could eat.

Lydia examined herself in the mirror. The long neck was artistic and free of blemish or wrinkle, even without the usual border of cascading black curls. The skin of her face was still youthful, the color of almond slices.

Appealing to a younger suitor, perhaps?

Her lips only slightly full, inviting. She turned her head to see herself from the corner of her eye. Her nose, not too long, flared just enough at the nostrils to make her look exotic, but not so much as to suggest a lineage.

Greek, or of Spanish descent, one could reasonably say...

Lydia picked up a coarse hair brush, the back plated in silver and adorned with her own initials. She tugged the bristles through the reddish brown nap that covered her head and relished the feel of cool air bathing her scalp.

What did you do, Sonja Pulaski?

She stopped moving her hands. Looked into her own violet eyes and smiled.

I have something for you, Sonja. What you did no longer matters. What matters from now on, is what I will do.

---<>---

October 19th.

Sam Briscoe entered the Tidewater Bank and Trust at exactly nine o'clock, acknowledging the 'good mornings' offered up by his two new clerks, Fields and Hannah. He gave them each a hearty smile, after enjoying his usual full breakfast at the tavern across the street.

He preferred a business atmosphere, and he believed using given names encouraged over familiarity. He also insisted they address him as Mr. Briscoe, and that was settled. When Sam was in control, things were settled.

The previous clerks, who had tolerated Binterfield, had been too willing to speak ill of him after his death. Sam could not trust them. They knew too many details, more than they realized, details that someone might put together in an uncomfortable sequence. He released them right after Herbert's funeral, but with a finesse Herbert lacked. Sam had urged them to find new employment 'away from the nightmare' they discovered August 16th. He wrote warm letters of recommendation for them and paid each a generous full month's salary in departure.

The engraved name block on his desk announced "General Manager", under his name. The massive oak desk was darker now. Some of the blood had worked its way into the grain of the wood, so he ordered it re-stained with the darkest mahogany oil. One of the previous clerks had suggested he have it replaced, but Sam would not consider it. He pulled out his new leather covered rolling chair and settled into it, gently patting the top of the desk and smiling at the memory.

He withdrew the document from his desk drawer where he had placed it the evening before. He read it again, but the written words had not changed, and he sighed. Lydia was the owner. Herbert had constructed his corporation such that even investors had no claim on its ownership, only its profits, and those were narrowly defined. Lydia was well educated and astute with legal matters. She had ensured Herbert's will allowed no distribution of his estate, and named her as the sole beneficiary. Sam was still only a figurehead, but figurehead to a beautiful woman who made his sexual dreams come true. His income, his position, his prestige all depended upon her good will. He would not argue with her on this matter. She directed the business of the bank from her parlor as completely as any chairman of any board.

"Sell the property in Lapidum," Lydia had ordered him. Known as the Pulaski farm, it was owned by the bank, and only rented by the Pulaskis. It was originally a two-room cabin, with large bedrooms added to each side later, and that followed by a generous front porch. The house commanded a beautiful view between two massive oak trees of the Susquehanna and Tidewater Canal and the Susquehanna River beyond the towpath of the canal. There was a gentle grassy slope from the steps of the front porch down to the bank of the canal. Ben's son Isaac had built a little two-plank wharf on the bank in front of their home, where the *Ugly Boat* would tie up when Ben came home. Herbert Binterfield bought the place from the absentee owner, only out of his hate for Ben, so he could raise the rent. Herbert sent Sam to inform the Pulaskis of the purchase and the significant increase of their rent, hoping they would default.

The document on Sam's desk directed him to place the Lapidum property up for sale at the asking price of one hundred thousand dollars, two hundred times the actual value, to ensure the Pulaskis inability to buy it for themselves. Sam knew the property would never be sold at the price, but the fact that it was being sold provided easy justification for the owner to evict the renters. Sam didn't really care about the impact on the Pulaskis, but the action was more typical of Herbert Binterfield.

There are other ways to settle this, Lydia. There are better ways to put Ben and Sonja Pulaski into their places. Ways that won't tarnish our reputations.

Sam placed the document with the others in the packet going to the lawyer in Bel Air. Maybe he could convince Lydia to use another approach while they waited on the lawyer to review the various papers going out that day.

Maybe.

It was not the way he preferred to settle the matter.

---<>---

November 8th.

Ben Pulaski stood between the dual wheels of the *Raven*, watching the sunrise paint golden light on the few

12

yellow and red leaves still hanging in the trees lining Spesutie Narrows. The empty masts and booms of the *Raven* matched the bare limbs of the trees. The *Raven's* anchors lay dead in the mud, undisturbed where they were dropped last April. Her shiny black hull now dulled by dust, ringed with a thin line of mud and haloed with floating debris.

November, and still no ice on the *Chesapeake Bay.*

The soft blue sky was lined with a fine strands of clouds and filled with seagulls diving for fish. After a long lazy drift from summer, autumn had finally yielded to her obligation and settled herself fully in residence with crisp cool air. The chill resurrected fond memories of thick wool shirts and sweaters. Sonja came up on deck toward Ben, wearing her favorite wool shawl, retrieved during her last trip to their home in Lapidum. Her gaze shifted from her husband to the southern tip of the island. A smile blossomed on her face. She pointed a finger toward the Bay.

The *Ugly Boat*, Ben's converted canal barge piloted by his son Aaron, sailed into the Narrows toward them with stiff sails shoved hard by a brisk northerly wind. Yelling and screaming, and the sound of banging pots bolted across the narrowing distance between the *Ugly Boat* and the *Raven*. Sonja and Ben dashed to the bow. The *Ugly Boat* was travelling far faster than she should be.

"Good God," Ben shouted. Then louder at the oncoming boat. "Veer away, God damn it! You're going to ram us!"

Red faces yelled in chorus at them from the deck of the *Ugly Boat,* frosty clouds rising from their mouths as they shouted. Adam Tuttle held up a rum bottle and shrilled like a savage, his face ruddy within the snow white frame of his hair and beard. Aaron waved wildly from the stern, his cheeks red and his ink black hair in windy disarray. He was standing barefoot on the storage box at the stern, one foot was resting on the tiller and steering with his toes. He too, had a bottle in his hand.

Ben shook his fist at the oncoming boat. "What the – veer off, I tell you!"

He turned toward Sonja. "They are going to ram us!"

Then he pushed Sonja away from the bow, knocking her off her feet and plopping her down in a painful thump onto the deck.

"Damn it, Ben!"

At the last possible moment, Aaron shouted "Jeremy!", and pushed the tiller hard to the right. The boat slid across in front of the *Raven* and over the shallows. The lee boards drifted above the muddy bottom, something a keel could never have done. Jeremy McMallery immediately released the bow anchor and dropped the sails, snugging the blunt bow of the *Ugly Boat* downward, almost to a perfect stop. The stern of the *Ugly Boat* swung against the *Raven* with a rude knock at the side ladder. Aaron launched himself from the boat onto the ladder and popped over the railing like a chattering red-faced frog, trading calls with Ben.

"They approved it, Pa!"

"The Maritime Court ruled?"

"Yes, Pa!"

Forrest McMallery, his son Jeremy, Adam Tuttle and Maggie Freidman scampered aboard behind Aaron and danced around Ben.

A smile spread across Ben's face. "They approved our claim, Aaron?"

"Yes!" he screamed

"Put your boots on, Aaron," Sonja yelled at him.

"How much? What percent are we allowed?" asked Ben

"All of it, Pa!"

"What? What percentage, Aaron? Did we get half?"

Sonja shoved into Ben, slapping his shoulder with both hands.

"You almost broke my tail bone, Benjamin!"

She continued to slap at Ben. He pushed her hands down as they came, ducking her swings, struggling to look back at Aaron.

"All of what, Aaron?"

"All of the ship, Pa. No one else claimed it! It's ours!"

Sonja stopped slapping and screamed the question. "It's ours?"

Ben pulled her close to him as the crowd from the *Ugly Boat* surged around them singing a jumble of different songs all at the same time.

"It's ours, Sonja," Ben said to her, reluctant to say the words. "This ship is ours."

She slapped him softly on his shoulder, and hugged him tightly. "It still stinks."

"The cargo won't mind," he said. "Not the cargo we will carry within her."

They hugged each other in the center of the jumping crowd. Sonja spoke into his chest.

"Can we go home now, Ben?"

"Yes. It is over at long last."

With a flurry of confused help, the merry mob scurried around the *Raven*, collecting all of the things Sonja had brought on board during their six month vigil.

Ben put his hands on his hips, surveying the growing pile on the deck. "This is going to take two trips, Sonja."

She stopped with another armload of sheets and blankets, her golden hair drifting down in front of her face.

She has to stay busy, Ben thought.

She blew the hair back up on her forehead and frowned at Ben. "Well, I don't want all this just dumped on the front slope of our house. I want it put up where it belongs."

Ben stared at her. *Hoagg had her. Tortured her. Just to bait me. All my fault.*

"You hear me?" she asked.

Ben forced a smile and nodded in agreement. "Yes, you're right. But, I think it means I need to stay on board and come back with the second load."

Sonja assumed command of the move, pulling Maggie to her side and directing the men and boys in moving her household.

"It will only last a couple weeks," Ben had said when he and Adam claimed the *Raven* as salvage. Over the weeks and months since Hoagg's death, more and more

15

was brought down from the Pulaski Farm in Lapidum.

Adam settled onto a chair pulled up from the captain's cabin below. His thin white hair free-floated around the sides of his head below his bald crown. His stubby pipe was a permanent fixture from his lower lip. "What the hell took the Maritime Board so long, Ben?"

Ben blew out his breath, glancing across the messy pile growing near the bow.

"According to lawyer Milton, the courts discovered a rat's nest of false documents pertaining to the *Raven*. It took them six months to identify its rightful owner, who was without family or known next of kin. Apparently Hoagg killed him, before they came here."

Adam released a small blue cloud of smoke around his pipe stem. "Just made himself captain, eh? Crew took to that?"

"Milton said he was already first mate. On a slaver, the crew is just interested in their share. They are hard to suffering."

"And now you own a slave ship, yourself. Still stinks, you know."

Ben folded his arms across his chest. "Not fully a slave ship, but Hoagg was converting her. Not only stinks in the cargo holds, but the idea of owning a slave ship stinks, too."

"'Cept you ain't gonna run slaves."

"No, Adam, I am not. And I won't run anything, if I don't start thinking about a crew."

"Well, you got yer carpenter sittin right here." Adam blew out a puff of smoke.

Aaron, Jeremy, and Jeremy's father, Mac, had most of the load settled safely on the *Ugly Boat* within an hour. Sonja stood at the squared off stern waving to Ben as the wind gently filled the sails and took her out onto the Chesapeake Bay. Moments later, Aaron shifted the tiller and sail boom to point the bow north.

Adam stood beside Ben, sipping from the rum bottle he had brought on board. Ben lifted it from Adam's grip and took a long drink.

16

"They not gonna be back before dark, Ben. Sonja won't let Aaron come out on the Bay at night."

"Aaron could do that as well as me, Adam."

"Ain't that, Ben. She's gonna have a chance to stuff him with a home cooked meal for the first time in half a year. No way in hell he's gonna want to or be able to get outta that."

"Is that why you stayed on board?"

"Oh, hell no, Ben. I just didn't want to help haul all that shit up the slope from the canal."

The sky was clear with no hint of rain. Ben and Adam pulled a canvas tarp over the rest of the pile of belongings and set weights at the corners.

Ben paced through the ship, paying new attention to her cargo storage details. The barriers at the bow and stern ends of the cargo hold still had to be opened. The central area had held almost fifty people crammed together. He removed a few loose manacles and chains, and threw them into the Narrows.

The slave platforms were partially gone. Only a pitiful eighteen inches from the boards they laid on to the next level of boards above their faces. Each slave placement was only two feet apart. Feces, urine and vomitus had simply run down the sluices into the bilge. Ben poured gallons of vinegar and water into the sluices and pumped it out into the Narrows, but still much of the odor remained. Ben returned to the deck for fresh air.

Adam noticed Ben leaning at the bow rail. "Coulda been worse down there, ya know. I think they only made a couple trips as a slaver, and a coastal schooner can't hold as many as the old Africa ships."

Ben shook his head. "That's like being in Hell and the devil telling you it's hotter at the other end."

With the smell of the holds flushed from his lungs, his stomach growled. There were still plenty of biscuits and fried bacon in the galley. He and Adam did not hesitate to eat more than their fill, chased with rum.

Later, Ben took pine boughs and cypress cuttings and placed them in the brick smoke pots he had set up in the cargo hold. As soon as the blazes arose from the waxy turpentine, Ben squelched them with of water. Smoke and steam churned within the cargo hold, driving Ben back up to the deck.

The evening breeze came cold but faint, and barely pushed the smoke back across the stern. Adam moved his chair to the bow and sat there smoking his pipe and patting his extended stomach.

Ben sat on a box near him. "You get enough supper?"

Adam shook his head. "A man ought'n ta let himself eat like that."

"It's a rare thing for us both, Adam. Still, it's hard to resist when just a couple people have access to supplies meant to feed a full crew of men and slaves for three months."

"Don't expect any of that bacon was meant for the folks in the hold," Adam said, speaking around the stem of his pipe.

They sat there in silence for a long while as the rest of the day settled below the western horizon. Adam set up a hammock on deck, preferring cold air under blankets to cypress smoke-steamed decks below. The need for sleep and the end of a long vigil finally sent Ben down to the large empty bed hanging from chains in the captain's cabin. He threw open the stern windows, appreciating the rarity in a schooner, and gave the room a general glance as he laid down.

I am the *captain of my own ship. My father would have been proud.*

---<>---

His legs were so heavy. The veins of his arms were filled with granite. He needed to move, but was paralyzed. He was hot. He was uncovered, and needed to remove his boots and shirt to be cool again, and to return to the call of sleep. He could not rise from its grasp. He rolled onto his side, his slumbering brain telling him to go back to sleep.

He should be cooler on his side, but he was not. More thoughts flashed through his head, sending him signals, like candles being lit far apart in a dark canyon. More and more candles were lit. His brain began to awaken. The smoke from his pipe burned his lungs, and he coughed, flipping his hand across his mouth to remove his pipe stem, but it was not there.

More candles were lit. The brightness was growing far too much. He was hotter than standing before the ship's furnace and he could not find his way back down to sleep.

He coughed and forced himself to sit up. Forced his eyes to open through the oily clumps that had entangled his lashes while he slept. He rubbed his eyes and coughed again. Looking through his matted eyelashes, still unable to open his eyes wide, the light was painfully bright.

He coughed again. His lungs burned, and he could not stop coughing. The heat was more than he could tolerate. He flung his legs off the bed, the heat on his face slapping his cheeks, loud cracking filled his hearing.

FIRE!

Ben stood and backed away from the fire. The forward wall of the cabin was engulfed in flames. He tried repeatedly to get to the doorway, to get up on deck, but the flames were too hot. They owned the wall and would not let him pass alive. He ran to the window to breathe in cleaner air, but very little fresh air could enter. Looking back into the room he saw the furniture in front of the door was already being consumed. Tongues of fire were licking up the forward wall. Frantically he searched around the room looking for something that could help, something that would tell him what he should do next. He stepped toward the door, but the heat was too painful. He threw his arms up in front of his face to shield his eyes from the fire. The cabinets on both sides of the room were showing flames from their interior. He was paralyzed with uncertainty. He forced himself to stand there, looking for an action to take, knew it must be him to do it, refusing to give ground, refusing to accept the reality.

Ben cursed the fire and threw whatever he could grab, but it only fed the fire. He had to step back. He could not advance to the doorway, to get on deck. Could not stand the heat anymore. He felt piercing heat on the top of his head and grabbed at the pain, pulling back a tuft of burning hair.

"God damn you to Hell," he raged at the fire as he backed toward the stern windows. His shirt began to smoke, the curtains on either side of him erupted into flames.

"Damn!"

He jumped through the stern windows, into the cold November water.

2

Ben splashed to the surface in the narrows, spitting water and yelling for Adam.

"Fire, Adam! Fire!"

He heard voices from the deck above as he clawed at the bank, the weeds brittle with frost. He pulled himself up and dashed barefoot to the gangplank. Up on deck there were two forms rushing in front of the flames, dumping buckets of water. Ben grabbed another bucket near the railing and dipped into the nearby fire barrel.

Ben yelled the question. "What the hell happened?"

Neither Adam nor the black man helping him responded while they dashed back and forth between the water barrel and the fire burning through the front of the raised roof to the captain's cabin. The fire seemed to be contained to that front cabin wall and the deck around the main mast. The water level in the fire barrel dropped low inside.

"Adam! Help me pick up the barrel. Let's dump it all at once on the fire!"

The other man bumped Ben's shoulder hard as he stepped in to grab the barrel on his own. In the firelight, Ben could see he was a broad shouldered black man.

"Who th-"

The man ignored Ben and dumped the barrel contents onto the fire. The hissing arising from the charred wood told Ben they were gaining on the fire.

Ben pointed toward the bucket tied to a nearby railing. "Get more water !" Then he took the bucket he had filled from the barrel before they dumped it, and ran down the steps to the captain's doorway. Most of the flames in the cabin were out. He threw the water on the forward wall. Adam had dropped the ship's bucket overboard and filled it, then joined Ben in the cabin, throwing his water on the remaining flames in the bedding. The large black man dashed into the room and poured another bucket of water over the last flame.

They stood panting in the darkness. A few red coals of simmering wood remained as ruby highlights in the darkness. The big man thumped out ahead of them as Ben and Adam rushed back up on deck for more water. The last three buckets full turned out the red pinpoints and filled the cabin with steam and the smell of charred wood and burnt fabric. The moonlight grew in the cabin as their eyes adjusted after looking into the flames. Adam grabbed a cutlass from the wall and poked into the burnt areas looking for embers, but they were out.

Adam moved through the doorway into the little stairway. His body was little more than a lighter shade of charcoal moving through the doorway. "I need to look at the base of the main mast. Make sure nothing is burning down there."

"What the hell happened, Adam?"

Adam spoke over his shoulder as he left the cabin, the anger heavy in his voice. "Ask Him."

Ben turned to the large form standing next to him. "Who the hell are you?"

"Cephus, Cap'n. I thought nobody was on board."

Ben coughed and pushed the man ahead of him toward the doorway, then up the steps to the deck. Cold water dripped from Ben's clothes, and he was shivering. "What do you mean by that?"

"I's sorry. I didn't know you was on board." Fragile transparent clouds drifted in front of their faces as they spoke

"Sorry? Did you start that fire??"

Yellow light bloomed in the stairway below deck. Both Ben and Cephus moved toward it. Adam rose up from below carrying an oil lantern.

"The bracing for the mainmast is charred and might be alright, but the wrapping is burned almost all the way through, and the forward cabin wall is too damaged to take much stress."

"Can you fix it, Adam?"

"You need a shipwright and someplace that can shore up a mainmast while making repairs. Nobody in Havre de Grace can do that. Maybe St. Michaels."

"Shit," Ben muttered. A small puddle of water formed around his feet. He opened and closed his fists, the muscles in his forearm rippling in the lamp light. He turned back to Cephus in the lamplight "You started this fire?"

"They kilt my youngest son. Throwd his body into the shallows somewhere near here. Kept my oldest shackled down in the bottom of this boat."

"So you set fire to it?" Ben held his fists up in front of him.

Cephus bowed his head, a ring of curly gray hair surrounded his wrinkled crown marked by an old black scar running into the hair line.

"This is my ship," Ben growled. "I didn't do a God damned thing to you or your sons!

"Your ship? No suh, it be them pirates' ship. This here a slave ship!"

Adam came up next to him. "Cephus, you just about killed us! All the pirates are gone. Been gone for months."

Cephus wrung his hands in the moonlight, slowly shaking his head. "I didn't know you was here. I didn't know. I come here looking for my youngest son's bones. I see this ship in the moonlight and..."

"So you decided you should burn it?"

"It a evil thing, suh. Slave ship never smell good again."

"I know you, don't I?" Adam lit his pipe and pulled out a stool from the table he and Ben had shared at supper hours before. He let himself down slowly.

Ben looked closely into Cephus' face. "You took Toby, didn't you?"

"Yassuh. Simon run off and Hattie had her hands full with this old man here."

"That young boy has been passed around a lot since his Uncle Jedediah was killed. Sonja took to him when he stayed at our farm," Ben said. "Where did you leave him?"

"Hattie took him back in, while I look for my boy's bones."

Ben sighed. "Little Toby will be safe with her. You gonna try to burn my ship again?"

"No, suh."

Adam slid the other stool over to Cephus who eagerly accepted it.

Ben stayed on his feet, staring out toward the faint dawn light gathering at the horizon. His teeth were still clenched, and he exhaled heavily. "You find your son's bones?"

"No, suh. They cut his throat and throwd his body out yonder. Throwd him out like he was trash! Laughing cause they knowd the crabs eat him. Black folks in the hold heard'em."

Still barefoot, Ben went down into the captain's cabin, then farther down to inspect the base of the main mast. His curses echoed up through the stairway to the deck. He came back up, stopping again in the cabin to put on dry clothes and his boots. Then he pounded the steps as he came back up on deck.

"What do you do, Cephus? When you're not burning other people's ships?"

"I can do mos' anything."

"Who's your master?"

Cephus looked up into Ben's face in the growing light. "Just God a'mighty, Suh. Massah Smith manumis me in 18 and 18."

"You got people waiting on you at home?"

"Got nobody left there. Toby with Hattie. Sadie gone to her grave and my oldest son got hissef a wife up in Baltimore. Only me and Thomas fo' a while, but he out there somewhere, now." Cephus pointed with his chin out at the water.

Adam shared a glance with Ben, and raised his bushy white eyebrows. "We're gonna need help getting this thing

24

over to St. Michaels. Might as well."

Ben looked down at Cephus. "You ever raise a sail?"

Cephus gave a practiced eye along the length of the *Raven*. "Massah Smith had a schooner 'bout this size when I was younger. He had me working it for a couple years. I can't climb up those masts no mo, but I reckon I can do mos everthing else."

Ben turned over one of the empty water buckets and settled onto it in front of Cephus. "I'm going to work the *Raven* as a cargo ship. Real cargo. Not slaves. But before I can do that, to fix the damage you caused, we have to sail it down to Kent Narrows and then down the Miles River to St. Michaels..."

Ben looked up at the dawn sky. "Might as well stay up and have some breakfast," he said. He pointed a finger at Cephus. "You stay the hell away from the galley fire, Cephus, while I cook the bacon."

Cephus brought another stool up from below while Ben was cooking, and when the *Ugly Boat* drifted against the hull after sunrise, Adam, Ben and Cephus were sharing biscuits, bacon and coffee around the table.

Just after sunrise, Aaron, Mac, and his son Jeremy swarmed on board the *Raven,* heading for the pile of household goods waiting under the canvas on deck. They stopped in surprise when they spotted the charred cabin roof and forward wall.

"What happened, Pa," said Aaron.

Ben did not look up from his plate. "Cephus burnt the bacon."

"Who's Cephus?"

3

Ben waved to Aaron as the *Ugly Boat* rounded the point for its trip back to Lapidum. At last, all the items Sonja had brought down from the house for their long vigil were on their way. After the experience with Cephus, Ben was determined to stay aboard until the *Raven* was in a ship yard in St. Michaels.

Adam trudged up the deck from the crew cabin at the bow.

Ben nodded to him as he came forward. "You all settled in, Adam?"

"Yeah, Ben. We have plenty of room down there. That cabin can sleep six."

"Are you still agreeable to sleeping in there with Cephus?"

"Long as he doesn't snore louder than me, we'll get along."

Ben scratched his head and twisted his shoulders around, working the tension from his muscles. "I wrapped some more rope around the base of the mainmast and the strut in front of it, but I don't think we should put any sail on it."

Adam puffed on his pipe and squinted up at the main mast rigging. "I think that's wise, Ben. We ought to get by with sails just on the foremast ." He sat down on a stool near the table still sitting up on deck. "No reason to wrap a mast on a schooner. It's stepped into the keel board. They musta sprung it comin back up from Charleston last spring."

26

Adam pointed his pipe at Ben. "Told you I crewed for your daddy, remember?"

"Yeah, I remember you told me," Ben said.

"But you don't remember, do you?" Adam smiled, waiting for Ben to think.

"I said I remembered you telling me that..."

"But you don't remember me. It still ain't come to you. Course I had a thick head of brown hair then. And a set of forearms that could crush a whiskey barrel. And a tongue that could call up the devil himself."

Ben stopped and looked closely at Adam.

"Your daddy told you to stay away from me, when you were on board." Adam said, still grinning at Ben.

Cephus looked from one man to the other.

Ben squinted at Adam, trying to imagine him as a young man, trying to call up memories of sailing on the *Osprey* with his father. Then he snapped his fingers, "You were 'Stormy'!" Ben walked around Adam, looking at him from different angles. "Stormy!" Ben slapped Adam's shoulders. "I can't believe I didn't see that. I used to think you were eight feet tall and made of iron!"

"And I thought you were the stupidest thing on two legs." Adam's cheeks turned red. "I was a lot straighter then, but I ain't gone to rot yet."

Ben clasped Adam's shoulders in joy, "Stormy...wait a minute," he said. "That was thirty years ago, and Stormy had to be in his mid twenties then."

"Hell, Ben," Adam chuckled, "I was only ten years older than you then and still only that now. Lost my top-notch and what's left on my head turned white, but I'm just fifty-three."

Cephus chuckled, "Well Adam, you and me the same age. You fit the British up here in the Bay, like I did in '13?"

Adam shook his head and pointed at Ben with his thumb. "Nah, his daddy took the *Osprey* and went to sea looking for them. We got caught up in new United States Navy and they sent us to a couple places before we got to New Orleans. We didn't see the Brits until '15."

"You was with Jackson at New Orleans?"

"Nah, I crewed the *Osprey* carrying gunpowder with

Ben's daddy, until we got run onto the rocks. Our crew got sent around where we were needed. But, Cap'n Pulaski was close by, and Ben there was right next to General Jackson."

"Really?"

"I was just a drummer boy, Cephus," Ben said.

Adam shook his head, "Not just that. When the British came, he had turned fifteen and picked up a musket. His daddy told me all about it on our way back to Maryland on a packet boat. Cap'n Pulaski said Jackson told him what he said to Ben on the day before the battle, 'By God, young'un, if I had a hundred like you, we'd just step out there and whip the Brits where they stand.' Your daddy was real proud of you Ben."

"He still around, your daddy?" asked Cephus.

Ben looked out at the water beyond the bow of the *Raven*. "No. I was in the Army a while and stayed down in Georgia and Florida during the Seminole Wars. A man gets caught up in his own life sometimes and all of a sudden he looks up and too many years have gone by."

"Happens to us all, Benjamin," Adam said.

Ben sighed. "I came back to Maryland in '25 ready to introduce my wife to him, but he had already died. Sonja and I stayed a couple days in Baltimore, but that woman he had married was eager for us to be gone. That's when we came up to Havre de Grace."

"We'll need a couple more hands to work this ship, Ben," Adam said.

Ben glanced up at the cloth pennant flapping at the top of the mast. "Winds have been blowing southward all morning. Bringing more cold air, but it'll make a good push down to St. Michaels."

Adam shook his head. "It won't do much. We'll be lucky to get more than two knots, maybe three, but I doubt it."

"We can set the night off Pooles Island, Cap'n," Cephus said as he crossed the deck to them.

Ben shook his head, "No. The water will be a little too busy to sit below the light house there. We can make farther than that this afternoon."

"No suh, Cap'n Ben," Cephus smiled as he spoke. "They a nice bay on the back side fo the night. Mosly slack water. We could up anchor at dawn, and make the run down to Kent Narrows befo sunset the next day."

"That makes good sense, Ben," Adam said, "Though I'd drop anchor down off Love Point tomorrow night, and make for Miles River that next day. We ain't gonna get farther than that at two knots. We're gonna be four days gettin to St. Michaels, assuming the wind holds."

"I don't know, Adam," Ben said. "We can get to Annapolis and back in three days with the *Ugly Boat*."

Adam shook his head no. "That's in a scow built barge 65 feet long and sitting four feet in the water, being pushed by the same amount of sail you're gonna have for a hundred and ten foot schooner drawing seven feet of water. The *Ugly Boat* would be twice as fast as what we got to work with."

Ben smiled at Adam and Cephus. "Gentlemen, I believe we have our course. Now if Mac and Jeremy can get back on board before the day is too far gone, we can set sail."

Well before noon, the *Ugly Boat* rounded the southern point of Spesutie Island and slipped against the bow of the *Raven*. Mac climbed aboard first, his muscular blacksmith arms propelling him up. As his red beard rose above the railing, he called out his messages.

"Ben, Aaron will come down to St. Michaels in four days to bring you back, since the *Raven* will have to stay there a while.."

Mac stepped onto the deck, then reached outside the railing to pull Jeremy up. Then Mac showed Ben a broad grin and reached outside the rail again.

"Got you another crewman, Ben."

Ben watched in curiosity as another person was yanked up onto the deck by Mac's strong arm. The new crewman almost flew over the railing as Mac yanked up. Canvas trousers, new boots, a new wool sweater, and handfuls of blonde hair escaping from under a wool watch cap, jumped on deck as the figure spun around.

"I'm through staying at home waiting on you to do something crazy, Benjamin Pulaski," Sonja said with a chuckle, her blue eyes sparkling and her hands planted firmly on her hips.

Ben stared at her for a long silent moment with no expression on his face. The twitch at the corner of his mouth was hidden behind his short black beard. "Yes, ma'am," he said, letting loose the weak hold he had on his smile.

Ben swept his arm toward Cephus, "This is Cephus."

As soon as hellos were exchanged, Mac offered a mock salute to Ben. "So what is your first order, Cap'n?"

"Now that we have enough people, we need to get rid of unnecessary weight. This is a cargo ship. I want to get rid of these damned cannon."

Mac looked around at the six deck cannon mounted on trollies. "Shame to waste them, Ben."

"Don't need'em," Ben said. "Don't need the weight."

"I agree," Adam said.

"Thank ye, Stormy," Ben said.

Adam frowned. "Nah, that name went away a long time ago. Adam's fine with me."

Sonja shared looks with Ben. "Stormy? And what happened to the cabin?? Was there a fire?"

"When I was a little boy on my father's schooner, Adam there was one of the crew. Said I was an angel of the sea..."

"Said you were the stupidest thing on two feet." Adam said.

"What about the fire?" Sonja asked.

"Tell you later," Ben said.

Ben and Cephus used the spar rig, already set up to off load their belongings, to raise each cannon off its trolley. As they were swung out over the narrows, the line was slipped and they splashed into the water. The lines were untied from the trolleys and they too were dumped overboard. Those were followed by two dozen cannon balls.

As the last trolley fell into the water, Ben announced,

"Well, we're a ton and a half lighter."

"So, what about the fire?" Sonja asked again

Cephus stepped close to Ben.

"I'll help you, Cap'n Ben, but I still ain't found my Thomas. You gots strong arms to help you git to St. Michaels. Can you trust me enough to come back by here?"

Ben tilted his head toward the stern.

"That your boat tied up at the stern?"

"Yes, suh."

"Don't you ever try to burn my ship again, hear?"

"No, suh."

Ben held out his hand. "I'm sorry you lost your son. I almost lost mine a while back. No man should know how that feels."

Cephus took Ben's hand. "I still gonna work off my damages, if you come back by."

Ben nodded. "There's a dead pine around the point that can be seen from the channel. Tie a rag on it if you want to come back on board. I'll look for it on my way back from St. Michaels ."

Cephus went down the gangplank and walked to his boat, while the little crew watched. Mac, Jeremy and Sonja traded questioning glances with Ben and Adam.

"Cephus set fire to the ship last night," Ben said.

"What??" came the chorus from Jeremy, Mac and Sonja.

"Hoagg's crew killed his youngest son and tossed the body in the shallows nearby," Ben said. "Cephus thought the ship was empty. So, he tried to burn it. Adam, Cephus and I put it out. Fire damaged the front wall of the captain's cabin. But, worse than that it burned the hemp rope wrapped around the base of the main mast."

"Masts on schooners don't get wrapped like that unless they're already damaged," Adam said. "That's why we gotta take this whore to St. Michaels."

"Cephus set fire to the ship?" Sonja asked. "And, then helped you put it out?"

"He didn't know anyone was on board. When he saw Adam, he started helping. When I got back on board, I

31

helped too."

"When you got back on board," Sonja said. "Where were you?"

"In the water."

"In the water?"

"Only way to get out of the cabin was to go through the windows. Same way you got out when Hoagg had you prisoner."

Sonja put her arms around Ben. "I never want to have to do that again."

Adam slipped his pocket watch back into his pocket. "Past eleven, Ben. We need to up anchor, if we're gonna make it to Pooles Island before dark," Adam said.

Mac and Jeremy cranked up the bow anchor and set the *Raven* to drift in the narrows. The current nudged her southward as Ben and Adam pulled up the foremast mainsail. With the boom at the bottom and the gaff at the top, holding the sail out into the mild wind, the bow slipped out of the narrows and moved toward the bay water. The triangular forward jib came out next, stretched between the bowsprit and the top of the mast then tied to the railing to balance the wind already pushing against the mainsail.

Using the wind and the push back of the keel, the magic that allowed sail boats to move even at angles to the wind, ushered the *Raven* away from Spesutie Island and into the Chesapeake Bay, heading south. Ben stood at the twin wheels, that made the *Raven* unique among schooners. She had wheels on both sides of the deck, one on each side of the Main Mast. The arrangement allowed the person steering the ship, to see around the low hanging sails no matter which way the wind filled them. Sonja joined him on the windward side, feeling the cold breeze on her face as it ran forward to push against the sails.

The wind pushed the short waves even faster than the *Raven*, so even as the ship sailed south, the waves ran up under her stern a little faster, causing the stern to raise gently and then slide back down, and the bow to move opposite the stern, creating a tail-first slow rocking motion known to sailors when on a 'following sea.' The motion was not disturbing and created a lulling sense to their travel toward Pooles Island.

As Adam had predicted, the travel was very slow, using only the forward sails on a two-masted ship. The sun was setting low over the western shore when the *Raven* found her way to the little bay on the eastern shore of the island. A fishing platform was already anchored there for the night, forcing Ben to come too close so he could then drop the forward anchor just beyond the platform. The lack of a sail in the stern made the maneuver awkward. The stern drifted closer to the fishing platform. Men on the platform yelled and cursed the sloppy schooner threatening them.

"Veer away, you damned fools! Your gonna sink us!"

The fishing platforms were barely above the water level. The compact cabins on them had their floors below the water level in sealed hulls, but the doors at platform level allowed too much water inside if the waves were high. Fishermen grabbed poles and pushed back against the hull of the *Raven*, while those on the schooner looked on helplessly. The stern quarter of the *Raven* drifted over one corner of the platform, driving some of it under water for a brief moment, to a torrent of profanities.

"Back off! Back off, God damn it!"

"Sorry friends," Adam yelled, "Our main mast is sprung. Only got forward sails?"

"No excuse! Ya had the whole Damned Bay to turn in! Back off or we'll fire at you!!"

Mac and Ben released the forward anchor of the *Raven*, and as soon as it bit into the bottom, the stern began to pivot out and away from the platform. One of the men on the platform pulled a rifle from one cabin and aimed it at the faces looking down from the *Raven*. He did not fire, but lowered the barrel and shook his fist at them as the stern drifted farther away from the platform.

The stern continued to swing to the south until the current pushed it parallel with the nearby shore. Adam dropped the stern anchor with the last of the light as darkness settled over the little shallow bay. The clear sky was replaced by clouds, pushed in by a slightly stronger and colder wind. Soon only the lights of the fishing platform and the ship lights showed reflecting off the gentle waves drifting toward the shore.

The surface of the little bay was relatively calm and allowed Ben and Sonja to start a fire in the brick and iron cook stove in the galley. The smell of fried meat soon drifted through the ship, joined by boiling potatoes, boiling coffee and ship's biscuits. The group shared the meal together in the crew's mess area in the open walkway between the masts on the lower deck. Mac found a keg of beer in the supply locker, and Jeremy found enough tankards for everyone in the storage cabinets of the crew's quarters.

Young Jeremy brought out a harmonica and played several tunes while the others shared rum. Adam leaned back in his chair and let his chin drift down onto his chest, oblivious to the continuing chatter.

"Are you going to be a blacksmith, like your father?" Sonja asked Jeremy when he had finished his last tune. Jeremy only shrugged his shoulders and glanced at his father.

"Lot of ironwork going to factories, these day, Mrs. Pulaski. Only reason I can help on this boat is because my work has faded. Not much coming in at Lapidum."

"Maybe it will get better," Sonja offered.

"I hear more people are moving to Lapidum. Mr. Friedman has bought into the hardware and is offering a lot of new things," said Ben

"Yeah, factory made tools," Mac said.

There was a solid bump to the ship. The deck canted slightly, but did not correct to level. Mac and Ben ran up on deck, Mac went to the lower side and Ben to the higher side to look down.

"Don't see anything," Mac said.

"Nothing here," Ben answered.

The ship lifted slightly with another wave, and then bumped again

"Hell fire," Adam yelled from the stairway onto the

deck. "We're running aground!"

Ben ran to the bow. The shore was barely visible in the starlight, a light line where the little beach rose out of the water.

"Looks about the same distance to the shore from the bow," he called out. "Adam, check the stern."

Seconds later, Adam called back. "We ain't drifting, Ben. Must be low tide, gettin us."

"Shit," Ben said.

"Ben, we still got a southerly breeze," Adam said. "If we bring up the bow anchor and lay the sails out on the landward side, it oughta swing the bow out inta deeper water."

"Mac, come help me raise the bow anchor," Ben yelled. "Adam, you and Jeremy raise the main sail. Sonja, you raise the jib."

Mac and Ben cranked the bow anchor off the bottom and it's chain was locked into place. As soon as the main sail rose up, Adam and Jeremy pushed the boom out away from the island as far as it would swing. Sonja had the jib sail pulled up to the top of the mast, and pulled the deck edge of the sail in the same direction as the boom. As the breeze filled both sails, the bow began to slowly drift out away from the shore. The movement gradually pulled the stern, pivoting it from the stern anchor until the bow was almost pointing directly away from the island. The length of the schooner brought the bow beyond the protection of the little cove, and a noticeable rocking motion set in.

A voice echoed over the water from the fishing platform, "Having trouble are ya?"

"Knew there was a sand bank at that spot," another voice called out.

"Kiss my ass," yelled another fisherman, and several voices laughed in the darkness.

As the ship rocked to the gentle waves, Sonja and Ben stepped into the captain's cabin. The smoked and singed bed clothes were piled in the corner, and clean cloth covered the bed. The cold breeze whispered outside the stern windows and along the canvas covering the burned openings in the cabin wall and roof, searching for a way to get in. The cold seeped in without the wind to push it, drifting invisibly down onto the deck and crawled across the cabin. The old quilt Sonja had brought back from their house in Lapidum was fortified by two heavy wool blankets over it. They pulled the covers up to their chins and rolled to face each other.

"I feel like I'm home, Sonja," Ben whispered.

"Being cold in a stinky ship feels like home to you?"

"No, not the ship. I mean us. For the first time since I came back from China, I feel like I'm home, with you."

"I hated you for a long time," she said

"I know..."

"No. You don't know. I mean, when you were dead. I hated you then, for leaving me. For leaving us."

He rubbed her shoulder and slipped his hand down to her waist, where it used to rest before he went away.

"This moment feels like before all that," Ben said.

"I can't go back there, Ben. Not in my feelings. Not yet."

Ben slipped his hand away from her, but she reached out and drew it back to her waist.

"I am at home with who we are now, Ben. You may feel the same inside when you sailed away in '38, but I cannot. You were gone for as long as you have been back."

"And I will stay..."

"Ben, I was your widow for two years. I mourned an infant daughter ripped from my arms. You never saw her. Never held her. I have loss you will never know."

They were silent, letting the ship rock them, drifting among their own memories.

"I am not the same person you left standing on the wharf in Havre de Grace. I wanted to die. I am harder. I am capable of killing."

Ben pulled her closer.

"I love you, Sonja. I always have."

"Then you have loved two women. This one shoved a pistol into a man's mouth and pulled the trigger, drove a glass shard into a man's neck and watched him bleed to death. This woman drove a marlin spike into a man's eye to get away from Hoagg. The woman you left behind died in the moldy basement recesses of the Binterfield mansion, alone and loathing herself."

"No. There are not two women, one left behind and a new one now. You are the woman I married, tempered into steel by what you endured, what you have had to do. Like me."

"No..."

"Sonja. You are the woman who threw herself off the *Raven* into the water with her hands tied. You are also the woman who bore two amazing sons and made stews from almost nothing while I hauled rocks to help build the canal..."

"I was the woman swept away by icy waters who let our infant daughter drown..."

"You were the woman who read from the Bible to us on Sunday nights..."

"No. Not anymore..."

"Yes. You are all those things, and I love you. If I could go back and never have left, I would, but..."

"But you can't..."

"No, Sonja. I cannot, but what I can do is ask you to share my life as you are."

She said nothing.

"Can you do that? Will you do that?"

"Yes."

"Then, I am home," he said.

They held each other close, letting themselves slip beyond borders and hesitations, merging in that place only lovers find.

It was late morning of the fourth day when the *Raven* edged to her anchorage, just outside the little harbor of St. Michaels. Ben and Adam stepped down into the schooner's rowboat that had followed behind them like a reluctant dog on a leash. They rowed across the mouth of the harbor to Navy Point, to find a shipwright who could heal the *Raven*.

4

It was late in the cool afternoon when the row boat returned to the *Raven*. The wide mouth of the Miles River offered a broad shallow bay and easy anchorage for the awkward schooner. Ben and Adam climbed on deck followed by a man with a heavy brown beard and deep set eyes. As the man settled on the deck, He stuffed his hands into a black wool sea coat, speckled with saw dust and frayed at the collar tips. His head twisted in all directions as he took in the specifics of the ship. Ben introduced the man to his crew.

"This is Robert Lambdin. He owns one of the shipyards in St. Michaels. He's going to..."

Before Ben could finish his introductions, Lambdin walked briskly to the stern passageway, slowing briefly as he passed the twin wheels, and muttering to himself. Ben and Adam followed him down. The hatch covers over the slave hold had been pulled back to allow in light, and freshen the air as much as it could be.

Lambdin stopped and turned on Ben.

"Didn't tell me you were a slaver." His eyes were kept in shadow of a pronounced brow and bushy eyebrows, all the more pronounced by his sudden frown.

"I'm not. We just took possession of her. Captain's dead. Crew's in jail."

"Ah. Heard about that. She the one hid in Spesutie Narrows kidnapping free blacks?"

"Yeah."

"You got papers showing you the owner?"

38

"Yes..."

Lambdin ignored the answer and continued his examination of the main mast wrappings, muttering to himself again. Then he examined the bracings, knocking timbers with a small wooden mallet he pulled from his coat pocket. He pointed the mallet at Adam.

"You'll do the cabin, right?"

"Yep."

"She's sprung, alright," Lambdin said to Ben. "You need a new one. If the previous captain and crew had tried to take her to Charleston this time of year, they would'na made it."

He looked keenly inside the slave hold, then stepped to the iron straps enclosing it at the stern, and turned back toward Ben.

"How come these are still up?"

"Just got word from the Maritime Board, and my papers, last week. The fire caused us to examine the hold and the mast."

"Good you had that fire."

"Well, I don't know..."

"Yep, you woulda drowned. You woulda filled her holds with shit and drove her hard in the winter wind. Profit is profit."

"Just like profit in a ship yard," Ben answered.

Lambdin chuckled. "That it is, Mr. Pulaski. That it is. You want these straps?"

Ben glanced at the iron straps and shook his head no. "I was going to drop them into the shallows like I did the chains and the cannon."

"You what??" Lambdin worked his mouth forming words that were left unuttered. "I can always use good iron, Mr. Pulaski. If my blacksmith don't have to make it, it comes cheaper to my shipyard." He muttered to himself again and folded his arms in front of his chest. "You let me have the iron straps... I'll remove these cages for you, and cut the cost of your new mast, which will not come cheap. And, if you retrieve the iron you threw overboard and bring it to me, I'll take even more off your bill."

Lambdin spun around and trotted up the steps to the

deck. He leaned back as he looked up at the rigging and then walked to the twin wheels, placing his fingers tenderly on the polished wood.

"Of course, you can have the iron straps, Mr. Lambdin. I'll be glad..."

"So your father was Lenz Pulaski?"

"Yes," Ben said

"Did you know the *Osprey* was built here in St. Michaels?"

"No, I didn't"

"My father, William Lambdin, had a ship yard here then. Couple years before he died. Don't remember anything about her. I was still in swaddling then. Just know the name."

Adam puffed on his pipe then asked, "You been here all your life?"

"Worked for John Graham as an apprentice. I was just a lumber monkey then, pulling down on ten foot saws, cutting planks."

Lambdin turned to face Adam. "What became of the *Osprey*? She'd have to be thirty years old by now."

"She broke up on the rocks just outside New Orleans in '15."

"You in the fight, there?"

"Both of us were," Adam said.

Lambdin walked away toward the railing, speaking over his shoulder,

"Alright, I'll do it. Gonna take a couple weeks to get a new mast. Needs ta be spruce. Better keep someone on board while she waits." He swung a leg over the railing and stopped, then pulled his foot back on the deck. "Better take a look in the cabin, anyway. Never seen twin wheels before. Better make sure nothing else is unique to this lady."

He skipped down the steps to the captain's cabin and was on his way back up as Ben took his first step down. They met face to face. Lambdin's smile was a fleeting flash and then gone.

"Nothing unexpected in there. We'll need to bring her

up against the dock to step the mast, but not before." Back on deck, he surveyed their anchorage and nodded to Ben.

"This is not a bad place to anchor, Mr. Pulaski. You're a hundred yards off Parrot Point and outta the main channel. I'd leave her here." Then he swung his leg over the rail again and climbed down into the row boat below.

Ben looked over at Sonja, standing with Mac and Jeremy, and smiled. Then he and Adam slipped over the rail down to the row boat.

As the three watched the rowboat make its way back to the dock, Sonja heard a conch shell horn blowing in the distance. Looking down the bay, she saw the main sail and jib above a boxed-end sailboat sitting high in the water, called the *Ugly Boat*. The conch horn sounded again and she waved her handkerchief so Aaron could see her.

Minutes later, the *Ugly Boat* kissed up against the *Raven*. Aaron and Maggie, chaperoned by Maggie's older brother Abraham, climbed aboard. Aaron had taken a full load of coal in the hull of the *Ugly Boat* as well as full loads in the *Turtle* and *Wilhelmina*.

"Coal prices are up again," he announced with excitement. "I took our whole 'fleet' to the coal market."

Sonja ran her fingers through his hair. "I'm so proud of you, Aaron."

"Me too," added Maggie.

Sonja touched Maggie's cheek gently and then turned to Aaron and Abraham. "When did you get back, Abraham? I thought you were in school in New York."

He shrugged his shoulders. "I don't think I can be a Rabbi, Mrs. Pulaski, and I missed home too much to stay any longer."

"And I'm glad he came home," Maggie said.

Aaron smiled and put his hand around Maggie's waist. As soon as he did, Abraham slapped his hand away, but not harshly. Abraham wagged a finger in Aaron's face.

"Just because I am not going to be a Rabbi, doesn't mean I am no longer a good older brother, Aaron Pulaski!"

Aaron and Abraham shared familiar chuckles.

"You had our 'whole fleet', did you, Admiral Pulaski?"

Sonja asked.

"Yes, Ma. It was like a duck with her duckling. The *Turtle* tied behind the *Ugly Boat* and the *Wilhelmina* tied on last. Luckily the wind was kind to us. That was a lot of weight to pull. I think we should add another mast like the *Raven*. I want to lash the other two barges side by side. Then I would only need one person on the tiller there and me on the tiller of the *Ugly Boat* in front..."

"Yes. Yes. Yes. Aaron," Abraham put in. "We heard it all a thousand times in the last two days!"

Mac playfully pulled on Maggie's auburn locks. "And where did you sleep last night, young lady?"

Abraham folded his arms. "She slept in the cabin by herself, as a young lady should. Me and my prisoner, slept in the forward hold like gentlemen."

"Were you cold, Maggie?" Jeremy asked. "It was like ice in the crew's quarters last night." Jeremy and Maggie were the same age, but Maggie had matured after the brutal loss of her Uncle.

"No. Aaron built a nice fire in the little iron stove."

Sonja snapped her fingers, "That's just what we need in the cabin here on the *Raven*!"

The new arrivals were still in animated conversations with Mac, Jeremy and Sonja as Ben and Adam climbed wearily over the rail and set their feet on the deck. The breeze that ushered the *Ugly Boat* so swiftly up to the *Raven* had fought Ben and Adam every inch of the way, rowing against it the quarter mile from the Mulberry Street dock out to their ship. Ben and Adam worked their shoulders in circular rotations, working the tension from their muscles and lower backs. Adam walked ahead to join the chattering group near the bow.

Ben lingered, watching Aaron and Sonja. In his mind's eyes, Aaron was still a little boy shedding tears as his father sailed away. He could not avoid the reality of his son now, with broad muscular shoulders, ruddy complexion, thick black hair and an infectious smile so like his mother's. Sonja too, was almost vibrating with joy and a smile so grand as he had not seen since the day she told him she was pregnant with their first born, Isaac. He stood there, captivated by her smile and her beauty ready to join her but not ready to let go of the picture he saw. He almost missed the expression on Aaron's face, who sent him a quick serious frown when no one else was looking.

There is trouble again.

Aaron stepped close to his father. "I have something to tell you, Pa..."

"Soon, Aaron," Ben said, putting his arm around his son's shoulders. "How are things on the canal?"

"As usual, Pa. The mules step the barges uphill through 29 locks to Wrightsville, cross to Columbia for coal, and then step downhill through 29 locks back to Havre de Grace. Day and a half up, day and a half down."

Ben yanked on his neck. "You know what I mean. How are the slave catchers behaving at the Line."

Aaron shrugged his shoulders. "Arrogant as always. Pushing across into Pennsylvania where they shouldn't be. Sometimes too pushy, but usually we have no trouble with them."

"Usually?"

Aaron exhaled and forced a smile, pulling them both toward the others. "Usually, but not always. Come on, Pa, I want to finish telling my latest story

Ben joined the group, listening to Aaron's tales of his most recent experiences in Wrightsville.

Rather than walk his mule along the platform built into the side of the covered bridge over to Columbia, a drunken canaller had decided to ride her. Half way across, the man passed out and fell into the river below, leaving his cantankerous mule alone and unwilling to be coaxed further by strangers. She tried to turn around and go back to the Wrightsville side, but there were a dozen mules in line behind her, each pulling their own barge. Others on the bridge finally had to cut the line to her barge, sending it drifting down the river after its drunken captain. Once the mule was freed, it jumped into the covered lane and ran braying through the streets of Columbia, finding new terrors at each corner.

Soon Ben was lost in the merriment of the moment.

After Aaron's last story, decisions were made for the following days. Mac, Jeremy and Adam would return to Havre de Grace with Aaron, Maggie and Abraham, once the other two barges were retrieved from Annapolis. Aaron had left them anchored in the shallows of Carr Creek, so he could sail to St. Michaels.

"That was an excellent decision, son," Ben said to Aaron.

Sonja would stay on the *Raven* with Ben. It was not until well after nightfall that Ben was able to speak alone with Aaron. Sonja and Maggie were settling down in the captain's cabin, when Aaron and Ben stood at the bow under one of the ship's night lanterns.

" I really don't know anything else, Pa," Aaron said. "Sheriff Mattingly saw me at the outlet lock of the canal basin as I was getting ready to pole out into the bay. He handed it to me and said to give it to you as soon as possible."

Ben fingered the folded paper in his hands. "And Mattingly said nothing else to you?"

"Just that he was sorry, but he said it was his duty to see it through."

Ben sighed and held the notice up into the light again. He had made great progress in learning to read during the last two years. There were a few written words he still did not understand, though he had always known his numbers. Even before he could read, he knew how to factor numbers in a ledger, running his own fledgling business on the canal. Now he had three barges. One could sail, which avoided towing charges by steam tugs for all three. And, now he had a schooner. But there were still some words he could not read, but he understood them when they were spoken.

NOTICE OF EVICTION...
FORTHWITH...VACATE...PROPERTY...NO LATER
THAN NOVEMBER 30TH...1843...

We are to be thrown out of our house!!
"This must be Briscoe's work! I always thought he was

just Binterfield's flunky, but he's just as bad," Ben said

Aaron placed his hand on Ben's shoulder. "What do we do, Pa?"

Ben sighed and gave a half smile to Aaron. "Well, first things first, Son. First we get the *Raven* masted. Then we go see George Milton, Esquire. I'm sure he can make this right."

Ben patted Aaron's arm. "Don't say anything to your mother about this. Not until we get back to Havre de Grace and deal with Sam Briscoe."

"Good night, Gentlemen," Sonja said as she walked toward them across the deck. Sonja pulled Aaron down and kissed him on the top of his head. Ben slipped the notice into his pocket. She touched Aaron's cheek with her fingertips. "Maggie is a fine young lady, Aaron."

"Yes, she is, Ma."

She reached out and pinched his ear, yanking it back and forth. "You keep her that way, young man."

"Oow! Yes ma'am. Of course I will."

She poked him in his chest with her finger. "You see to it. Now, look away." Then she gave Ben a long deep kiss on his lips.

Aaron smiled at them, but Sonja just frowned back and said, "Shut up."

Aaron's smile quickly faded as his mother walked away, but Ben's did not.

"Do you love Maggie?"

"Yes, Pa."

"You are seventeen, Aaron. You are a man. So, are you man enough to do what it takes to be worthy of her?"

"Sure. I'd do anything?"

"Could you do the hardest thing a man can do?"

"There is nothing I wouldn't do, Pa."

"I waited two years on your mother, before she could marry me."

There was silence between them. Ben patted Aaron on his shoulder and they wandered toward the crew's quarters, Aaron still deep in thought. So was Ben.

Binterfield is dead and still corruption seeps out of that bank like a rotting outhouse.

45

5

Ben and Sonja were wrapped in wool layers, standing on the deck of the *Raven* at dawn, watching the *Ugly Boat* sail up the broad Miles River. In six miles, after it cleared Tilghman Point, Aaron would steer west and then south through Eastern Bay, and finally return to the Chesapeake Bay below Kent Island. Even after he retrieved the two barges he left anchored outside Annapolis, Aaron would still have an arduous sixty-mile journey north to Havre de Grace, mostly against the wind. He would tack back and forth across the wind, gaining only precious northerly yards each leg. The *Ugly Boat*, with her two cumbersome ducklings towed behind her, would go nearly two hundred miles on her zig-zag route up the Bay, before she could finally enter the canal basin. The final five miles up the canal to Lapidum and the Pulaski Farm would be behind the leisurely pull of mules walking ahead on the towpath. It would take six days for a trip that only took Aaron two coming down. The freedom of moving without the burden of paying a steam tug came at the cost of time when sailing against the wind. The wind was both the free magic that moved sailing vessels on the water, and the curse that kept them away from home when it blew against them.

When the *Ugly Boat* had sailed beyond the distance where a waving arm could be seen, Ben and Sonja released their hollow smiles and made their way down the ladder into the rowboat. The boat rocked briskly even in the sheltered space next to the *Raven*. Sonja sat in the stern, trying to sink deeper into her wool clothes, as Ben rowed the boat fully into the wind. Ben pressed his straw hat firmly on his head, as one-foot waves shoved under their stern quarter, rocking the boat like a hateful nanny. Ben had the advantage of working up his body temperature as he rowed toward Parrot Point, while Sonja shivered and brought the collars of her coat around her face and held on to her seat. Half way there, they encountered a much larger rowboat heading into the wind, toward the *Raven*.

"Good morning, Pulaskis," yelled Robert Lambdin. A frosty mist followed his words into the air.

"Good morning, Mr. Lambdin," Ben answered. "How are you today?" He squinted at the silhouettes painted from behind by a hard sun rising above the land, stabbing his eyes with light but offering precious little warmth.

"Another cold day, sir, but still no ice in the water. Odd for November, but welcomed."

"Do we need to turn around and accompany you back to the *Raven*?"

"Not necessary, Mr. Pulaski, unless you don't trust me to remove all that iron strap without damaging your ship."

"By all means, Mr. Lambdin," Sonja answered with a smile.

"Yes of course, Mr. Lambdin," Ben answered with his own smile as well. "We're happy to have it gone."

"Excellent, sir. Oh, and another thing, Mr. Pulaski. Your Mr. Tuttle said he would do the carpentry on the cabin, and I am sure he would do a beautiful job for you..."

"Yes, Mr. Lambdin?"

"Well, I thought I'd bring Freddie here to put a decent patch on your forward wall and roof to keep out the chill... until you got home"

Ben nodded. "I appreciate that, Mr. Lambdin... I guess you can just add that to our bill."

"Nonsense, sir. Your iron will cover that and much more. And sir..."

"Yes?"

"We have a little iron stove that came off a wrecked canal barge. Floated down this way a couple years ago, after the ice gorge up on the Susquehanna. Thought you might like to have it to heat the cabin, for the lady, sir..."

47

"The lady would love that," yelled Sonja.

Lambdin looked at Ben, then shifted his glance to Sonja. "Thank you, Mrs. Pulaski. We have it here with us, and will be happy to install it, with Mr. Pulaski's permission..."

Ben slapped his hands, seeing the sparkle in Sonja's blue eyes, "So be it, Mr. Lambdin. I believe you have made Mrs. Pulaski's morning a most enjoyable one. Thank you, sir."

"Should be easy work, since you already have a burnt hole to put the stack through."

Lambdin touched the brim of his cap to Ben and Sonja, then nodded to his crew to continue rowing. Sonja showed a bright smile and a happy face, and then retreated back into the cocoon of her outer coat.

As Lambdin headed toward the *Raven*, he turned around in his boat and yelled back to Ben. "If you need a Tavern for a good meal, go to Samuel Harrison's Inn on Cherry Street." He pointed a direction across the town's harbor. "Put in at that little cove on the north side of the harbor !"

Sonja waved thank you as Ben continued to pull at the oars.

"That sounds wonderful," Sonja said to Ben.

Ben nodded and showed a small grin as he looked over his shoulder to their new destination. His rowing distance had just increased from a hundred yards to almost half a mile. To Ben's satisfaction, the breeze blowing across the river gentled significantly once he was inside the little harbor. The waves that had been slapping against the stern quarter of the rowboat disappeared. The churned muddy dark green color of the river water was replaced by translucent lime-amber. The harbor waters hosted dozens of wandering Mallard ducks and little black coots, smacking the surface water between their bills for morsels. Few trees grew near the harbor, which held several boat yards, each with boats in various stages of birth. Still, there was enough barrier to the wind for the early morning sunshine to warm Ben's face and Sonja's back. She relaxed her shoulders and straightened her back, abandoning the shriveled pose she had held since leaving the *Raven*.

The bow of the rowboat kissed up onto the muddy sand near the end of an oyster shell road coming down a gentle slope from the town. Ben pulled the boat farther up the narrow shore, helped Sonja out and stood to stretch his back and shoulders.

"Ought not to leave her there," said a fisherman coiling his rope on a nearby dock.

Ben turned toward the voice. "Why not?"

"Cause at low tide your whole boat will be outta the water, fighting you every inch putting her back in. Tie her up over here and let her float til you get back."

Ben smiled at the man. "Thank you. I'll do that, but how do you know I'm coming back."

The man relaxed his shoulders and tilted his head to one side. "Cause I don't know ya, so yer a visitor, and ya came from that wounded schooner out there." He pointed out into the river with his thumb.

"Yep. That is so. I'm told there is an Inn close by here," Ben said.

He pointed his thumb up the oyster shell road. "Harrison's. On your left. Almost spitting distance from here." Then he nodded to Sonja, "Ma'am." And turned back to his rope.

"How do you know she's wounded?" Ben asked the man.

He did not look at Ben, but out at the *Raven*. "Ya came in with forward sails only and nothing hanging from yer mainmast. You was either wounded or stupid, and ya didn't row like you were stupid."

Ben took the bow line in his hand and pushed the rowboat back into the water, then stepped over onto the narrow dock near the fisherman.

"Don't guess you miss much," Ben said. "Figured it all out just watching us?"

He looked back over his shoulder with a smile, "Well...plus I seen Robert Lambdin head over there with a crew, and he fixes busted boats."

He chuckled to himself then turned around to face Ben and held out his hand. The man was much younger than he sounded, but his hand was coarse and calloused.

"Tom Kirby. I own one of the boat yards here."

"Ben Pulaski. And the lady over there is Mrs. Pulaski."

Tom nodded in Sonja's direction, "Ma'am." He turned back to Ben. "Saw that odd boxed end sail boat come to ya yesterday afternoon. If ya don't mind me asking, what kind of boat was that?"

"It's a converted canal barge. Damaged in '39, so I had the stern and bow chopped back like a scow, and put lee boards on either side to act as keel."

Tom nodded as if he understood, but frowned. "Odd looking thing. How does she handle?"

"Like a coffin. But she can move herself and pull my other barges without the need to pay steam tugs."

"She go up the canal too, then?"

"The mast slides up and lays flat. Then we leave it at our farm in Lapidum, and the mules take us to Wrightsville."

Tom's eyes were wide open and his interest peaked. "There's some interesting boat building in all that."

"My son's idea."

"She gotta name? Surely she wasn't named after the pretty lady over there, begging your pardon."

"I named her *Brzydka Łódź*. A phrase my father used to use."

"What's it mean?"

"*Ugly Boat.*"

Tom dropped his hands to his side and laughed out loud. "Good for you!" Then he tipped his chin toward the *Raven*. "So that's the slaver been kidnapping free blacks in the upper Bay?"

"That is the ship the pirates were using, but it's mine now. And Robert Lambdin is on her right now taking the cage straps out of her hold ."

"It's a harsh business, that."

"Yes it is," Ben said. "One that I will not pursue."

Tom nodded and turned his back to Ben, coiling his

50

rope.

Ben tied the row boat's bow line to a nearby post in silence, and walked away from Tom without speaking further.

Careful Ben. He may feel the *same or he may not. This is still Maryland, here. The eastern shore is still slave country. Delaware, Maryland and Virginia are all slave states.*

Ben carried a frown as he caught up with Sonja.

"Benjamin Pulaski, this 'pretty lady' wants to go inside somewhere," she said. "Thought you two were going to gab all morning... til slavery came up."

"You don't always know what people think about things like that," he said, "and people have had their houses burned for saying what they think."

The Inn was a wide two story brick building barely two hundred feet from where they landed. The short brick walk from the road to the porch stairs invited them up. The painted lettering below the name on the wooden sign above their heads stated "1799." Sonja had made coffee and breakfast at dawn on the *Raven*, before the *Ugly Boat* set sail, but that had been hours ago.

They were bathed in warm air laced with the scent of sweet breads and fresh coffee as they entered the front room. The tavern had several small tables attended by two women moving eagerly back and forth from the kitchen. The fireplace at the back wall was generous with a shoulder high mantle. It filled the room with heat, the pleasant sound of crackles and pops and added the aroma of burning oak to the air. The morning sun peeked in through a side window, but circles of yellow light were still painted on the walls around the flames of mounted brass oil lamps. The tables were thick oak and maple, shiny from long use and worn round at the edges. They were all filled and the mumble of morning conversations were punctuated by forks and knives tapping on pottery dishes. Sonja caught the eye of one of the serving girls who motioned to a single man sitting in the corner. Almost as if by cue, the man stood and dropped a couple coins on the table. He smiled at Ben and Sonja as he walked by to the door. By the time they made their way to the table, it was cleared.

The serving girl arched her eyebrows in the timeless silent question of taverns.

"Coffee, please," said Ben as he held the chair back for Sonja.

"Do you have cobbler?" asked Sonja.

The girl's smile lit up her face and brightened the faint natural redness of her cheeks.

"Why, yes ma'am. Momma's apple cobbler is the best ever."

Sonja smiled at her. "Then let's each have some."

The girl glanced at Ben with her eyebrows arched high in question. "Sounds good to me," he said, seating himself.

Sonja tapped her fingertips on the table and frowned as the girl rushed away to the kitchen.

"What?" Ben asked.

"Someday, when I tell someone what I want, they will just do it, without looking to you for permission."

Ben smiled at her and patted her hand, and opened his mouth to speak.

"Be careful what you say, Mr. Pulaski," she said, but her frown could not overcome the half smile working its way across her mouth.

He leaned forward and whispered to her. "Don't recall being asked permission the day you stuck a pistol in Herbert Binterfield's mouth."

"Sshshsh," she hissed. "That's not anything to say in public, Ben."

"Just wish I had been there. Nathan Brown described it to me, not too long afterwards."

The smile faded from her mouth and her eyelids drooped. "Poor Nathan. He always wanted to help…"

They held hands across the table until the girl returned with coffee cups and two plates holding generous servings of apple cobbler. As soon as she set them on the table, she was off again to the kitchen as Ben and Sonja stared at their empty cups. Almost immediately, the other girl who was obviously a sister, poured fresh coffee and set a small bowl of coarse sugar on the table. Sonja used the diminutive spoon in the bowl to add a thin sprinkle to her coffee. They ate in silence, each hoping for better moods to visit them.

A heavy set man burst into the Tavern, leaving the door open behind him and striding into the middle of the morning customers.

"Where's Hoagg," he demanded in a hoarse baritone voice.

He looked around the room, not seeing the face he sought. One of the server girls came to him as the other closed the door.

"I was told the captain of that slaver was in here," he said to the girl as she approached him, causing her to step back.

Ben stood at his table.

"It is no longer a slaver, sir," Ben said calmly. "And I am her captain."

The man charged to their table and snatched out a chair. He thumped his elbows on the table as he sat, leaning over his forearms in a barely contained whisper. The smell of black coffee mixed with whiskey was heavy in his breath.

"What the hell are you doing here in St. Michaels?"

Ben drew his hand across in front of his waist and placed his hand on his knife handle.

"Be careful of your actions and your voice, mister. My wife and I are eating."

The man leaned back in his chair, and took in a deep breath.

"I need a moment with you - *Captain*."

Ben tightened the grip on his knife handle and drew it slightly from its sheath. The blood thundered through his ears, muffling the sounds within the tavern. His face turned crimson. Sonja placed her hand on his arm.

"Ben..." Then she faced the rude man. "You should step outside, sir."

The man noticed the intense look in Ben's eyes and the glint of Ben's emerging blade reflecting the lamp light in the room.

"Yes. Uh...yes. Kindly come outside when you have finished eating, Captain."

The man stood and walked briskly to the door. Ben took in several deep breaths.

"I was fighting it, Sonja. I was..."

"Go see him, Ben, but no more of that. You promised."

Ben sipped his coffee and took in another two deep breaths. He withdrew his knife from its sheath, holding it low and out of sight of other customers. He set it gently next to Sonja's plate and left it there as he walked outside.

The man stood down on the brick walkway. As Ben approached, the man held out his hand in greeting.

"Ed Covey."

Ben did not accept his hand, but kept his own in his jacket pockets. "What the hell was all that about, mister?"

"I apologize for being so bold to you and so curt in front of your wife..."

"What business do you have with Randall Hoagg?"

"Never met him, but Binterfield told me about his business. He collected my consignment from one of my men. Binterfield said I would get top dollar. Said that ship would not come in these waters."

"Binterfield is dead. Hoagg is dead."

Covey only hesitated an instant. "Who are you?"

"Benjamin Pulaski."

"I don't care one way or the other about that, Captain. And I don't care to know how you took the ship, but I do care about my consignment. Are you going to honor it?"

"There is nothing to honor, Covey. All the kidnapped blacks on the ship were freed last summer. The *Raven* is now a mercantile cargo ship. Here for mast repairs."

Covey worked his mouth, but no words made their way out of his throat. "I own shares," he said at last. The words sounded like the last breath of a dying man.

"There are no shares," Ben said and turned to walk away.

Covey grabbed his arm. "I have legal shares signed by me and Binterfield binding the cargo of the *Raven* for sale

54

on consignment. I will attach your ship for my loss, Pulaski."

Ben jerked his arm away from the man's grasp. "The ship has no attachments, Covey. The Marine Board made a final decision two weeks ago."

"No...no...I was not informed..."

"It is settled, Covey. I hold her papers. I own the *Raven*. Me and my equal partners who shared the vigil to hold her until the Board decided. Your shares are worthless."

Ben turned to walk back into the tavern.

"God damn you, Pulaski," Covey called after him.

"Yeah," Ben answered over his shoulder. "I hear that a lot."

The sun was well up in the morning sky above the town buildings when Ben and Sonja left the tavern.

"Thirty cents, Benjamin! For coffee and cobbler? Good Lord! What would a full breakfast have cost us? I'm surprised you didn't say something in there."

"It will be even worse in Annapolis, Sonja. Besides, Aaron had plenty of money from selling the coal in Annapolis."

"Really. How much do we have?"

Ben leaned in close to her ear and whispered. "Fifty Dollars."

"On you? Isn't that dangerous?"

Ben patted his waist. "Most of it is in a money belt."

They walked past another street and onto the town's main street. Shops were opening and wares were being displayed in windows and beside entrance doors. St. Michaels was fully alive and in business. Sonja spotted a clothier shop and pulled Ben toward it.

"You need gloves," she said. "And that straw hat is starting to fray at the edges. You need something worthy of a ship's captain."68

6

Aaron steered the *Ugly Boat* and its two cantankerous ducklings behind a spit of land at the northern end of Kent Island. The spit held a weathered stand of shadbush and loblolly pines that provided meager but desperately needed shelter from the northerly wind. The sun was setting over a low tide and he intentionally ran the *Ugly Boat* aground, just to keep it from drifting farther south. Abraham was not accustomed to the rocking waves that slapped against the side of the boat all day and had retreated pale to one of the bunk beds after emptying his stomach overboard. His sister, Maggie, attended him with cool wet cloths on his forehead. The boats had struggled since sunrise to tack back and forth across the wind. The *Ugly Boat* was at the front, her sails shoved to the side by the wind, and barely making headway, dragging the two other empty barges behind her with Mac and Jeremy at their tillers. Aaron released the chains holding the lee boards down in the water, brought down the main sail and released the jib sail as the hull kissed onto the sand in the little cove. He sank onto the storage trunk that served as bench in the stern and let the tiller float loose, leaning forward to ease the knots in his lower back.

Mac pulled hand over hand on the tow line from the *Ugly Boat,* bringing the *Turtle* onto the sand next to the *Ugly Boat*, and stepped over onto the deck near Aaron. He shook his bulky blacksmith arms from the effort and took a length of tow line to the bow to loop it around a post there. Aaron joined him pulling back on the line to winch the *Turtle* up on the sand. Then Aaron and Mac moved to the deck of the *Turtle* and repeated the same steps for the *Wilhelmina*. Jeremy joined them to pull the last barge into the shallows and then the three men squeezed down into the cabin and out of the wind. Chilled fog drifted from their mouths as they spoke.

The dim yellow light from an oil lamp barely lit the single room. Steep steps through the small door in the roof two feet above the deck, brought them down into the efficient cabin. Bunk beds lined two walls from a common corner. Three thick beams, the ribs of the barge, marked both ends and the center of the cabin walls. The end beams held the front and back walls of the cabin. The side walls were the wooden hull of the barge, half their height below water level. A short cast iron stove squatted in a bed of river rocks at floor level. Thick iron brackets in the back of the stove were bolted into the center beam and again from the back of the stove pipe going out through the roof. In the other corner from the bunks, narrow benches served as storage trunks and seating at the modest table. The rest of available wall space was covered in shelving with slats to keep the contents in place.

"Towing those barges in line behind the *Ugly Boat* just isn't working," Aaron said as he bent down to start a fire in the compact stove.

Jeremy rubbed his hands together and exhaled into them. "Couple times out there, the *Wilhelmina* was almost beside you, Aaron. Couldn't do anything with the tiller. The wind took me wherever it wanted."

Mac patted him on his shoulder. "You did all you could, son."

Aaron pushed in all the split wood the growing fire would take and closed the door. "How are you doing down here," he asked Maggie when she handed him the coffee pot.

They touched fingers as she passed it to him. "Well enough, Aaron. Better, now that we've anchored."

"No anchor, Maggie. I ran us aground for the rest."

"Oh no," she said. She pulled her wool shawl tighter around her shoulders, the bright blue of the shawl matching her gingham dress. Her brown eyes lingered on

Aaron. Her lips were moist and her face full of all the life her fifteen years granted her.

"Not to worry, young lady," said Mac. "It's just a brief respite on a sandy bottom until the tide comes back in to toss us off it."

"Until then, I think we need to tie the *Wilhelmina* and *Turtle* side by side," Aaron said. "They will show less side to the wind that way."

Jeremy held his hands over the growing heat of the stove. "Maybe after we get warm and have some coffee?"

"Oh, yes, please, Aaron," said Maggie. "Let us get warm and have some hot food. This is the first fire we've had in the stove today."

"It was too dangerous, Maggie..."

"I know Aaron, but it's not now."

Jeremy pulled the bean pot from its storage cupboard below Abraham's bunk and unhooked the top. "White bean soup, folks. Let's heat this up!" White bean soup still remained the traditional portable meal among canallers, and the little group was hungry to have it.

While the bean soup heated, Aaron, Mac and Jeremy went back up on deck and began lashing the *Turtle* and the *Wilhelmina* side by side as a pair. Aaron glanced across the barges, their history floating in his mind. Both barges were almost mirror images of the *Ugly Boat,* except they had no masts or sails. All three had modest single cabins in the center, similar to the one in the *Ugly Boat*, with cargo holds before and after the cabins. They were Pennsylvania built to haul coal, pulled by mules up and down the Susquehanna and Tidewater Canal between Havre de Grace and Wrightsville.

The *Ugly Boat* had been left unfinished and damaged by an ice gorge, during the terrible time when the town thought his father was lost at sea. When his father returned, he took the remnants of the barge and converted it into an ungainly scow, a square ended sail boat common in the upper Bay. Blowing into their hands and rubbing them together after tying the last knot, the three dashed back to the cabin of the *Ugly Boat*.

They managed to eat a hot meal and talk a few minutes before all five drifted off to sleep sitting on benches or the edges of bunk beds. Groggy from too little sleep they were soon bounced awake by the incoming waves of a rising tide lifting the hull and then dropping it hard on the bottom. Aaron dashed up the steps followed by Mac and Jeremy. The wind was a hoarse whisper, but building, and bringing a winter bite.

"Stay on board and help work the sails," Aaron said to Mac and Jeremy.

"Just as well," Jeremy answered. "Tillers weren't helping anyway!"

Mac yelled to Aaron, his body illuminated by the light shining from the low cabin windows barely peeking above the deck. "Not sure we oughta sail on in the dark!"

"We got wind and the bay is eight miles wide north of here!" He looked up at a sky filled with bright cold stars. "And we got stars and starlight!"

"What do ya have in mind for a course?"

"I want to make a straight run across the mouth of the Patapsco to North Point, then tack there to north west. That sound reasonable to you?"

Mac smiled and nodded, then bent to his task.

The wind had stayed northerly, but the angle of the shore where they rested gave them enough of a working angle so the *Ugly Boat* could sail off the spit with the pair of empty barges behind her. It was far colder than when they went below and the ratlines to the mast hummed in the wind.

Abraham and Maggie stood in the stern holding on to ratlines running up to the top of the mast.

"You two might as well go below, for now," Aaron said to them.

"I want to help," said Abraham.

"So do I," said Maggie.

Aaron pointed to Abraham and then toward the bow. "Go forward and help Jeremy with the jib sail."

Aaron turned back to Maggie. "Please go below and put out the fire, then put on some pants. You can help Mac with the boom. We're going to run hard across the wind!

The boat's gonna lean a lot. Too little wind and we slow down and get pushed back south. Too much wind and we capsize! It's all on how we keep the sails against it."

The wind shoved hard against the main sail, billowing it out with a harsh pop. The boat leaned dramatically away from the wind, the upper edges of the deck on that side dipped into the waves. The stern drifted slightly toward the south until Jeremy and Abraham pulled tighter against the jib sail, helping the wind push the bow back on course. Maggie's eyes grew wide and she looked at Aaron in fear.

"Go below," he yelled.

The tied barges behind the *Ugly Boat* slewed southward. The bows still loyally followed the short line to the stern of the sail boat, but their sterns swung downwind. Aaron shook his head.

Nothing to be done about that. Those barges are only empty boxes, but they will be dragging against us.

Mac yelled to Aaron. He pointed up and said, "And we're getting moonlight!"

The last of the low lying clouds were brushed away and the moon bathed the world in faint silver light.

Aaron picked the star to follow to North Point, examined the fullness of his sails then smiled and leaned into the tiller, letting the *Ugly Boat* surge ahead.

The wind stayed on useful headings the rest of their journey and on the evening of the fourth day they dropped anchor on the Susquehanna Flats, just outside the canal basin at Havre de Grace. Mac took the rowboat to shore, to arrange for entry through the lock and to retrieve the mules left boarded in the canal company barn during their absence. The mast and sails of the *Ugly Boat* were lowered and strapped to the deck, leaving her as helpless as the other two barges. The *Turtle* and the *Wilhelmina* were untied as a pair and put bow to stern, in line behind the *Ugly Boat*. Long poles were unleashed from the deck and pushed against the sandy bottom of the flats, moving the lead barge ahead slowly, drawing the other two along behind. The water level of the river and the canal basin was the same, so the lock was kept open for all three barges to pass within.

Abraham stood at the bow of the *Ugly Boat* watching Mac tie the tow line onto the rig of two mules standing in line, one behind the other. "Alright Aaron, tell me how all this works."

Aaron pointed over the water of the basin. "The Canal Basin is a man-made lake, several acres of mostly still water. It's fed by water coming down from Wrightsville, forty-five miles up canal."

"So, it's just a ditch,?" Abraham said.

Maggie poked Abraham's side with her elbow and sent him a frown.

"So, it's a BIG ditch," Abraham added

"It's a big ditch with locks in it," Aaron said

"What do you need those for, anyway. I remember they just take too much time to get through," said Abraham.

Aaron snorted. "Thought you went to a fancy school in New York, Abraham. Didn't they teach you anything."

"Lots, Aaron. About lox, but not locks."

"What? Did they or didn't they?"

Maggie jabbed Abraham with another elbow.

"Never mind, Aaron. Tell me about the locks."

"Water flows downhill. They teach you that in New York?"

"Funny, Aaron."

"Barges need flat water deep enough to float them when they're full of Pennsylvania coal. That makes it easy for mules to pull them..."

"Yes."

"The canal is divided into stairs that step downhill from Wrightsville. Each lock maintains the water level for their "stair", but their main job is to raise or lower the barges between two different water levels."

"Which is done how, Aaron?"

"Each lock is a holding pen that can raise the water level within it, using the flow from Wrightsville, or lower it by releasing water downstream."

"By opening and closing the big gates at the end of the locks. Right?"

"Wrong, Abraham. At the bottoms of the 'BIG' gates are small iron doors that can be opened or closed with tiller handles on top of the 'BIG' gates." Aaron used his hands to mimic the water level and the motion of the doors. "Open them and water level within the lock drops. Close them and the water level rises."

Abraham stared out over the canal basin. "So, I think I understand. So where do the barges go to dump their coal?"

"I know that much," Maggie said. "They have to be towed to Philadelphia or to Baltimore..."

"Or to Annapolis," added Aaron.

"I was going to say that, too," Maggie said. "By steam tug or by very smart people who have a sailing barge."

Mac whistled to get their attention. "We gonna sit here all day?"

Maggie looked over the other two barges. "Aaron, I thought the steering barge had to be in back?"

"Yeah, Maggie, usually. Mac thought we could pull all three with two mules pulling the *Ugly Boat* and the other two barges behind. I don't think one tiller is going to be able to guide three barges..."

"And so..."

"And so, what?"

"Shouldn't someone be at the tillers of the other two barges..."

"Oh Shit! I was talking to Abraham..."

Before he could say any more, Maggie and Jeremy ran back and leaped from the stern of the *Ugly Boat* on to the bow of the *Turtle*. They ran the length of the *Turtle*. Maggie yanked on Jeremy's sleeve as they neared the stern of the *Turtle*, causing him to slip and fall. She giggled and ran onto the stern locker, launching herself onto the *Wilhelmina* just as the tow lines were stretching out. She dashed to the stern of the *Wilhelmina*, grabbed the tiller and turned around waving at Aaron. Red-faced, Aaron made his way quickly to the tiller of the *Ugly Boat*, then signaled Mac they were ready to go.

Slowly, the mule team pulled on the lead tow line and

gradually moved the trio of barges past the barges waiting for tows, past the canal company mule barn and toward the open area of the canal basin. The space between the barges opened to the ten feet of line between stern and bow. Ahead, the surface of the basin was like a mirror, reflecting the pale blue November sky streaked with strands of fading clouds.

The towpath ahead was both a pathway and a wall, caught between the weight of the manmade lake water, and the surging force of the untamed Susquehanna River on the other side. The river was engorged with the recent rains and roiled with undulating humps and frequent splashes against the outside of the towpath like a wild animal trapped just below the surface and begrudging the area of the basin stolen from it.

Gradually the countryside of the west bank edged back toward them as the mule team continued their steady pull, drawing the long rope leading out from the bow of the front barge, taking them closer to the mouth of the actual canal. Most of the trees on the hillside had been cut down for lumber or fire wood, some of the stumps sprouting saplings bearing the colorful leaves of the majestic trees that stood there before. Palmer's Island rose out of the middle of the river blocking the view of Perryville back down to the east. Great Blue Herons squawked complaints at being disturbed during morning wades in the shallows and flew majestically away over the river. The green tinted water of the Bay was left behind and replaced by the murky water of the canal or the hard cobalt of the river beyond the towpath.

Within an hour Mac and the mule team came abreast the Pulaski Farm on the left. Mac made dramatic arm movements pointing across the canal toward the farm. Aaron could see Mac's movements, but did not yet have a clear view of where he was pointing.

"Oh no," Abraham shouted from the bow, and he too, pointed at the Pulaski house.

Moments later, Aaron passed in front of the massive oaks that guarded the slope up to the house. He stood up, his mouth wide open.

"Hey," he shouted to the men coming out of his house. "What the hell are you doing?"

He threw open the locker top and yanked out the pistol kept there in oiled cloth. He yelled at Abraham over his shoulder as he leapt from the *Ugly Boat* onto the towpath.

"Take the tiller, Abraham. Bank them and stake them!"

Aaron dashed along the towpath up to the swing bridge at Lock number nine, clumping across the muddy wood and then turned back down toward his home. He was catching up to Mac as they both charged along the path over the little wagon bridge to their property and up toward the porch. Two men were coming out of the house carrying his mother's chest of drawers between them. Aaron slid to a stop in front of the porch, turned to face the men, cocked his pistol and pointed it at the men's faces.

"I'm going to kill the next man that moves!"

7

Ben wandered along Talbot Street in St. Michaels while Sonja was left to spend rare moments in the millinery shop talking about dresses. He had left the packages they had acquired during this additional day of shopping stacked in a corner of the shop with the ladies. He silently admitted his satisfaction with the new black hat Sonja had helped him select on their first day in St. Michaels. The new clothing styles drawing men's coats in to a narrow waist with high collars and the man capped off with a high top hat, were nothing but silly to Ben. The low crown version was far more sensible. The new goat skin gloves were also a treat to keep his hands warm while he walked through the cold late morning.

Can't use them for work. Tear them to pieces. Canvas will be fine for that.

He came to a tavern he had visited before and stepped inside. A stout box stove sat in front of a bricked up fireplace that left only an opening for the stove pipe to pass. The collection of drinking men and the iron stove was more than enough to warm the room. He stepped up to the bar and nodded to the tender.

"Good morning, Mr. Pulaski. An ale for you, sir?"

He turned around to the keg pin without waiting for an answer and filled a wooden mug.

"How goes the work on yer schooner, sir," the tender asked as he served the ale.

"The mast came in this morning, William. Mr. Lambdin tells me he will step it tomorrow."

William nodded as Ben drank from the mug.

"I guess you're eager to get back up to Havre de Grace, then?"

"Yes, I am. Not, that I haven't enjoyed the week spent here in St. Michaels."

"That's kind of you, sir."

"Not at all, William. Mrs. Pulaski and I..."

"Hey, Pulaski," Ed Covey said as he yanked on Ben's arm.

Ben turned on him with a frown. "I already told you..."

Covey held his palm up. "Relax, Pulaski. I ain't going after shares any more. I got business for ya."

"What business are we going to have together?"

"Passengers, 'Captain' Pulaski. I've got passengers for you that need to go to Havre de Grace."

Covey pointed his thumb over his shoulder toward the window panes. Outside stood three black men, standing close together. One was shirtless. The other two wore coarse burlap pullovers. Even from the distance, Ben could see the copper tags each wore on a string around his neck.

"I don't deal in slaves, Covey."

"I ain't asking you to. I got three bucks that I'm renting to a lumber mill over that way. We got more niggers than we got work for over here. They're gonna eat me oughta house and home, if I don't find work for them somewhere. I was gonna keep'em on the farm until spring with the money I was going to get from the one I put on your boat, but..."

"It wasn't my boat then, Covey."

"I ain't gettin back into that, Pulaski. I just want to ship'em to Havre de Grace. Nobody else going that way for a while. I'll pay you for it..."

"I'm not chaining them up."

"You don't need to, Pulaski. They behave good. Broke'em in myself. Have'em sit on your deck or down in the cargo hold. They'll stay put."

Ben took another drink for his mug. "Alright. I should have the new mast in tomorrow. Assuming the rigging is put in right, and my son comes back with the crew, we'll

66

leave the day after. Have them at the dock on Mulberry Street at sunrise."

Covey smiled.

"And get that man a shirt," Ben said, pointing at the window as he walked away.

Covey shook his head and sighed, speaking to Ben's back. "He's got one. Won't wear it." Then he added, "But other than that he does what he's told. Broke him myself."

Moments later Ben approached the millinery shop, just as Sonja stepped out.

"I was just going to look for you," she said.

"Let's have a midday meal at Harrison's Inn."

"Oh, that would be lovely. We haven't been back there since that rude man interrupted our cobbler. Let me tell Miss Tallon that we will return shortly for our packages."

She was back outside in seconds, and looped her arm into Ben's as they walked.

"I ordered three dresses, Ben. I hope you like them. And, the cost was reasonable..."

"I am certain it was reasonable, and I am also certain that anything you wear will look beautiful on you, even if it was just a flour sack."

She blushed and patted his arm. "Where did you amble off to?"

"I was having an ale with that same rude man, Ed Covey."

"What?" She stopped on the sidewalk, looking up into his face.

"Well, truth be told, he approached me on business." He placed his hand against the small of her back and they began to walk again.

"What business would you have with such a man?"

Ben chuckled. "That's almost exactly the question I asked him."

"And..."

"And... I agreed to take three of his slaves as passengers to Havre de Grace."

She stopped again, placing her hands on her hips. "Why would you agree to do that, especially for him?"

Ben folded his arms in front of his chest and stepped

against her. In a hushed tone he said, "First, I get them away from him. He is known as a slave breaker and has a vicious reputation here in Talbot County."

"I hope I like your 'second' better than I like your 'first'."

He smiled at her and touched her cheek. "Second, Mrs. Pulaski, my fire-breathing wife, they will go as passengers and be treated like human beings on our ship."

"I am still without a 'why', Mr. Pulaski. Does that come in a 'third'?"

"Third. Once in Havre de Grace, I intend to introduce them to people who could help them to Pennsylvania."

"Such as a young barge captain, who tows a second battered barge named *Wilhelmina*, that has a secret compartment for such things," she whispered.

Ben smiled again and touched the side of his nose.

"Is there a fourth?" Sonja asked.

"Yes..."

"Well?"

"Fourth, that rude man will pay me money to take his slaves away from him, and set them free."

Sonja stepped next to him, smiling and hugging his arm in hers, pulling him toward the Inn, "Let's eat."

Later, while the sun was still high in a pale blue cloudless sky, Ben rowed toward the *Raven* across the little harbor, kissed by a gentle breeze out of the north. As Ben pulled on the oars, pushing them out of the harbor, Sonja leaned to one side holding her hand over her eyes looking ahead at their ship.

"There is another mast. Have they mounted it already? It looks smaller than I expected."

Ben let one oar drag in the water and pulled with the other, spinning the rowboat to an angle where he could see the *Raven* clearly.

"It's the *Ugly Boat*," he said with a broad grin. "Aaron is already back!"

Ben dug deep into the water with both oars and sent the rowboat gliding toward his ship. Within short minutes they came along side, scurried up the side ladder and hopped through the entry port in the railing.

Aaron stood nearby with his hands in his pockets. Sonja was to him first and gave him a big motherly kiss on the cheek and hugged him, but his eyes were fixed on his father. Ben stopped several feet in front of him, eyeing his stance and the worried look on his son's face.

"What is it, son?"

Aaron shrugged, looking more like the little boy he once was. "They came early, Pa."

"Who came early? Early for what?" Ben stepped next to his son and placed his hand on his shoulder. "What happened, son?"

"The bank. The realty company. They evicted us from the house. From the farm."

Sonja filled her face with a frown. "What? Who? Why?"

Ben shook his head. "It wasn't supposed to happen until later in the month..."

Sonja turned on him in fury. "We're being evicted and you knew it was going to happen!" She turned back to Aaron. "How much time do we have?"

"It already happened, Ma. When we got back to the farm, men were taking everything out of the house and putting it on the front slope"

"What?"

Ben put his hands on her shoulders. "Sonja, we had plenty of time to talk this out with the bank. I don't believe Sam Briscoe would..."

"Whatever you believed was dead wrong, Benjamin Pulaski! When did you know about this? How long have you known?" She looked over the water at the little town of St. Michaels. "You've known since we got here, didn't you?"

She swung her hand to slap Ben, but he grabbed her wrist and stopped her in mid swing.

"Damn it, Sonja. You have to calm down!"

She pulled away from him and crossed her arms. "All right. Tell me."

Aaron started to speak, but Ben held up his hand. "I need to tell her about the note, then you need to tell us the details of what happened."

Aaron nodded and blew the air out of his lungs.

"Sonja," Ben said, "We have known for a while that Binterfield valued the farm at twenty times what it's worth, just to keep me from buying it. That's when he raised our rent. When Aaron came from Annapolis he had a note from Binterfield's realty company that actually owns the farm..."

Sonja blew her breath out. "Go on."

"The notice said we had until November 30th to settle matters. I figured this was something Binterfield put in motion before he was killed. I found Sam Briscoe held captive in the hold of this ship when we took it from Hoagg. I set Sam free. That is when he got my knife. I gave it to him to get away. So, I figured he would be more than willing to stop the eviction, since he's managing the bank now and the realty company. Today is only the 18th!"

Ben turned to Aaron.

"When I got back to the Farm," Aaron said, "there were men taking all our things out of the house. I thought they were stealing, so I pointed a gun at them and told them to stop or I would shoot."

Sonja gasped and brought her hand up to her mouth. Ben looked out at the opposite shore.

"Another man came out from the barn and tried to knock the gun out of my hand. It went off..."

"Oh God," muttered Sonja.

Ben held his breath.

"The bullet shattered a window pane and Mac knocked the man down, out I think, cause he just laid there. The two on the porch dropped the chest of drawers and came for me and another man came out of the barn..."

"Was anyone hurt seriously?" Ben asked.

"No, well, not so they won't heal, I don't think. The first man Mac hit has a broken jaw, and the next one has a broken arm, and then that last one lost some teeth..."

"Good God, Aaron," muttered Sonja.

"I think I got a broken rib, but it all stopped when the deputy held his shotgun on us."

"Are you all right, Aaron?" Sonja asked.

He nodded. "Doc Harper looked at me at the jail..."

"At the jail," Ben snapped. "They took you to jail? Or did they take the men who were stealing?"

"Us," Aaron said. "Seems the men were all deputized and there was a full deputy with them."

"Mattingly?" Ben asked.

"No, but I think Mattingly just deputized him."

"Then what, Aaron?" Ben asked.

"Folks from Lapidum had gathered around after the gun shot. I guess after Hoagg's raid at our house, they didn't know what else could happen. Everybody came with rifles or pitchforks and started yelling at the men from Havre de Grace. The deputy said he was going to take us all to town to sort it out, and Mr. Freidman came along to watch them. Oh, and Mr. Nilson said they'd keep all our things in his storeroom until we come to get it."

"So, all our things are not still laying out in the elements," Sonja asked. "Did they break much?"

"Some, Ma."

She frowned and exhaled deeply. "Well, I'm relieved you're not shot or locked up..."

"Mr. Mattingly let me go. Said to come tell you what happened. He locked up Mac, but said it would only be a couple days. I found the lawyer, Mr. Milton and told him everything."

Ben nodded. "Is Mac with you?"

"No, Pa. He's still in jail. A judge gave him 30 days for hitting a deputy, so Jeremy stayed home to get things for his Pa. And Abraham stayed home while his father went to town with us, so we didn't have much of a crew."

Ben sighed. "I'm glad as well that you are all right. I don't imagine I could have done any better..."

Aaron looked down at the deck, then jerked his head up. "Oh! Oh! I didn't tell you yet! I brought Uncle Edward!!"

"What?" Ben and Sonja spoke at the same moment.

"What Uncle Edward," Sonja asked, the frown crumpling her face.

"Me, Uncle Edward," the man said as he walked up the

71

steps from the food locker below. He was chewing a piece of smoked ham and carrying other pieces in each hand as he stepped up onto the deck. He held his arms open to Ben. "Hello, Little Brother," he said with a wide grin.

Sonja stood with her mouth open, staring at the stranger. "What brother, Ben? You have a brother?"

"No. I do not," Ben said. He pointed a finger at Edward. "Get the hell off my ship, before I throw you off."

8

Edward kept his arms wide, still smiling. "We are brothers, Benjamin . Don't deny it!"

Ben's face was twisted in anger. He looked around among the people near him. He spotted the pistol stuck in Aaron's belt and snatched it up. Sonja saw him grab the pistol, saw him level it toward Edward.

"No, Ben! No," she screamed.

Ben aimed the barrel at Edward's face. "Get off my goddamned ship, or so help me God..."

"Ben, we had the same father," Edward said. "I am coming to you because you need help and I'm a damned good seaman. Been a first mate..."

Ben kept the pistol aimed at Edward's head while he cocked it with his thumb. Ben's breathing stopped. The blood exploding through the arteries in his brain deafened him within his own personal hurricane. Only Edward was clear in his vision, all around him was a blur, and the blackness was crawling in from the edges.

"No, Ben," Sonja yelled, but he did not hear her. She reached in front of him and slapped the gun barrel to the side.

The pistol emitted a steel click and the hammer fell on the firing nipple, but there was no gunshot.

Ben stared at the pistol, then glared at Sonja. He took in a deep breath and his face let the snarl slip away. Aaron took the pistol gently from his father's hand. Ben took in another deep breath, but kept his glaze on Edward and pointed back toward the *Ugly Boat*.

"Go now," Ben said, "while you're still alive."

The grin that had been pasted to Edwards face, drooped closed, and his eyes filled with ice. He turned slowly and walked to the railing and slipped over the side, down onto the deck of the *Ugly Boat*.

Sonja placed her hand on Ben's forearm. "Ben…"

He exhaled again. "It is a difficult story, Sonja. Not one I will spread on this deck. Later. I promise."

Aaron's eyes were still wide on his father, and took a half step back as his father moved toward him. Ben stopped and held up his hands to his son.

"Tell me how he came to be with you, son."

Aaron swallowed hard, glancing between Ben and Sonja. "Well, Pa…"

Ben placed his hand gently on Aaron's shoulder, and smiled at him.

Adam Tuttle sat down on a nearby keg and began filling his pipe. "Too damned much excitement with you Pulaskis." He chuckled to himself and shook his head slightly, as he pointed his pipe stem at Aaron. "I've seen Ben's father in that same state, more than once. Only he didn't have the grace of your mother's hand on the barrel."

Ben looked back at Sonja. "And I thank God I did, this time."

Aaron cleared his throat. "When I came through the outlet lock yesterday morning, Mr. McGraw said there was another Pulaski in town looking for his brother Benjamin. He said he told the man he could ride up to Lapidum on number 26 with Dan Bartlett. Told him I had already gone up that way the day before, but you were still in St. Michaels."

"Chatty, wasn't he?"

"Aw Pa. You know Mr. McGraw. He passes on more news about folks on the canal than the Madisonian."

Ben motioned to those around him. "Let's go down into the captain's cabin and get warm."

Once settled around the new iron stove, Ben turned to Aaron. "So how did Edward Leonard come to be on the *Ugly Boat*?"

74

Aaron and Sonja exchanged unspoken questions hearing the name Leonard and both gave small shoulder shrugs.

"I had just talked with Dan Bartlett not ten minutes before hearing from Mr. McGraw, so I walked back to his barge and found Unc...Edward there. He told me he was your older brother and was looking for work. Since Mac was in jail, I thought..."

"You thought correctly, son. You were thinking like a captain. We need a crew..."

"So, is this Edward a Leonard or a Pulaski," Sonja asked. "And why do you hate him so?"

"Later, Sonja. I promised you later, but not..."

"Not what? Not in front of the people you were willing to have as witness to you murdering a man?"

Ben exhaled, and settled onto a bench below the stern windows. He pulled his pipe and tobacco pouch off the nearby shelf and began speaking as he filled his pipe.

"Edward is Edward Lenz Leonard. He is named for his mother's father and his own father, Lenz Pulaski. Edward's mother was a very popular serving girl at a tavern in Baltimore when my father was a young man. They spent time together. Apparently, a lot of time together."

He tamped the tobacco in his pipe. He held a slender twig over the lantern for a flame to light it. As he puffed the tobacco into embers, Sonja waved her hands back and forth through the smoke drifting up from both Ben and Adam.

"Good Lord," she snapped. "This cabin is far too confined for that." She threw open one of the stern windows and sat on the bench next to Ben, elbowing him to move back to her chair.

Ben frowned at his wife's odd dislike of tobacco and settled into the wooden chair by the stove.

"This was the story my father told me as we sailed down to Louisiana in his schooner *Osprey* in '15. Miss Leonard went off with the captain of a New England ship and he did not see her for over two years. During that time he met my mother and they were married. When I was still an infant, Miss Leonard showed up at my Father's door with a three year old boy, claiming it was his. I can only imagine the strife between my parents over that day. He never said much about it."

"Your father turned her away," Sonja asked.

Ben smiled at Sonja. "I wish you had met my mother. She would have liked you so much. You both share the same fire..."

"Which means what, Ben?"

He chuckled. "My father would not hesitate to sail into the teeth of a gale, if his duty demanded it. But Hurricane Marie was a storm where he would only reduce sail and run ahead. No, he did not turn Miss Leonard away."

Aaron was mesmerized by the family tale. "So what..."

Ben rolled his eyes. "So, my mother had her in and drained her of every fact floating around in the woman's head." He smiled. "Mother should have been a lawyer, if women did such things. In the end, my mother decided my father could neither prove nor disprove his obligation. Without and disproof, she insisted he accept the obligation, especially since the New Englander had sent the woman packing back to Baltimore."

Sonja leaned forward, resting her elbows on her knees and her cheeks in her hands. "Did you see him often as you grew up?"

"When I was eight, Miss Leonard died and Edward came to live with us a while. He stole some of my mother's jewelry, lied all the time and started fights with me and our cook's son. That following year after my mother died, Edward became almost uncontrollable, so my father turned him out as an apprentice on a fishing boat."

"And you still begrudge him from that," Sonja asked.

"No. As I said, it was a difficult story. My father re-married in '13 to a woman who took advantage of him. I was in the Army in Georgia when he passed away. Edward and my step mother laid heavy claims against my father's estate. Evidence of my father's generosity to Edward over the years was also used as evidence of parentage."

Ben stopped to puff on his pipe and shifted in his chair.

He looked only at Sonja.

"Much of the estate was sold off between them to pay lawyers as they sued each other. It was squandered. That is why the house was cold both physically and emotionally when we visited there on our arrival from North Carolina. All my stepmother had left was the house and her own caustic nature. Everything outside the house was Edward's, and he ran up huge debts in my father's name."

Ben joined Sonja on the bench at the stern windows.

"When Congress finally paid patriots for their losses fighting the British, the money that was supposed to replace my Father's schooner, simply went to cover a portion of Edward's debts. The name Lenz Pulaski is still considered an untrustworthy debtor. Edward ruined my father's name and I will not have him using that name while I live. He piles up debts and then runs away, leaving them unpaid. We must be careful of him."

Adam tapped his pipe onto the stove and brushed his ashes into the fire box. "So, does this mean you'll not try to shoot Edward again?"

"Yes, Adam. It means that. It also means I will use him as a crewman to help get us back to Havre de Grace."

Ben turned to Aaron as they stood up. "I will not waste the wise step Aaron took bringing him here. After that I will be rid of him."

Aaron smiled at his father and accepted his rare hug.

Ben held his son by his shoulders. "Do you have the other two barges anchored somewhere nearby?"

"No, Pa. I left them in the canal basin, so I could come here as soon as possible."

"Good man. I'll need you to tie the *Ugly Boat* to our stern and help me work the ship. You all right with that?"

Aaron gave a broad smile and stepped out of the door and followed Adam up toward the deck.

Ben turned back to Sonja. "I'll need you to help pull a line or two, as well."

Sonja punched him in his arm. "We've been married twenty six years, and you are just now telling me about Edward?" She punched his arm again and walked out of the cabin.

Aaron walked to the railing and called down to Edward. "Edward, come back up on the ship and greet the Captain"

Edward grinned and tilted his head. "No Uncle Edward?"

"Nope."

Ben was standing by the starboard wheel when Edward came back on the *Raven*. Edward examined the dual wheels keenly.

"Never seen a schooner with dual wheels, Ben."

"Two things, Edward. One. You don't refer to yourself as an Uncle, Brother or a Pulaski. Two. You do not hesitate to do what I tell you, when I tell you to do it. If you do either of these things, I will throw you overboard and let you swim to shore, if you can."

Edward gave a thin smile that did not reach his eyes. "Is there a three?"

Ben paused a moment. "Yes. I am going to re-load my pistol. My wife may not be able to save you next time."

Edward nodded without expression and said nothing else. Ben pointed to the crew quarters in the bow.

"I am only letting you crew with us back to Havre de Grace. Your behavior will determine what happens after that. Now, stow your things and stay out of my way."

Ben stood at the wheel looking along the deck of the *Raven*, as Edward went forward.

One hundred and thirty feet long. Twenty three feet abeam. Two masts. Up to seven sails. She should have a captain, five crewmen and a cook. We're going to have to make do with a total of five individuals. One a woman with plenty of heart but not the brawn or seamanship. Another with experienced seamanship and a bad heart. One a young man just learning how to sail. One seasoned sailor come back from the dead. And one, an untrustworthy liar.

Ben shook his head and blew out his breath. He glanced up at the wind pennant flapping from the foremast.

"Shit."

The wind had veered and strengthened. Coming colder from the north.

9

Dawn was a slice of pewter above the black tree line on the other side of the Miles River when Ed Covey's rowboat thudded against the hull of the *Raven*. Ben had just started a fire in the new cabin stove and stepped on deck while water brewed for coffee. Without invitation, one of Covey's slaves slipped over the railing and stood peering into the fading darkness on the deck before helping Ed Covey up the side ladder.

"Damned bold of you," Ben said, lighting a nearby lantern.

"I'd get beat if I didn't get up here quick," the first man said.

"And that's a fact," Ed Covey added behind him, then elbowed the slave to the side so he could approach Ben, crunching frost under his boots. He held out his hand to Ben. "Morning, Pulaski."

Ben did not accept his hand.

"Next time you climb onto my ship without calling out, you might get shot."

Covey chuckled. "Well, you might waste a well trained slave, Pulaski. I always send'em ahead of me."

"Good to know, Covey. I'll be sure to aim for the second figure climbing up."

Covey ignored the comment and snapped orders to the first slave. "Get the others on deck, Albert."

The other two clanked on board, working around the chained manacles each had looped between their wrists. One was still shirtless and neither of the other slaves wore coats.

"I have manacles for Albert as well, Pulaski. He will behave, but feel free to chain them all together in the hold to avoid the bother of watching them. Also, here is the transportation permit for the three of them. Their destination and claimer are written on the ticket." Covey handed the other manacle and the paper to Ben.

"Key," Ben snapped.

"Oh, Albert has that. Trained him myself. He'll do what you tell him."

Ben took the manacle and papers and sighed. "Ten dollars," he said.

"We agreed on nine, Pulaski."

"We agreed on three per man. Three manacles are a dollar extra."

Covey sniffed and counted out ten silver dollars to Ben, then handed Ben another paper and a pencil.

"Sign for'em."

Ben dropped the coins into his coat pocket, hesitated, then took the paper to the lantern. It was similar to the transportation permit, but assigned responsibility for the slaves to Ben. After reading what he could, he pressed the paper against the foremast, signed it and returned it to Covey.

"You lose'm, you buy'em," he said. "They're worth three hundred a piece." Then he returned to the railing and stepped down into his rowboat.

Sonja joined Ben with a cup of coffee billowing steam in the crisp air. She glanced at the slaves standing near the mast and retreated to the captain's cabin. Seconds later she returned on deck with old wool shirts of Ben's and one of his old coats. She handed the coat to the man with no shirt, and the shirts to the others.

"Thank you Sonja," Ben said as he approached them. "Gentlemen," he said to the slaves, "no one wears manacles on the *Raven*." He addressed the first slave. "Albert is it? Please remove the manacles from the other two men, and place the manacles in the storage box near the foremast."

"What about the key, suh?"

"You keep it, Albert," Ben said. "You men go down into

the main hold nearest the galley. There's a man down there named Adam cooking breakfast. Help him for now. By the time we all eat, the crew should be here from the dock to step in the new mast. I'm sure your help will be needed."

The center passageway in the hold held a fold out plank table to serve as the table for the crew. Benches were hung in the storage areas and brought out for meals. Ben and Sonja joined them for breakfast. With the crew shortage, there was enough room for the slaves to sit at the table as well, but they stood aside unwilling to sit down.

Ben looked at them when he entered. "Sit down men, we have plenty of food and Adam is a tolerable cook.

"I'm a damned good cook," Adam added, sticking his head out from the little galley.

The slaves looked at each other and then at Ben. "This be trouble for us, Massa. It be best we eat on deck or not at all," Albert said."We ain't never 'loud ta sit with white folk."

Adam walked past them to set a large platter of fried bacon on the table at the end nearest the slaves.

Edward watched it all with steel eyes. Aaron watched it in amusement.

"Eat," commanded Ben.

The one who had come aboard without a shirt leaned forward. "Shit. I ain't no white man. Don't wanna be. But I can eat the hell out of bacon!" He slipped into the bench next to Aaron, who pulled the platter close. Then Aaron pulled an empty plate in front him, grabbed a handful of bacon and dropped it onto the plate, then slid it in front of the man.

"What's your name," Aaron asked.

"B'gamba," he said.

Albert frowned and shook his head heavily. "No it ain't. You been named Thomas. How many times you get beat for that?"

"He lets me be without a shirt," B'gamba said. "Long as I work like a mule, he lets me be."

82

"He don't let you be B'gamba. He calls you Thomas, and you do what he say Thomas do."

"I say all I gotta say cause I don't wear that shirt and he knows it."

Edward snatched his coffee cup and stood up from the table, then left the hold for the main deck. All three slaves stiffened and went silent.

"B'Gamba," Ben called out, and all heads turned toward Ben. "Pass the bacon."

As the platter moved to Ben, he caught B'gamba's attention and nodded in Edward's direction. "This is not his ship. It is mine." Then he looked to Albert. "Sit, eat, or go on deck hungry, but we've got work to do this morning." Ben glanced at the third slave. "What's your name?"

"Ezekiel," he said.

"Sit and eat or go on deck, Ezekiel"

Ezekiel slipped effortlessly onto the bench next to Albert. Adam brought a second platter of bacon and a platter of biscuits to the table and slipped in next to Aaron. Within seconds all three platters were empty, and within minutes all plates were empty.

Ben and Sonja were the last to leave the table. Ben turned to Sonja, "Would you mind washing up the plates?"

She met his glance with an empty stare. "Would you mind sleeping in the crew's quarters?"

Ben hesitated a moment, allowing a narrow smile on his face. "I guess Adam can get to them later."

Robert Lambdin arrived, sitting in the stern of the large rowboat with a crew of four men at the oars. They towed an odd barge to the free side of the *Raven* and tied on to its hull in several places to stay parallel with the ship. The gin pole stood like a stubby mast on the barge. The base of the *Raven's* new main mast was linked to the lower part of the gin pole, with the top of the mast laying far out over the water. A heavy rope was looped around the mast several times near the top, holding a ring of pulleys, each dangling its own rope, all of it looking like a long legged spider. The whole arrangement looked far too ungainly for the small barge, but the barge held the arrangement securely in the calm water. Lambdin boarded the *Raven* with a curt nod to Ben and keeping his eyes on the new mast.

"It's a fine Douglas Fir for you, Mr. Pulaski."

Ben held his breath as the mast was fully raised on a pulley near the top of the gin pole, and then the base of the mast swung from the barge with the help of a boom until it was centered over the hole in the deck where the previous mast stood. Sonja stood next to Ben, sensing his tension.

Ben leaned next to her ear and whispered, "If they drop it now, it will pierce the hull and the *Raven*'s back will be broken."

Sonja could not look away from the operation and whispered back, "I wish you had not told me that."

Lambdin halted the operation with his men at the ropes and checked the setting for two angles, then motioned for his men to lower the mast into its new home. When it was only inches from being seated, Lambdin motioned Ben to join him below deck.

Lambdin examined the set of the mast hovering inches above its intended seat, a thick ring of carved oak pinned to the top of the keel beam, forming a cup to secure the mast for years to come. He nodded to Ben. "Do you have a coin for the stepping."

Ben hesitated for a moment, then fished a silver dollar from his coat pocket.

"Almost forgot," Ben said. "Been a long time since I was part of a mast stepping." He kissed the coin, then hesitated again before calling Sonja down in the hold. Lambdin smiled broadly as Sonja came down.

"Good morning, Mrs. Pulaski," Lambdin said. "It is an exceptional honor your husband has called you for."

"Kiss the coin," Ben said. "Then we place it under the mast for good luck wherever we sail."

Sonja took the coin, kissed it and said a silent prayer as she held it in her hand, then returned it to Ben. He dropped it down into the mast step and nodded to Lambdin, who yelled for his men to lower the greased mast into place. The fit was perfect. There was no space between the mast and the ring that enclosed the step. Lambdin's assistant applied long braces against the mast base and began wrapping the heavy rope around it. Soon other men came down to join in pulling the line taught. Ben, Sonja and Robert left them to their work and went on deck. Adam, Aaron and the slaves were already at work, preparing main sail rings, pulleys and booms under Edward's keen direction.

"Looks like you've got yourself at least one good seaman, Mr. Pulaski," Robert said.

Edward heard the comment and looked without expression toward Ben. Ben said nothing, but gave his half brother a nod of approval.

"I know you're eager to be away, Mr. Pulaski, but I'd like to have my crew go over all the lines before we leave you. I'm sure your man there will see it done well, but my reputation is on both the stepping and the rigging."

"Thank you Mr. Lambdin."

Lambdin went to the railing where one of his men had placed a parcel and returned to Ben and Sonja.

"With your permission, Mr. Pulaski, Mrs. Lambdin has sent aboard a gift for Mrs. Pulaski." Without waiting for a response Lambdin handed the parcel to Sonja. "Feel free to open it, Ma'am," he said.

It was a light blue southwester raincoat edged in bright yellow with a matching sloutch hat and lined inside with soft shearling wool.

"It's a might heavy, but my wife swears by hers and will not go to sea with me after October without it," Lambdin said.

Sonja gently rubbed the shearling fur against her cheek, smiling under sparkling blue eyes. "This is a generous gift, Mr. Lambdin. I will always think of you and your wife when I wear it."

Lambdin nodded without comment, then returned to the hold to inspect the progress of his men.

By ten o'clock that morning, the rigging was correct,

Lambdin and his crew had returned to his boat yard and all of *Raven*'s sails had been hoisted onto the booms of both masts, ready to be unfurled. The wind remained gentle, no more than a cool breeze, and had shifted to come out of the south. It was perfect for the direction they needed to sail, so Ben ordered the anchors raised and sails set. Watching his small crew, he noted that Edward was acting as a good first mate.

But we will see, thought Ben.

The southward turn in little Eastern Bay at the mouth of the river, went smoothly and they were out to the main channel of the Chesapeake Bay before noon. The *Ugly Boat* galloped obediently at the end of her tow rope a hundred feet behind them. Ben had the sails on the *Raven* tightened to take more of the wind and lean gently from its push, after Edward set them perfectly. Ben smiled with his hands on the ship's wheel, feeling the response to the rudder, while Edward stood nearby watching the sails the way a good mother watches her children at play. Adam stood next to Ben for a moment watching the sails and Edward's attention to them.

"Say what you will, Ben," Adam said only loud enough for Ben to hear him. "...but that Edward knows his sails."

Ben grunted as Adam went below. Sonja sat on a storage locker near the stern ladderway, uncomfortably warm in her new southwester, even though she sat full in the wind, not yet ready to give in and remove it. Adam began cleaning up the dishes in the galley, putting on a stew for supper and setting the iron yokes to hold the pot on the stove. Albert and Ezekiel sat together on the deck near the midship railing. Aaron and B'gamba were at the bow watching the edges of the bay slide past in the distance, each gesturing boldly as they spoke between smiles and laughs.

"You have to get away from the yarn mill in Havre de Grace. Night is the best time," Aaron said.

"Why not as soon as we touch ground in that place? Or just before we reach it? I can swim like a fish."

"Yes, you could do that, but it will hurt my father. And

men will catch you right away. I think your Albert would see to that."

B'gamba frowned and looked back toward Albert. "Yes. Albert will want to go home to Covey. Covey has him trained like a hunting dog. I have watched him bring back runaways. There is thick beef for Albert, and bloody backs for the runaways. Sometimes much worse."

Aaron glanced back toward the stern, then toward the bay ahead of them, pointing as if he was discussing the land with B'gamba. "There are people who will help you get past the slave chasers. Pennsylvania is only fifteen miles from Havre de Grace. They do not hold slaves there."

B'gamba nodded his head. "Yes. I have heard of the Pennsylvania, and the place called Canada. Is it in Pennsylvania?"

"No. Canada is a thousand miles from here, I think, but Pennsylvania is only fifteen miles up the canal."He glanced over his shoulder again. "We have a special barge. It has a little space in the cargo hold that no one knows about but us." He hesitated, "We can get you to freedom."

B'gamba stared into his eyes for a long moment. "Your father knows of this?"

"Yes." Aaron paused. "That is why he cannot be linked openly to an escaped slave. They could put him in jail. Some people would want to burn our house... well if we still have a house."

"How can you promise this, when you are losing your own house?"

Aaron rubbed his forehead. "Barges are like moving houses, because each one has a cabin in the center. Barges stay in the canal basin at either end of the canal for days or even weeks. We move when we want to within the canal."

B'gamba looked out at the bay and smiled. "I must see this canal that will float me to freedom."

Aaron placed his hand on B'gamba's forearm and squeezed it tightly.

"You two seem to be getting along well. You ready to do a little work to keep the sails trimmed," Edward said.

87

He patted Aaron's shoulder while giving B'gamba an icy stare. "Move it, Thomas," he said.

Edward pointed B'gamba toward the stern. "Tighten up on the line to the main mast sail, back there. Tight, you hear? Make sure Cap'n Ben approves before you quit."

Then he steered Aaron with him toward the nearby jib sail lines. "Be careful with him, Aaron. That kind can get you in big trouble. One minute you think they're trained and timid, and the next minute they cut your throat and run away. They may act like people, but they can be savages and will attack you like mad dogs. Your father may not see me like family, but I want to look out for you. I knew you were family the moment we met." He slapped Aaron on the shoulder like a friend after the lines were tightened and he walked away with a smile. "Be careful, young master," he said.

As Edward walked past Albert and Ezekiel, he kicked their ankles.

"Get your asses below and help Massa Adam."

He came to stand at his assumed place to the side and slightly forward of Ben, folding his arms and looking around the ship, taking in its details.

"So this was a little slaver, was it," he said over his shoulder to Ben.

Ben heard him but did not respond.

"Damned good business," Edward said. "Good money. Demand is high. Prices are up."

That evening they anchored off Meeks Point near Still Pond Creek on the eastern shore, after a steady five knot run for eight hours.

Ben and Sonja joined the crew at the crew table again for supper. "Today was a good trial run," Ben said. "I'm sure we can go faster tomorrow."

"We could easily reach seven or eight knots before Havre de Grace, Ben," Edward added.

Ben took in a deep breath and barely hesitated. "I think so Edward. You did a good job with the sails today."

Edward smiled and patted Aaron's back next to him. "Thank you, Ben, as did young master Aaron. He's a good sailor."

Ben looked at Aaron. "Yes, I think he's a better sailor than I am. He steers the *Ugly Boat* as if it simply follows his thoughts."

"Adam," Sonja said, "that was an excellent stew."

"Well", Adam said, "even after chewing through all the salted beef and pork on board for five months, we've still got almost a hundred pounds hanging in there. Gonna need some potatoes and vegetables. Tell you what we really need, though...oysters! Boats oughta be full of'em in Havre de Grace. What ya' think there Cap'n?"

"While we straighten things out with the bank tomorrow, why don't you go get some for us," Ben said.

Edward stood up from the table and patted his stomach. "Good food, Adam. Thankee, sir," he said then turned toward the slaves. "You boys get some pads from the storage locker behind you, and make your beds here in the galley after we clear out...if that's acceptable to Cap'n Ben," he said turning toward Ben.

"It'll have to do," Ben said. "This isn't a passenger ship."

After short periods on the deck for pipes and cigars, and sips of rum for Ben, Adam, Edward and Sonja, the *Raven* closed up for the night. Adam was the last one to the crew's quarters, and took a meandering pathway through the main hold, offering to share a few more ounces of rum with Albert, Ezekiel and B'gamba.

Only Albert accepted the rum. Afterwards, he went to the stern storage locker where he retrieved two sets of the manacles and chained Ezekiel and B'gamba to the few remaining restraint bolts still embedded in the hull braces.

Late in the night, Ben awoke from recurring bloody nightmares that had returned since the fight to free Sonja from Hoagg and take the *Raven*. Walking through the ship, Ben found Ezekiel and B'gamba chained in the main hold. He had Albert remove and return the manacles to the storage locker. Then under Ben's direction the four of them removed the last of the restraining bolts. Before leaving them to find what sleep was left in the night, he confronted Albert and tapped him firmly on his chest.

"Albert, when I order that no one is chained on the *Raven*, that order is to be obeyed. It is why you are not in chains at this very moment," Ben said. Ben gripped the restraining bolts in his hand as he stepped up onto the deck, then threw them overboard.

10

Ben stepped onto the wharf in Havre de Grace and was immediately approached by Abigail Hannah. Her perpetual smile had been replaced by a grim line at her mouth and dark circles under her eyes. She wore a stained canvas dress and carried a small leather satchel hung across her chest by a worn leather strap.

"Gotta pay a docking fee, Ben," Abigail said.

"Never seen a woman doing this, Abigail," Ben said.

"I was lucky to get the work, Ben. After Robert was murdered, the canal Superintendent spoke to the town council for me. My late husband's brother works at a bank, and helps some, but I still got children to feed."

Ben fished one of the silver dollars from his coat and placed it in her hand.

"Is this new? Never had to pay for the *Ugly Boat*."

"Still won't, Ben, least not the first day, then a dollar a day after that. For schooners and Bay ships, it's a dollar first day and five dollars each day after. Town council wants'em moved out of the way for other incoming ships. We're barely keeping up as it is. "

Ben smiled and nodded his understanding, then quickly returned to the deck of the *Raven*. He pulled on Edward's sleeve and drew him near to Sonja.

"If we have to leave the *Raven* to go up canal, I need Edward here to slip away from the wharf and anchor off shore, then send a rowboat back for us. The town'll charge five dollars a day for us to stay here after today."

Sonja gasped and her eyes widened. "Five dollars a

day!"

Ben left them to their animated conversation and crossed the wharf toward Oyster Street. The bell above the door to the Tidewater Bank and Trust jingled as he entered. He approached the first teller window, but before he could speak, he heard Sam Briscoe's voice boom out from the back of the bank.

"Mr. Pulaski! Come on back here, please. We need to talk."

Ben glanced at the unfamiliar faces in the teller windows, then turned toward the little gated railing separating the entrance from the desk area. The gate opened silently on new oiled brass hinges and whispered into place against felt braces behind him as he walked to the desk.

Briscoe stood up as Ben approached and held out his hand. He showed the face of an undertaker plying his trade.

"This was not my decision, Benjamin," he said.

Ben hesitated, then accepted Briscoe's offered hand. Briscoe smiled at the acceptance and motioned Ben to sit in the padded velvet chair facing the desk.

"Heard Binterfield was dead," Ben said.

"Yes," Briscoe spoke softly, gently patting the desk top. "It was a loss to some."

"Not to me. I see by the name plate on your desk that it was not a total loss for you either."

Briscoe nodded solemnly, his eyes still on the desk top. "No, not a total loss..."

"So why are we being evicted?"

Briscoe brought his head up and almost pleaded his whisper, "I could not stop that, Benjamin. Herbert started it, but Lydia pushed it on. She has a great hatred for Sonja."

Ben crossed his arms. "Herbert Binterfield told my wife that I was dead. He reduced her to a destitute widow and then hired her as a servant to clean his house. Why the hell should Lydia hate Sonja?"

Briscoe looked quickly toward the front of the bank.

92

"Please, Benjamin, let us speak civilly to each other. Much has gone on in the past that we should leave there."

Ben took in another deep breath and slowly let it out. "So how do we put this eviction notice behind us?"

"I have a plan that will enable me to help you back into your farm, but it will take a few months..."

"Months? We must move out for months? Are you serious?"

Briscoe dropped his voice to a whisper, "I can be fired, Benjamin. We can both be out of house and home. Things will soon happen that will change that. In the meantime, I will do all I can to help you find a suitable dwelling..."

"We have a suitable dwelling, and I damned sure intend to keep it."

"I'm sorry, Benjamin, but your only choice now is to move out for a few months or move out forever. Understand, Lydia owns the property. In her current mood, Lydia would be happy to burn your farm and leave it in ashes."

Ben stood and slapped his hands on the desk, his face red and the artery in his neck pulsating.

"Please, Benjamin. Go speak with George Milton, your lawyer."

Ben glared down at Briscoe, then spun around and stomped out of the bank. The two tellers left their stalls and stood near the door, blocking the entrance, should Ben return. Briscoe went to the front and patted them each on their shoulders.

"It will be all right, gentlemen. Thank you."

Briscoe returned to his desk. Withdrawing his handkerchief from his pocket, he polished away Ben's palm prints on the desk top and returned to his seat.

Moments later, Ben paced the floor in front of George Milton's desk. The small office above the First National Bank barely afforded room for either man to walk around the desk.

"I'm sorry, Ben, but this paper is legitimate. There is no law that requires they give you any notice at all, but they have given you time to get your possessions out."

"This is not right, George! No one will buy the place!

This is just Lydia Binterfield taking out her vengeance on Sonja – and me."

"It may not be right, Ben, but it is legal. And even if what you say Briscoe told you is also correct, you have no choice but to move out. And...you have no guarantee he will actually help you move back in later. You should think about finding a new house for you and your family."

Ben stomped his foot. "God damn it, George!"

"There are other things to consider as well, Ben."

Ben spun around to face him."What else?"

"Shipping traffic is overwhelming this little town. Every cottage, house and closet is rented out to canallers, and journeymen. I can't think of a single dwelling that would hold four adults..."

"Adults? My sons are not adults. No, Isaac is at college. So, it will be three of us. Me, Sonja and Aaron."

"Well, your Aaron is an adult, now, Ben. He must have a room separate from you and Sonja, don't you agree?"

"Well, yes, of course..."

"I do know of someone that might be able to help you.."

"Who, George?"

"Mamie Stewart."

"Who?"

"Widow Stewart, Ben. William Stewarts' wife."

"Oh yes, I met him once. About a year before he died, I think. Then, yes, met her once, too. Nathan Brown lived there. Boarding house on Union Avenue?"

"Yes. That's it. Built of red oak. She has a room for rent. Quite nice, I hear. Or heard. Nathan remarked about the large room facing Union Avenue. It was across from his room on the second floor. Said it was ...sumptuous. That was the word he used."

"Well, if I can't find anything else, maybe I will go talk to her."

"Ben. You won't find anything else in Havre de Grace, unless you sell one of your boats for a month's rent. I urge you to go there straight from here. That room won't be open for long."

"Well, we always have the *Raven*, George. We can

sleep there."

"Tsk, tsk, tsk, Benjamin Pulaski! Sonja spent seven months on that thing. Do you honestly believe she will be happy spending another two months, or more, on it? Returning to the farm is NOT an option. Go see Mamie!"

Ben left Milton's office, made his way down the outside steps quickly and headed for the *Raven*. A brisk three block walk brought him to the wharf where the *Raven* had tied up earlier in the day, but she was gone. Fifty yards out in the Susquehanna Flats, the *Raven* sat in calm waters at the edge of the main channel, where her keel was safe from finding the shallow bottom at low tide. The *Ugly Boat* was no longer tied to the stern, and no one appeared to be on deck.

Ben cupped his hands around his mouth and bellowed out, "Ahoy *Raven*!" Some people nearby turned to look at him, but quickly returned to their chores or errands. No one came on deck to wave that they heard. He shouted again.

"Here I am, Benjamin," Edward spoke from a rowboat just below the edge of the wharf. Ben stepped to the edge and looked down. Edward was leaning back on the stern bench with his feet crossed on the mid bench and his hands folded behind his head.

"Oh. Thank you, Edward. I had forgotten I asked you to do that, and..."

"And you expected me to be off somewhere doodling."

"Well, I didn't know what...My apologies."

Edward gave a sloppy salute and pointed relaxed finger toward north.

"Sonja and Aaron took the *Ugly Boat* and went up the canal. Apparently he left one of your mules at the canal stable. They said you could meet them there when you can." Then he flipped his finger toward the west. "Adam is asleep on the ship."

Ben placed his hands on his hips and looked around, blowing out his breath and frowning.

"What?" Edward said.

"I wanted Sonja to go look at a boarding house with me."

Edward shrugged his shoulders and raised his eyebrows.

"I'll be back," Ben said. Then he spun on his heels and walked to Union Avenue.

On the corner of Union Avenue and Bourbon Street sat a well constructed house with five gables. Smallish windows looked out from the third floor, flanked on each side by cypress shutters. Large windows were on the second floor, also with cypress shutters suitable for their size. And, on the ground floor, tall narrow windows stood proud and crystal clear, hung from the window frames ready to be thrown open in hot evenings or shuttered against the storms. A few houses on Union Avenue had been painted as was a growing fashion among expensive homes, but the Stewart house had not succumbed to covering its natural wood. It was covered by lapped red oak planks. The window and door frames were made of white oak. In the several years since the house was built the white oaks had faded, but the red oak planks had taken on a dark pink hue. Ben sighed and closed his eyes momentarily.

A Pink House.

He stood looking at the house as a stylish couple strolled along the edge of the wide shady lane holding hands. The couple slowed as they meandered past Ben.

"Good god," mumbled the man.

The woman giggled softly. "I told you it was pink."

As they walked on, Ben dropped his chin and let out a long slow breath. Then he straightened his back, marched briskly up the walkway and knocked firmly on the door.

Within seconds a very attractive petite woman opened the door. Her Nanticoke lineage was subtly displayed in her high cheekbones and the intensity if her brown eyes. The skin of her face was smooth and unblemished, making a secret of her age as it was with the oriental women Ben had seen in China. She frowned at him and glanced at the edges of the door. Her stance was confident, challenging.

"We have a brass knocker, sir. Banging on the door like

that may loosen the hinges. May I help you?"

Ben took a half step backward. "I need to speak with Mrs. Stewart," Ben stuttered, realizing who she was even as he spoke the words.

"You already are, sir. How can I help you?"

"Room..."

"What?"

"Room. Large room?"

"Do you wish to rent a room, sir?"

"Yes, please. For me and Sonja, but not Aaron. No, not Aaron, he can sleep on the ship."

"All right. Would you care to come in and see the room?"

"Yes, please." He held out his hand. "I'm Ben Pulaski..."

"Yes."

"Yes?"

"Yes. We met once before, Mr. Pulaski. George Milton told me yesterday you would be needing the front room on the second floor for you and your wife. I assume that's Sonja?"

"Yes. Sonja is my wife."

Mamie chuckled and pulled him into the house. "I actually met Sonja a couple years ago, before you came back from the grave, when she worked for that bastard Binterfield." She flipped her finger over her shoulder toward the staircase and turned away from him, speaking over her shoulder as she went up.

"I tried to hire her to come work here, but she said she owed him money and would stay to pay her debts."

"She thought I was dead..." Ben said to her back as he followed her up the stairs, his voice echoing in the stairwell.

"Cheated her on her land and made him his servant over the debt," Mamie said. "The bastard. George told me."

Ben stopped.

"George is awfully chatty for a lawyer. I didn't know that about him."

Mamie laughed. "He stayed with me a while. He had

the room before poor Nathan took it. Mr. Milton left me when his house was built." She turned around and looked down at him. "You will be chatty with me too. Everyone who stays here is. Your Sonja will, too. I am very easy to talk to." She wrinkled her nose and chuckled again. "And I love to hear about everything." Then she spun around and showed a hooked finger over her shoulder, motioning him up the stairs.

The landing on the second floor presented a well decorated parlor that opened on to an uncovered raised porch through glassed doors. Within the parlor were several comfortable looking covered chairs and foot stools, arranged around a small iron stove on the left guarded by brass spittoons on either side. Against the right wall was a polished mahogany counter, arrayed with etched glasses, several bottles of whiskey and a carved cigar box set on white linen.

At the left corner, closest to the landing, was another door. A brass oval was mounted in the center of the upper half with the number 1 engraved in its shiny surface. Mamie flipped her hand around the hallway as she pulled a key from her apron pocket.

"Rooms two, three and four are over there. Five, six, seven and eight are on the third floor." She unlocked the door, but stopped before opening it. She spun around and tapped Ben's chest with her index finger.

"Each room has a wash stand, with bowl, basin and chamber pot. If you are neat, the chamber pot is cleaned by the maid and returned. If you are not, the chamber pot is not returned, and you will use the outhouse among the roses at the far edge of the garden."

She pushed open the door. There was a generous high bed under a covered canopy with matching heavy curtains tied to each corner post, night stands, cabinets, dresser, two chests of drawers and a large chest at the foot of the bed. Two large front windows looked out over Union Avenue through intricately laced curtains, and a side window overlooking Bourbon Street. To the left was a smaller room holding the wash stand and chamber pot cabinet, with another small curtained window. The wide yellow pine flooring was almost completely covered with a woven oriental rug, similar to rugs Ben had seen in China.

"This will be wonderful," Ben said.

"Of course it will," she said. "Twenty dollars a month. Half now," she added, holding out her hand. "Supper is precisely at six o'clock. If I am late, you must wait. If you are late, you may not find any food. Biscuits and sliced meat are set out in the kitchen each morning at five thirty. What's there is there. Leave some for the others," she said, "although they may not leave any for you," she added with a throaty chuckle.

Ben smiled and reached into his coat, withdrawing ten silver dollars and placing them in her palm. She bounced them in her hand listening to the metallic ring.

"Excellent. He has money and puts it out as soon as I say. We will get along splendidly, Mr. Benjamin Pulaski. Now run get your Sonja."

11

Ben returned to the Farm to find Sonja sitting alone on the porch. The front door behind her was open, showing a room devoid of all furniture. He sat down next to her and wrapped an arm around her.

"Where are Aaron and the others," he asked.

"Gone. Everyone. Everything. Gone."

"Gone where, Sonja?"

She swept her hand across the leaf filled yard and into the air toward Lapidum.

"Everything has been taken out and placed elsewhere, except for our clothes in the front bedroom. Mac was kind enough to take all our furniture up into the loft of his blacksmith shop. It will be dirty when we get it down, but it will be dry. Dishes, pans, utensils and most of the lanterns went into Delbert's storage room in the back of his dry goods store."

Ben nodded his head, looking out at the river between the empty branches of the twin oaks, but seeing the faces of his friends.

"They are good friends to us, Sonja. And I assume Lars agrees with Delbert to keep our things in his warehouse?"

"Not his anymore," Sonja said, leaning her head on Ben's shoulder. "Lars sold out to Delbert while we were on the *Raven*. He moved to Bel Air to live with his son. Took the white dog that Aaron likes with him."

"I'm sure Delbert gave him a generous payment." He squeezed her shoulders within his arm. "I suspect the Freidmans will be our in-laws within the year."

Sonja straightened her back and looked into his eyes. "Not this year anyway. This year only has five weeks left." She paused, searching his eyes for a tell. "Has Aaron said anything to you?"

Ben smiled. "No, but it's hard not to see that it will be soon." He looked down at the canal.

"Where are the barges? I didn't pass them on my way up here."

"There was nothing left for Aaron to do here. He has decided to live on the *Ugly Boat* until things are settled."

Ben looked hard into Sonja's eyes, but said nothing.

"Miss Freidman has gone home...like the lady she is," she said. "I told Aaron to go on to Wrightsville for a load of coal. Better than him lingering around here, steaming for a fight with those deputies. Jeremy and Abraham have gone with him to help handle the barges through the locks."

Ben sighed and nodded his head.

"Well then, Mrs. Pulaski. Let us return to Havre de Grace and settle into our new room at Mrs. Stewart's boarding house. I will walk down to Mac's blacksmith's shop and borrow a wagon for our things."

Sonja pushed on her knees to stand and then stepped into the house, speaking over her sagging shoulders as she went. "All that's left in here are two small trunks for clothes, and our coats."

As Ben took a step into the yard, Sonja stopped in the middle of the front room, spun around toward the open door and placed her hands on her hips. "I want my stove taken out of here! I will not leave it so that bitch can sell it along with my house!"

An hour later, Mac's loaned wagon sat in front of his shop, while the mule harnessed to the wagon munched brown grass at the side of the hard dirt road. Sonja sat on the seat with her arms folded across her chest under her shawl, looking out over the river. She watched a blue heron glide over the shallows beyond the towpath and remembered the brassy taste of fear as she laid bound in the bottom of Hoagg's rowboat. She absently rubbed the scar on her upper thigh where Hoagg's crewman had forced his blade to make her scream.

"I hope you're burning in Hell," she mumbled to herself.

Inside the blacksmith shop, Mac and Ben grunted as they shoved the stove onto the last empty storage shelf in the back of the shop. Ben shook hands with Mac as they came out the front of the shop, and Mac tossed his hand up in a friendly wave to Sonja. She did not see him. Nor did she see Ben as he pulled himself up onto the seat next to her. Her face was still turned out toward the river, but he knew she did not see that either.

They both had such moments now. Sometimes the nightmares that always stood at the edge of day, slipped between the sunshine and the nightfall, and raged again behind their own eyes. Sometimes her memories exploded into the daylight, like his own raw memories of three squalid years a prisoner in China. He never knew which demon was dancing in her brain at any moment, nor the chorus of his own.

Was it the agony of watching our infant daughter swirl beneath the ice when she thought I was dead? Was it the terror she endured on the Raven before she flung herself into the water with bound wrists?

Ben left her to her silence, allowing her to return in her own time, when she could claw back up from the dark pit that pulled at her.

He flipped the reins on the haunch of the mule and clicked between his teeth. The mule leaned into her harness and pulled the wagon down the road the few yards to the swing bridge turned out over the canal. She clomped her hooves on the wood planking, then down onto the packed earth of the towpath. She turned south toward Havre de Grace, leaving Lapidum behind them.

The sun was beginning to settle onto the stump dotted hillside west of town as Ben drove the wagon along Union Avenue. The gnawing demand for firewood and logs for wood planks had denuded most of the hills around Havre de Grace. Except for the poorest households, coal was burning in iron stoves and fireplaces, feeding the slate colored cloud hanging over the town in still air. It added more ash to rooftops and on to surrey tops without carriage houses for the night.

Mamie swooped from the front entrance and descended upon Ben and Sonja as soon as the wagon came to a halt.

"Sonja, my dear. Welcome to the Pink House." She smiled and put her hands on her hips in exaggerated motion and then pointed a dainty finger at the wagon. "You are the wife of a sea captain, who commands the noble *Raven*, and yet he brings you to my house in a workman's barrow?" She flipped a finger gently under Ben's bearded chin, giving him a mock frown, "What were you thinking, Benjamin?"

Mamie slipped an arm under Sonja's, pulling her along into the house. Within seconds Mamie had Sonja in the middle of the front room on the second floor. Mamie rolled out her hands above her shoulders with a flourish and pirouetted.

"This shall be your abode," Mamie said. "Your sea captain has done you well, has he not?"

Sonja beamed and sat on the bed, closing her eyes to the softness and the texture under her palms, and then took in the view of the room. The four poster bed was framed above, draped with dark green wool, fringed in bright yellow. Matching enclosures were suspended from the frame and tied against each post with yellow ribbons.

"It's beautiful, Mamie."

"The bed curtains overlap generously. They will keep you and your hubby snug and warm at night," Mamie said.

Boot steps clomped on the floor in the landing, and a man's head jutted into the doorway.

"Welcome to the Pink House. Mrs. Pulaski," Sam Briscoe said.

Mamie fixed him with an evil stare.

"Your hat, sir. This is not a barn."

Briscoe snatched his hat off his head and absently ran his fingers through his ink black hair.

"My apologies Mrs. Stewart...and yours as well, Mrs. Pulaski..."

"Step aside," Ben said from behind Briscoe. He brought in the first trunk and set it on the floor at the foot of the bed.

"There is something I wish to show you, Ben," Briscoe said, and motioned Ben in his direction."

Ben and Sonja exchanged glances. Ben shrugged his shoulders and followed Briscoe to the rear of the second floor. Mamie ignored the interchange and continued to show Sonja around the room.

Briscoe met Ben at the door for the rear-most rented room. Ben's eyes were wide open.

"You stay here?" Ben said

"Yes. Been here almost two years, but not for much longer. Here, look at this."

He handed Ben a folded letter on Bank Letterhead. It was a letter of credit from The Tidewater Bank and Trust Company to Benjamin Pulaski in the amount of one hundred thousand dollars. Ben swallowed and opened his mouth to speak, but nothing came out.

"I can't give it to you yet, Ben. All of the money has not been moved into that account yet, but I wanted you to know I am doing everything in my power to keep my word to you."

"I...I," Ben stammered.

Briscoe slipped the paper from Ben's fingers and returned it to a wooden box set beneath a silver cross hung on the wall above his small desk at the rear of the room.

"Why are you doing this, Briscoe?"

"Ben, I did many things for Herbert Binterfield. Many of them were crooked, but watching him single out you and Mrs. Pulaski for his unending hate, was more than I could endure. I had already resigned when he was murdered. However, Mrs. Binterfield begged me to reconsider and has since made me bank manager." He took in a deep breath and straightened his back. "I am now in a position to rectify some things that weigh heavily on my soul, Benjamin. The hatred he heaped upon you and which still lingers without cause in his widow, is one of the greatest wrongs I intend to right."

"Briscoe. Sam, I don't know..."

"I don't begrudge you for hesitating to believe me, Ben. So, I am committed to proving it by my actions."

Briscoe held out his hand in friendship and Ben reluctantly took it.

"Now, go help your wife settle in, Ben. And I will see you both at dinner."

Ben stood in the landing as Briscoe withdrew into his room and gently closed the door. He then went down to the wagon and brought up the second trunk. After he set the trunk next to the other one, he stood by the window staring down at Bourbon Street.

"What?" Sonja said.

Ben shook his head. "Briscoe just apologized for everything he and Binterfield ever did to us. He is in the process of helping us get the farm back."

"What? Do you believe him?"

"I don't really know, Sonja. He certainly acts...sincere..."

"So do wolves, Ben."

"He seems to have had an epiphany of sorts..."

"Epiphany doesn't sound like one of your words, Ben."

He spun on her. "I don't have to know how to spell it or write it, to know what it means!"

She looked into his face with a small smile. He grinned and looked down at his feet.

"Don't forget, Sonja, you read it to me in the bible hundreds of times before I finally learned to read it myself."

She leaned into his face and kissed him on his cheek.

"You can say epiphany any time you feel like it, Benjamin."

"Oh, hush," he said and pulled her lips to his. After the kiss, he added. "He has a cross hanging over a little desk in his room.

Sonja's eyebrows went high on her forehead.

Back in his room, Briscoe flipped the cross off the nail over his desk and replaced the knife holder that typically hung there. Then he opened the desk drawer and withdrew his ivory handle knife. He stood there a long moment looking at the reflection of his eyes in the highly polished blade. He lay down on the bed with one hand resting on the pillow behind his head and crossed his boots at the foot of the bed. He absent-mindedly toyed with the knife, tracing the tip gently down his abdomen in a long lightning bolt design and chuckled to himself.

He snickered in a child-like voice, "One of the greatest wrongs I intend to right."

He drifted off to dreaming sleep. In it he stood before the bank again, when Pulaski hit him in the face so hard he sank onto the dirt and dust of the street, blood gushing from his nose. When he got up onto his feet he was in the basement of the Binterfield house, immaculately dressed in a fine English suit. Lydia was naked on her knees, holding up a silver platter with his knife laid on a blue silk cloth. Ahead of him, stood the long walnut table from Mamie's dining room. Everyone he had ever despised was tied in chairs around the table. In the center of the table lay Ben Pulaski, spread-eagled with his hands and feet nailed into the walnut. He took the knife from Lydia and slowly sliced long pieces of flesh from Pulaski's abdomen then laid them in the plates before his guests, as Ben Pulaski screamed.

"Down to supper, old man!" The roomer next to Briscoe knocked on the door again, and then clomped down the wooden steps to the main floor. Briscoe quickly replaced his knife in its holder and washed his face at the basin. He was down in the dining room before Mamie set the evening roast at the center of the table. Mamie's kitchen helper filled glasses with beer or wine as requested, as Briscoe took his customary spot near the head of the table. The silverware was aligned perfectly next to each plate, in two neat rows, like soldiers at attention, along the long white table cloth. Light from candle chandeliers hanging overhead gleamed off polished silver in rows of yellow stars. Ten faces sat around the massive table, and ten more would have found room without touching elbows. In a lull of dining room chatter, Mamie said a blessing then turned to Briscoe.

"Would you kindly do your usual honors with the meat, Mr. Briscoe."

Briscoe stood and bowed to Mamie and the other boarders.

"It is always my distinct pleasure, Mrs. Stewart."

He beamed as bright red juices from the roast trickled down onto the silver serving plate, and expertly sliced exactly equal pieces of rare meat for each guest. His smile was greatest for the Pulaskis

"And to our new neighbors in this wonderful household," he said as he laid meat on their offered plate.

Mamie held up her glass in salute, joined by the others.

12

On board the *Raven*, Adam Tuttle stood near one of the ship's tandem wheels with his arms folded across his chest. Edward stood near the railing ladder way, holding the line to the rowboat.

"Your choice, old man, " Edward said. "You gonna row with me to that dock over there, or am I gonna leave you stranded on this ship without a rowboat."

"Edward," Adam said, "you told Ben you would stay aboard until he gets things settled about his farm."

"I've stayed all I'm going to, Adam. Now either come along or get left behind. I'm not staying out here one more hour listening to men and women laugh and drink at those taverns over there."

"How come you have money for taverns this evening? When you showed up in St. Michaels last week, you were penniless?"

"I delivered those three slaves to the lumber mill while Ben and Sonja went to the bank," said Edward.

"And?"

"And the lumber mill owner gave me a couple dollars for my trouble."

Adam shook his head. "Old man Jackson doesn't give spit for anybody's trouble. If he gave you money, it's because you convinced him he owed it!"

Edward spun onto the side ladder and began stepping down into the ship's rowboat.

"All right. All right," Adam said. "I'm comin with ya."

Minutes later, as the rowboat touched against a

dockside ladder, Edward sprung from his seat and trotted along the dock. Adam stood to grab the ladder, his white bearded face only inches above the level of the dock. Edward spoke over his shoulder as he walked away.

"Don't wait for me, old man. I ain't comin back tonight."

"You comin back at all, Edward," Adam asked.

"Probably, but I need some time for myself and maybe a woman or two. And I'm sick of bacon!"

Edward stopped, blew out his breath and turned back to face Adam. He smiled at the view of Adam's head bobbing like a white bushy jack-o'-lantern above the dock's edge in the growing darkness.

Edward pointed north. "There's a tavern on Oyster Street that serves decent food at a fair price, old man. Tell Carl I sent you."

Then he turned and walked up toward the lights and sounds on St. John Street.

Adam plopped down onto a seat board in the rowboat. He yanked the bow line back into the boat and pushed against the dock ladder, sending the rowboat out into the river. He grabbed the oar handles and rotated the blades down into the water, then leaned back as he pushed the rowboat back toward the *Raven.*

We got free smoked meat hanging in that galley, and Edward turns his nose up at it.

"I like bacon," he said to the rowboat.

And rum. Still got a couple kegs of that, too.

Adam was standing on the deck near the ship's lantern, patting his full stomach and smoking his stubby pipe when the steady metal clang of a public clock in town struck eight times. Under a whale oil street lamp mounted on the dock, a man and woman stood close to each other, waving in his direction.

"Lord Benjamin and the Lady Sonja," Adam whispered to himself with a smile. He returned their wave and bellowed across the water, "All's well, Cap'n."

The couple turned and walked back up Bourbon Street. As Ben and Sonja approached the front door of their new residence, the door flew open and Sam Briscoe nearly skipped down the steps.

"Good evening," he said as he tipped his top hat and trotted by.

Ben and Sonja had only a moment to smile and nod his greeting as he flitted away. Sonja glanced over Ben's shoulder watching Briscoe stride north.

"Headed to the Binterfield House, no doubt," she said.

"And how would you know that, without a doubt, Mrs. Pulaski?"

"Mamie knows everything, Ben."

"Yes. So she says." Ben held the door open and walked with Sonja up the mahogany staircase to their room on the second floor.

Four blocks north on Union Avenue, Briscoe rounded the corner of Franklin Street and slipped out of the street light onto Freedom Lane. The lane allowed common deliveries, and servants entrances at the rear of houses facing Union Avenue and Stokes Street. The lane also presented two rows of outhouses, poorly disguised among aromatic plants covering rear fences. The rear pathway to the Binterfield Mansion also took him past its own outhouse, reminding him of Herbert's resistance to paying for regular emptying. He twisted his nose at the embarrassment of entering by way of the outhouse and servants door, but he still needed to keep his affair with Lydia secret.

At least I have my own key, and no longer have to suffer getting Junie or Sissy to open the door, with their sneering pompous looks.

"Sell you both," he muttered to himself as he turned the key.

Well past midnight, Briscoe slipped back out the rear door of the Binterfield mansion and walked quietly down the brick path to Freedom Lane. The night soil cart was parked on the opposite side of the lane. The cart mule waited patiently while two men spoke in low tones as they dredged one of the other outhouses. The stench from the cart was aggressive, even in the cold air. Vapor rose off the open barrel sitting at the back of the cart. A black man rounded the corner from the brick outhouse, leaning away from the weight of his full bucket, his face was hidden behind a frayed cloth tied over his mouth and nose. The faint aroma of camphor scented the smell of excrement near him.

"Is this your business?" Briscoe said.

"No, suh," he mumbled, then nodded toward the nearby outhouse. "Be his," he said. "Matthew," he said in a hoarse whisper.

Another man wearing a face cloth and a heavy apron stepped out and stood facing Briscoe.

"What is your fee?" Briscoe said.

"Dollah," the man said.

Briscoe fished a silver coin from his pocket and handed it toward the cart owner. He waited for the man to open his palm under where he held the coin, so he could drop it without touching the man. Briscoe pointed to the Binterfield outhouse.

"You do that one next. And don't spill. You leave it clean, hear?"

"Yassah. Always do. I'm the best in town?"

Briscoe frowned at the man, unable to see his eyes. "There are others?"

"Yassah. Hava da grace gots fo'"

"You go by Matthew? Your...business?"

"Yassah."

"Do it right and I'll have you do it on a schedule."

"Yassah. That be good. Massah Binafeel, he always wait too..."

Briscoe had walked away, trying his best to hold his breath until he reached fresh air. At the corner, emerging from the night shadows into the lamplight, he turned toward the sound of the taverns on St. John Street.

Late the following morning Mamie allowed herself a rare second cup of coffee, leaning against a heavy wood block preparation table in the center of the kitchen. One wall of the kitchen, was windowed from ankle to high ceiling, bathing the room in bright morning light. The white oak framing had not yet been touched by paint, as was becoming the fashion. Several glass enclosed shelves were mounted in front of the windows holding dozens of porcelain Staffordshire blue stain plates and matching bowls. The back wall, where older houses had cooking fireplaces, was bricked to receive the smokestacks from a matched pair of knee-high iron box stoves with a brick oven between them, fronted by an ornate iron door. The left hand stove held a large water tank and outlet to serve hot water as needed. The wall holding the kitchen entrance from the dining room and the doorway to Mamie's private suite provided dozens of closed wooden cabinets.

Sam Briscoe entered the kitchen and stepped before her.

"I rarely see you in the morning, Mr. Briscoe. I am sorry, but any food or coffee was gone hours ago..."

He waved her comment away.

"No, I...um... have a question for you. It may be too delicate, but I need the advice of a property owner."

"Really," she said, putting her hands on her hips with a flourish. "What information could a man of such esteem seek from a boardinghouse keeper?"

Briscoe frowned at her.

"Mrs. Stewart. We both know that you are a shrewd business...person."

She tilted her head and smiled, but said nothing, holding his attention with the arch of her eyebrows.

"It is about...well...night soil," he said

"What?"

"I am trying to arrange for such service for the Binterfield estate. I understand there is someone known as Matthew that performs...such service. How do I...how do you...contact him for...regular service? And are there others that I should consider?"

"Ah, so you are not about to whisk me off my feet with delicate platitudes. Is this so, Mr. Briscoe?"

"Well, er...no. What?" he said .

Mamie chuckled and barely touched his forearm with her fingertip, like a fleeting butterfly.

"Just having a little joke with one of my boarders, Mr. Briscoe."

She brought the same finger tip to the side of her cheek and tapped gently three times.

"Yes. Now that I think about the Binterfield house, it sits back against Freedom Lane, as does this house at this end. Matthew takes care of almost all...privies on Freedom. Of course, my husband had already started using Matthew long before he passed away..."

"Oh. I did not mean to bring that..."

She placed two fingertips on his forearm, quickly retracted.

"Have no concern. Mr. Briscoe. It was only a reference of time. As I recall, William sent word through Matthew's wife, Eudora. I'm sure there are other ways, but she is my connection to him."

"Eudora?"

"Yes, sir. She works in the home of Dr. Harper on Adams Street. May I pass a note to her for you?"

"Oh...yes...yes, that would be very helpful. Thank you."

She placed a finger tip on his forearm, glancing at his sleeve. "Sir, you have hurt yourself? There is blood on your cuff."

Briscoe twisted his arm to see the outer side of his cuff.

"Oh, just me being sloppy last night."

"Oh?"

"Yes...I...I helped my brother with a shoulder of venison he was given as partial payment for horse shoes. He is so clumsy with knives. Hammer and anvil are his tools. He is more at ease with smashing hot iron than making a delicate cut in meat.

"And you. Mr. Briscoe, are our artiste with the blade, are you not?"

"Well, there is a skill to meat cutting. Our father was a humble butcher, and I believe I acquired his sense of satisfaction with a good clean cut."

"Ah," Mamie said, "Just as both the wood chopper and the carver work with wood, one is a hacker while the other is a sculptor. Yes?"

Briscoe bent his head and shoulders in a bow, looked

deep into her eyes and shared a boyish smile of genuine affection. "Why... yes, Mrs. Stewart. How very astute and kind of you to put it that way."

He kept his smile as he turned slowly away, and left through the front door.

Moments later, as Sonja came into the kitchen with two empty coffee cups and saucers, Mamie was still standing near the center table, smiling.

"A pleasant memory, Mamie?"

Mamie sighed and flashed a broader smile.

"No, just a curiosity of thought. How are you this morning, Sonja?"

"Bored, Mamie. I have forced myself to stay in that beautiful room, since Ben left earlier, but I must have something useful to do. At home I would be...busy. Let me help your kitchen girl."

"My kitchen girl only helps with breakfast and supper."

"Then let me help your maid."

Mamie folded her arms over her chest.

"There is no maid. No. No, that is not entirely true. I am the maid."

"What?"

"Sonja. Do not be troubled. Make yourself comfortable on the settee in the parlor and let me fix you a cup of tea, then I must be up to my daily duties."

"You. You clean the rooms?"

" They do not clean themselves, unless there is a secret that you used in your home in Lapidum?"

"No. I just...You are so refined. I cannot imagine you..."

"Sonja, I love playing the part of the society woman. I did it for years under the care of my wonderful husband. There was nothing he would not have done for me. No fight he would have not taken on for my honor. No enemy he would not have faced down for my pride. He separated himself from the family that bore him, so he could live with his Indian maiden..."

114

"But, surely..."

"There are no 'surelys'. You are among the few who are not aghast at an Indian living as a white man's woman...wife no less. And, married in a church, too. He made that happen for me. And then he worked himself to death paying the debts he amassed treating me like a white woman. Even in the census, he bribed the census taker to enter me as Greek."

Sonja placed her hand on Mamie's arm.

"In North Carolina, there are many families who share Cherokee blood. As it is in my family."

"Ah, yes, Sonja, but you look like a Nordic queen. I look like what I am, the daughter of a Nanticoke Indian woman and a white man. And the blood of my mother is stronger in me than that of my father."

"Enough of this, Mamie. If there is work to be done in this house, let's get it done! Let me feel useful!"

Within three hours, all beds were made, night jars were emptied, wash basins were cleaned, water pitchers cleaned and refilled, floors swept, wicks and candles trimmed, lantern and candle glass cleaned, and dishes washed. In the early afternoon, with a fresh ham cooking in the brick oven in the kitchen, Sonja and Mamie relaxed on the settee in the parlor, chatting as old friends.

"It was a hard time for me, Sonja. I was losing my home soon after losing my husband, far away from my family."

Sonja nodded with tears framing her eyes, picturing her own home on Pearl Lane, pushed off its foundation during the ice gorge, screaming at the empty spot in the ice water where her infant had been pulled away from her. Ben reported lost at sea. Dead. Both dead.

Alisha!

"He was in the ground only two months," Mamie said. "when the bank began to foreclose on the house," She eyed Sonja. "This was far more house than William could have ever afforded. The mortgage was doomed from the first day. Binterfield knew that. I am sure he did, but I knew none of that then."

Sonja sat in silence, knowing she could say nothing at

such a memory, knowing the insult to the moment it would be to say 'yes, I did that, too'.

Mamie chuckled and pointed up toward the back of the house.

"It was poor befuddled Mr. Briscoe who was tasked with informing me of the foreclosure and handing me the note." She fixed Sonja with her eyes. "This was before he moved in as a boarder. I believed he lived with his brother's family, then."

"Did he help you with the foreclosure?"

Mamie let out a small dry laugh. "No not that one. He prefers to let things run their course, I think. No, it was something else entirely..."

Mamie stared long at Sonja's face.

"Something else, entirely..." Mamie said again, then stood up, turned toward the kitchen and paused. "I miss having family...I never had a sister," she said with her back to Sonja. Then she spun around to face her again. "Did you really try to shoot Herbert Binterfield in his bank?"

Sonja hesitated. "Well...how...how did you hear such a thing?"

"People tell me things that they would never tell another soul..."

Sonja raised her chin and answered firmly. "Yes."

Mamie blinked. "One of my previous boarders said it was so, but in strictest confidence. I believe that if he was still alive he would be my friend still. He was the best friend God ever sent me, except for my William."

"Can you name him?"

"Nathan Brown," Mamie said.

"Oh," mumbled Sonja. There was a sadness in her eyes and a slight tremble in her lower lip. "He was my friend as well, and my husband's friend. We were near him when he died, taking the *Raven*."

"Sonja, it seems that we can share anything with each other. Like sisters, we can speak from our deepest hearts. I do not have to pretend to be anything but what I am."

Sonja smiled up at her.

116

"Be my sister, Sonja."

Sonja's eyes went wide. She tilted her head and peered deeply into Mamie's eyes. Then she smiled and stood up. Stepping close to Mamie, she placed her hand on her shoulder. "I will," she said, then held her a brief moment.

They shared smiles, then Mamie gave a broad child-like grin, grabbed Sonja's hand and pulled her through the kitchen. "You must see this," she said over her shoulder as they stepped out the narrow back door and then turned down into what appeared to be a root cellar.

In the darkness under the house, Mamie lit a candle, covered it with a glass and held the candle holder out in front of her. Taking Sonja by the hand again, she drew Sonja farther under the house, lighting what appeared to be an ancient stone walled basement.

"This was the basement of the original house on this site. It was burned by the British in 1814. William had our house built well beyond this basement in 1835."

Mamie placed the candle holder on a nearby rock ledge, and then pulled down a modest wooden chest. She turned to look into Sonja's face in the yellow candle light.

"No one knows about this except me...and now you."

She opened the chest and blew dust off the contents. A yellow metallic reflection almost sparkled in the candle light, casting faint spots of yellow light on the heavy wooden beams above their heads. Mamie giggled like a school girl and lifted one of the coins full into the candle light, then handed it to Sonja.

"Is this..."

"Yes. It is a gold coin. And it has many brothers and sisters in this box."

"Your William, had these down here?" Sonja said.

"No." Mamie giggled again. "They were buried in my garden. In rotting leather pouches where my potatoes grew. Placed there many years before my William had this house built, maybe even before the house that was burned here in the second war with England."

Sonja examined the coin carefully in the candle light. "It looks like the picture of a woman with a big nose on this side and the date 1760. There are flowers and a crown on this other side. And, there is writing around the edges of both sides, I think."

Mamie giggled with excitement. "The *woman* is King Louis the 16th of France. The *flower* is a special flower. It is the fleur-de-lis of France. There were French gold coins buried in my garden!! I found them only days before the bank was to repossess my house."

"So you made your bank payments with some of these coins?"

"Oh no! I didn't want anyone to know I had gold coins! I used William's old musket ball tools and melted some of them down into nuggets. The jeweler gave me much more for the gold than Binterfield would. And that let me keep the house until I had enough boarders for income."

"I have seen a coin like this coin before, Mamie. Adam Tuttle wears one around his neck on a chain. He knows the story, or at least 'a' story about the coins."

"Really. Then we must have this Adam Tuttle to supper one evening."

Sonja dropped the coin into the wooden chest, then closed it. Mamie grunted softly as she placed the chest back up on the rock ledge.

Back upstairs, Mamie wrote a short note and the two ladies walked toward the Harper home on Adams street. Mamie guided them onto the service lane at the back of the Harper house. She stopped at the fence on the far edge of the Harper's yard, near the back corner of the brick outhouse. Mamie pulled on a loose brick, and showed the spot to Sonja, although Sonja no longer looked at her. She was staring at the little shanty at the other back corner of the yard.

As Mamie held up the loose brick in one hand and her folded note in the other, she followed Sonja's stare.

"What is it, Sonja?"

"I lived there for almost a year, Mamie."

"What? That shack? You?"

"It was a hard time for me and the boys. Ben was dead. Alisha was dead. The house was gone – taken by the river...the ice gorge of '39..."

"I remember that..."

"We had nothing. Binterfield took me in as a house servant to work off the debt to the bank...Wallace Harper was our doctor. He let me stay here, so I could move out of the Binterfield house."

Sonja looked at Mamie with tears rolling down her cheek. "When Ben finally came home, I couldn't feel anymore. I just slapped his face and told him to leave."

Mamie coughed. "That was stupid, Sister."

"Yes. Sister. That was stupid. But Ben didn't leave. God knows why."

"And then?" Mamie said

"And then one day, after Binterfield tried to smash Ben down as he had smashed me down, I rode into town from Lapidum, shoved a pistol into Binterfield's mouth, and pulled the trigger."

Mamie's eyes went wide, and her eyebrows shot up. "God almighty, Sonja!"

Sonja wiped the tears from her cheek. "The pistol did not go off. His spittle had fouled the firing powder." Sonja looked Mamie deep into her eyes. "Now we have firing caps on our pistols."

"Good that he is already dead, then."

"Yes, Mamie. Good that he is already dead. But, even from the grave, that bastard Binterfield reaches out to take our home, through his wife and Sam Briscoe."

Mamie put her arm around Sonja's waist, still holding the loose brick. "You are not going to shoot one of my boarders, are you, Sister?"

Sonja sniffed and chuckled. "No. I have no current plans to shoot Sam Briscoe."

"Good, then watch me mail this note to Eudora, so Mr. Briscoe can have the Binterfield outhouse cleaned out."

Afterwards, Mamie slapped her hands together, freeing them of brick dust. "And so now you and your Ben live happily ever after, since you did not shoot your former employer..."

"Until one of Ben's old shipmates kidnapped me and Ben killed half his crew getting me back..."

Mamie stopped and stared at Sonja. "You were on the

slave ship that Mr. Briscoe and the Sheriff had to storm?"

"Briscoe?" Sonja said. "He was a prisoner on the ship, too. And all he did was steal Ben's rowboat and run away!"

"I must hear this whole story!" Mamie said. "All I have heard is town rumors and apparently false embellishment from Mr. Briscoe."

"We can talk all about it tomorrow, after we do our chores, Mamie."

"And, hopefully, the note we left for Eudora will begin her husband's regular service of the Binterfield's outhouse."

As they walked away, Sonja added, "Knowing what I do about the Binterfield estate, I suspect it will take Matthew several trips to haul all the shit coming from that household."

Mamie's laugh was heard well onto the next block.

13

The cloudless morning sky was a dull steel blue. The air was full of water and it felt like snow was coming. Delicate ice plates floated slowly on top of the current, drifting down from a sluggish Susquehanna River, slipping over the Flats into the Chesapeake Bay. Ice crystals laced the edges of the dock, mooring posts and the waterline of anchored ships. December was close, and still the ice was not thick enough to be of concern.

Ben stood on the Havre de Grace dock, waiting for Adam to row across from the *Raven*. Adam's breath bloomed out from his mouth like puffs of white smoke, with each pull on the oars. As Ben stood watching, Deputy Sheriff Mattingly approached him.

"Morning Benjamin," Mattingly said.

Ben glanced over his shoulder, but did not smile. "Morning, Lyle."

Mattingly withdrew his notebook and pencil from his coat pocket. "Still having trouble answering all the questions I have about that knife of yours, Ben."

Ben sighed and turned to face him. "You asked me where my knife was. I said I remember giving it to Briscoe, and told you to go ask him about it."

"Yes, and I did. And he showed me his own knife, which looks a lot like yours, and which he still has. Yours however, I pulled out of Herbert Binterfield's chest."

"...Which I did not put there, Lyle..."

"...Which I had to take from you once, when you threatened to kill Binterfield with it, standing out in front of his bank. Maybe I should not have given it to Mrs.

Pulaski to take home."

"That was two years ago, Lyle. Briscoe is lying to you"

"Hate can steep a long time waiting for an opportunity. I also remember that you busted Sam Briscoe's nose the same night you threatened Binterfield. Dropped him in the middle of Oyster Street with one punch. Right in front of me. You can't seriously expect me to take your word over his, Ben."

"It is the truth, Lyle."

"Yes, and he claims the truth as well, but which truth is the real truth? Where were you last night, Ben?"

"Why?"

"Havre de Grace has another dead body to be investigated."

"Who was it?"

"Sailor on one of the schooners up from Annapolis. I am told he spent part of the night drinking with your brother. Edward, I believe?"

"Edward is neither a Pulaski nor my brother."

Mattingly flipped through his note book. "You do not care for Edward, it seems. He told one of the serving girls in the Susquehanna Tavern that you threatened to shoot him while you were in St. Michaels."

Ben shrugged his shoulders. "She probably never met Edward..."

"Oh they met, Ben, and spent the night together. So, is the story so?"

"That is a difference of opinion about something that happened out of your jurisdiction, Lyle."

"According to my notes, the dead sailor and your...Edward had an altercation over card cheating and the sailor stormed out of the tavern."

"Well, then it sounds like you should pursue all that with Edward Leonard, not me!"

"You canallers tend to stick together, and at first I thought maybe you might have had a hand in dealing with the sailor, but obviously not. You still haven't answered my question."

"Which one?"

Mattingly huffed. "Damn it! Where were you last night?"

"Second floor, front room of the Pink House. All night."

Mattingly made a few notes in his book, mumbling, "Yeah, that's what the widow Stewart said."

Ben's face turned red. "Then why did you even ask me?"

"Sometimes you get different answers to the same question, and the real truth is wedged in between."

Ben stared at Mattingly in silence. Vapor rising over his head and shoulders in the cold air.

"This sailor was cut up just like Binterfield, groin to breastbone. The cut was shaped like a lightning bolt, " Mattingly said. "Just too many people dying in my town under suspicious circumstances." Mattingly turned and walked away, making more notes in his book.

"What did Mattingly want, Ben?" Adam asked as he climbed up onto the dock.

Ben shook his head with his eyes on Mattingly's back. "There's been another killing, and he still can't let go of the suspicion that I killed Binterfield."

Adam huffed. "Benjamin, there are dozens of men, and women, who would have loved to push a blade into that man's heart. Don't fret about it."

"My 'fret' is over what that deputy can put together as a truth that fits in his mind. Have you seen Edward this morning?"

Adam shrugged his shoulders. "He's still got wild oats in him, Ben. He went to the Taverns up on St. John Street last night, looking for comfort and ale."

"So Mattingly told me."

Adam kept his gaze at Ben's face.

"Is there something else, Adam?"

"Two things worry me about Edward, Ben..."

"Well? What are they?"

"One, he got old man Jackson to pay him for delivering the rented slaves we brought from Covey. And, two, he told us in St. Michaels he just passed through Havre de Grace looking for you. But last night he told me if I went to the Oyster Street Tavern to 'tell Carl he sent me'!"

Ben put his hands in his pockets. "I wonder how long that sneak was hanging around here? Maybe waiting so he could present himself to Aaron as my brother."

"That's what I was suspectin," Adam said.

"You up to strolling along St. John Street to help me look for that liar?"

"I certainly am, Ben."

Ben and Adam walked briskly up Congress Street and as they rounded the corner onto St. John Street, an enclosed carriage stopped abruptly only inches in front of them. Ben slapped the door to the carriage and shouted at the driver.

"Idiot! Your horse almost stepped on my foot and you blocked us as we were walking! Watch where you're going!"

With his comment made, Ben began to step around the carriage. He pulled at Adam's arm, but Adam did not join him. Ben paid no further attention to the carriage, but looked back at Adam to see why he was not moving. Adam was staring into the carriage with a broad smile on his face. Ben followed Adam's gaze, peering into the carriage. Sitting next to the driver and leaning forward so Ben could see his face, the passenger waved at Ben. Ben frowned as he looked at the pale faced man with clean shaven chin and mutton chop sideburns.

"What the...Good God! Anthony! Anthony Renowitz!"

Ben jammed his hand into the carriage in front of the driver and took Anthony's hand in his own. As the two friends vigorously shook hands, vibrating the poor driver between them, another smiling face came from the rear of the carriage.

Ben's voice bellowed within the small carriage and drew attention several yards away in all directions. "Isaac!"

Ben leaned in to grab his son and yanked him bodily over the driver, who had to fold into his own lap to allow Isaac out. The son was taller than the father, but Ben held Isaac around his waist in a bear hug with his feet off the ground, shaking him like a stuffed rag doll, his head bouncing from side to side.

"Isaac! What a wonderful surprise! We did not expect to see you until the Spring!"

Ben released his grip on his son and stepped back with his hands still on his shoulders. Isaac was dressed in a trim fitting gray tunic, lined in front with three rows of shiny brass buttons, over gray trousers.

"You look very professional son. Very impressive in the uniform!"

Isaac looked down at his own tunic and grinned, almost whispering, "Mr. Renowitz had this waiting for me in Philadelphia. My class won't really receive our uniforms until July 4th, but he said I could wear it home for Christmas."

Ben nodded and glanced at Anthony, then back at his son. "So, how are you?"

"Well, father..."

"Father?" said Ben.

Isaac blushed. "I am well and happy up there, Pa. I am learning so many amazing things at the Point. The cadets are from all of the states. It is harsh, but exciting. The senior cadets treat us like slaves, but it's only what they call hazing. Thank you so much for writing President Jackson..."

"It was a pleasure to do, son. I was just happy he remembered a brash drummer boy in New Orleans. I can't wait for your mother to see you!"

Anthony had slowly stepped out of the carriage and was shaking hands with Adam.

Isaac's stomach growled and he grinned as he rubbed it. "Oh, I have dreamed about Ma's cooking! I can't wait to settle into my room with Aaron and walk around the farm. I have missed all of that."

Ben froze. "Yes, well...I am afraid we no longer live there, Isaac..."

Isaac's eyes flew wide open. "What? Oh, you're joking with me. I almost believed it for a moment. The senior cadets pull so many pranks, it had me ready for..."

"No, son. I am afraid it is true."

Anthony placed his hand on Isaac's shoulder and then Ben. "I couldn't bring myself to tell him about that, Ben. Maybe I should have prepared him."

Ben looked at Anthony, realizing how gaunt and frail he looked within his black suit. "You knew? When? How?"

"I will tell you more, later, Ben. But, for now enjoy presenting your soldier-son to his mother and brother. I have taken a room at the Harford Hotel. Let's meet for supper there in the tavern. Six o'clock?"

Anthony was almost breathless after the short conversation. He nodded to the driver, who took him by the elbow and assisted Anthony getting back into the carriage. After seating himself, Anthony smiled at the worried faces watching him, and focused his attention on Ben.

"Apparently my left lung no longer works, Ben. My physician in Philadelphia tells me that you and Doctor Harper saved my life, cauterizing my wound there on the ship."

Anthony coughed several times and wheezed, then took in a deep breath. "He says it has shriveled." He took in another deep breath then waved his fingers. "We will talk more, later."

The driver snapped the reins and the horse trotted away with the carriage.

Ben, Adam and Isaac shared solemn faces for a short moment then replaced their grins. Ben noticed Isaac's suitcase on the boardwalk, and snatched it up.

"To the Pink House," Ben announced.

"Pink House? What is that," Isaac asked.

Adam lingered, as Ben put his arm on his son's shoulder and directed him up Congress Avenue. Ben called over his shoulder, "You too, Adam. I want you to meet Mrs. Stewart."

Five minutes later, the front door of the boarding house burst open to the sound of heavy boots and chattering men, assaulting the stairway to the second floor.

"Sonja! Sonja!" Ben shouted in the stairwell, but when

he arrived on the second floor their room was empty. He tossed Isaac's bag on the trunk at the foot of the bed.

"We'll settle that later," Ben said.

Isaac was in a dizzy confusion looking around the second floor parlor and peeking into his parents' room, asking unanswered questions and following his father. Next they clomped back down to the main floor and entered the parlor and then the huge dining room, commanded by the monstrous walnut table. Isaac continued to mumble, hoping for answers while gawking at the contents of rooms as he flew through them. After finding the kitchen empty and performing a quick three-person pirouette at the kitchen door, Ben hustled Isaac and Adam into the foyer.

"Damned if I know where they are. The place is empty for all I can see."

"Why are you here, Pa" Isaac asked.

"Put out from the farm, Son, but don't expect that to last long..."

"But, where will I stay? Where is Aaron?"

"Oh Aaron and Jeremy have taken the barges to Wrightsville for coal. Aaron lives on the *Ugly Boat*... for now.

Ben grabbed Adam's arm. "Let's show Isaac the ship!"

"You row," Adam demanded.

"No, Adam," Isaac said. "I have been sitting in carriages and trains for three days. I will row."

"Excellent," Ben said and gave his son a hearty pat on the back.

With that, they charged out of the house and headed back down Bourbon Street to the docks.

As Isaac rowed with mechanical momentum toward the *Raven*, he continued to pepper his father with questions.

"So the bank wants to sell our farm? It's Binterfield again, right, Pa? But, how can he sell our farm?"

"We don't own the farm, Son. We rent it, or we did. And it's not Herbert Binterfield doing this, it's his wife. Herbert Binterfield is dead. Murdered."

"What? How did that happen, Pa?"

"Devine Intervention," Adam said with a smile. "Probably in answer to a lot of prayers from here abouts."

"Mrs. Binterfield has put the farm up for sale, and had us evicted," Ben said.

"Can't we buy it, Pa? I thought our shipping business was doing real good."

"It was and is, Son, and it's going to get better with the *Raven*. But the witch Mrs. Binterfield made the house so expensive, no one will be able to buy it."

Isaac frowned and shook his head, "But if it is too expensive to sell, how can she expect to sell it? It don't make sense."

"Here we are," said Ben as he reached his hand out to grab the *Raven's* ladder.

Adam tied the bow rope onto the ring bolt near the ladder as Ben and Isaac went up and then joined them on deck. Ben took Isaac on a tour of the ship, pointing out all the changes made since they took the ship on Spesutie Island.

Standing down in the main hold, Isaac looked around and said, "Well, it looks better and even smells some better. Smells like...sweat...and...bacon."

"Bacon? I can cook up some more, if you're hungry. I got biscuits left over from last night," Adam said.

Ben patted Isaac on the back, "Young men are always hungry. Let's fire up the stove, Adam."

Ben and Isaac pulled out the benches lined under the suspended plank table, then went up on deck. Adam sliced more bacon in the galley and tossed pieces into the heating cast iron pan on the ship stove. Isaac and Ben ambled around the deck, checking lines, looking at the changes to Havre de Grace and chatting.

"It doesn't really have anything to do with money, Isaac. Mrs. Binterfield has hatred to spare and appears to send most of it at your mother. Sonja hated being in the house, and I think Mrs. Binterfield hated having her there."

"Is it because Ma shot at Binterfield in the bank?"

Ben absently looked around the deck. "Perhaps, but

let's not mention that where others can hear, son."

Isaac glanced over his shoulder. "No one is here..."

Ben raised his hand, "Yes. I know. It was only a cautious reminder."

Isaac nodded and sighed. "So, I can stay here at night? The captain's cabin looks very comfortable, and with the little iron stove in there, it should be warm."

"At supper last night, Mr. Whiggington, a gentleman who keeps a room at the Pink House, mentioned he was leaving to visit family in Vermont for the Christmas season. So, we might be able to rent his room for you."

"Bacon!" Adam announced.

As they walked to the steps Ben placed his hand on Isaac's back. "How long can you stay with us, Son?"

"Mr. Renowitz arranged for me to be gone from the Point until after Christmas."

Ben stopped at the landing in front of the cabin door, "Will this cause you difficulty catching up to your studies when you return?"

Isaac shook his head. "No, Pa, my instructors say that I am already ahead on my academic subjects. And my cannoning instructor says I am his only cadet to arrive having already fired one. Besides, many of the cadets will be gone home as Christmas nears."

"Wonderful!" Ben said and patted him on the back again. "I know your mother will be overjoyed at your visit, as am I."

Gray smoke boiled out of the little galley as Adam stepped into the main hold coughing. "It's out. It's out," he said between coughs. They pried up the wooden battens holding the canvas covers over the main hatches to let out the smoke.

"Bacon grease fires up worse than whale oil," Adam said.

The morning wind was cold but gentle and out of the north, pushing the stern southward from the anchor chain at the bow. Smoke rose from the cargo hold and drifted over the captain's cabin, while the three men ate bacon and biscuits at the bow. The crunch of hard fried bacon sounded like beavers chewing dried wood.

14

Sonja screamed his name with delight when Isaac entered the room, and engulfed him in hugs and kisses. The tears she shed in May when his train left were finally swept away by new tears of joy at his return. She abruptly held him at arm's length, unable to release his shoulders, but wanting to look at her son.

"I was so hoping you might be able to come home at Christmas time, but never hoped for such an early visit."

Then she drew him into another hug and several more kisses on his cheek before he was able to step back and adjust his uniform. Red-faced with his hair disheveled, he glanced at his father standing next to him.

"You might as well give in and let her have her way, Isaac," Ben said through a broad grin as he picked up his son's cap off the floor. Pride for his son beamed from his face. "Resistance is useless."

Sonja yanked him back into another motherly embrace, then pulled him to the stuffed chair, while she sat on the nearby chest at the end of the bed, still holding his hand.

"You look wonderful in that uniform, Isaac."

"Well, I just got it yesterday, Ma. None of my class have theirs yet. We won't be given them by the Point until July. This one is a gift from Mr. Renowitz..."

"Mr. Who...oh, Anthony. Is he having you call him Mr. Renowitz, now?"

"No. I think he would be fine if I called him Anthony, but at the Point... it's a matter of respect."

"You have lost weight, Isaac," Sonja said. "And you are taller..."

"Straighter," added Ben.

Sonja leaned back to look out toward into the hall. "And where is Mr. Renowitz, Ben?"

"He went on to his hotel room, Sonja. You would not have recognized him. I almost did not."

"He is recovered from his wound?"

"He is frail and pallid, Sonja. He is not bleeding, of course, but I suspect he may never fully recover from Hoagg's wound. He moves as an old man..."

"But with a quick wit and clear memory, Pa. He was talking almost the whole way here from Philadelphia..."

"How long were you in Philadelphia, son," Sonja asked.

"Just the night, Ma. He had a man come get me at the Point. The Commandant knew all about it. Let me go from class as soon as Mr. Wolcott arrived."

"Horace Wolcott?" Ben said. "Harsh scar down his face?" Ben traced a line with his finger from his forehead to the edge of his jaw.

When Isaac nodded, Ben spoke to Sonja. "Horace sailed with Anthony's Grandfather as a ship's boy until old man Renowitz gave up the slave trade. Stayed on as a family servant up there."

Sonja sighed and turned back to Isaac. "Now, tell me what they feed you."

"Each day has its own meal, Ma. Each Monday is the same, each Tuesday is the same, but different from Mondays. And the best meals of the week are on Sundays. We hunger for Sundays..."

Ben put his hand on Isaac's shoulder. "You had a chance to tell me and Adam all about this earlier, but your mother is going to want to know just how many peas they served you on Wednesdays and the exact sizes of the potatoes they served on Thursdays..."

"I will not," said Sonja

"I will go down stairs and see what mischief Adam has gotten into," Ben said with a smile, leaving Isaac and Sonja to talk.

Downstairs, Ben found Adam perched on the edge of a parlor chair chatting with Mamie. Adam had his gold coin necklace dangling from his hand, showing the coin to her. She pretended to never have seen such a coin.

"I hope you saved the grindings from the hole you made in the coin, Mr. Tuttle."

"Of course! It bought me an ale at the Rodger's Tavern," Adam said and then sighed as he glanced at both Ben and Mamie. "Truth be told, the cook there is an old mate from my sailing days, and he probably would have given me the ale anyway."

Mamie tapped a gentle fingertip on Adam's hand before she drew it back. "So, there are many people who know of your... Spanish coin?"

"French, Ma'am. The coin is French. And, no, few know I have it. I only show it now because Sonja told you about it."

Mamie smiled. "People like to tell me things. It may be a gift or a curse, but they do."

"Depends on where and when it is shared, and whose ears hear it," Ben said.

She fixed Ben with a warm smile. "Ah, that is so, Mr. Pulaski," she said and rocked a pointed finger toward Ben. "...but I never share when it could hurt good people."

Ben looked down on her and returned her smile. "I do believe that Mrs. Stewart."

"Your Isaac, where will he sleep at night," she asked.

"I had hoped you might rent Mr. Whiggington's room, but I hadn't..."

"Of course you hadn't, but you will not rent Mr. Whiggingtons room."

"Oh..."

"I will not charge a mother to have her son close by at Christmas."

"Oh no, I couldn't..."

"Of course you could, Mr. Pulaski," she said as she stood. "Mr. Whiggington and Mr. Barnes have both gone back to their homes until after the new year. Their work fades at this time of year and they spend time with their families elsewhere."

"Yes, but..."

"Yes. And no but, sir. They pay to keep the room in their names, and yet the rooms are empty," Mamie said, wagging her finger at him again. "Your Isaac will stay in Mr. Whiggington's room, and your Aaron, when he returns, will stay in Mr. Barnes' room. Your sons will join you and your wife...and Mr. Heiden on the third floor. Poor Mr. Heiden still has his family in Austria, but too far for holiday travel, I am afraid. So, your family will be my family this Christmas!"

"But, but...Mrs. Stewart, we can't possibly..." Ben spoke at her back as she disappeared into the kitchen.

Mamie's voice echoed from the kitchen. "No Buts! And Mr. Tuttle will join us for dinner tonight!"

Ben and Adam traded smiles. "We have our orders, Adam, and we dare not disobey."

Adam kept his smile as he spoke, "Need to go check on my shop, Ben. Haven't been there in weeks, now. I'll come back for supper."

Ben followed him out the front door, and as Adam turned south along Union Avenue toward Concord Cove, Ben pulled his wool coat closed and headed toward the Harford Hotel.

After a brisk walk, Ben knocked on the door to room number three. The man who had been driving Anthony's buggy opened the door. The man nodded, opened the door to a large room and motioned to a stuffed chair set near a fireplace lit by bright yellow flames dancing within the bricks. The heavy drapes had been drawn closed across the window, and the candles within the room were lit. Opposite a large four poster bed, one corner was hidden behind a folding screen where Ben heard splashing water.

"That you, Benjamin," Anthony asked from behind the screen. "Just washing the train soot off me. Be with you in just a moment. Jerrod, pour Ben a brandy – no wait, he likes Rum."

Ben took off his coat while Jarrod presented him a cut glass holding faint amber liquid reflecting the firelight.

"Thank you," Ben said, but Jarrod only nodded. Ben spoke toward the folding screen. "Your man doesn't say much, Anthony."

"Doesn't say anything at all, Benjamin. Been like that all his life. Camilla hired him when we returned home after...after you and Hoagg tried to kill me."

"Me?? Hoagg drove a harpoon through your chest and pinned you to the damned mast! I never tried to kill you!"

Anthony laughed unseen. "You shoved a red hot iron bar into the hole in my chest while I screamed. Close enough!"

"God damn it, Anthony! You know full well Dr. Harper guided my hands and sealed your wound to save your useless life!"

Anthony laughed again. Water splashed loudly. Jarrod grabbed a folded towel off a nearby stand and dashed behind the screen.

"Just joking with you, Ben," Anthony said from under a working towel.

Seconds later, Anthony stepped from around the screen, tying a woven red cord around the waist of a heavy robe and wearing matching carpet slippers. He quickstepped to the liquor stand, coughed several times as he poured himself a drink and then settled gently into the stuffed chair next to Ben. He held his glass out to touch with Ben's. His glass trembled as it rang softly in unison with Ben's. Anthony seemed exhausted by the activity of leaving the bath and making his way to his chair. He took a sampling from his glass and coughed again.

Anthony glanced at Ben and swept his empty hand to the side. "Don't be too concerned, Ben. I'm not dying yet. It just looks that way." Then he laughed again.

Ben sipped his rum, swallowing it as he gazed into the fire. The room was becoming too warm for him. "What do you need, Anthony? I greatly appreciate your bringing my son...but a gifted train ticket would have done as much, with you having to drag yourself down from Philadelphia."

Anthony took a greedy drink from his glass."One of my friends has been kidnapped."

Ben sat up straight in his chair. "In Philadelphia?"

"Yes, but he is no longer there. He has been taken down south. He is a black man and the bastards took him to be sold into slavery."

"Anthony, that is...I mean, I am sorry to hear that, but what..."

"I need you to go buy him."

"What? Where?"

"Charleston, South Carolina."

"Anthony, I can't go to Charleston. I am really sorry for your friend. He must be terrified, but I don't think I could help..."

"You have a ship, Ben, a schooner. It is a known slaver. It came from Charleston."

"How do you know where..."

"An old friend of the family sits on the Maryland Maritime Board..."

"That's why I got the ship...got it free and clear...no other claimants..."

"Yes, Ben. But, you were already on it, claiming it. When my friend, Robert Hannibal, was taken, and I looked for something I could do, I began to connect the dots..."

"And the dots came to me."

"And they came to you, Ben."

"And the reason you brought Isaac, was to sweeten the pot?"

"Yes. That, plus I think highly of Isaac. Camilla and I were greatly impressed with him, when he helped me return to Philadelphia after you and Hoagg attacked me. Bringing Isaac was a pleasure."

"No, Anthony. I cannot go to Charleston. I cannot buy slaves. You know that I used to ignore the whole issue. Growing up here, it was just part of...the way things are. It is the law. Every time we take a barge across the line into Pennsylvania with slaves hidden on board, we risk losing the barge, or worse. And we've been taking that risk since you were here, but..."

"It has to be done. Not just for my friend, but for anyone we can help. We have to do more."

Ben looked over toward Jarrod, sitting in a chair near the door.

Anthony waved his hand at Ben and sniffed. "Jarrod is part of this, Ben. Even if he could talk, he would never. He is devoted to this."

"Why?"

"He was a slave, because his mother was a slave. She died getting him to Philadelphia."

Ben spoke to Jarrod. "Aren't you afraid of being in a slave state?"

Jarrod rose from his chair and stood before Ben. He shook his head no, then smiled and opened his coat, showing the pistol in his belt.

Ben turned back to Anthony. "Abolitionists are being hung in the deep south, Anthony. Their property in the south is burned," Ben said.

Anthony signaled to Jarrod, who went to a nearby chest of drawers and withdrew a thick envelope. He offered the envelope to Anthony, but Anthony pointed him toward Ben, so he dropped the envelope into Ben's lap.

"Anthony, you are far too ready to risk the *Raven*; to risk my life," Ben said. He opened the envelope finding a thick stack of money and several legal papers.

Ben's face flushed crimson. "Don't you dare try to buy me, Anthony Renowitz..."

"That's not for you, Ben. That's to buy my friend, and for other things." He held up his hand and began to tick off fingertips with his thumb. "There is also a bill of lading for merchandise to be picked up in Annapolis and taken to Charleston. There are consignments for lumber and Carolina Rice, to be picked up in Georgetown. There is a letter of introduction from Grayrocks Plantation in Saint Mary's County to the slave brokers Lebeaux and Chambers. There is also..." Anthony sighed.

"Also what, Anthony?"

"A license in your name granted by the states of

Delaware and Maryland, to engage in the purchase and sale of slaves in any American slave state or the Caribbean."

Ben threw his glass into the fireplace, shattering it against the bricks in a cloud of crystal shards sparkling in the flames.

Red-faced, he stood and pointed a finger at Anthony's nose. "You are going to get me killed, and the *Raven* sent to the bottom of Charleston Harbor!"

He stormed out of the room.

Jarrod started in Ben's direction, but Anthony called him back.

"We will give him time, Jarrod. He is a stout friend and has a good heart. He will come back...I hope, for Mr. Hannibal's sake, I hope."

15

Ben marched along St. John Street and then down to the docks. He stood at the edge near a single-mast work boat, looking out over the Susquehanna Flats. His eyes were unfocused, looking but not seeing. Seagulls circled and plummeted into shad schools rippling the surface near the middle of the river, snatching away silver morsels twitching in their beaks. Thin ice, almost transparent, drifted lazily in front of the docks, twirling slowly in the slack current. He breathed deeply, sending vapor clouds out in front of his face, and opened his coat to the cold breeze slipping in off the water.

A man's voice drifted up from the workboat. "Well now, I've seen that posture before. Don't know if it's safe to come close."

Ben glanced down at the speaker, who wore a bright blue knitted cap, then blinked hard and examined the boat.

He has a man's voice now.

"Aaron!"

"Are we going to war, Pa?" Aaron smiled as he said it.

Ben blew out his breath and took in a deep fresh one. "No, son. I just needed a moment to send my anger out to the water."

Ben stepped down onto the deck of the *Ugly Boat* and grabbed his son in a brief hug. Letting go, he said, "Your voice is that of a man's now. Every day you show me again that you are no longer a boy."

Ben reached up to Aaron's chin and pushed his face to the side. "What happened to your cheek?"

"Nothing much. Just a serious discussion with one of the slave catchers hanging around the Maryland side of the Line..."

"About what, Aaron?"

"About his authority to search my barges."

"He did that to you?"

"Only in self defense, Pa," Aaron said with a wide grin. "I had just split his lip and knocked out a tooth when he tried to step on deck of the *Ugly Boat*.

"What else happened?"

"It all stopped when Jeremy pointed a shotgun at the guy and his friend."

Ben frowned and shook his head slowly. "Tension stays high there. Free state above, slave state below and our barges move back and forth across that line. Were they waiting for you when you come back down from Wrightsville?"

"Yeah, but I did what you did once, and offered free transportation to Havre de Grace for any man with a gun and a dislike for slave chasers." Aaron chuckled. "The slavers had four waiting at the line, and we had nine standing on deck when we came through the lock back into Maryland."

Ben put his hand on his son's shoulder. "Be careful, son. Pulaskis seem to be drawing trouble these days."

Aaron smiled. "Can you tell me?"

"Anthony Renowitz is in town."

Aaron chuckled. "It is usually Ma who gets angry when he is around."

Ben sighed. "I'm afraid my anger is only a mild show compared to what will come from your mother..."

"Is it safe for me to come home, Pa?" Aaron chuckled again. "And speaking of home, were you able to stop the bank..."

"No. We are out of the farm for now."

There was a harsh silence. Ben stared out over the water. Aaron looked down at his boot toe as he traced a curving line in the coal dust on the deck.

"Where will you stay, Pa? On the *Raven*?"

Ben blinked and shook his head. "Not for now, son...As

a matter of fact, Mrs. Stewart has open rooms for both you and Isaac."

"Really?" Aaron folded his arms in front of his chest. Ben noticed his large biceps and forearms, barely retained in his thinning wool jacket.

"You need a new coat," Ben said.

"I like this one." Aaron noticed his father also looking at his cap. "Maggie knitted it for me. Very warm. When is Isaac coming?"

"He has come, son. He is with your mother now."

"What? Then let's go there!"

Aaron grabbed Ben's upper arm in a firm grip and pulled him up on the dock. They moved together up the slope toward St. John Street, when Aaron abruptly stopped. "Where are we going, Pa?"

"To the Pink House."

On North Union Avenue, Lydia Binterfield sorted through the remaining personal effects of her late husband in the drawing room of the Binterfield Mansion. Of the three large piles that her house slaves had created in the middle of the room, only a few items remained. One item that intrigued her was an Irish boot pistol with folding trigger. Herbert attended to it far more than he did to her. It was a cap and ball pistol that barely reached from her wrist to her finger tips. It had a highly shined walnut handle, engraved brass band around the mechanism , and a short barrel. The polished cherry wood box that held it also had eight lead balls, eight patches of wool cloth, eight copper firing caps, a short ram rod and an ornate powder flask. Since each notch and nook in the box held an item and none were empty, she guessed the pistol had never been fired. After placing the pistol in different locations in her wardrobe, she determined the pistol would fit comfortably in her purse, a coat pocket or in her bodice. She hefted it with her hand and smiled, then began to load it.

You will stay close to me, little one.

A few blocks away from the Binterfield mansion, Sam Briscoe sat at his desk in the Tidewater Bank and Trust Company frowning intently at the man sitting in the guest chair.

"What do you mean, by saying Mrs. Binterfield cannot own the bank..."

"She is a woman, Mr. Briscoe..."

"Yes, but Herbert's will was written to ensure she gained complete control of his estate. Maryland law is enforceable in this matter, regardless of tradition..."

"We have legal claim that predates the will and was signed by Herbert Binterfield ten years ago. It is a binding business contract that no Will can usurp."

"That is a lie, sir," snapped Briscoe.

The cold gray eyes of the visitor remained fixed on Briscoe's even as his hand slipped down onto the handle of his pistol. "Be careful of your words, sir."

Briscoe glanced down at the exposed pistol and licked his lips. "Oh, well, yes...that was an excessive statement. My apologies, sir."

The man's posture relaxed. "Apology accepted, Mr. Briscoe. Let me elaborate. My father, James Williamson, advanced Mr. Binterfield sixty percent of the funds necessary to open this bank. By legal and binding contract, in the event of the bank's failure, sale, or other distribution, the entire proceeds go to my father's estate."

"Why would Herbert Binterfield sign such a ridiculous contract," Briscoe asked.

The man sighed and lowered his voice. "At the time, Binterfield was practically penniless and he was hell-bent to marry Lydia.."

"You knew Lydia, I mean, Mrs. Binterfield."

"She grew up on our plantation in Saint Mary's County, Mr. Briscoe. Herbert Binterfield looked upon my father as his future father-in-law..."

"Lydia is your sister?"

The man sighed again, and lowered his voice to a whisper, to which Briscoe had to lean forward to hear. "Hell no. James Williamson is my father, and he admitted to being Lydia's father, at least after his wife, my mother, died. No. Lydia's mother is a slave, as is Lydia."

Briscoe sat bolt upright, slamming his chair against the edge of the desk, blinking his eyes several times. The noise attracted the attention of his clerks.

"Pay attention to your numbers, gentlemen," he shouted. He turned back to the visitor. "Mr. Williamson, I find this all very difficult to believe."

"Since she was so light skinned, and resembled his own mother, my father sent Lydia to school in Europe so he could pass her off to some gentry fool. However, although her suitor was penniless, Herbert came from a decent enough family in Philadelphia."

Briscoe stared at Mr. Williamson in a long uncomfortable silence. The clock across the street in front of the Hardware store struck four times. Briscoe clapped his hands twice, and spoke out to his clerks.

"Business is too slow, gentlemen. Close up your stations and go home. I will pay your full day's salary, none the less. Have a good evening."

The two men bobbed their heads in servile gratitude and scurried out of the office, locking the front door behind them.

After they were gone, Briscoe continued his conversation without whispering.

"Lydia is a slave?"

"Yes, Mr. Briscoe." He studied Briscoe's face for a moment. "You are pursuing her?"

"I...I...work at the pleasure, I mean...I work for Mrs. Binterfield...er...I did until now, I mean...oh, Hell! What terrible news!"

Mr. Williamson chuckled. "Fear not, Mr. Briscoe. You may pursue Lydia without interference from me. As the major stockholder in the bank, I see no reason not to leave you in your position as manager. You appear to be doing a good job. Interest income is satisfactory, and I admire how you address your employees."

"Really," Briscoe answered almost boy-like.

"Just recognize your obligation to me and pay me my 60 percent of all profits as Herbert did for years, and as

Lydia has not been doing these last few months. She didn't even send word that Herbert was dead."

"She didn't? Then how did you know to come here," Briscoe asked.

"I came here looking for a runaway slave that killed my brother and caused the fatal heart attack of my father. I received word from the town constable that he was living nearby."

"Do you know his name?"

"Simon Bond. If he still goes by that."

Briscoe began coughing. "Yes...yes...I know him. He stayed on the Pulaski farm these last few years."

Williamson stood up. "Where? Can you get some men together? Slave catchers? I will pay well..."

"You're too late," Briscoe said, working hard to suppress the small smile trying to escape into the open. "He is gone, but is wanted for murdering a ship captain."

"Do you have any idea where he might have gone?"

"The Pennsylvania Line is only fifteen miles from here. He's probably liquored up in one of the black slums surrounding Philadelphia."

Williamson remained on his feet and studied the clock on the back wall. "It is too late to contact a local lawyer. I have a name to ask for, but I will have to pursue that tomorrow. I want to update the contract with this bank, naming you as our representative and promoting you to Director. I reward loyalty, Briscoe, but do not tolerate failure."

"What is the lawyer's name," Briscoe asked.

Williamson fished a card from his vest pocket and read it. "George Milton."

"Oh, no. You do not want that man. I hear he is an abolitionist."

"Shit. Can no one be trusted up this way?"

"I can," Briscoe said with a smile. He wrote another name on a slip of paper and handed it to Williamson. "This lawyer has helped me many times with real estate contracts. He can be trusted."

Williamson hesitated briefly when Briscoe offered his hand, but then smiled and took it.

"I will see you tomorrow, Mr. Briscoe."

Briscoe nodded and smiled in return.

That lying bitch! A God damned slave!

He sat down and withdrew a silver brandy flask from a lower desk drawer, loosened the top and took a satisfying drink. The flask was new. The edges of the engraved letters SB were still fresh and sharply defined. Ideas were spinning in his head.

What to do first? Marry Lydia? Yes, marry her then she has an accident, or falls victim to the horrible killer loose in the Havre de Grace nights.

He chuckled to himself and took a long second drink from the flask.

Maybe blame it on Pulaski? Maybe he has another knife in his room I could take. How sweet that would be! Let the law hang him!

He placed his feet up on the desk and laughed out loud, taking another drink from the flask.

"She has ordered me around like I was dirt," he said out loud. "Like one of her slaves! But SHE is the slave! I will tell you tonight, bitch! No more begging at your God damned feet!"

He took another long drink, draining the flask, then tossed it back in the drawer and wiped his mouth with the back of his hand.

"Tonight, I will let you know what I know. You will do as I say or I will sell you! I will be kind and marry you. Keep you as a white woman, and you will beg me to slip between your legs so I will keep your secret!"

In the open drawer next to the cast aside flask lay his own ivory handled knife, brought from the Pink House to keep Pulaski from finding it. The keenly sharpened edge gleamed in the lamp light.

"Maybe I will feed you tonight," he said to the blade. "The artiste! The sculptor!"

Briscoe stood up and kicked his chair back against the wall. His head bobbed slightly and his stance leaned away from the desk, but he steadied himself by grabbing the corner. He took out the knife, slipped it into its scabbard and slipped it into his coat pocket. He walked to the front door and let himself out with his key, but did not pull the door completely closed behind him, nor did he lock it back with his key.

Briscoe whistled as he left Oyster Street and walked along St. John Street. He stopped in at his favorite tavern for dinner, but in the middle of his order he canceled it and requested a bottle of bourbon. The owner brought him a plate of sugar cookies when he delivered the bourbon.

"A gift from the wife," he said to Briscoe as he set them down.

An hour later Briscoe left the tavern, going into the dark and leaving behind most of the cookies, most of the bowl of she-crab soup the proprietor had served him, and an empty bourbon bottle. He had difficulty getting his key into the keyhole of the Binterfield back door.

Hearing the rattle at the door, Junie yanked the door open to investigate, and pulled Briscoe onto his knees. When he stood, there were smudges on the knees of his pants.

"Clean these things," he bellowed at her.

"Yassah, yassah. I clean dem right now, suh," she promised.

"Down in the basement with you," he ordered.

Sissy heard the voice and came running to assist her mother. Briscoe grabbed her by the arm and shoved her after Junie. "Both of you get down there. Get clean cloths and water to get the dirt off my pants. Now!"

He followed them down to the wash area and sat on the table used for folding. "Sissy! Get me a bottle of brandy from the storage room! Junie, if these pants are ruined I will have the skin flayed off both of you!"

"I gets it, suh, I gets it good," Junie said. "We fix it like new, Massah Briscoe."

"Massah. That's good Junie. You call me Massah. After I marry your mistress, I will be your Massah. And I will sell your black ass down to Mississippi if you ever sass me again! You hear me?"

Sissy offered him the brandy. He snatched it out of her

hand and took a long drink.

"You black bitches always sass me! I see it! I hear it!"

"No suh. No suh. I nevah sass you, Massah Briscoe."

"You sass me every time I come here, you lying bitch. You think you can look down your nose at me, like your mistress does. I will turn your body into fish bait! Chum!"

"We no sass you, Massah," Sissy pleaded.

"You both sass me, God damn it! You think I don't see the way you look at me," Briscoe yelled and set the brandy on the table. Then he snatched his knife from his coat, threw the scabbard across the room and slashed across Sissy's arm. Blood poured down on the floor and Sissy screamed at the top of her lungs.

"Oh lord God. Oh Lord God," Junie screamed. "Please don't hurt my baby!"

Briscoe stood and reached out, pulling the girl toward him as he drew his knife across her belly. Sissy screamed again and fell to her knees. Junie screamed and began slapping at him, but he slashed at her with his knife, cutting her arm, her breast and her cheek. Both Sissy and Junie were becoming stained with blood. Briscoe stood over them holding his knife in the air, prepared to slice again. Blood had splattered on his face and stained his arms and hands.

"What is going on down here," Lydia yelled. "Sam, have you gone insane? Get out of this house!"

He turned toward her, weaving slightly, his eyes white within a mask of red blood. He pointed his knife at her.

"Shut up, you bitch! You treat me like dirt under your feet! You God damned slave! I know what you are!"

"Sam! How can you say such a thing to me?"

Spittle ran off his lip as he spoke. "Your half brother came to see me today. Your father helped Herbert start his bank, but your mother was a slave!"

"That is a lie, Sam! You're drunk and someone has told you lies!"

"James Williamson Junior visited me today. Your mother was a slave in Saint Mary's county. You cannot own anything! Your half brother will contract with me to

146

run the bank and send him the profits you haven't..."

"What profits?"

"Herbert sent them 60 percent of the profits for the past ten years! Something you failed to do!"

"I never heard of this. Samuel, please! Listen to me"

"Samuel, please," he imitated her voice. "You will satisfy me in any way I choose, then I will listen to you..." He stabbed the air in front of him with each syllable. "as your master!"

"No! You will not be my master!"

He pointed the knife tip off to his side. "I will marry you, Lydia. And you will sleep in my bed, but if you do not please me..." He pointed the tip at her again, tapping out each word. "I will tell all of Havre de Grace your true heritage!"

"You can't do that, Sam!"

Again, he pointed the tip off to his side. "You think I want the town to know that I am sleeping with a nigger? No, but you will do everything I desire, if you want to stay out of the tobacco fields!"

She turned and ran upstairs.

"Get back down here, you bitch," he yelled and ran after her.

Briscoe caught Lydia in the Foyer. He grabbed her arm, yanking her to the floor in front of him. Lydia slapped his face and dashed for the stairs. Junie and Sissy slipped upstairs and ran to the back door.

"Get out of here, Sam," Lydia yelled. "You are drunk! You do not want to do this!"

He lunged at her with his knife, cutting her dress sleeve. She tried to run up the stairs, but he grabbed at her with his other hand. He ripped open her silk bodice, exposing her corset. He grabbed at the top of her corset and yanked her toward him, loosening the garment. Lydia fell against him, her mouth close to his, breathing heavily with his breath, then she smiled at him.

"Yes," she said in a husky voice, and kissed him.

He loosened his grip on her corset and lowered his knife. He inhaled her scent, drew her into a deeper kiss and she folded her body softly against his, pressing her pelvis against him. He slipped his tongue into her open mouth.

She bit down fiercely onto his tongue and ripped her chin away, tearing the edge of his tongue, then spit it out and jammed her thumb into his eye.

He screamed and mumbled curses as she spun away from him. She ran to the front door. He reached for her but she slipped beyond his grasp and opened the door. She dashed onto the front porch.

"Help! Someone help me!"

A passing couple stopped to stare at her.

Briscoe lunged out onto the porch and grabbed the back of her head, pulling her wig off in his hand. She turned to face him and he swung at her with his knife and cut the palm of her hand.

She screamed again, "Help me! Help me!"

The man accompanying the woman in the road, stepped toward the Binterfield house. Another man came running down the avenue following Lydia's screams.

Briscoe punched Lydia's face, spinning her around and driving her down to her knees onto the top brick step. He grabbed the back of her corset and pulled her onto her back. He sliced across her upper arm. She screamed in pain and tried to roll away from him. He kicked at her head, but missed. She crawled down the steps on her hands and knees, screaming for help. Briscoe jumped over her and landed on the walkway in front of her, blocking her escape. Blood poured from his mouth, his curses garbled in the spewing blood. He stabbed her in her shoulder as she tried to stand. Lydia struggled to pull something from her pocket, but her injured shoulder and hand burned in bloody pain. She could not bring it out.

One of the men from the road grabbed at the hand holding the knife, but Briscoe yanked the blade through his palm slicing him to his bones. Briscoe punched him in his face with his other hand.

Other people were gathering in the avenue. Briscoe swung the knife blade at them, then turned it back toward Lydia. Spittle flung from his lips as he yelled to them.

"She is a slave! Look at that nappy hair! Her mother was a slave and her father was her master! She pretended to be white and fooled poor Herbert, but not me!"

Lydia managed to get to her feet. She twist her skirt around to pull out the boot pistol. She pointed the pistol as Briscoe's face.

She spoke quietly to him. "Sam. Stop this. Come inside."

He pointed the tip of his knife at her, his chest heaving. He stepped toward her.

She kept the gun aimed at his face. "Stop! Stop, Sam! Stop right now!"

Briscoe lunged at her, snarling "You God damned nigger slave!"

His face was only inches from the gun barrel as his knife cut along the side of her bodice. She screamed, but could not hear her own voice as the gun exploded, sending a surge of pain up through her elbow. Fiery black powder and smoke engulfed his face. The back of his head exploded in a ruby spray onto the bricks behind him. He stood frozen for an instant. His face was pocked with burning cinders. His eyes were wide open in surprise, below a bright red hole in his forehead. He collapsed into a lifeless ragged pile on the walkway.

People rushed around Lydia to help her. Someone yelled out to find the Deputy Sheriff. A man gently slipped the pistol from Lydia's hand. One of the women placed a shawl over Lydia's bleeding shoulder, another handed Lydia her wig.

"Don't you fret, dear," she whispered as she helped Lydia straighten it. "My hair thinned to nothing years ago, and I have always admired your beautiful wigs."

16

Deputy Sheriff Lyle Mattingly kneeled by the crumpled body of Sam Briscoe. Briscoe's face was down against the walkway bricks. His head was ringed on the bricks in a halo of thickened blood. The ugly back of his head had filled with blood, like a small overflowing birdbath and run forward just above his ears. An ivory handled knife was still gripped in his cold right hand, its blade caked with blood. Mattingly rolled him onto his side and noted thinner blood on his face, his hands and the front of his coat.

"That doesn't look like it came from your head, Mr. Briscoe," Mattingly said to the body. "I think I need to go inside and see what mischief brought you onto Mrs. Binterfield's walkway."

He looked carefully along the walkway and up the steps, then walked through the open front door of the Binterfield Mansion. The trail of people going in and out of the house led into the parlor off to the right of the foyer, like a line of ants to spilled sugar. A man near the doorway to the parlor handed him the boot pistol. The barrel was split at the end. Lydia Binterfield sat in a wingback chair near the fire with a heavy shawl over her shoulders and Dr. Harper hovering nearby.

"Mrs. Binterfield," Mattingly said, "I am sure you wish nothing but privacy at this terrible moment, but I need to ask you questions about the details of Mr. Briscoe's attack."

Lydia stared into the fire and did not turn her head,

but slowly nodded her acceptance. Dr. Harper stepped closer to Mattingly and spoke in a low voice.

"She has received two doses of Laudanum, Deputy. Her responses may not be as clear as you wish."

Mattingly bowed his head slightly to Harper and looked down at Lydia. Her bandaged right hand rested in her lap on top of her other. There was another bandage high on her right forearm. Her ripped silk bodice showed at the opening of the shawl, light blue soaked with blood. Harper pulled a parlor chair next to her and signaled Mattingly to sit in it.

"She has stitches in her shoulder as well, Deputy. I would prefer she not be tempted to raise her head nor bend up her neck muscles," Harper said as he stepped away.

In an almost toneless chant, Lydia answered Mattingly's questions and described Briscoe's deranged attack on her house slaves and then her.

"He had been fixated on me since my Husband's death," she told him, "maybe from even before that. I suppose when I asked him to stay on at the bank as manager, he misread my intentions."

Mattingly gave only a flicker of a glance at the comment, and a slightly raised eyebrow. Havre de Grace gossip was far faster than the new telegraph.

"And where are your house slaves now, Mrs. Binterfield?"

She focused her eyes on his and frowned. "Well, I don't know. I haven't needed anything other than what Dr. Harper has provided, since...I suppose they are in their quarters...in the basement." Then she returned her gaze back into the fire. "Could someone place another log in the fire," she asked of no one in particular.

One of the other men in the room picked up a piece of split oak from the iron rack next to the fireplace, while three women stood at the edge of the room looking around and chatting among themselves in animated whispers. One of them stepped away from the others. Nadja Lister, wife of the undertaker, bent over to Lydia's ear and whispered.

"Do you remember me, Lydia?"

Lydia looked at her with unfocused eyes.

"Nigger trash," Nadja said, then gave a beaming smile as she left the room.

Lydia stared after her.

"Where is the doorway to the basement, Mrs. Binterfield," Mattingly asked, but she did not respond.

Dr. Harper tapped him on the shoulder and pointed into the foyer. "Toward the back. Third door on the left. I have already given both women stitches and dressings. Mrs. Pulaski is probably still with them."

"Mrs. Pulaski? Oh yes, she worked as a domestic here when her husband was believed lost at sea. I suppose she is...friends...with them."

Mattingly left the room and made his way down to the basement. At the bottom of the stairs the floor was spattered with blood in an open area holding a smooth-topped work table on one side. A narrow hallways split off to the sides in both directions.

"Hello," he called.

"We're back here," a woman's voice answered.

The hall was dark except for faint yellow light laying on the floor from a doorway at the right. The small bed to the side of the room held a young black woman with bandages on her right arm. Another blood spotted bandage was visible across her abdomen, within a large split in her dress. Two wooden chairs were pulled close to the bed occupying most of the rest of the room. Near the head of the bed an older black woman sat with bandages on her left arm and right cheek. A slice in her dress near her right breast was partially pinned shut, but a fresh white bandage peeked out from the opening.

"I need to speak with these two, Mrs. Pulaski. May I take your seat for a few minutes?"

Sonja reached over and patted Sissy and then kissed Junie on her unharmed cheek.

"I'll just be in the folding area, ladies," she said to them, and then fixed Mattingly in a firm gaze. "Deputy Mattingly has some important questions to ask you. Just tell the truth and he will treat you kindly."

Mattingly sighed and gave her a half smile, then spoke to Sissy and Junie, "That's right...ladies."

Sonja drifted toward the folding table under the lamp light. She heard a sound in the storage room. Ben sat at a narrow table with a burning candle next to a bottle in the center. He held a small glass in his hand and offered it to her.

"Brandy," he said. "The bottle was already opened and sitting on the big table out there."

Sonja accepted the brandy, took a drink and then exhaled a long breath. "If they tell Lyle what they told me, Briscoe brought it all on himself."

She handed the glass back and Ben took a drink. He shook his head.

"I watched Wallace sew up Sissy. She was really lucky."

"Lucky??"

"Yes, lucky. The inner skin wasn't broken. I'm sure it hurt like hell, but Briscoe only cut her outer skin. He didn't actually open her belly. She's young and will heal quickly. If she and her mother avoid infection, it will all only be a bad memory and scars for the telling."

"A very bad memory. Ben, I know I should have stayed with them while Wallace worked, but..."

"But, nothing. Sonja. You came to their aid as soon as you heard," Ben said.

"And then I ran away from the blood. It was too much, too soon. I watched poor John Bartlett when Hoagg cut him open in our house..."

"Let it go, Sonja. Don't tie those two acts together."

"It's all coming back, Ben. Flooding over me like a nightmare, even as I stand here now."

She pulled up her skirt and bloomers, exposing the fresh scar on her thigh. She rubbed her fingertips over the wound.

"The man that did that is dead, Sonja. So is Hoagg," Ben said.

She pushed down her skirt, picked up the glass and drained the remaining brandy. "I think I understand why veteran soldiers drink so much. " She set the glass down

153

and touched Ben's hand. "Don't refill it."

"You could refill it for me, if you would be so kind, Ben," Mattingly said from the doorway.

"Do you find anything that would cause more trouble for Junie or Sissy," Sonja asked as Ben refilled the glass and leaned forward, handing it to Mattingly.

The Deputy took a long drink, then held up the glass to the candle light. "Very nice," he said. "No, I heard nothing that would make me believe that, unless of course, their master says otherwise...and then, if the late Mr. Briscoe stated a truth as he died, there could be the question of who is the master of those two women back there."

He rolled his eyes and took another drink, and sighed. "Now you two never heard me say that last part, right."

Both Ben and Sonja shook their heads no.

Mattingly took another drink and rolled the empty glass in his hands. "Ben..."

"Another?" Ben asked.

"No. Thank you. I...uh..."

"Yes, Lyle?"

Sonja leaned against Ben and placed her hand on his other shoulder. She joined her husband's waiting stare at Mattingly.

"Ben...I believe all my questions about your knife are fully answered. So...I am done with that."

"Good," Ben and Sonja spoke together.

"But, why?" Sonja asked. " Was his attack on Lydia and his behavior in front of everyone, as well as his cuts to Junie and Sissy finally enough?"

"No, Mrs. Pulaski. I was coming to arrest Sam Briscoe, anyway."

"What?"

Mattingly shook his head and held out his glass. "I believe I will have another, if you would be so kind..."

Mattingly took his full glass and sat upon a wooden crate.

"There was another murder tonight. Sliced groin to gullet, just like the others. Like a lightning bolt."

"Briscoe?" said Ben

154

"Had two witnesses this time. One was a black night cleaner, but what clinched it was the word of a white sailor; a stranger in town. The sailor saw Briscoe do it and then saw his face in the lamp light."

"I thought it might have been, but I was never sure. I just knew it wasn't me, and you didn't believe me, Lyle," Ben said.

Mattingly sipped at his brandy and nodded.

"Well, this sailor followed him to a tavern and heard the keep call him by name. Then he come looking for me."

" Awfully bold action, Lyle," Ben said. "Especially for someone not from around here..."

"He wanted that reward, Ben."

"What reward?"

Mattingly chuckled and shook his head. "For One Hundred Dollars! I must have twenty reward posters tacked up around town, and you never saw one, Ben?"

Ben shrugged his shoulders and glanced at Sonja, who shrugged her shoulders as well.

Mattingly chuckled again and absently withdrew the boot pistol from his pocket and showed it to Ben and Sonja. The split barrel was ugly testimony that it could never be fired again. Mattingly half chuckled.

"She put in at least a double charge, maybe more. But if she had put just a couple grains more, this little thing would have blown her hand off and only scarred Briscoe. As it was, she held a hand cannon that would have shot through a wild boar. And given that two balls are taken from its box, I suspect that aided in spreading Briscoe's brains out on the walkway"

"That's just what it did," Ben said.

"Guessing from what I saw in the box that held it, which she just showed to me," Mattingly said, "this was the first time it was loaded and fired."

"How special for Mr. Briscoe," Sonja said with a smile that held no mirth.

Ben offered the brandy bottle to Mattingly, but he waved it away.

"Kindly leave it open down here, if you would Ben. I may need to...investigate... down here again before I...Oh

155

No!"

"What?"

"I still have Mr. Leonard locked up at the office! Plum forgot about him!"

"Leonard?" Ben said. "Edward Leonard?"

"You know him, Ben?"

"He's... off my ship. He is your witness? And you have him locked up?"

"Already had a couple false accusations and stupid reports. Wanted to keep him where I could get back to him if he was lying..."

"Let's go get him," Ben said

"Let's wait a moment," Sonja added. "We've had enough excitement tonight..."

Ben halted in mid motion and smiled. "Yes, he can just wait there until in the morning. Do you mind, Lyle?"

"No. Actually, I still have plenty to do here. He's safe and warm there, with a nice cot to sleep on."

The three traded smiles and Mattingly walked back up stairs. Sonja made a quick visit to Junie and Sissy to let them know that no more trouble over Mr. Briscoe would come their way. Then they walked up the steps to the main floor and headed for the front door.

"This is the first time I have ever used the front door of this house," Sonja whispered to Ben as they walked.

Just as they reached the foyer, where blood splatters had slapped the walls of the staircase and droplets had meandered down thin red lines, Lydia emerged from the parlor.

Ben and Sonja stopped to face her. Ben nodded to her without her reaction. Sonja and Lydia were locked in a momentary gaze.

"Junie and Sissy do not have mortal wounds, Mrs. Binterfield," Ben said.

"So Dr. Harper told me," Lydia answered without taking her eyes from Sonja.

"Kindly close the door as you leave, Sonja," Lydia said, passing them as she walked up the stairs.

Ben pulled the door as they went out, but Sonja caught

it and pushed it back open.

They stopped in the street. The wind had calmed. The sky overhead was cloudless and full of stars in a near silent night. Breath clouds hung in front of their faces, Sonja's was twice the size of Ben's, rolling out in long puffs. Sonja's face was well lit in the lamp light, with her chin up and her face set. She glared at Ben with arched eyebrows.

Ben smiled with the light behind him and whispered from the darkness, "I have nothing to say, Mrs. Pulaski."

The public clock on Oyster Street clanged twice as they stood there. Ben slipped his arm under his wife's and said, "Let's go to bed."

Sonja blew out a long slow vapor cloud into the cold air and turned away with him.

At 8:00 O'clock the next morning, Lydia stood at the doorway to Sissy's room. Sunshine poured in through the tiny slit window near the unfinished ceiling, filling the room with light. Junie was slumped in the chair next to Sissy's bed, snoring. Lydia cleared her throat and Junie awoke with a start.

"Oh! Oh, Misses Binafeel! Oh, I so sorry. Doctah give me medicine. Oh, I so sorry..."

"Just fix me coffee, Junie...let Sissy sleep. Just fix me coffee and take care of your daughter, this morning. You can start cleaning up the house this afternoon. Be sure to get all the blood off." She started to turn away, then turned back. "Start with the walkway and the front porch. Hopefully they have taken Mr. Briscoe's body away."

"Yass'm. Yass'm," Junie said as Lydia walked away.

Three hours later, Lydia walked along the boardwalk on Oyster Street, approaching her husband's bank. Two ladies strolled toward her, looking beyond her and chatting loudly about the weather. They neither slowed their pace nor acknowledged her, boldly forcing her to step off the walkway to let them pass.

One of the women whispered, "Nigger," as they passed

Lydia grit her teeth and made the remaining steps to the bank's front door. She stopped a few feet inside the office area gate and looked at the man sitting behind the manger's desk.

James Williamson laid down the pen and stood up. "Come in Liddie. Come sit."

She sat stiffly in the visitor's chair. "James..."

He smiled and reached out to pat her arm. "You look beautiful, Liddie. While we can speak privately, please call me Jimmie. You always did."

"What are you doing, Jimmie? This is my bank. It's in Herbert's will."

"Herbert's will is of no consequence, Liddie..."

"But in Maryland, I am told..."

"You were told only what you were meant to hear. Herbert signed everything over to us in the event of...well, let's call it tragedy. We have an overriding contract, a Maryland contract. We now own everything he did, his bank, his house, his slaves..."

"and me, I suppose, Jimmie."

"No Liddie, not you. And pity is the case. You cannot be his wife, of course, and you were not his negotiable property. Legally, you no longer exist."

"What?"

"Unfortunately, Liddie, last night you killed the man I had just appointed as director of the bank and holder of Herbert's property, with my blessing to pursue you romantically, domestically, whatever."

"And now," she asked through gritted teeth.

"And now, Liddie, I need to stay up here and run this damned bank until I can find a trustworthy white man to do it."

There was a long silence.

"Am I to be evicted? Or will you move into Herbert's room."

"I am sorry, Liddie. If we were in Saint Mary's County at Grayrocks, you would be welcome to stay in your old room to come and go freely, on the property. But, here..."

"But here?"

"The bank has a public trust, that I cannot embroil in a racial scandal." He took in a deep breath, then blew it out and let his shoulders sag. "You may stay in the house until the day after Christmas - I will not have you on the streets Christmas Day."

"And what happens after Christmas Day, Jimmie?"

"Then you must be gone from here. You may return to Grayrocks, or go stay with our uncle in Georgetown. I believe he calls his plantation 'Palmetto Haven'. Your sister is already down there. I sent her there after father died. It was far too complicated, even for Grayrocks.

"She is my daughter," Lydia said.

"We both know who her sire was. Pick your term. Her grandfather was her father and her sister is her mother. It is simply too complicated for me, now."

Lydia stood up, tears painting water lines down her cheeks. James reached out and took a gentle hold of her wrist.

"I always thought of you as my sister, until we found out, Liddie. Much of that affection still lingers, in spite of the reality of your status. I will provide you funds, wherever you choose to go. Just send me word and the name of a local bank. I will tell them I am your brother, so you won't be bothered by objections to a single woman wanting a bank account."

"Am I dismissed, James?"

He sighed again. "Not yet. I have a business question."

She returned to her seat. "Yes?"

"You have a property for sale not far from here, in a place called Lapidum. It is assessed at $100,000, but the previous valuation was $1,200, and even that appears inflated by twice . Can you help me understand that?"

17

Ben and Sonja sat with Mamie in the parlor when the knock came to the door. When Mamie opened the door, Lydia Binterfield stepped inside. Ben and Sonja exchanged quick glances, walked to the staircase and went to their room upstairs, avoiding eye contact with Lydia. Moments later as Ben and Sonja came back down buttoning their coats and slipping on gloves, Ben noticed Lydia and Mamie sitting together in the parlor. Mamie smiled and nodded to Ben as he passed, but Lydia focused her attention on her tea cup and Sonja had her attention on the front door. The Pulaskis left the boarding house without speaking and walked down toward the town docks.

"I wonder what Lydia has to say to Mamie," Ben said, stepping off the stone walkway onto the street.

"I don't give a damned what that woman says or thinks, Ben."

Ben smiled and adjusted his hat in the gaining breeze as they neared the docks.

"Ah, the Pulaski fleet is at anchor," Ben said, pointing to the barges tied with the *Raven*. The *Ugly Boat* looked tied against the hull of the *Raven*, their bows pointing north against the current from the river. The *Turtle* and the *Wilhelmina* lounged in single file, tied one behind the other, from the stern of the *Ugly Boat*. All three barges were riding high in the water.

"Looks like Aaron sold all the coal in Annapolis and came back empty," Ben said

Sonja could see figures moving about in the deck of the

Raven. The sun bathed the surface of the upper bay in warm golden light, but the temperature was still just barely above freezing. A figure wearing only a shirt stepped up on the roof of the *Raven*'s cabin and waved energetically at them.

"Aaron!" Sonja called. "Put your coat on," she said, knowing he could not hear her. She pulled her knit muffler higher under her chin.

Ben looked down along the edge of the dock and shook his head. "I don't see our rowboat," he said. "No way to get out there to them."

The white shirted figure disappeared from view, and within seconds, a rowboat rounded the bow of the *Raven* coming toward then. Two men sat on the oar seat, wedged against each other, each pulling hard on an oar and leaning far back with the strain. The little rowboat skittered across the short choppy waves, almost coming off the water at moments. Sonja could hear the bravado claims and yelling between her two sons, as they competed between themselves driving the boat to their mother and father. Less than a minute passed before the rowboat thudded against the dock and Aaron threw the bow line up in the air for Ben to catch. Aaron was off the boat and up the ladder to street level before Ben could tie the line. Isaac was immediately behind Aaron, their cheeks deep red from the chill and their breathing still rapid from exertion.

As soon as Aaron was engulfed in his mother's hug she pushed him back out, still grasping his arms and inspecting his face.

"What happened to your cheek, son?"

"Um...hit by a piece of coal when they loaded the barges in Wrightsville."

Ben and Aaron locked eye contact for a split second.

"You can't fool me, young man," Sonja said.

"Wha..."

She smiled. "I know as well as any canaller that you have to cross over to Columbia to load the coal."

She pulled his chin around and gently tapped his bruised cheek.

"Well," Sonja said. "At least you got it cleaned. You be careful. Hear me?"

"Yes, Ma."

Moments later, Ben and Sonja were seated in the rowboat as their sons pulled them toward the *Raven*.

"How are the coal prices in Annapolis, Aaron," Ben asked.

"Falling a little more, Pa, Nowhere near the money we took in when the Steamships were outbidding the colliers. Still, it's near three dollars a ton and we're paying a dollar-seventy five in Columbia and ten cents a ton at the outlet lock."

"Aaron brought in a hundred and sixty dollars, Pa!" Isaac said. "In three days! When I get commissioned, that will be over six months pay for a Lieutenant."

"It would be a quarter less, if we had to pay steamer tugs to pulls us," Ben added.

"And, it all stops when the water freezes, Isaac," Aaron said. "Pa, we may not get another chance to pull to Columbia this winter. The river and the bay are almost ice free, but the canal is already sluggish. The freeze is close."

"Without the farm, we need to be cautious about where the barges spend the winter," Sonja added.

Ben nodded his head in agreement. "Better that they are in the Havre de Grace Canal Basin, than stuck up in the canal where we can't watch over them. There were some break-ins last winter near the Line. One barge burned to the ice line."

"Do you think that was intentional, Ben," Sonja asked

"More likely someone started a fire in the stove and let it get out of hand," Ben said. "Desperate people do stupid things."

"I think we can get one more trip to Wrightsville, Pa, then leave'em sit in the basin full of coal. Lots of people in Havre de Grace have started burning coal here instead of wood. Not enough trees left close to town to feed all the fires in town."

"That's good thinking, Aaron. And maybe we still have time to put some goods in the barges to sell in

Wrightsville, before you go."

Aaron looked over his shoulder as they neared the schooner.

"Ahoy *Raven*. Captain approaching!" he said

Ben laughed and gently slapped Aaron's arm. "You are the nautical one, aren't you."

Aaron and Isaac smiled and said in unison, "Aye aye, Cap'n!"

Sonja stood up as the bow of the rowboat nudged against the side ladder. "Alright, you sailors, help your mother up and make sure she stays dry!"

On deck, they were greeted by Adam and Edward and two new faces. Ben frowned at Edward.

"How were your accommodations last night?"

Edward gave him a wry smile. "Warm enough, Ben. Deputy Mattingly was a thoughtful host, but I would have enjoyed it more if he had not locked me in."

Ben grinned. "He mentioned he had secured you until your information could be verified."

"Apparently it was, since he paid me the reward. What has been done with that Mr. Briscoe."

"He was shot."

Edward stiffened his neck. "Mattingly said nothing about that."

"Wasn't him doing the shooting. It was his..." Ben looked at Sonja. "His..." Ben continued.

"His paramour," added Sonja.

Edward held his hands palm up and raised his eyebrows.

"His woman friend," one of the strangers said and patted Edward on his shoulder.

Edward raised his chin. "Ah. I see. Oh, Ben, this is Harry Rodgers," Edward said, indicating the man who had spoken. "And this is Jarrod Frieze."

Ben slowly accepted their hands, still eyeing Edward. "Are you a relative of the famous Commodore," Ben asked as he took Harry's hand.

"Only remotely, if at all. We're at the poorest end of that name, Cap'n."

Ben took Jarrod's hand. "So what brings you to the

Raven?" Ben eyed Edward, then turned his attention on the visitors. "I know who brought you, but I don't know why."

The two men exchanged quick glances. "Well, Cap'n," Harry started, "Edward said you were in need of seasoned sailors and I grew up on schooners, mostly out of Baltimore."

"I'm from Newport News, grew up on ships. I spent three years on a revenue cutter out of Philadelphia, Cap'n," Jarrod added. "Ain't nothing on a ship I can't do or learn."

"Well...I don't know..." Ben said

"Your man already paid us the sign-on bonus, Cap'n. And I already used almost half of it on lodging, bath and a big breakfast. It's been hard since..."

Ben turned toward Edward. "What sign-on bonus? How much? Where'd you get it?"

Edward stepped close to Ben, his hands tense by his sides. "Ten dollars each. Took it from my reward. You need crew and these men can do a good job. Met them last night and they can use the work."

Ben blinked and turned back toward Harry and Jarrod. "Why are you out of work?"

Harry chuckled and pointed toward the docks. "You see any good sized ships there? This is the only hull with more than one mast." He folded his arms across his chest. "Edward said you needed crew. If that wasn't true set us on shore."

Ben turned back toward Adam, Sonja and his sons, but their attention was directed elsewhere at seemingly nothing. He glanced at Edward and then the other two men.

"Yes. I need crew...and you appear to have more than enough experience. Fifteen dollars a month. You have your meals on board unless you don't want them. In port you can come and go as you please, once the cargo is delivered or brought on board and your assigned duties are completed. You'll get a crewman's share of each cargo sold."

Harry and Jarrod both nodded in agreement. Ben shook their hands again.

"I will bring up a ship's log and have you both sign on."

Then, Ben sighed and turned back to Edward. He sighed again.

"...Thank you...Edward. I will repay you for the sign-on bonuses..."

"No," Edward said "I am intent to prove to you I am an honorable man."

"We'll see," Ben said, then turned and went to the captain's cabin to retrieve the ship's log. The ship's log book was just a ledger used to record important activities and cargo on the ship. Ben picked it up off the captain's desk and held it loosely in his hands, remembering when he could barely read the words or write his own name when he returned from China.

Simon taught me.

He gripped the log firmly and trotted up the steps onto the deck. He printed his own name as co-owner and captain, then had Sonja sign in as co-owner and crew and then Adam. He had Edward, Harry and Jarrod sign on as crew, then he dated the entry, wrote his signature below it and snapped the ledger closed.

"Done," he said. "I want to go to Annapolis and pick up hardware and porcelain and anything else that may sell." He looked at Aaron, who stood not far away wearing a frown.

"Aaron, you remain as captain of the *Ugly Boat* and responsible for the other two barges. Rest for a couple days while we go to Annapolis. This will be a good exercise for the new crew and we can move far quicker with the *Raven*. If we hurry, we can fill the barges with goods and send you to Wrightsville one more time before the freeze."

Aaron's frown began to soften.

Ben added, "I suspect Miss Friedman might not be too disappointed to have you visit her some, while we are gone."

Sonja smiled at him. "And you will be the perfect gentleman, correct young man?"

"Yes, Ma," Aaron said.

165

Then she tugged on Isaac's sleeve. "And you will come to Annapolis with us, so you can tell me more about your experiences at West Point!"

"Adam," Ben said, "would you and Edward please show Harry and Jarrod where to bed down and help them bring their gear on board..."

"Already on Board..." Adam said, "...Cap'n"

Ben blew out his breath and shared a frustrated face with Adam. "Very well. I want to leave at first light in the morning and be anchored back here the morning after."

He put his arm around Aaron's shoulders. "No sense taking the barges into the basin tonight, son. Just anchor them here, fore and aft, and come back to the Pink House with your mother and brother."

Ben looked at Sonja and smiled, then turned back to his sons. "Aaron, after we get back to the dock, take two dollars from our coal profit and rent horses for you and Isaac from the canal company barn, for an afternoon visit to Lapidum. Just be back by sundown for supper."

Sonja nodded her agreement and gently squeezed Ben's arm. She drew his eyes with hers, tilted her head slightly and flicked her eyes toward Adam, then raised her eyebrows.

Ben smiled at her.

She doesn't always need words.

"Adam," Ben said, "You are invited to join us for supper at the Pink House."

"Well, er, Ben I thank you but...er..."

Sonja pointed a finger at Adam's nose. "You will come, Adam Tuttle."

"Yes, ma'am," he said and then turned back to Ben. "Thank you, Ben."

Edward stepped closer to Ben. "Just in case you thought of inviting me, Ben, I am happy to stay on board tonight."

"I would think what's left of your reward would be screaming to be spent in town," Ben said.

Edward rubbed the back of his neck and squinted up at the sun sinking in the afternoon sky "There is a lady in town that warned me to stay away. Apparently she has a husband with a hot temper who was supposed to be in Maine, but returned home last night to find her sitting in my lap in a tavern. Sleeping in Mr. Mattingly's jail was not totally unwelcome."

Harry and Jarrod both chuckled.

"I am happy to stay aboard, Cap'n" Jarrod said and Harry nodded in agreement. "But for different reasons," Harry added. "To sleep in a bed without paying for lodging is a blessing. And I hear from Edward the ship's galley is well stocked."

"It is," Ben said with a smile.

The sun had set and the candles lit in the Pink House dining room as people began to file in at 6 o'clock that evening. The house had filled with the aroma of roasted venison, lamb, and duck. Even Sonja's stomach growled in hunger. The table was covered in Irish linen and laden with stewed potatoes swimming in butter, and a rainbow of pickled vegetables from Mamie's root cellar. The table was immaculately set with shining silverware and sparkling crystal goblets. Guests entered from all directions, from the parlor, from the foyer, and from the once-flowered veranda where men were having cigars.

Mr. Heiden, the Austrian boarder from the third floor, mumbled in a heavy accent to another as he found his seat, "Is this another American holiday? Should I have brought a gift of some sort?"

Mamie came in behind him and placed her fingertip gently on his arm, "Not at all, Mr. Heiden. Just a lovely setting for a gathering of lovely people."

Mamie addressed the others. "There are place cards on the table before each seat. Kindly take the chairs at your names."

She gave a quick inspection of the table and reached out to Ben, squeezing his wrist and pulling him from the gathering crowd.

"You wish to have your farm back, yes?" she whispered.

"Yes."

"Then I will need another yes from you before the

dinner is over."

She released her grip, then swept herself into the kitchen, where she and her helper were busy preparing the meat dishes for presentation.

Ben, Sonja, and Adam were seated next to each other with an empty chair next to Ben. Aaron and Isaac were seated across from their parents. Next to Isaac came Harold Lister, the town's undertaker, and his wife Nadja. They were settling into their chairs as James Williamson entered. James was seated next to Ben, with whom he shook hands and introduced himself.

"Mamie mentioned you were taking Mr. Briscoe's room, Mr. Williamson. I expect we may see a lot of each other over the coming weeks."

"Perhaps," James said.

At that moment Lydia entered the dining room from the foyer and froze in her step. Mamie rushed in from the kitchen and began helping her with her coat. Mamie held out her hand toward the table, "There, dear, your place is waiting for you."

Shed of her heavy coat, Lydia reluctantly walked around the table to the setting beside Isaac and directly across from James. Lydia and James eyed each other in cold silence. James took in a deep breath.

"Lydia," he said.

"James," she responded, locking his eyes with hers.

Sonja stiffened and glared at Lydia. Ben watched Lydia in surprise. Adam rolled his eyes, suppressing a small twitching smile, and followed Lydia's progress as she took her seat.

The room silenced. Boarders glanced among themselves.

"Ladies and Gentlemen," Mamie announced. "This beautiful lady is our guest of honor. Mrs. Lydia Binterfield." Mamie focused a smile at James. "Mrs. Lydia Williamson Binterfield," she added.

Mamie placed her hands on her hips and smiled broadly to her dinner guests.

The room remained silent.

18

Ben and Sonja exchanged questioning glances as the remaining guests were seated. Mamie and her helper brought in the meat dishes to the welcoming murmurs and clapping hands of those at the table. Four platters were delivered, each holding generous slices of venison and lamb, surrounding a roasted duck and artfully decorated with wild celery, winter kale, nuts and dried fruits. None needed passing, as was boarding house tradition, since everyone was within reach of one of the magnificent meat trays. Next came bottles of wine from Boordy Vineyards and Pikesville Rye Whiskey.

Soon conversation had returned to full volume and joviality spread down the table amidst small talk and pleasantries. Mamie worked the dining room the entire meal with her helper, neither sitting down for more than a few seconds at a time. When, at last, fruit pies and coffee were brought out, men were loosening vests, women were leaning back and drawing deep satisfied breaths.

Mamie tapped her crystal goblet several times with a spoon and then stood to receive the attention of those at the table. "We are sorrowful for Mrs. Binterfield's loss, and are grieved by her recent attack, but even in mourning and recovery she is showing this generosity to her friends." Mamie swept her hands over the table.

"This dinner is a gift to us all, and we appreciate it," Mamie added. She began clapping her hands and was joined by several of the people at the table, followed by quizzical looks from James Williamson and Sonja Pulaski.

"While not everyone shares her loss for her departed husband," Mamie said. "Mrs. Binterfield is correcting something that should never have happened..."

The room fell silent again.

"We all know of the travesty endured by the Pulaskis due to unfortunate actions by the Tidewater Bank and Trust under both Mr. Binterfield and Mr. Briscoe..." Mamie nodded toward Ben and Sonja. "Mrs. Binterfield wishes to inform all here tonight, that the property known as the Pulaski Farm is being returned to the Pulaski family."

Clapping and cheering thundered around the table. Sonja's eyes flew wide and her mouth opened with the beginning of a great smile. She turned to Ben, but he continued his stone faced stare at Mamie. She squinted her eyes at him and pressed her lips into a thin line, then returned her attention to Mamie, but stealing quick glances at Ben's face from the corner of her eye.

Mamie held up her hands and continued. "As one would expect for the widow of a wealthy man, Mrs. Binterfield has inherited significant holdings, but her heart aches from her experiences and she has chosen to leave us to heal..."

"She is leaving the Bank and all her holdings in Havre de Grace in the hands of her trusted...brother...Mr. Williamson..."

James' eyes widened slightly. He maintained a stiff gaze on Mamie, while the others were looking toward Lydia in growing admiration.

"Mrs. Binterfield has chosen to assume responsibility over family holdings in South Carolina, and will be leaving our lovely Havre de Grace, the day after Christmas..."

Mamie turned toward Ben and Sonja and held out her hand, drawing the guest's attention toward them.

"aboard the schooner *Raven*, with our own Captain Ben Pulaski at the helm. Yes?"

Sonja dropped open her mouth and turned completely in her chair to face Ben. Ben gritted his teeth under a smile and kept his gaze on Mamie.

"Yes," he said.

Sonja continued to stare in disbelief at Ben while the others clapped.

Ben rested his fisted hands on the table in front of him. He let his unfocused vision drift to the empty space in front of his plate and forced several deep breaths. Then he gulped his whiskey glass dry.

Harold Lister patted him on his back. "Winter voyage to the south. I envy you, sir," he said.

Mamie clasped her hands together over her heart and beamed to her guests.

Lydia, offered her wine glass toward James in toast, and then drained the glass.

Sonja pinched Ben's arm and delivered a hoarse whisper to his ear. "And when did you decide to do that?"

Ben raised his chin slightly and took in a long breath, then let it out in a rush of air that set the candle flames in front of him dancing. "Just now. God damn it," he muttered

Dinner guests began rising and heading out of the dining room. Sonja stood without speaking to Ben and walked out of the room. Ben caught a glimpse of her in the foyer taking the staircase. He reached for the whiskey decanter and refilled his glass, then patted his coat pockets feeling for his pipe and tobacco pouch. Someone else patted him on the back but he ignored the person. He glanced toward the foyer again, but Sonja was gone. Lydia lingered there only momentarily staring directly at him and smiling broadly. She mouthed 'thank you' and turned away. He picked up his glass and the decanter and moved toward the veranda door. When he came before it, he was deciding which item to set down to open the door, but Adam was there to let them both out.

The cold wind had settled and the side yard was silent. Light slipped through the dining room windows and joined the yellow circle from an oil lamp in the nearby corner. Ben set the decanter on the lamp table between two chairs positioned closest to the house, and settled into one of the chairs. Adam set another decanter next to the one Ben had placed and sat in the other chair. Neither spoke as they twisted in their seats to pull out pipes and tobacco and pocket knives. Adam filled his pipe first and pulled down a piece of dried vine still curled around a porch post, then held it over the oil lamp flame until it began to burn. After he lit his pipe he handed the burning twig to Ben.

"How did you like Liddie's show in there," asked a man's voice from a darkened corner across the veranda. His outline was lost in the deeper blackness of bushes behind him. A point of ruby light grew bright as he drew on his cigar.

"Ah," Ben said when he realized the name was a nickname for Lydia, and the speaker was James, her brother. "Was it Lydia's show, or was it Mamie's, Mr. Williamson?"

"Call me James, please. May I address you as Ben?"

"Please do. A room full of misters and madams is more than I wish to..."

"Wish to, what, Ben?"

Ben waved the rest of the comment away, knowing James could see him perfectly well.

"James, this is Adam Tuttle, my ship's carpenter and friend...and one of the co-owners of the *Raven*."

Adam grinned around the stem of his pipe. "Your pleasure, sir," he said to James.

"Oh, it was Liddie's show in there, Ben. No doubt about it. When did Liddie approach you about taking her to Georgetown?"

"Georgetown? Is that where she's going?"

James laughed like a tavern drunk. "You didn't know?"

Ben took a long sip of whiskey. "No. None of it."

James continued to laugh until he began to coughed. "Forgive me, please..." and he coughed several more times, then took another drink of whiskey.

"In her own way, Mamie that is, let me know that I was about to get my farm back, and I would have to say yes to her during dinner, but I sure as hell wasn't expecting this."

"Is this how it is done in Havre de Grace, Ben? Does

one come to the Pink House to learn the official news from Mamie?"

"I wasn't aware of that," Ben said "I have only just arrived here and have nothing to add to what we saw at dinner."

"No. I suppose not, Ben. But Mamie was a willing ally for Lydia this evening, for the same reason as you.

"Oh?"

"Liddie asked me to write off two accounts. Yours and Mamie's. Both of you own your properties free and clear. That is no small gift, Ben."

"No. And I appreciate it, James. Taking your sister to South Carolina, to...Georgetown, is a small price to pay, to get our home back."

"She's not really my...well, I suspect you know the truth."

Ben said nothing in polite silence. Adam stood and stretched, then tapped his pipe empty over the edge of the veranda.

"I think maybe one or two pieces of duck may be just the thing to chase this whiskey."

Adam went back inside while Ben and James remained on the veranda talking.

An hour later Ben slipped into their room. The lamps and candles were out, so he lit one in the wash room to shed light in the sleeping area. A blanket and pillow were laid out on the floor next to the bed and Sonja lay on the bed with her back toward him. He picked up the blanket and pillow and tossed them onto the bed, then knelt on the mattress to kiss Sonja's cheek. She yanked the covers up over her face so he could not kiss her. He kissed the top of her head and gently slapped her bottom.

"You can stay mad as long as you like, or at least until you hear what really happened, but I am not sleeping on the floor, woman."

Ben went to the wash room, blowing out the candle when he was through, then climbed into bed. He lay down on his back thinking about sailing the *Raven* to South Carolina and about meeting with Anthony again.

"Might as well do'em both," he mumbled before he drifted into deep sleep.

The room was still black when Ben heard a loud thump and felt sharp pains to the back of his head and his elbows. He sat up disoriented, feeling for the edge of the bed and looking for shapes in the darkness when his hand slapped the floor next to him.

"Damn it to Hell," he said and climbed back into bed.

He rearranged his blankets and rolled onto his side facing Sonja, who once again had her back to him. He reached out until he could place his hand against the small of her back.

"Don't you dare," she said. "Don't you d-"

Ben pushed her off the bed.

At sunrise Ben and Sonja lay in each other's arms in a twisted nest of blankets and loose feathers. Both their heads rested on the same pillow. The other pillow lay almost empty of feathers, but every surface in the room was covered with them.

Ben rose and washed his face, then dressed and went down stairs for coffee. Mamie's kitchen helper was busy cleaning pots and pans and dishes, but there were piles of sliced meat and bread on the kitchen counter and coffee was just finishing its boil. She poured Ben a steaming cup and went back to her duties. Ben ambled into the parlor and found Adam asleep on one of the settees, with his lower legs hanging off the end.

Ben sat in a nearby chair and sipped at his coffee, slurping to cool it.

Adam snorted the aroma of fresh coffee and sat up, his wiry white hair sticking up in the air and dark circles under his eyes. He scratched his head and yawned and walked on socked feet into the kitchen, following the scent of coffee. He returned with a large red mug, steaming from the top.

"Played poker with Mrs. Mamie last night," he said.

Ben sipped his coffee, speaking through the steam. "How late?"

"Dawn," Adam said and yawned again.

"How much did you lose?"

"Almost all, Ben. Even bet my lucky gold coin I found on Spesutie Island."

"Oh, now I am sorry you lost that. I think it really was one of those gold coins stolen from Lafayette when he marched through Havre de Grace."

Adam chuckled and set his mug on the table in front of the settee. He reached into his pocket and pulled out his coin, with the hole drilled near one edge for his necklace that held it.

"Oh good," Ben said. "You didn't lose it..."

Adam kept chuckling as he laid down two more French gold coins just like it, and stared hard at Ben.

"Those came from Mrs. Mamie, Ben. Laid them down like they were just American coppers."

"How did she come by them, Adam?"

"Didn't say. She just threw up her hands when she lost that last deal, and said she was going to bed. Said I could sleep on the settee and went off to her rooms. Damndest, thing!"

Ben and Adam drank their coffee in silence, staring at the three gold coins on the table. When they had finished their coffee, Adam scooped the coins into his pocket and they returned their cups to the kitchen. They bundled up in heavy coats and stepped outside. The air was still calm but a wet cold nipped at their noses. Just as Ben was closing the door, Aaron and Isaac came out as well.

"We'll row you out to the *Raven*," Isaac said.

"Just take Adam, son," Ben said. "I need to speak with Anthony first. I will fetch your mother after that and be down at the docks in about an hour."

At the Harford Hotel, the hallway outside room three was only dimly lit by a glimmer lantern held away from the wall by a brass rod. Shafts of early morning sunshine were only beginning to find their way into the hall. Ben pounded on the door twice before he heard someone stirring in the room. He was about to pound on the door again when the sound of muttering and cursing arrived at the other side of the door and the latch was released to open it.

"What in the name of..."

"Good morning, Anthony," Ben said as he brushed by Anthony and headed for a stuffed chair in the sitting area. "Tell me about your friend Hannibal, and how you know he is taken but not yet sold, and is to be sold in Charleston."

Anthony padded to the desk at the foot of his bed and picked up a cup of cold coffee left from the night before. He slipped the arms of wire-rim octagon spectacles into the hair above his ears and examined several papers lying on the desk. Finding the one he wanted he limped to the heavy chair set next to the window.

"Robert Hannibal is the son and grandson of free men," he said, then eyed Ben over the top of his lens. "Not freed men, but free men, Ben. There is no maternal lineage to him that includes a slave. There is no legal precedent to claim he is a slave in any southern state. This was blatant kidnapping." He stopped again and locked eyes with Ben.

"I understand, Anthony. I know very well that the child of a slave woman is a slave..."

"In the south..."

"In the south, and Maryland is part of the south. Yes, I know that, now answer my questions."

"Kidnapping is becoming rampant, Ben."

"I know that all too well, Anthony. Has the blood-letting of taking the *Raven* from Hoagg that gave you your limp escaped your memory?"

"The limp is from gout. It is my lung that was forfeited taking the *Raven*. My lung that you and the good Doctor Harper fried with a red hot iron."

"Stop it, Anthony. He kept you from bleeding to death, or drowning in your own blood after Hoagg pinned you to the mast with a harpoon!"

Anthony sighed and lay the papers in his lap. Anthony was younger than Ben, but looked far older. His color still remained pale. "Allow me my petulance, Benjamin. I am now in almost constant pain from one thing or another..."

"Hannibal, Anthony. Tell me what you know about

Charleston."

He picked up the papers from his lap, but looked at them only briefly. Holding them was only a reminder.

"Robert was taken in Boston. He had inadvertently slighted a plantation owner from South Carolina. We think the plantation owner had ruffians drag Robert aboard his ship when he sailed south. Robert was taken to the man's plantation, conditioned for servitude, treated horribly for several weeks, and is now destined for the auction block in Charleston.

"How do you know all this?"

"We have spies in many places, Ben."

"And, just who is 'we'?"

"Most of 'We' are members of the Philadelphia Abolitionists Society, but not an official division of it. There are many of us who feel compelled to take direct action, rather than simply advocate for abolishment. Many of us are prepared for 'severe' actions. My grandfather made us rich selling slaves, so I must..."

Ben waved away Anthony's coming dedication.

"I heard all that when you first talked me into helping you hide slaves in your barge with secret compartments." Ben turned in his seat, taping the scar on the side of his head. "You will remember, old friend, I was almost killed at the Line, crossing into Pennsylvania past slave catchers."

Anthony wagged his finger at Ben. "But we got across."

"I almost didn't."

"If we do nothing more, it's to our shame."

"If we do nothing more, it will change on its own, Anthony. Slavery has become all too complicated to remain. It's like a carcass in the water being nibbled by the crabs"

"You're a fool if you believe that, Benjamin Pulaski! And I know you don't. You've been saying that for years, but it rings hollow on my ears."

Anthony took off his spectacles and pointed them at Ben. "You grew up in Maryland, a slave state yes, but in the upper Bay. Here it is a legal obligation. In the deep south it makes men rich beyond dreams, and they will kill

177

to keep it. You grew up around the slaves of others since childhood, paying it no attention, but now you have a good friend who is also called a slave. Is it changing for Simon? Is it getting better...for him?"

Ben stared into the dark fireplace. Tiny pinpoints of ruby coals sat like miniature stars in an ashen sky. A lazy wisp of smoke struggled free of the ash and drifted toward the chimney.

"No."

"But you still say that it will change."

Ben sighed. "It was once a belief, Anthony, and then a hope. Now it is just a comfortable lie to answer questions in public. While..."

"While you and your sons hide runaway slaves in your barge. That same barge I left behind after we took the *Raven*, when I thought I was going home to die."

"Yes. All that." Ben's voice was weary.

"It's time to do more, Ben."

Ben sighed again and watched one of the tiny coals fade out and join the ash. He spoke to the fireplace. "When do you need me in Charleston?"

19

Ben and Sonja climbed aboard the *Raven* under a nearly cloudless blue sky. Sonja had covered herself in a heavy wool sweater, a new seaman's wool outer coat and canvas pants. She and Ben turned back toward Isaac and Aaron sitting in the rowboat below them.

"You boys behave," said Sonja.

"We're going to set the anchors for all three barges, and then take another trip back to Lapidum today. We want to visit our friends there and let them know we're coming back," Aaron said.

"I am still in happy shock over the news, Ma," said Isaac.

Ben leaned over the railing. "You two be careful, and say hello for your mother and me to our neighbors. And be back on board the barges in the morning. We'll be bringing goods on consignment, so we can't sit on them in a frozen canal all winter. We need to..."

"We need to get the barges to Wrightsville and the damned coal to Havre de Grace!" Aaron finished Ben's command, mimicking his father's voice.

Ben playfully wagged his finger at Aaron and gave his sons a broad smile. Sonja showed them dancing fingers that passed for a little wave as her sons rowed the few yards away to the side of the *Ugly Boat*. Isaac and Aaron scampered up on its deck and threw quick waves as they ducked down into the cabin.

While she waited for her sons to comeback on deck to wave them off, Sonja stood beside Ben at the tandem wheels and swept her hand up toward the rigging.

"Ben, tell me again about the rigging."

Ben spoke slowly and emphasized each word as if he was talking to a child.

"The wind pushes the sails and that makes the ship go..."

Sonja poked him hard in the chest.

"Don't talk to me like that, Benjamin. I know how sails work from being on the *Ugly Boat*. Main sail powers the boat. Jib holds her bow straight ahead. The keel turns the push of the wind into forward motion, and the rudder keeps her on course. Right?"

He smiled at her with a sparkle in his eyes. "Yes."

She poked him again. "So, what's different here?"

He nodded and pointed toward the bow. "Two masts. The one in front is the Fore and the one back here is the Main. Sails attached to each mast are named for their mast and their position on the mast, like the main sail and the main topsail."

"And the ones at the bow hanging from the stay line are jibs. I understand," Sonja said.

"Well, except that one big one over the bow hanging from the stay line has a boom at the bottom and is called the staysail."

"But it works like a jib, right?"

"Right."

"And booms let us put the sail in better positions to catch the wind. Right?"

"Right, Sonja."

"Thank you," she said and turned facing the bow, pulling a knit cap down over her curls. She looked back over her shoulder with an impish smile. "Let's go then, Cap'n."

With *Raven*'s anchors up and free of her bonds to the *Ugly Boat*, she was already drifting backward, pushed southward by both wind and tide. The Foresail and Staysails snapped as they filled with the wind and yanked the bow of the *Raven* completely in the opposite direction, like turning a horse. Harry and Jarrod dashed back to hoist the mainsail, while Edward and Sonja raised the jibs at the bow. The deck of the ship leaned slightly away from the wind as the sails took the pressure and forced the ship forward. Ben stood at the windward side ship's wheel and steered the ship southward along the main channel. Sonja stayed at the railing trading waves with Isaac and Aaron. Ben gave a quick wave from the wheel as the *Raven* came alive. Compared to the stodgy *Ugly Boat* with its single main sail and blunt bow, the *Raven* seemed to leap ahead and race with the wind. Ben watched the shore as the *Raven* glided past.

Must be making six knots. Twice the speed of the Ugly Boat! We can be in Annapolis by sundown!

They were sailing less than an hour, when Edward spotted a capsized skiff to the west of their course. He grabbed the telescope from near the wheel and examined the little boat bobbing in the mild chop.

"Ben, er, Cap'n! Looks like an overturned boat to starboard. Maybe someone hanging on to it."

Ben turned the wheel and the bow began to swing toward the troubled boat. "Shit. Lower the main and staysails, and drop the foresails half way, so we keep steerage."

"That's shallow water out there," Jarrod said.

"Better get to the bow, Jarrod, and pole the depth, so we don't run aground," ordered Edward. He continued to assume the role of first mate. Ben was satisfied with his decisions, so he did not interrupt Edward.

"We're empty in the hold," Ben said to Edward, "so we can float in seven feet, but I do not want to go less than that."

Edward nodded and returned to his inspection of the capsized boat.

"Looks like a girl," he said.

Sonja ran to the bow to watch their progress toward the boat.

"Seven feet," yelled Jarrod.

Edward spun around to face Ben. "Drop anchor, Cap'n?"

"Do it."

"Drop anchor, Harry."

181

Ben had not noticed that Edward had already motioned for Harry to stand by the anchor. Edward ran to the stern and pulled in the line to *Raven*'s trailing rowboat. As soon as the rowboat bumped against the *Raven*'s hull, Edward untied the bow line and jumped into it. He pushed off against the hull, grabbed the oars and began long powerful pulls, sending the rowboat skimming toward the overturned skiff. Edward grabbed the arm of the girl clinging to the boat and pulled her into the rowboat. Her face was almost blue. She stared open eyed at the sky and did not move. Edward slapped her face, then rolled her onto her side and began slapping her back.

After several slaps the girls screamed, "Stop!", then began coughing and shaking violently.

Edward grinned at her as she tried to slap his face. "Welcome back girlie!"

Within seconds Edward returned to the *Raven* and with help from Harry and Jarrod, they lifted the girl onto the deck. Sonja rushed forward with a wool blanket and wrapped it around the girl.

"Mos?"

"Y-y-y-es ma-aam," the girl stuttered.

Sonja turned to Ben. "This is the girl I had seen before in town." Sonja turned back to the girl. "Child, you can't be more than five or six, why in the world were you trying to row a boat by yourself?"

Ben stared at the little girl. The color of her eyes matched Sonja's. Where Sonja leaned over the girl, her hair fell against the girl's face and one could not tell where the girl's hair stopped and Sonja's began. Both were golden blonde and naturally twisted in cascading tight curls.

Alisha would be her age.

Ben turned away for a moment and took in a deep breath. "Take her into the captain's cabin," he ordered.

"I'll start a fire in the stove down there," Adam said over his shoulder as he padded from the crew's quarters in the bow toward the captain's cabin.

"Another boat coming, Cap'n," said Harry. He pointed

out toward nearby Spesutie Island.

Half way between the *Raven* and Spesutie Island, a large black man pulled long deep strokes, creating a foamed bow wave as he moved rapidly toward the *Raven*.

As the second rowboat came against the *Raven*, Harry hooked the bow of it with a gaff, holding it in place.

"Is that child all right?" said the man in the boat.

Ben joined Harry at the rail and looked down into the rowboat. The man looked up and smiled.

"Almost didn't recognize this ship and you, Cap'n Ben," he said.

Ben smiled back at the man, "Hello, Cephus. Were you coming after that girl?"

"Yes suh. I seen her comin off Shad, thinkin she awfully small to be out in that chop. I was on my way after her when I seen your ship turn in. Thought you'd run aground fo sure. Lucky tide still be up."

"Come up on deck, Cephus. It's good to see you."

"Like to Cap'n Ben, but I gonna go tie a line on that skiff and pull it back to sho 'fore it gets lost for good. Miz Tatum gonna need that thing."

"You know the girl's family?" Ben said.

"Just Widow Tatum and her Mos on Shad Island, til fishing season. She the watch lady."

Cephus looked back over his shoulder at the overturned skiff.

"Cap'n Ben, I needs to go git that thing."

Harry released the gaff hook from the bow and Cephus pushed off from the *Raven* with his oar. Ben turned from the railing and headed toward the captain's cabin. Edward spoke as Ben passed him.

"You know him, Ben?"

"Yes. He tried to burn this ship. Good man."

Ben pattered down the steps from the deck to the cabin.

The cabin was warm. Adam was at the little stove feeding in another piece of wood. There was a small pile of wet clothes in the floor. Sonja sat on the side of the bed with one hand resting on a pile of wool blankets. The little girl's head barely stuck out from under the blankets, like

183

a turtle peeking from under its shell.

"It just happened, Ben," Sonja said. "She saw us and stood up to wave us down. The chop flipped the boat, but she was able to grab onto it."

"What was she doing out in a boat by herself...in this water?"

"Her mother is very sick, Ben. She says her mother has been lying in bed four days and burns with fever. There is just the two of them on that island."

"Yes. Cephus just told me."

"The man who..."

"Yes, that one, but he went to get her skiff and tow it to shore."

"Hattie ain't far from here, Ben," Adam said. "She's better than most doctors. Knows medicine plants. Healed me more than once."

Ben absently pulled on his beard. "Shad Island...buy boats dock there during fishing season. Adam, do you know if anything as big as the *Raven* docks there."

"I don't know, Ben, Chesapeake Bay buy boats, even the new steam ones, are shallow water boats. Need no more than four or five feet under their hulls even when they're full."

Ben scratched the side of his neck. "We'll try to get as close as we can, but looks like we'll need to send the rowboat to take this girl back."

"I'm going with her," Sonja said.

Ben slowly shook his head. "Sonja, we have got to get to Annapolis. We should do what we can, but..."

"Go on without me. Pick me up on your way back."

"Maybe Cephus could go get Hattie," Adam said.

Ben was frowning at Sonja, but spoke to Adam. "He's not coming back to the ship. He's pulling the skiff back to Shad island."

"Then I need the rowboat to go get Hattie."

"You up to that, Adam?"

"I'd be going with the wind, Ben."

"Yes, but what about coming back, Adam?"

Adam rubbed his chin and chuckled. "Hattie's strong

as a mule. I'll have her spell me going to Shad."

The wind had picked up when Ben returned to the deck. Adam buttoned up his coat and swung a leg over the railing above the ship's rowboat.

"Maybe you should not do this, Adam," Ben said

"Then who, Ben?" Adam pointed at the other crew "They don't know Hattie. Where she lives. What she looks like. And she don't know them."

He slipped over the railing and down into the boat. The wind pushed against Adam's chest as soon as he rowed away from the protection of the ship's hull. Ben could see that it was an easy pull toward the shore.

Edward stepped next to Ben, watching Adam row away.

"So how do we get the little girl to her island if we can't dock there? Adam just took our only rowboat."

"Cephus will be there. He will come to the ship."

Ben and Edward watched Adam row. With the bow anchor in the sand the wind had pushed the stern of the *Raven* toward shore.

"We're facing a lee shore, Ben, and the tide is dropping."

Ben faced Edward with a mirthless grin.

"Let's see if we're good sailors."

With shortened sail, *Raven* was worked to skim the edge of the shallow, running across the face of the wind and edging foot by foot toward the deeper channel. The wind increased again, slapping the sails hard toward shore, trying to push the keel onto the bottom. Just as the water began to shallow ahead of them, and the hull hissed as it gently kissed the sandy bottom, the crew fully raised all sails and then pulled the booms hard against the wind. The pressure gave her a surge of speed and the *Raven* shot ahead toward the channel as they neared Shad Island and clawed into deeper water. The ship had developed such forward speed that both bow and stern anchors had to be dropped to keep her from flying past the island. The bow anchor bit first , snugging the *Raven* low by the bow until the stern anchor bit. For a few moments, the hundred and ten foot schooner rocked bow to stern like a great rocking horse, while the crew dashed from sail to sail, snatching them down.

Almost breathless, the four men came together at the tandem wheels, shaking each other's hands and grinning like school boys.

"Damned fine seamanship, gentlemen," Ben said as he took their hands. He clamped his hand on Edward's shoulder as he offered his other hand. "You've brought me an excellent crew, Eddie," Ben said, using a childhood nickname without thought. "Thank you."

"You are most welcome, Bennie," Edward said, accepting Ben's hand and placing his left hand on top.

Sonja came up on deck holding Mos' hand. The girl wore a pair of Sonja's trousers, the legs rolled up several times, and a heavy seaman's coat with the sleeve dangling loose below her fingertips like a broken wing penguin. Sonja carried the girl's clothes in a canvas bag.

"If you boys are through playing, I need to get this girl back home and help her mother."

20

Cephus reached the overturned skiff, fished out the bow line and tied it to the stern of his rowboat. Ben watched from the *Raven* as Cephus pulled the skiff to the shallows of Shad island. Once he emptied the water and righted it, he dragged the boat far above the high tide line. He disappeared from shore for a few moments then came running back to his rowboat, waving his arms at the schooner and rowed with a panic back to the *Raven*.

Breathing easy after his pull from Shad Island helped by the wind, Cephus climbed aboard the *Raven*.

"Miz Tatum bad sick, Cap'n Ben! She was laying in the floor and got blood in her mouth. She need a healer! You know Miz Hattie?"

"Adam has already gone for her, Cephus," Ben told him. "Step down into the cabin and get warm."

"Then will you take me and Mos to help with her, Cephus," Sonja asked.

"I takes you right now Miz Plaski. Don't need no rest. I takes you right now. "

They both looked to Ben, who gave them a quick nod. He reached out and squeezed Sonja's arm.

"Sit low and be careful, Sonja."

She patted his hand. "I know what to do, Ben."

Cephus was already slipping over the side back into his rowboat.

"Come on Miz Plaski," he said.

As they pulled away Edward pointed toward the other shore where Adam had gone. "Looks like Adam and a bushy haired black man."

Ben chuckled as he peered at the oncoming rowboat. "That's Miss Hattie." He slapped Edward on his back. "If you want to live, don't you let her hear you calling her a man."

Adam looked up at Ben and smiled as he passed the *Raven*, rocking back with each surging stroke from Hattie's arms, propelling the ship's rowboat toward Shad Island. They touched sand just as Sonja and Mos stepped into the treeline, heading to the house.

The wind was broken by the trees, and the change from loose sand to firm ground gave Sonja and Mos better footing to get to the house quickly. It was dark inside. The sun was not welcomed. No candle or lamp was lit. The wind outside rattled the windows, but the air inside was hovering with the cold smell of decay, like the deeper hold of an old ship on the verge of rot. There was also the pungent scent of sickness. Mos dashed ahead to her mother's room on the lower floor. Following her, they passed a near empty kitchen displaying a sparse assortment of dishes and a modest cook stove with the door open to a darkened firebox and nearby empty wood basket. The floor was almost spongy under their feet. Mos kneeled beside her Mother's bed and murmured to her, stroking her fevered brow, pushing tangled hair away from her face. There were spots of blood on the faded striped pillow bunched under her head. Sonja held her breath a moment, until the woman stirred and opened her eyes.

Hattie marched into the room tossing a series of orders over her shoulder to Adam behind her.

"...and get a fire in the stove in the kitchen."

She pressed her way next to the woman, parting the others like a ship's bow through timid waves. Hattie placed her hand gently on the woman's forehead.

"Miz Tatum, it's Hattie. We gonna git you well, sweetie."

She leaned near the pillow to smell it and then smelled near the woman's mouth. She shook her head slightly with a pensive frown.

188

Turning to face Mos, she asked, "What's her given name, child?"

"Rachel, Miss Hattie."

Hattie leaned close to Rachel and whispered into her ear.

"You bad sick, Rachel, but you ain't gonna die, lessen you don't do what I tell ya."

Rachel opened her eyes and gazed at Hattie a brief moment, then nodded her head.

"Cephus, you get buckets of bay water and bring them up to the kitchen. You get the water downwind, you hear, not from the current and not foamy. Put the biggest pot in the kitchen on the stove once Adam starts a fire and boil me some water. All you can. Sonja, you go through this house and find me some more bedclothes. Mos, you go find your momma something clean to put on."

Minutes later in the kitchen, Hattie pulled a series of dried herbs from her bag, dropped them into a small pot of water and placed it on the stove next to a large pot of water waiting to boil. Adam had discovered a large wooden box held closed by a brass lock, sitting in a storage room. The words "Company Property" were painted on top. In spite of dire warning from Mos, Adam had pried off the top and pulled out several supply items intended for the spring work on the island. Fat candles were pulled out and lit in both the kitchen and the bedroom. Adam found bars of soap at the bottom of the chest and Hattie ordered two of them dropped into the largest pot. Hattie then pulled a bundle of sage from her bag and held it to the flame growing in the stove. With sage smoke billowing from her hands, she walked through the rooms on the lower floor, waving the bundle in the air, spreading the scent and making her way back to the bedroom.

"Sonja, you take this sage and do what I just did in all the rooms upstairs. If any of it is left, throw it in the fire down here."

She returned to the kitchen and glanced quickly around the room. Cephus had returned with his second load of bay water.

"Adam, you get that laundry stick in the corner and stir

189

the soap in the big pot, so it don't stick to the bottom. Cephus, pour that last bit of water into the little pot, then go get more firewood for the stove. I want it sweatin hot in here. Adam when it gets that way, you open the windows in the front room. It smells like rotten death in here and we ain't lettin nothin in this house to come take Mos' Momma."

Hattie blew into the bedroom and snatched the gown from Mos' hand. She sniffed it hard and crinkled her nose.

"You go stuff that into the soap pot Adam is stirring, then you come back in here and collect the gown your Momma is wearin."

Sonja had returned from upstairs holding a bedsheet. Hattie snatched it from her hands and smelled it. She smiled and spoke to Sonja."We gonna wrap Rachel in that sheet, while we boil her clothes."

As the two women removed Rachel's gown and began wrapping her in the sheet, tears flooded into Sonja's eyes. Her body was emaciated, only slightly more than her skeleton. She was bruised in dozens of places, filth was painted in patches almost everywhere and she had a gash on one leg that looked rotting.

Barely able to utter the words, Rachel whispered, "I've been awful sick, Miz Hattie."

Hattie pulled Rachel against her bosom and embraced her.

"We gonna get you well, child."

Mos entered the room , just as Hattie flipped the sheet around Rachel. Hattie handed her Rachel's gown.

"You go tell Adam and Cephus that woman's work is goin on in here now, and if either one tries to come in here without my invite, I will slit their throats."

Mos could only stare blankly at Hattie.

"Go on, child. You tell them exactly what I said."

Sonja stared at Hattie as Mos left the room.

"Of course you didn't really mean that?"

Hattie neither smiled nor frowned.

"I don't say nothin I don't mean."

Soon after Mos scampered from the room, Hattie

headed out the door as well, speaking over her shoulder as she closed the door.

"I need to see to washing them gowns and look for more clothes upstairs. You watch over her, Sonja."

Rachel opened her eyes and stared hard at Sonja. The woman reached up with skeletal fingers and gripped Sonja's arm.

"You that Pulaski woman. Seen you in the store with my Mos."

"Y-yes."

"When I die, you come get her."

Sonja stroked her arm gently and whispered to her.

"You're not going to die, Rachel. Hattie knows what to do. She'll get you well."

Rachel dug her fingers deeper into Sonja's arm.

"Can't nothin cure consumption. I been coughing up blood for months."

Rachel raised her head and shoulders, pulling Sonja closer. Her eyes wide open staring deep into Sonja's.

"You had other children. God knew that. Knew I had none and never would!"

Sonja's throat tightened.

"What?"

"God answered my prayers and brought her to me."

"Rachel. What ..."

"Take her when I die!"

Rachel released her grip and collapsed back onto the bed unconscious. Sonja was shaking her shoulder when Hattie walked back into the room.

"She passed out," Hattie asked.

Sonja could only nod to her question, still staring at Rachel.

"Just as well. She needs to sleep a while. Here, help me with these bed sheets."

Sonja worked with Hattie in a fog of confusion, only barely functioning, lost among the hurricane of thoughts.

Three hours later, heat drifted through the house and the air was scented with warm oak and sage. The wood piles were replenished and bowls of Hattie's broth had been served. Adam and Cephus had caught two giant

191

striped bass, still laying in the shallow waters around the island in spite of the approach of winter. Some of one fish was pan fried in the kitchen, but the rest was chopped into a fish stew that had just begun to boil. Adam and Cephus hovered over the meager table, gingerly picking greasy pieces of fish from the iron pan and sucking air trying to cool their bites taken too quickly from the heat.

"Adam Tuttle," Hattie wagged a cooking spoon at him, "that fish stew broth be much better for you than this fried fish."

Adam just looked back at her with a bulging grin like a little boy, as he continued to gobble the fish and suck more cool air around his latest capture.

The kitchen door opened, pushed by Ben Pulaski carrying a large bag on his shoulder.

"I thought this might be useful," he said setting down a canvas bag containing several bags of flour.

Hattie beamed at him and snatched up one of the bags of flour. " Now we get some bread made!"

Sonja heard Ben's voice and flew into the kitchen.

"Was it a hard pull," she asked as she hugged him.

"Wind's dying down. We're safely anchored in the channel not far from the island. We'll stay anchored there for the night and leave early in the morning."

He pulled out another small bag and held it under her nose.

"Oh, coffee," she cooed, then looked around the kitchen. "I have seen a grinder."

"Edward ground it in the galley before I came. Glad he did."

Mos brought an empty bowl back into the kitchen, then sniffed at the coffee.

"Mama doesn't get coffee. Says it costs too much."

"Well she'll have it if she wants it." Sonja spoke as she gently stroked Mos hair and the girl smiled up at her.

"It's nice to have visitors, here," Mos said. "We don't have town people here, just the fishermen in the spring."

"What the hell are you people doing in here?"

They turned to see Rachel Tatum standing with a cane,

her hair combed back and wearing a fresh clean dress.

"Get out!!"

"Miz Tatum, honey, you need to get back in bed," Hattie said.

"The hell I do! I need all you people to get out of my house!"

21

Rachel stood with fire in her eyes, glaring at everyone in the kitchen. Mos stood behind her with her mouth wide open, her eyes flipping from her mother's back to the faces of Hattie and Sonja.

"Miz Rachel. Honey," Hattie said. "We only here to help you. You been awful sick for a few days. Mos come get us. We gonna get you better, but you need to go lay back down for you get another chill."

Hattie took steps toward Rachel.

Rachel reached out with a skeletal hand and grabbed Hattie's sleeve, yanking her forward. "Yes. Fine. Thank you Hattie." Then Rachel scanned the room and focused on Cephus. "You, too, Cephus. I thank you for being here."

Rachel released her grip on Hattie's sleeve, then reached behind her and yanked her daughter next to her. She pointed a skinny finger at Sonja's face. "You get from here," she said. "I don't need you or your men folk around me or my daughter. Get out!"

She pulled her daughter tightly against her.

Ben frowned back at the woman. "Appears to me she is fit enough now, Sonja. Adam, let's get back to the boat."

Sonja shared a worried look with Hattie, who smiled back at her.

"Don't you worry, Miz. Sonja. Me and Cephus can take care of things now."

"Get the hell out of my house," Rachel yelled again.

Ben grit his teeth and gripped the upper arms of Sonja and Adam. Then he kicked the kitchen door open and pulled them outside.

"Ben, we can't..." Sonja started.

Ben released Adam and Sonja's arms and spoke through gritted teeth. "That woman is being cared for and we are no longer needed."

He marched off toward the beached rowboat from the *Raven*.

Sonja remained standing in the brushwood between the house and the beach.

"But, Ben..."

Adam looked back over his shoulder as he followed Ben. "Come on, Sonja. We been thrown out, and I ain't swimin back to the ship."

Still, she stood there, looking back into the house, listening to the woman's words over and again in her mind. Then she realized the woman was staring at her through the crusted glass. When their eyes connected in recognition, Rachel threw the curtain closed, coughing as she did. Sonja bowed her head and followed Ben and Adam to the rowboat.

Ben launched the rowboat and rowed back to the *Raven* in quick silence.

Edward met Ben at the railings, as Ben climbed on deck then helped up Sonja and Adam. Sonja went straight to the captain's cabin, passing Edward without speaking.

"Thought you folks were..."

The remainder of Edward's question was left unsaid.

"We were not welcome," was Ben's only response.

Edward found Adam's eyes, but he only shrugged his shoulders to Edward's raised eyebrows.

"Crazy damned woman," Adam muttered, shaking his head and crossing the deck to the crew quarters in the bow.

Edward caught the questioning glances from Harry and Jarrod, giving them a half smile, and shrugging his own shoulders.

"Still doesn't look like we're leaving here this afternoon," he said. "All is put in its place and the anchors are well set. Bring us up a pitcher of rum, Harry. Oh, and fetch five tumblers. I suspect we'll have company before supper."

"Do I still need to do that cooking chore, Edward? I mean, seeing that Adam is back..."

"Adam's not the cook, Harry," Edward said. "We take turns 'til we get one." He added with a broad grin. "And it's still your turn."

Supper was small and quiet. Ben said very little, only responses necessary for ship operations. Sonja did not venture from her cabin and Ben did not withdraw to it until the small hours of the night. Adam shared a few pieces of information, but nothing could explain the bizarre turnaround of the Tatum woman. Only Sonja suspected the real reason and she refused to let herself wander down that dark painful path.

At dawn Cephus rowed Hattie in his boat to the *Raven*. Sonja roused from bed and followed Ben barefoot to the railing wrapped in an old quilt.

"I's ready to come crew for you, Ben," Cephus said.

"Did that woman run you off too," Ben asked.

Edward and Jarrod joined Harry near the wheel, since Harry was still on night watch. The three came close to the others to hear what has happening.

"Miz Tatum's gone back to bed and is listening to me," Hattie said. "I think she'll be all right, and I don't need Cephus to do what else needs to be done."

"'Cept my boat," Cephus added. "Hattie keepin it to git back and forth to Shad Island."

"All right, Cephus, as long as we understand about fires, you can crew for me."

Jarrod stepped forward. "What? Is he going to join the crew?" He gripped the railing, looking down at Cephus, then at Ben. "He ain't crewing with me, not if he thinks he's going to sleep in the crew quarters."

Ben turned to face Jarrod fully.

"He sleeps where I tell him to. You all do."

"I ain't sleeping with no nigger," Jarrod said. "You can just put me off in Annapolis and I'll find a white man's ship."

Ben turned his attention back on Cephus. "Does it

matter what you do on this ship?"

Cephus answered Ben's question, but he was facing Jarrod. "No, suh, Cap'n Ben. I worked on schooners befo'. Won't no man of any color work harder than me. I made you a promise and I aims to keep it, unless you don't want me."

"Are you men fools?" asked Hattie. "Cephus be the best cook outside of Baltimore."

Sonja leaned closer to Ben. "Ben, he cooked most of those games meats we had at Mamie's dinner..."

"You want to be the cook, and lend a hand with the lines when needed?" Ben asked Cephus.

"Can I have my own hammock in the hold near the Galley, Cap'n Ben?" Cephus kept his eye on Jarrod. "I'm p'ticular who I sleeps near."

Ben smiled. "The job is yours if you want it, Cephus. I expect you to cook for everyone on board – except Jarrod. I'm sure he won't want any food cooked by you..."

"Now hold on, Ben," Jarrod said. "I never meant anything like that..."

"Hattie, will you be all right to go back on your own?"

She plopped her fists on her hips. "Unless you needs me to row your ship out into the channel for you, Cap'n Ben."

Ben grinned down at her and turned to Jarrod, speaking loudly. "Jarrod, see to the needs of our new crewman and help him get settled in the galley." Ben leaned closer. "We'll discuss your status on this ship again when we arrive in Annapolis."

As Hattie rowed back to the island and the others tended to their duties, Adam remained at the windward wheel, smoking his pipe. Ben walked casually to his side, stuffing his own pipe with fresh tobacco.

"All right, Adam. What is it?"

"You'll find damned few men on the bay that will share quarters with a black, Benjamin."

"I know, but I needed to counter Jarrod's blatant behavior to me. I need him as much as I need Cephus to crew this ship. It isn't like the *Ugly Boat* where two or three of us can do it all. I'll give him a chance to accept things as they turned out. I need for both of them to work things out on their own."

Adam stared into the dawning southern horizon without looking at Ben. "You sound just like your Pa." He turned his face at Ben. "You may not sink this schooner after all." Then he winked and went to the crew quarters to roll up his bedding for the day.

At full dawn the *Raven* moved along the face of a timid morning breeze, scooting southward over the bay to Annapolis. Once he cleared the eastern shore of Spesutie Island, it was Ben's intention to exercise his ship and his crew on this southern course. He had twenty five miles of arrow straight sailing in a modest wind, so he intended to haul up every sail he had and send every crewman through their full range of duties with the lines.

Once the ship leaned away from the wind as far as she needed, Ben placed Adam on the windward wheel and Sonja on the lee wheel, with instructions to Adam to let Sonja take all the control she could. He was determined to exercise his own trust, as well.

The pounding in Sonja's chest was matched by the effort of her own breathing as she struggled with the strength required to steer the ship across the wind. She also struggled to keep her face passive as she screamed with joy inside, knowing she was steering the ship almost on her own. She lost her wool cap in the breeze, but ignored the loss, letting her hair strands leap around her head like a flag in the wind, and she gripped the wheel with all her strength.

Adam yelled to her, but she did not understand at first. Adam had to yell her twice more to gain her attention. Almost too engrossed to turn away from the bow sprit to look at Adam even for an instant, she glanced quickly toward him, like a child afraid to look down from a height. Adam was grinning. Ben was standing near him, grinning at her as well.

"You have the wheel, Madam!" Adam said and stepped away from the windward wheel.

The monster of 130 feet, shoved by the increasing wind

ramming into almost a half acre of sail above her, was entirely in her hands. The rest of the crew stood nearby, but the lines were set and the wind was steady. The *Raven* dashed along the face of the wind, galloping over the increasing waves. The pitch of the deck had risen unnoticed to her as she thrilled in the ride, and braced herself on the deck, while only her hands controlled the beast. It was a moment she would never forget, and one she swore at that moment she would have again.

Too soon for Sonja, Ben had Adam return to the wheel for tacking into the Severn River and making their approach to Annapolis Harbor. Not yet commanding the confidence himself to dock with the wind, Ben had the rowboat lowered, and the *Raven* pulled into the berth pointed out by the harbor master. The afternoon was still early, so Ben made quick contact with merchants who had offered consignments to him in the past. With help from various store clerks and stockmen along the waterfront, the crew soon had the holds of the *Raven* crammed with merchandise. He brought on board some working metals for blacksmiths and metal smiths from Havre de Grace to Wrightsville, but most of his cargo were finished goods for the mercantile stores. Too big for the ship's holds, Ben had four bales of cotton strapped on the deck and covered in canvas to keep them dry.

The crew, except Cephus, was off exploring the public houses of Annapolis. Cephus had been in almost constant motion since he rescued Mos the previous day, and had already gone to sleep in his hammock. In the early evening, as the sun began its dip to the west, Ben sat on the edge of the roof to the captain's cabin, smoking his pipe. He admired the view of the full deck and was satisfied with the cargo. Sonja came to sit next to him, propping her feet on an overturned bucket that provided a step up from the deck.

"This trip alone will provide all the money we need for the winter, give winter payoffs for the crew, and help us settle back in to home at Lapidum," Ben said.

She looped her arm under his and laid her head on his shoulder.

"I was terrified that we would never go home again. After all we endured overcoming Hoagg and holding onto the ship, I couldn't believe God would take our home."

There was a pause before Ben spoke.

"He took our daughter," he said.

There was more silence between them for a long moment.

"Yes..." Sonja started, but said nothing more, and then heavy silence returned.

While she looked at the wheels and drew her emotions back from their cruise south, Ben let his eyes flitter around the deck, retracing his struggles in the fog. Moments later, as darkness slipped into the shadows, Ben pointed the stem of his pipe toward the portside wheel.

"I think Findley and Jenkins died just there," he said.

Sonja turned to him in the growing darkness.

"You've got to stop that, Ben. Remembering their names is too good for them, and too cruel on you."

"They were human beings..."

"They were animals, Ben. And if you had not killed them, they would have killed us. Don't you dare waste your thoughts on them!"

Ben nodded in agreement, knowing she could no longer see him. He looked up at the first stars showing themselves in the night sky.

"I think..."

"What, Ben?"

"I think killing should be hard..."

She waited.

"If it ever becomes easy, a man has lost his soul. I think... that's what happened to Hoagg. I think he lost his soul."

Sonja placed her hand against his cheek.

"I remember hearing Mickey once tell you," she said, then tried to imitate the accent of their Irish friend,

> "You're a darlin' man,
> Benjamin Pulaski. I only wish I
> could visit the kind world ya keep
> in yer head, 'cause I've never

been to such a place."

Ben chuckled at the memory and put his arm around her, pulling her close to him.

"The Middleton Tavern is only a short walk from here. They serve a wonderful roasted duck and a spiced mulled red wine. I think we should celebrate your successful tour at the wheel."

The sound of heavy snoring rumbled out from the smoke stack in the galley, as they stepped down the gangplank onto the cobble stone dock.

The following morning provided a surprise for the boats and ships moored in Annapolis. December brought the rising crews and captains a white world of snow. Six inches fell during the night and the snowfall continued in soft fat flakes, covering all exposed surfaces in a thick blanket, and limiting visibility to only several yards. Ben and Adam stood on the deck frowning at the snow. The smoke from the galley rose heavy gray and sluggish in the damp air. No wind slipped overhead and the houses around the dock wore halos of coal smoke, floating like jellyfish around the chimney tops. The air was scented with coal, frying meat and coffee. The snow hushed the usual morning sounds. Chilled breath hung before speakers, unwilling to move away, clouding the space between red cheeked faces.

Ben and Adam joined Edward at the outward rail and gazed at the harbor where the water was covered in snow.

"How bad is the ice, Edward," asked Ben.

He smiled and shrugged his shoulders, keeping his hands in his heavy coat pockets. "There is none, Ben. Snow just floating on top of the water."

Adam shook his head slightly, speaking around his pipe stem. "Fickle Bay weather. You never know what she'll bring. Storm or calm, you never know."

Ben leaned over the rail and watched the slight undulation of the snow rocking on the surface. "Temperature is barely at freezing. That's good news for canallers, if it's the same up in Havre de Grace."

"Soon as we can see a hundred yards, we could move

201

out of the harbor," Edward suggested.

"If there is wind," Ben added, looking into Edwards face. "In the meantime, let's get the crew up and into breakfast. I can smell coffee and bacon from the galley. Cephus is already at it."

Ben slipped down into the galley and filled a tin cup with fresh coffee, then made his way back to the landing before the captain's cabin door. Sonja was fully dressed and straightening up the room as he set her coffee on the small table. She had pulled on a heavy wool sweater and trousers. A replacement wool watch cap hung from one of the chair backs. The little iron stove warmed the room, even though the window curtains were pulled open showing the brilliant white carpet of snow outside and filling the cabin with light.

"Are we able to sail, Ben," she asked, taking up her cup and blowing on its contents.

"There's no ice below the snow, but there's no decent wind yet. Maybe by mid day."

"What about the canal," she asked.

"We won't know that until we get back there. I certainly don't want to be stuck with all the merchandise we have on board."

"Ahoy *Raven*," shouted a voice from outside.

Sonja grabbed up a heavy cape, Ben grabbed his coat and both scampered up the stairs to see who was calling.

A man stood bundled in heavy coat, standing in the snow beside a mule drawn cart filled with small barrels.

"Are you Ben Pulaski," asked the man.

"I am," said Ben.

"I have your order of rum, sir."

"I ordered no rum."

"Your stern says this is the *Raven*. And I am to deliver to her captain, Ben Pulaski."

Ben lit his pipe, giving himself a moment to think about the man's information. He frowned at the man. "On whose order," Ben demanded.

"Mr. James Williamson, sir."

"We just left Havre de Grace yesterday, and nothing

moved faster than this ship. How could you have such an order?"

"Telegraph sir. Came this morning. We have served Mr. Williamson's needs before. He has an account with us. Said to catch you before you sailed and put this on board."

Ben and Sonja traded glances and Ben shrugged his shoulders. He called for Edward to bring the crew to the gangplank. "How many of your barrels are for Williamson?"

"All of them, sir. Forty eight barrels. Five gallons each."

Ben turned to Edward. "Have the men stack them in the mess area. There is no other place to put them. And tie them down. If we get into weather, I don't want us awash in wasted rum! We'll have to just sit wherever we can, if we have another meal gathering before we dock in Havre de Grace."

Sonja locked eyes with Ben. "Forty eight barrels of rum?"

"Two Hundred and forty gallons," he added

"He mentioned nothing about this to you when you were on the veranda with him?"

"Nothing."

Sonja gave Ben a stern look.

"Nothing," he repeated.

After stowing the rum barrels, the snowing thinned noticeably during breakfast, as people sat where they could while balancing their plates. By the time the crew cleared the snow from the decks and off folded sails, a modest breeze had arrived. The *Raven* moved gingerly out of the harbor under partially raised main sails.

At noon the *Raven* was on a northerly course ahead of a strengthening wind when the Sun broke through the clouds and melted the remaining snow from the rigging and the water surface. The wind brought chill, but nothing to indicate a freeze was coming.

During their run toward Spesutie Island, the sky cleared and the sun drove the temperature well into the fifties. The crew traded grins with each other, as they peeled off heavy coats and performed their duties in almost spring-like weather. On reaching Spesutie, Ben kept the *Raven* toward the central channel through the Susquehanna Flats and almost directly toward the canal basin outlet lock. There he dropped anchor near his barges.

Aaron had kept the barges outside the lock, so they could off load all the merchandise brought from Annapolis, except the barrels of rum which became a constant topic of jest. The mast of the *Ugly Boat* had already been stowed, so as soon as each barge was loaded, it was poled through the outlet lock into the canal basin, where Mac had the mules ready to pull the barges toward the canal. The *Turtle* and the *Ugly Boat* were tied stern to bow and poled to their waiting mule team. The *Wilhelmina* was poled to a separate team, since the canal locks could not accept more than two barges at a time. Aaron sent Jeremy ahead on horseback to let the mercantile stores know that he was coming, so they could prepare their purchases. Ben barely had time for a quick "Good Job!", yelled across the water to Aaron as the barges slipped into the canal basin.

Sitting much higher in the water, Edward worked the main sails to move the *Raven* crab like up to the Havre de Grace docks, with only a gentle bump as the hull settled against the rope wrapping around the pylons. As the sun began to slip over the tree line at the western edge of town, a wagon holding four men pulled by two horses trotted to the dock and waited for the gangplank to be lowered. One man carried a ledger and approached the ship.

"Mr. Pulaski?"

"I am," answered Ben.

"Sir, I am George Watkins, and I am here to pick up an order of rum barrels for Mr. Williamson."

"They're all here. Send your men on board and Mr. Leonard will show you where they are."

While the men handled the rum barrels, Sonja patted Ben's arm and left for the boarding house.

After several trips into the ship and back to the wagon,

an argument erupted between Mr. Watkins and Edward. The two men approached Ben at the portside wheel, each telling the other "No!" Mr. Watkins handed Ben an envelope addressed to Captain Pulaski.

22

Ben accepted the envelope, but looked to Edward to tell him what was wrong.

"He says he has all he's supposed to take, but he isn't finished."

Ben looked to Mr. Watkins. "And your comments?"

"Please read the letter, Sir." He raised his ledger between them. "I have picked up what I was directed."

Ben opened the envelope and held it up to the ship's lantern, then chuckled.

"It appears you are both correct. Mr. Watkins you were directed to pick up thirty barrels of Rum." Then he turned to Edward. "The remainder are *Raven*'s, for our trouble."

As a childlike grin spread across Edward's face, Ben held up his hand. "I will need to come to a decision regarding the disposition of *Raven*'s payment. For now, I want each barrel in the mess area numbered, locked in storage, and the key brought to me."

Edward's grin dissolved into a deep frown as Ben signed Mr. Watkins' ledger.

Ben let the crew decide whether to spend the night on the ship or elsewhere. Adam joined him going down the gang plank.

"I need ta check on my wood shop, Ben," Adam said. "I'll be back on the ship in the morning."

Ben arrived at the Pink house just in time to join the other boarders for dinner. Sonja had already ensured there would be servings for her and Ben. There was little table talk except for Sonja's description of her experience piloting the *Raven*, which entertained the table. As soon as the meal was finished, Ben followed James Williamson onto the veranda for pipe and cigar while Sonja joined Mamie in the parlor.

Sonja balled her hands into fists in her lap as they sat. "When did you and Lydia decide to have Ben take her to South Carolina," Sonja asked.

"We decided nothing, Sonja. I apologize for the abruptness of my announcement."

"Abrupt? It was a shock that we would do anything for that woman..."

"Mr. Williamson approached me that afternoon..."

"So, you planned with him..."

"No. Sonja. There is no planning with him or Lydia. He told me he was taking over the Bank and offered to forgive my mortgage completely if I would host Lydia."

"You certainly did that well."

"Sonja, I had only short moments to do what I did. I barely had time to let Ben know he could have your farm back."

Mamie placed her hand on Sonja's. "It all happened so fast, but I knew I could not overlook the opportunity, nor could Ben."

"So what happens next, Mamie?"

On the Veranda, James poured a brandy for himself and Ben while Ben lit his pipe.

"Lydia is to be out of the Binterfield House the day after Christmas," James said.

"When you return from South Carolina with verification she has been delivered to my Uncle's Plantation, I will deliver your ownership papers for your farm in Lapidum."

"Without further debt?"

"That is my intention," James said as he handed a brandy to Ben.

"Intention?"

James chuckled in a whisper. "I know your experience with Herbert was strained..."

"The bastard was a cheat and a liar..."

"And I want to establish a better relationship with you

207

than Herbert allowed. The rum..."

"Yes. What about the rum? Why so much?"

James sat in the chair next to Ben and loosened the top button of his coat, and spoke in a soft voice. "Ben, Herbert left the bank in a precarious position with many of the more significant depositors. I intend to ply them with gifts of rum over the Christmas holiday."

"And the other barrels?"

James waved the question away. "Just priming the pump."

Ben frowned in the lamp light of the veranda. James sighed and withdrew two envelopes from his coat and offered one to Ben.

"That is my letter of intent. Our Quid Pro Quo, promising you unfettered ownership of the Lapidum property upon delivery of Lydia to Georgetown."

James blinked as Ben snatched the envelope from his fingers and held it to the light.

"Really, Benjamin, we need to trust each other if we are to do business together."

Ben looked above the letter at James. "What business?"

"Your man Anthony visited me while you were in Annapolis. He informed me you were entering the slave trade with your schooner..."

Ben lowered the letter into his lap and stared at James in silence.

"Is that not true, Ben?"

Ben's breathing slowed and tightened in his chest. "Yes," he said.

James tilted his head slightly and returned the second envelope inside his coat, then drained his glass. "Excellent. Please come by my office tomorrow, and let's discuss the remaining details of our joint venture."

James smiled, and rose from his chair. "I will visit my...Lydia... tonight and inform her you will leave the day after Christmas for Georgetown." He chuckled again. "Surely the woman can manage to have her clothes packed within three weeks." As he reached for the door he spoke over his shoulder. "Oh, and please make room for her maid, Junie, to accompany her."

Ben was sitting alone on the veranda, toying with the empty brandy glass in one hand and still holding the letter of intent in the other, when Sonja joined him an hour later. She sat next to him in silence, pulling her coat tighter around her and slipping her hands into her pockets.

"We are to be slave traders," he said.

Her head jerked up and she looked into his face. In quiet monotones Ben informed Sonja of his arrangement with Anthony, the letter of intent from James, Ben's admission to James, and of his appointment with James to discuss their business venture.

"It must involve slaves," Ben said to her last question.

In the following silence, Sonja began to cry. Ben put his arm around her shoulder and she leaned her head against him. "God forgive us," she said into his coat.

Shortly after sunrise, Ben stood in the hallway of the Harford Hotel, banging on the door to room number three.

"Open up, Anthony!"

There was a metallic click from the inside and the door was flung open by a tall clean shaven man displaying a scowl on his face. "What the hell do you want? Who are you?"

"Anthony Renowitz," Ben said, looking past the man into the room."Where is he?"

"This is my room," the man bellowed and shoved Ben away from the door, knocking him down, then slammed it shut.

A clerk ran down the hall to Ben and helped him up. "Mr. Pulaski. We can't have you doing this. Mr. Renowitz checked out yesterday, but he left you a letter."

Ben followed the clerk to the registration desk, where the clerk snatched an envelope from a small file on the desk and handed it over. Ben's name was neatly penned on the front. Ben frowned at the envelope and ripped it open, letting the pieces fall to the floor. Only a name and address were written on the paper inside.

Mr. George Milton, Esq.
South Washington Street
Office above the National Bank

As a disgruntled clerk picked up the pieces to the envelope from the floor, Ben shoved the door open and marched to South Washington Street. A few blocks beyond Granite Lane, he came to the bank, then stomped up the outside stairs past the sign saying "G. Milton, Esq." Without knocking, he entered the office. The outer area held two chairs against one wall. He marched past them and opened the door marked "Private".

George Milton looked up with a surprised smile, then relaxed his face into a frown. He stood to face Ben, saying "Sit down, Benjamin."

Ben put his hands on his hips and spoke with heavy breathing, "What the Hell..."

"Sit down, Ben or I am not talking to you."

Ben brought his hands above his waist in balled fists. Milton kept his eyes locked on Ben's.

"Ben, I can match you blow for blow, if that's what you intend, but there are things you need to know."

Ben took in several deep breaths and relaxed his hands, then sat in the chair next to Milton's desk. George reached past Ben and closed his door. He sat back down in his padded chair, straightened his vest and pulled a file from his desk.

George spoke in a quiet voice, "Did you not agree with Anthony to purchase a particular slave in Charleston?"

"Yes," Ben spoke through gritted teeth.

"And did you not understand what was to become of the particular slave?"

"Yes."

"So what are your specific questions this morning?"

"Anthony has arranged for me to be in business with James Williamson!"

"Please keep your voice down, Ben. Did Anthony not tell you he would acquire the necessary papers and bone fides so you could make the purchase in Charleston, as a

210

legal agent for such things?"

"Yes, but..."

"But, you thought what? That it would all be secret?"

"Yes. I did not expect..."

"To have to play the part to a public audience?"

"I did not expect that. I did not agree to that."

George sighed and laid the file on his desk, then clasped his hands on it. "Ben. This is a dangerous thing you have agreed to do. You cannot only pretend to do it in Charleston. You must carry that role before anyone who might know you anywhere. This is a slave state..."

"God damn it, I know that..."

"Then you must know that your role begins here and now, and will go far beyond just one purchase."

Ben stared at him in open mouthed silence, only broken by the tick of the mechanical clock sitting on top of the wooden file cabinet next to George.

George's eyes went wide."Good God, Ben. Did Anthony not make that clear to you? It was the reason he arranged for you to gain possession of the schooner."

Ben's mouth shut into a firm straight line, a severe frown settled his eyebrows low over his eyes, and a dark cloud formed in his eyes.

George lowered his voice even more. "This is a long term effort, Ben. Our group is opening a new front to purchase those slaves we can, and bring them north. If we have to allow a few to go to the fields, while we rescue many more..."

"No. I will not be a party to placing anyone in bondage. Not even one."

George took in a deep breath and blew it out. "Anthony said you might change your mind about the role, but he led us to believe you were committed – fully informed and committed. Damn him. Always the rouser and rarely the detailer."

"Who is 'we'?"

"There are others both north and south of here that wish to see an end to slavery. Until that happens, we will do what we can to send as many escaped slaves north, but that is not without our own risk. It is better you only know who you need to know to accomplish your duties."

"I have to leave the day after Christmas. You need to find other options for me than delivering slaves to plantations. You need to find them before Christmas!"

"I cannot promise you that, Ben."

Ben stood up. "Then do your best to take my ship from me. I slaughtered men to take it from Hoagg. I will not release it without a fight, and I will not forfeit my home again."

Ben stormed out of the office and returned to the *Raven*. He ordered Edward to moor the ship fifty yards from dock and not let anyone on board that did not have a note from himself, except Sonja or his sons. At least one crewman was to stay on board at all times.

"What about Christmas Day, Ben?"

Ben stood a moment in silence, staring at the water. "We'll bring her back to dock the day before Christmas and Christmas Day. The day after Christmas we will load the belongings of Lydia Binterfield and her maid, Junie. We will be sailing to Georgetown, South Carolina, and then to Charleston."

"And the rum, Ben?"

Ben chuckled at the question. "Take barrel number 18. Have it shared out a pitcher at a time. You need one man sober at all times. I'm going to trust you to manage the ship, but I will be coming out frequently."

Edward grinned and knuckled his head in the old fashion way of sailors to their captain.

"Might as well go to Oyster Street, and get on with it," Ben muttered to himself. As he walked away he spoke again to Edward, "I expect Cephus to be treated well as a crewman."

"Of course," Edward said.

Ten minutes later, Ben sat in the leather bound chair next to the large mahogany desk at the rear of the Tidewater Bank and Trust. James poured him a cup of coffee and set the pot back on the little wood stove against the rear wall. James held his hands out to the stove then rubbed them together as he sat down.

"The little stove is earning its keep this morning, Ben."

James leaned back in his stuffed chair and sipped his own coffee cup. Setting it down, he cleared his throat. "So, Ben, I wish to invest in your cargo."

Ben nodded his head and sipped at his coffee.

"This is a common investment for southern banks," James said, "so I would like to discuss the kinds and amount of cargo you have in mind."

Ben spoke over his coffee cup. "Mercantile, Cotton, Sugar..."

"And slaves," James added.

"Where there is adequate profit and minimal risk," Ben answered.

"Good. I like a captain who avoids risk. May I also suggest rice."

Ben shrugged his shoulders.

"Rice appears to be of little interest here in Havre de Grace, Ben, but I assure you the rest of the world is very interested in it, especially the type grown in South Carolina."

"It is? Is it profitable?"

"My dear Ben, Carolina Gold rice is the most sought after rice in the world. Georgetown exports more rice than China! My Uncle's key slaves come from a region in Africa known for its rice cultivation. The Gullah slaves have transformed Georgetown into dozens of rich plantations."

"I am not planning to sail to Africa, James..."

"No. No. No, of course not. With the British and American bans on the African slave trade, it would be far too risky. No, we have second and third generation rice slaves in Georgetown. Many are placed as supervisors over the most important steps. No, the rice plantations have the expertise. What they need is more labor."

Ben continued to sip on his coffee.

"Of course, on an enterprise ship, especially where the captain is the prime investor, the selection of cargo rests with him. And by the way, I am very glad to hear you are considering multiple cargos. It rarely works well for single cargo ships, unless they carry huge amounts. No, a schooner needs to carry variety, and make profit with each. Scooting in and out of several harbors with minimal time and back for more in short order. That's the way with a schooner."

Ben finished his coffee and set it on the edge of the desk.

"My brother needs slaves," James said. "He can get them for less from me than from Charleston, and I can get more for them than in Southern Maryland. And truth be known, we have over bred in Saint Mary's County. I need to be shed of some."

"How many do you need me to take to South Carolina?"

"Ten."

Ben's stomach growled and he clenched his fists below the edge of James' desk. "Where would you like me to bring them on board?"

"I can have them ready at the harbor of Solomons in Calvert County, at the mouth of the Patuxent River. It is not be far from Grayrocks, in Saint Mary's County, just a healthy day's walk to the Patuxent and a short boat ride across the Patuxent. It would be an easy and quick call for the *Raven*."

"I will assume their ownership there?"

"Yes. I ask that you get the best price for them, after your share of the profit, of course."

Ben frowned and cleared his throat. "And I am obligated to only sell them to your Uncle in Georgetown?"

"Well, Ben, to be blunt, I really don't care. He was never really close to my father and I hardly know him. If you can get a better price, elsewhere, so be it. This is a business venture, not a family outing."

"And your investment, James?"

James withdrew an envelope from the desk and handed it to Ben. "Three thousand dollars in property on consignment. My ten slaves."

Ben took in a deep breath and slowly released it. "I believe you are an honorable man, James, but if you will kindly understand, I will have this reviewed by my lawyer."

James extended his hand. "On the contrary, your action only adds to my trust of our relationship. May I expect my signed copies tomorrow."

Ben accepted his handshake, adding "Barring he is not hung in the meantime."

James released a hearty laugh and patted Ben on the back as he left the bank.

23

December 9, 1843. Havre de Grace

Ben and Sonja Pulaski sat next to the desk in the cramped office of George Milton, Esq. and were introduced to Mr. Lionel Renowitz. George left the three alone and went for a walk, saying "Certain conversations should not include him." Lionel was a junior partner in the Philadelphia accounting firm of Watson, Jackson and Renowitz. He was also the nephew of Anthony Renowitz. Lionel had devised a method of record keeping for the voyages of The *Raven* he believed would allow Ben to avoid delivering slaves to plantations, but still allow him to purchase them in South Carolina.

"So, you see, Mr. Pulaski, you will need to keep three sets of cargo ledgers for your ship. One you will show to deep south authorities while you still have purchased slaves on board, the second set you will show to Eastern Shore authorities while you still have slaves on board, and the third set you will be able to show Maryland authorities in Havre de Grace. You will need to show your slave purchases in all three sets. The Deep South Set will show your intention to sell them elsewhere in the deep south, and justify still having them on board. The Delaware Set will show your intention to sell them in Delaware. The Maryland ledgers will reflect sale of the slaves in the deep south, and the profits thereof."

Ben frowned and rubbed his forehead. "Are three sets of ledgers really necessary, Lionel?"

"Since the Society began to raise money to buy slaves

216

into freedom, we have always struggled with the anticipation of allowing some of them to go to plantations to verify our agents. This ledger method was actually designed by a friend of yours and ours, Nathan Brown. He learned the multiple ledger approach from his employer at the Tidewater Bank and Trust."

"But why three sets, Lionel," Sonja asked

"You will need to tell three separate lies. As you sail away from Charleston with slaves on board, you must be able to show a measure of proof that you are only taking them to another deep south location, where the demand and profit is high. They will not believe you if you tell them you are taking slaves to Delaware, where the prices are lower."

"Alright. That makes sense to me," Ben said and Sonja nodded her agreement.

"Once you are in the lower Chesapeake Bay, with slaves still on board, you will need to tell authorities you bought the slaves in Southern Maryland for delivery to the Eastern Shore of the Bay. There is sufficient price difference, though small, to justify the cargo, especially if you have multiple cargos."

"What if we are stopped well south of Southern Maryland," Ben asked.

"We actually discussed that possibility in Philadelphia, but we could not devise a legitimate set of books to fit the situation. Nor could anyone think of a legitimate reason for a Maryland ship to be stopped there. Uncle Anthony suggested you use your deep south ledger and claim the slaves have woodworking or masonry skills. It would justify higher prices within the Bay."

"God protect us from a fourth set of ledgers," Ben said.

Lionel nodded in agreement. "You will actually take the slaves to the Eastern Shore, to be released to our representatives at locations we will identify to you later. On your return, you are to meet with an agent of the Argyle Corporation in St. Michaels. Do not forget that name. And finally, you tell your Maryland investors you have sold your slaves in the deep south, other cargo elsewhere, and then share out the profits. You must never let the wrong authorities see the other ledgers, or you will go to jail – or hang."

Ben scratched his head. "And you will pay me to purchase the slaves and have enough to show profit from their sale."

"Yes, Mr. Pulaski, as much as we can to maintain the illusion, but you must make sufficient profit on other cargos to fund your operations. The money we give you for profit must go to your slave trading investors."

"Bank drafts? Correct," asked Sonja.

"Whenever possible, Ma'am, paid against the Charleston firm of Lebeaux and Chambers." He faced both Ben and Sonja. "Be sure you only speak with Chambers. Lebeaux is a fanatic against our cause, and must be feared. Chambers has no cause except our money, which he hides from his partner."

"Mr. Williamson is providing 10 slaves for our first voyage. They are valued at $300 each, and he expects a profit of $300 each from his Uncle. If we are to give a plausible reason for not selling to the Uncle, we should bring back more than $600 for each slave. That will be a draft for $6,000."

"No Ma'am, we will have to show a profit for the *Raven* as well, so the draft will be for $8,000, but the amount paid Mr. Pulaski will be $6,000."

"I don't like that, Lionel. That means we have to falsify records here in Maryland. Please consider providing an owner's draft and an agent's draft. We can always say Ben deposited his fee in another bank elsewhere."

Ben nodded his head in agreement. "I like that much better," he said

Lionel smiled and made several notes in his journal. "I like that much better, as well. Thank you Mrs. Pulaski."

They stood and shook hands.

"Tell your Uncle I said he is a son of a bitch," Ben said.

"If you will permit me, Mr. Pulaski, I would prefer to tell him you called him a bastard. That will allow me to avoid besmirching my grandmother."

"Bastard, he is then," Ben said with a wide grin,

supported by serious nods from Sonja.

"Be sure to contact Mr. Lebeaux as soon as you dock in Charleston," Lionel added.

As they walked down the outside stairs, Sonja leaned close to Ben. "We need to decide how to handle the slaves while Lydia is still on board..."

"No more here. We'll discuss that later in the room."

After a few quiet minutes strolling up Union Avenue, Sonja spoke. "I wish we could get into the house before we leave, I would love to spend Christmas day there."

Ben patted her arm. "It is still locked up. We will not get the key until we return. Beside, Mamie is planning quite a Christmas meal at the Pink House."

"Yes, I know, but..."

"Well, at least she has assured me Lydia won't be joining us. James has invited guests there for Christmas dinner, and said she would be spending the rest of Christmas day packing."

Ahead Sonja spotted two familiar shapes walking briskly toward them. Isaac and Aaron waved energetically as they approached, and as soon as they were in arms reach, each son took a turn picking up his mother in a swinging embrace while Ben watched in joy.

"Pa. I think we have time for another trip to Wrightsville."

Sonja glanced at Ben with a frown.

"Aren't you empty of all the merchandise I brought from Annapolis," Ben asked.

"Yes," Aaron said. "And we've sold all the coal we brought back down. We should go get another one."

"And go up empty?" Ben asked.

Aaron glanced quickly around them and moved closer to his father. "Almost." Then in a whisper, he said "There is some cargo in Wilhelmina".

"I think it wise to leave the *Wilhelmina* in the Wrightsville Basin over the winter." Isaac said. "We have Pennsylvania friends there who will watch it and keep the wrong kind of person from snooping around inside."

"Friends we can trust all winter," Aaron added.

"Quaker friends who have too many sons and too

many daughters for one small farm on the edge of town," Isaac said.

"Two of their sons will spend the winter on board, and will crew for me next season," Aaron said.

Ben nodded his approval and patted Aaron's shoulders. "Good thinking, son."

"I thought of it," said Isaac.

"Only part of it," said Aaron, playfully hitting his shoulder with a fist.

Ben stood in silence a moment, then said, "I think I will come with you."

"And so will I," added Sonja."It's one way to get us all together for a few days. And in a place we own, even if it is a barge."

Aaron put his arm around his mother. "Three barges and three cabins."

Isaac cleared his throat loudly and gave Aaron a stern look.

"All right. Two cabins we can use," Aaron said.

--<>---

The next day the *Turtle* moved slowly toward the canal at the tug of the mules with the *Ugly Boat* tied snugly to her stern. Sonja and Ben sat on the supply box near the tiller, guiding both barges in tandem. Behind them followed the pair of mules pulling the *Wilhelmina*, guided by Jeremy. The front pair of mules walked next to Aaron, while Isaac walked the mules pulling the *Wilhelmina*.

"Why did you have those two barrels of rum brought off the ship, Ben?"

"Gifts," he said.

"For whom," she asked.

He looked into her face with a mock surprise. "For whom? When dost thou sayeth whom?"

Sonja slapped him on his arm. "When I feeleth like it, sir."

Ben smiled and looked back as the mules pulled them across the last of the basin and drew them into the narrow canal. "They are for the slave catchers, at the line."

She stared at him for a moment. "You can't be serious."

He turned to face her again. "I am a slave trader and I want them to leave my son alone. Maybe this gift will encourage them to consider our brash-mouthed son in a more favorable light."

She raised her eyebrows and looked deeper into his eyes.

"If we must play the role, we must seek what little advantage it brings us," Ben said.

She said nothing else, but kept her arm looped in his until they approached lock number 9. They stood up so Ben could retrieve the conch shell from the locker under them and blow it three times, letting the lock tender know they were coming. As soon as both barges were snugged inside the granite walls of the lock, the upstream sluice gates were opened and the cavern began to fill. As the *Turtle* and the *Ugly Boat* rose within the lock, Ben stood on the deck holding a small barrel in each arm. He handed one off to the first armed man who approached them.

"Here. Let's take these up to the barn and share it with the boys," Ben said.

The man followed Ben to the barn, where several other armed men gathered around him. One older man with a short beard stepped forward, squinting at Pulaski's face. "Don't I know you, farmer?"

Ben faced him squarely. "There has been more than one run in between you boys and my family, and it's time to clear the air."

"What's in them little barrels?" the older man asked.

"Rum," Ben said, which was greeted with happy murmurs among the slavers.

"Boys," Ben said, "I am a slave trader and I've got a shipping business with contacts from Maryland to South Carolina. Now I don't want any of the property I sell to be running up here, so I appreciate you being here doing your jobs for your employers." He folded his arms and let his eyes float around the faces watching him. "Now, I also have a coal and mercantile business running up and down this canal. I have three barges: The *Ugly Boat*, The *Turtle* and the *Wilhelmina*. And I don't need my people getting into pissing contests crossing back and forth between

Pennsylvania and Maryland. I would appreciate it if you could just leave my barges alone and let my people do their jobs while you do yours."

Ben set the other barrel down and turned his attention back on the older man.

I suspect you're probably their leader," Ben said.

"Sort of," he said.

"What's your name?"

"Geoffrey," the man said and extended his hand to Ben.

"Geoffrey, this is good Jamaican rum. It ought to keep you boys a little warmer, and give you something to sip besides burnt coffee and river water. I leave it to you to share it out as it should be. Consider it an early Christmas present."

Several hands patted him on the back followed by a scramble for cups and pitchers and quickly emptied coffee pots. As soon as Ben walked back to the lock and stepped onto the deck of the *Ugly Boat*, Aaron whistled at the mules, which had already stepped up the tow path to take up the slack in the tow rope. The *Turtle* and the *Ugly Boat* slipped through the open lock gate and moved quickly into the upper canal holding pond. There was no other barge in the pond waiting to go down canal, so the lock tender closed the upper gates. Then he opened the lower gates, spilling the water from the lock into the lower level and rocking the waiting *Wilhelmina* below.

"I feel like I need a bath," Ben said to Sonja.

"But, if it will help Aaron..." she started.

"I would go do it again," he said.

Sonja handed him a small crockery jug with the cork removed. "Adam sent it along, just in case. He said it was corn whiskey."

Ben brought the jug to his lips and took several swallows. He coughed a couple times and grinned at her. "Thank you ma'am. I believe that will do."

Sonja took a long drink from the jug and then replaced the cork without saying a word or making a sound. Ben looked at her in astonishment. She smiled at him and took the jug down into the cabin, from where Ben heard several strangling coughs echo in the cabin.

He leaned over the cabin hatchway and yelled into the shadows. "And whom is coughing down there?"

"Oh shut up," she answered, and followed her remark with several more coughs.

Twelve miles north of The Line the three barges arrived at the lock in York Furnace, Pennsylvania. The sun was setting over the western hillside and the barges were staked at the edge of the upper canal holding pond. Another barge, labeled with the number 26, was already secured in the pond for the night. Several men filed out of a barn next to the Locktender's house and down to the *Wilhelmina* in the fading light, where Aaron had placed the gangplank. Aaron and the five men stepped down into the cabin and shortly a procession of men carrying boxes on their shoulders emerged from the barge and walked up the hill back to the barn in the fading light. The men were joined by other forms in between them and a procession of boxes, like ants in a trail, began to pass slowly to and from the barge for several minutes. Lastly, only Aaron returned down from the warehouse to the barge.

Ben lit a lantern on the *Ugly Boat*, and joined by Sonja and their sons, they strolled up the gentle slope to the warehouse. Inside, a crowd of people greeted them with hugs and handshakes.

Aaron and Jeremy stood next to stacked empty wooden boxes, grinning at Ben and Sonja. Smiling faces known to them greeted them near the door, while the escaped slaves from the *Wilhelmina* filed to a table in the back of the barn spread with food and coats. There, mugs of apple juice, slices of meat and pieces of bread were served by three Quaker women. Out of the small crowd, a tall lean man much older than the rest, stepped forward and swept Sonja up into a hug.

"Papa! I was expecting to see you up at the house," Sonja said into his shoulder as she returned his hug.

"Couldn't miss the fun, daughter!"

Ben patted Burl Jundt on his back as he hugged Sonja.

"Good to see you up and about," Ben said.

The barn doors opened and three Quaker men entered. "We need to get the visitors loaded in the wagons. They still have miles to go."

Each of the men quickly approached and said goodbye to them, then headed out the door. Outside, three wagons were hitched to strong farm horses and layered in dry hay, holding several folded wool blankets for the visitors. The escaping slaves moved out swiftly holding small sacks, some still chewing food in their mouths. Each had acquired an ill-fitting winter coat, but not overly worn and still in good condition. They climbed into wagons according to their preferences, spreading blankets over their laps as the wagons moved into the night under a partial clear moon.

"It still isn't safe here," Burl said. "Slave catchers come up this way often," he said to Aaron and nodded toward the wagons. "Those people still got a ways to go before they can breathe easy. Time was, all they had to do was step a foot onto Pennsylvania soil, but it isn't like that anymore."

Burl walked out with his arm around Sonja's shoulders, speaking over his shoulder. "Any one not having a warm bed for tonight, come on up to the house. We got more beds than we need, and hot stoves.

"We'll sleep down here on old number 26," a voice said, "and go back to Lapidum early in the morning."

"Is that you, Dan," Ben asked in the growing darkness, but there was no answer.

After the short walk up the slope to Burl's farmhouse, they mounted the steps to his porch by the light of a lantern in the front room. Inside, the curtains were drawn open and the room neat, but dusty. As everyone entered the room, Burl poked the coals and placed a small log in the fireplace to rekindle a fire, and then went into the kitchen to bring the fire in the woodstove to life. After placing a pot for fresh coffee on the stove, Burl returned to the front room, rubbing his hands and smiling.

"It has been so long since everyone was here, just

224

Aaron lately, I..."

He stopped in mid-sentence, watching them exchange glances and fidgeting with their hands.

"Burl," Ben started, "We really..."

"No you don't Benjamin. I know a 'gotta get going' look, when I see one. I gave too many of them to my wife and daughter over the years. No, what you folks really need to do is sit your asses down and visit with me! At least one night!"

Sonja glanced at Ben then turned to her father. "Yes, of course. We would love to spend the night here. Is, um, is anyone else in the house with you?"

He laughed. "You mean that crazy Esther? No! She is long gone since you, Doc Harper and the York County Sheriff tied her up. No, she ran away and didn't come back!"

Burl watched the shocked glances pop between Isaac and Aaron. "Well, it looks like I have some stories to tell the boys! Sonja, did you not ever tell them?"

"Only some of it, Papa," Sonja said.

"Only very damned little," added Ben. "I want to hear them as well!"

24

Early the next morning, Burl walked down the slope to the lockhouse with the four Pulaskis, holding his arm around Sonja's shoulders.

"It's about time we had a house full of family up there," Burl Said. "Been just Aaron visiting me here lately. At least he kept me up on the news of you folks claiming that boat, and of Isaac going to West Point."

Burl tussled Isaac's hair and pulled gently on his ear. "You boys are both smarter than most. I'm proud of both of you."

"We're proud of them too, Papa Jundt," Ben said.

Jeremy MacMallery joined them at the Locktender's house.

"Thought you would have come up to the house with us last night, Jeremy," Aaron said.

"Nah. I stayed on Number 26 with my Dad and then had breakfast with the Calverts."

Burl nodded his head at the name. "John and Emma are good people. If it hadn't been for them and Sonja, well, we talked about that last night."

"Are you sure she's gone for good, Papa," Sonja asked.

"Yeah, people like that burn their bridges, then go off looking for people who haven't heard their lies."

They reached the upper canal holding pond, chatting a few more minutes while Aaron and Jeremy brought the mule teams down from the barn. The barges were light and riding high in the water. They were pulled swiftly up the canal by the mules as the Pulaskis waved back to Burl.

"Did you tell Papa about your slave trading," Sonja

asked Ben.

"No. I am barely clear about it myself. I am not prepared to have that conversation with a man like him."

In Wrightsville, the barges followed obediently as the mules pulled them across the bridge to Columbia. Wrightsville was the northern end of the canal, but the coal was loaded on the far side of the Susquehanna River in Columbia. The mile long bridge was the longest covered bridge in the world, boasting an additional walkway along its side, where the mules could pull the barges. Within the shadow of the slender bridge, barges tracked single file on the water, like a line of huge black beetles. The barges sat much lower in the water on the return trip, their holds gorged with Pennsylvania coal. Back in the Wrightsville holding basin, Aaron introduced the young men who would spend the winter in the cabin of the *Wilhelmina*.

"I recognize you boys from last night," Isaac said as he shook their hands. "You drove two of the wagons."

The young men scanned the area around them for stranger ears, but then smiled and nodded their heads yes.

Aaron leaned close to Isaac. "We need secrecy even up here, Brother. Just in case."

The younger of the two Quakers smiled broadly. "We are brothers, too."

"The holds are full of coal," Aaron said. "Use all you need to stay warm, and share with your family as they need it."

"Thank you," the older brother said and leaned closer to Aaron. "We will have the occasional visitors in the barge, you must know, waiting for the right time to cross the river."

Aaron nodded. "Just keep prying eyes away from the special areas built on the cabin."

Isaac stood watching his younger brother. After they shook hands with the Quaker brothers again and walked away, Isaac said, "I am so proud of you Aaron. You are a brave man."

Aaron shrugged his shoulders and looked at Isaac

227

from the corners of his eyes. "It's what you would do."

"I hope so," Isaac said.

Late that afternoon the *Turtle* and the *Ugly Boat* slipped ponderously down the canal, sitting low in the water with holds full of Pennsylvania coal. The second team of mules from the *Wilhelmina* stood in a makeshift stall at the bow of the *Turtle*. The slave catchers gave lazy waves as the barges passed through Lock 9. On the lower side of the lock, Aaron and Isaac switched the teams, and with fresh mules on the tow rope, they brought the barges to Lapidum before Sunset.

They staked the barges at the edge of the canal in front of their home. Knowing they could not yet go into it, they lingered to gaze up at it between the massive oak trees standing as sentinels in the front yard. They left their mules in the canal company barn, and stopped only a few minutes at Freidman's Mercantile and McMallery's Blacksmith, to make preliminary plans to return to their home in January or February. Ben told both to help themselves to the coal in the barges, in gratitude for storing their furniture. Jeremy stayed with his father at the Blacksmith's and gave his farewells to the Pulaskis. Ben and Sonja had not yet met the new lock tender's family and did not stop to visit. The new family replaced poor Mr. Bartlett's family, the locktender so brutally murdered by Randall Hoagg the previous year.

The lamps around the canal basin had been lit when the Pulaskis walked passed it into town. They followed Ben to the dock, where he stood under the lamp post and yelled to the *Raven*.

"All's well," Edward yelled back, so Ben waved at him and turned with his family toward Union Avenue. The lighting was dim in the front room of the Pink House, when the Pulaskis entered, but as they began to walk up the steps, Mamie flew out of her room and came to the foot of the stairs.

She placed her hands on her hips with a flourish and scolded them with a smile on her face. "You thought you could just sneak by and not help me eat all the food prepared for dinner? I suspected you would be back this evening. Come. Eat!"

She slipped ahead of them and began lighting candles in the dining room. Several covered dishes sat along the table arrayed in front of four plates, silverware and goblets. She dashed into the kitchen and grabbed pot holders to lift a meat tray kept warming on firebricks set on the stove.

After setting the meat in front of her guests and uncovered the other dishes, she flew into the kitchen to retrieve two bottles of wine. After uncorking them, she fidgeted with the bottles filling glasses and hovering nearby, but not sitting with them as she had previously.

Ben reached out and gently took her forearm. "Please sit with us."

As she sat next to Ben, he continued to hold her forearm and took up Sonja's in his other hand. "We do all we can to hold on to our homes," He said.

Mamie nodded, shifting glimpses around the table. Sonja met her glance with a soft smile.

"I have agreed to do what I must to get our farm back. It is my decision. You put me in a position to accept that opportunity. Thank you."

Mamie sighed, then took in another deep breath. "I wasn't sure, I mean, there was no time..."

"Thank you, sister," Sonja said.

Mamie's eyes glistened in the candle light as she smiled at Sonja.

"So," Ben said, "are you satisfied with what Mr. Williamson promised."

"Oh yes. My mortgage will be forgiven completely..."

Ben leaned closer to her, "Still, you should keep your coins well hidden."

Mamie frowned and looked at Sonja.

"No," Ben said. "I learned it from Adam."

"Oh! That scoundrel! I told him to keep that to himself."

"Hopefully, he has only mentioned it to me," Ben said.

Mamie shrugged her shoulders. "More wine?" Mamie asked.

Isaac and Aaron both snatched up bottles and refilled their glasses. Sonja gave them stern glances, then softened to smiles.

They are men now, she thought.

The mistress of the Pink House and all her guests slept soundly that night.

At six o'clock the next morning, Junie rapped hard on the front door to the Pink House.

Mamie's morning girl opened the door.

"My mistress must see Cap'n Pulaski as soon as possible," Junie said.

"My mistress does not arise until 6:30," the girl said.

"And my missus take a cane to my baby girl if I don't do what she tell me," Junie said as she pushed the door open and stepped into the foyer.

The girl placed a hand gently on Junie's shoulder. "Please have a seat in the parlor while I go get Captain Pulaski."

Moments later Ben clomped down the stairs with tussled hair and a frown on his face. The morning girl escorted him into the parlor and sat him before a fresh cup of coffee. Junie sat across from him, a half filled cup of coffee in her hand. Junie said nothing until Ben had taken a second sip of coffee.

"Suh, Miz Binafeel need you to show her around your ship, so she can decide where she gonna stay, and where I'm gonna stay."

Ben took a third sip and sighed. "You and Lydia are going to sleep in hammocks strung on the open deck all the way to Georgetown."

A small smile slipped across Junie's face and her belly pumped with laughter she dare not release.

Junie pulled back her smile and kept her composure sullen. "Dat be fine with me, Cap'n, but I spect Miz Binafeel not gonna feel that way bout it."

Ben looked at Junie with a poker face. "You tell your mistress that I dashed up the stairs saying I would be happy to meet with her on the dock before my ship at 9:00

this morning."

"Yas suh," Junie said.

"Now," Ben continued, "I think it would be a sin to waste this delicious coffee that has been prepared for us."

They sat together in silence until each cup had been emptied, at which time Junie stood and curtsied to Ben saying "Captain Pulaski." Ben stood and bowed to her saying "Miss Junie." And each slowly left the room.

I think this trip gonna be lots a fun, Junie thought as she walked back to the Binterfield mansion. *An Miz Binafeel gonna be in a hateful bad mood the whole damn way.*

At 9:30 that morning, the Binterfield carriage pulled up to the dock where Ben and Sonja had been pacing, waiting for Lydia. She was helped down by the driver, who she instructed to wait. Lydia put on her gloves, straightened her hat and coat, glanced at Ben and Sonja then scanned the length of the dock.

"Is your ship not here, Captain?"

Ben nodded and pointed out the *Raven*, moored fifty yards from the dock, and then down to the water level where the ship's rowboat floated at the end of its bowline.

Lydia approached him with a frown growing on her face. "Must we go to the ship in that little boat?"

Ben only smiled and indicated the boat with his hand, at which time Sonja took his hand and quickly stepped down the ladder from the dock to the rowboat, taking the bow seat. Lydia sighed heavily and made her way down the ladder with surprising agility, taking the mid seat and leaving the stern seat for Ben.

"No ma'am, Lydia, you need to sit in the stern, unless you intend to row us to the *Raven*."

Lydia huffed, but shifted her position as Ben stepped over her and took his seat in the middle. The wind was cold but still and the surface of the water was almost calm. It took only a few minutes to row to the *Raven*, where Harry and Jarrod laid boat hooks at the bow and stern to make the climb on deck easier for the ladies. Once on deck, Ben introduced the crew. Lydia responded "good morning" when introduced to Edward, Harry and Jarrod, but only nodded when introduced to Cephus, who stood back from the rest. Adam sat on a small barrel at the far side of the ship smoking his pipe. His only response was to extend one finger of the hand holding his pipe and letting a cloud of smoke rise in front of his face. Lydia managed to say "good morning" to him.

Sonja led the way for Lydia, pointing to the bow and the stern.

"Lydia there are two ladder ways down to the lower decks. Each one has a landing half way down. At the bow landing there is the door to the crew's quarters, and at the stern, the door to the captain's cabin. Both ladder ways continue down to the cargo deck. That's cargo hold where the galley, eating table and storage areas are."

Sonja motioned for Lydia to follow her and then stepped down the stern ladder way to the landing for the captain's cabin. Ben walked down behind them. Sonja entered the cabin and stood by the far side of the bed. Lydia stuck her head in the cabin and glanced around the little room.

"It will have to do, I suppose," she said.

"We will share the cabin," Sonja informed her. "I am going as well."

Lydia gave a soft chuckle and turned to Ben. "I will have a private cabin, Captain."

"Not on this ship, Lydia. It's either here, in the cargo holds, or in the crew's quarters at the bow, except there are no empty bunks left in the crew's quarters. However, I will be happy to re-join my wife in here and allow you to take a bunk in the crews quarters, at the bow. I'm certain they won't mind your company."

"This is not acceptable," Lydia said.

"There is no other option, Lydia."

"I will not..."

"Lydia, this is your transportation. Agreed to in writing by your brother. As of the day after Christmas you will have no other place to lay your head except this cabin, until we land you in Georgetown."

Lydia's face turned bright red. "No..."

"If I have to chain you in this cabin, I will," Ben said. "I now hold a trading permit to carry slaves."

Lydia's eyes went wide open.

" I can chain you in here or down in the hold, as I choose," Ben continued." You will behave yourself on my ship and treat my wife and my crew with respect, or I will deliver you to Georgetown in God damned chains!"

Lydia pressed her lips together breathing heavily through her nose, her fiery eyes on Ben's face.

Sonja reached out and placed her hand gently on Lydia's arm. "Let's make the best of this, Lydia."

Lydia closed her eyes and slowed her breathing, pulling her arm away from Sonja's hand. She looked back into Ben's face. "What about the accommodations for my maid, Junie?"

"Since we are not carrying much cargo," Ben said, "We are putting up temporary privacy dividers in the hold for Junie, and all your luggage that will not fit in this room."

"And for my private activities," Lydia asked.

"We will provide you a chamber pot and a wash basin. You and Junie will be responsible for both. Sonja will have her own."

"Where will I eat" Lydia asked.

"You will be welcome to join us at the group table in the hold, near the galley. It is called a mess by sailors, but I do not like the term," Sonja added.

"May I discuss my meal requirements with the cook? Cephus is it?" Lydia asked.

"You will eat what we all eat," Ben said.

Lydia's lips remained pressed into a thin red line, the frown deepened above her eyes, and a single tear slipped down her cheek. She swallowed. "Very well, Captain Pulaski," she said. Will you kindly take me back to the dock?"

Lydia's following visit with James at the bank, was short and bitter. James could only reaffirm what Ben had said to her. He also informed her that Sissy would not remain in the Binterfield household. He confessed to using Sissy's freedom as enticement for Junie to go with Lydia to South Carolina. Sissy would be living in the household of Dr. Harper with his freed housekeeper until other plans were made.

"Liddie," James said, "I wanted you to have a companion who went willingly with you, not some sullen stone who would run away at her first opportunity. I am trying to help you, but we cannot change reality."

Lydia stared at her hands.

James sighed. "You are a colored woman in a slave state, Liddie. Your options are very few. You have made your choice to go to Uncle Jeremiah's plantation, and I have contracted to get you there."

Lydia left the office without speaking, returning to her carriage in cold silence and ordering the driver to trot out of town on the road toward Bel Air. Nearing the road to Lapidum, Lydia ordered the driver to take her in that direction. Minutes later the carriage stood in front of the Pulaski farm. She stepped out and walked around the gentle front slope between the great oaks, tears streaming down her face. As she neared the front steps, she picked up a fist-size rock and hefted it in her gloved hand.

"God damn you, Pulaskis!" she screamed and hurled the stone through a window pane. She screamed several more times and dropped to her knees. The driver jumped down from the carriage and went to her side to comfort her.

"Get the hell away from me," she screamed at him.

The driver stepped back to the carriage shaking his head as "Mac" MacMallery walked up from his blacksmith shop, wiping his hands.

"Is everything all right up here," Mac asked.

"Woman's trouble, I think," the driver answered.

As they stood together, Lydia stepped back up into the carriage and slammed the door.

"Let's go," she yelled to the driver.

As the carriage moved down the lane to Stafford Road and turned up the steep hill, Mac examined the front porch of the Pulaski house.

"I better put a piece of wood over that broken window pane," Mac muttered to himself.

25

Christmas Eve, 1843. The Pink House.

Ben and Sonja joined the crowd of people milling about in the parlor and the dining room. Isaac stood uncomfortably erect in his West Point uniform, while Aaron moved only slightly easier in his new wool suit, high collar and double wrapped neckcloth. Both wore trim stylish coats that nearly stopped their breathing. The crowd flowed ponderously between the two rooms and the foyer exchanging Christmas greetings, sampling the array of cakes, pies and cookies placed on the table, and sipping wines and whiskies set up at the far end.

The House was overly warm from the iron stoves and numerous candelabras. Many of the younger men took all opportunities to step out onto the Veranda overlooking the snow-covered side yard through cigar smoke, and relishing precious moments when they could undo a button or two before going back inside. The women suffered inside bright colored dresses among damsel smiles and miniscule sweeps past the cool air from the Veranda door that more experienced folks continually left open. Adam stood near the Veranda door, not far from the whisky tray, frequently fingering the neckcloth snaking under his chin, until he finally managed to loosen it. Edward, Jarrod and Harry came late, but dressed as well as they could, after the *Raven* had been tied to the dock, and they had filled themselves with roasted duck prepared by Cephus. They moved directly to the Whiskey tray.

Mamie's morning girl had accepted Mamie's extra pay to spend the Eve serving the guests and keeping the treats replaced. Cephus preferred to sit in the kitchen and keep an eye on the warming trays, while sipping the mulled wine Mamie had served him. Sissy joined Eudora at her first paid duty, to help serve the guests. Wallace and LuAnn Harper were painted with smiles watching how well Sissy moved among the guests. She was without the perpetual slouch she had assumed while living at the Binterfield Mansion and was meeting the guests with full eye contact and her chin proud.

Ben stepped next to Dr. Harper. "Pity Junie can't be here to see how well her daughter is doing."

"Only a Mother could make such a sacrifice," Wallace said. "Giving up seeing her daughter grow to set her free."

Sonja stood nearby, listening to Wallace's comment, a tear glistening in her eye.

"I will have none of that," Mamie scolded Sonja with a smile. "You will be happy tonight. I demand it," she said with a sparkle in her eye and then floated away to see other guests.

Kling! Kling! Kling! Mr. Heiden tapped a crystal goblet on the table. "Ladies and Gentlemen, my friends of Havre de Grace, I have accepted Mrs. Stewart's request to read a very special poem for this Christmas Eve. Please join me in the parlor, as you can."

Mr. Heiden settled into the large wingback chair commanding the parlor, and opened a leather bound journal in his lap as others took nearby seats. Many of the dining room chairs had been added to the parlor, and side tables removed to provide sitting places. Unusually snug with all the guests, several sets of eyebrows arched as knees touched between them. Some young men and women obviously enjoying the contact.

Mr. Heiden cleared his throat dramatically, and held the book up in front of him. "This poem was written several years ago by the English man named Clement Clark Moore. It has been passed among admirers of the poem, and I think some of us here have heard it before, but it is yet to be published, I am told. My niece copied it in her own journal of poems, which she gave to me when I came to this country a year ago."

He cleared his throat again. "I hope you enjoy it." Then, releasing his baritone voice softly, as if he were speaking with a child, he began.

"T'was was the night before Christmas, and all thro' the house,

Not a creature was stirring, not even a mouse..."

Heads tilted and childish smiles spread among the guests sitting nearby and those standing in the archway to the dining room. Adam and Cephus left after the poem. Adam preferred to sleep in his woodshop. Cephus rowed across Concord cove, still free of ice, to spend the night in his own house, even though no one else was there.

Christmas day was quiet in the Pink House. Some boarders had left days before to be with their own families at Christmas. Mr. Heiden and the Pulaskis were joined upstairs by some of the *Raven*'s crew, using the empty rooms. Mamie had insisted, and three of the men were happy to have a warm bed and thick mattress for the night. The guests snacked on left over foods and pastries and shared gallons of hot coffee, content to be in a warm house, in preparation for sailing the next day.

James held a Christmas Farewell Dinner for Lydia, convincing the guests she was going to South Carolina by her own desire to overcome the loss of her husband. Sissy joined Junie to prepare the meal and serve the guests. Afterward Sissy spent her last night in the mansion with her mother. Late that night, James returned to the room in the Pink House originally rented by Sam Briscoe.

The next day was a flurry of activity, as the crew rejoined on the *Raven*. Ben and Sonja moved their final possessions from the Pink House to the *Raven*. Isaac gave hugs to his mother, father and brother and boarded the ferry to cross to the Susquehanna River. After more hugs, Aaron made his way down to the canal basin and began his walk along the towpath to the *Ugly Boat*, where he would live for the next few months.

Mamie made no effort to hide her tears as she hugged Sonja. "I have been so alive while you and Ben lived here," she said. "I am happy that we both have our homes free from that damnable bank, but my sadness in missing you is without description."

"I will miss you, Sister," Sonja told her. "And we will visit frequently when we come back."

Mamie yanked Ben down to her shoulder and trapped him in another tearful hug. "You take care of my sister, Captain."

"Thank you for everything, Mamie. Your Pink House was heaven-sent when we were heartbroken over the loss of our farm. I can't thank you enough for your kindness."

She pushed him back to arm's length and spoke with arched eyebrows and pouty mouth, "Then you must think of something to please me, sailor."

Ben blushed with a smile, then let his face grow serious and whispered to her, "You must take great care to keep your coins secret. Trust that secret with no one else, Mamie."

She released him and pushed him toward Sonja. The sparkle was once again in her eyes and her smile beaming. "Go back to your wife, sailor. I am done with you."

Sonja smiled through flowing tears as they turned and walked away from the Pink House.

Mamie spun around and marched into her house, closing the door behind her. As she stood in the foyer of the empty house, she stomped her foot and said to herself, "This house is too God damned big." She took in a deep breath and blew it out through pouting lips, adding, "and it needs to be dusted."

It was 10 o'clock before the wagon arrived bringing Lydia's trunks and baggage, with Junie sitting in back. A polished carriage came in behind the wagon and the driver helped Lydia down. She was wearing a long blue cape, edged in white fur, a matching hat and white gloves. She walked down the line of luggage taken from the wagon and tapped three large trunks, then turned to face Ben.

"These are to go into the cabin. The rest can be stored safely with Junie," she said

Ben folded his arms and shook his head no. "Pick one trunk and one bag for the cabin. The rest goes into storage. Junie can bring you what you need, one at a time as you need it."

Ben went on deck and down in the hold to speak with Edward who was overseeing the luggage storage.

"How is it going down here, Edward?"

"Between Junie's cabin and Cephus' cabin..."

"Cephus' cabin?" Ben asked.

"We figured since Junie was getting one, and Cephus is our cook, we put up some more partitions on the other side of hers to make him one."

"Did you make the other compartment I discussed with you?"

"Yes, but that's part of the problem. I didn't know Mrs. Binterfield was bringing so much. What's going in the compartment, anyway?"

"Slaves," Ben said.

Edward stopped still, looking at Ben for an explanation, but none came. "We delivering some more, like we did from St. Michaels?"

Ben let out his breath. "No we're buying and selling."

"What?? Since when?"

"Since I was given a permit."

"For Maryland?"

"For anywhere it's legal. I didn't think you'd have a problem with it, Edward. You were warm enough to it coming from St. Michaels."

"Well, I guess I don't. I'm just... surprised, Ben."

Edward held Ben in his eyes for a moment, then looked away. Ben returned to the deck to watch the rest of the luggage come on board. In the captain's cabin, Lydia had Junie hang a blanket down the middle of the bed, Lydia was standing in her side of the cabin with her arms folded. Sonja was standing on the other side of the cabin, wearing a deep frown and her arms folded as well.

Ben pointed his finger at Lydia. "I don't want to hear what's going on right now, but you hear this Lydia, If you

aggravate my wife I will put you in the hold with Junie."
He turned to walk out, then spun around and faced Lydia
again. "Furthermore, our next stop is in Solomons, where
we will take on some slaves from Grayrocks. If you cause
any trouble before we get there, I will put you off in
Solomons. My letter from James, my contract, requires
me to deliver you to the family plantation, which at the
time he wrote the letter, 'he assumed' would be in
Georgetown. I can just as easily place you in the hands of
the Grayrocks overseer."

Lydia's eyes were wide and filled with fire, but she said
nothing and nodded her head in understanding.

Ben kept his attention on Lydia and pointed at Sonja.
"Your destination is in that woman's hands."

As Ben left the cabin, Lydia turned to Sonja saying, "I'll
have Junie take down the blanket."

"No, Lydia, it's a good idea. We will leave it up. Let's
add another to divide the length of the cabin. That will
allow a little privacy for both of us. And I don't want to
hear any more of your hateful treatment of Junie."

It was noon before the rowboat was hauled out of the
water and placed on chocks on the deck at midships, and
the *Raven* was untied from the docks. There was a gentle
southward wind telling Ben they would not make
Solomons that day. At 5:30 they pulled down the sails and
dropped anchor in Hawks Cove just north of Back River.
During the night, the temperature dropped to the low
thirties, but still no ice formed on the bay. On the
Susquehanna and Tidewater Canal near Lapidum, the
temperature dropped into the mid-twenties, signaling the
beginning of the winter freeze on the canal.

Mr. Friedman invited Aaron to have supper and spend
the evening with his family, begrudgingly accepting the
likelihood that Aaron would marry his daughter, Maggie.

The train from Philadelphia to New York passed into a
heavy snowfall, and even with the small iron stove in
Isaac's car filled with burning coal, frost grew at the inner
edges of the windows.

By Sundown the following day, the *Raven* sailed into

the mouth of the Patuxent River and then poled its way into the little harbor at Solomons. The ten slaves were led down the short pier to the *Raven* by the Overseer.

"Thought you'd be here yesterday. We had to put these nigras in a barn overnight and then had to watch them all day," he said to Ben.

Ben took the ledger from the man, had Jarrod count the slaves, and signed for the cargo. Ben returned the ledger to the overseer without speaking, and the man left in silence. The harbor master came to the ship to collect seventy five cents for mooring the *Raven* and had Ben sign his ledger. Afterwards Ben went down to the hold to see the slaves.

"Did they provide a key, Edward," Ben Asked.

Edward held it up so Ben could see it.

"Unlock them," Ben ordered. "Gentlemen," he said to the slaves, "I don't want to keep you chained, but I need you to stay in here. It will be warm in here tonight, you will be fed in a few minutes, and you will have blankets for the night. We have a long journey. You will get a chance to get some fresh air in small groups and visit the head..."

"What de head," one of the slaves asked.

"Our outhouse at the bow of the ship," Edward answered.

"Just shut up and move when you're told," Jarrod added. Ben glanced at him with a stern look, and noticed Edward was showing the same face to Jarrod.

When Ben stepped out of the slave partition, Cephus was standing there with a frown on his face. He leaned toward Ben, their faces only inches apart. "You say this ship never used for slaves again, Cap'n Ben. I can't be on such a ship. Men who catch slaves killed my boy. I wish it burned when I set fire to it."

Ben gripped his upper arm. "Come up on deck with me, now."

On deck, Ben grabbed Cephus' arm again and pulled him off the ship to the dock.

"If you puttin me off that's good, but not here Cap'n Ben, please."

Ben pulled him farther along the little pier until they

241

were well away from the ship, and spoke to him in hushed tones. "Cephus, I need to tell you a secret that could get me killed. Can I trust you?"

"I don't know if I can trust you, Cap'n Ben."

"Cephus, we are going to set these men free." They stood in silence a moment. Cephus looked to Ben to hear more.

"Cephus, it will take a while. We have to sail to Georgetown and put off Mrs Binterfield. Then I have to sail to Charleston to create a record that those men below decks have been sold. Then we will sail back to the Eastern Shore and place them with men who will take them north to safety."

Cephus kept his frown. "Why you don't just sail back across the Bay from here?"

"Because I would get caught as soon as I sailed back to Maryland. I would get caught and this ship seized. But if we do it the way I described, we will free these ten men and maybe a hundred more."

"How is that?"

"I am working with a society in Pennsylvania that wants to buy slaves at auction to set them free. They are doing many things to free slaves, this is just one way."

"I don't know, Cap'n Ben."

"Help me this trip, Cephus. Let me show you how it works. For now, help me feed these men and keep them warm. Help me keep them hidden until we come back. If you don't like what I've done, you can go home when we return to Havre de Grace."

Cephus looked into Ben's face a long moment. "All right."

They turned around to return to the ship and faced Edward, standing only a few paces away.

"Is everything all right, Ben?" Edward asked.

26

"Is there something you need, Edward," Ben asked.

Cephus whispered, "All right, Cap'n", then turned and walked back to the ship.

Edward stood in silence, his face in darkness from the dock lamp behind him, his eyes locked on Ben's face.

"I said is there something you need, Edward," Ben said.

"Um...it's about Jarrod..."

"What about Jarrod?"

"He heard about the slaves on board..."

"And?"

"He wants to make sure that the share of the cargo you promised includes them."

Ben sighed. "Yes."

"His share when they are sold," Edward asked.

"They will be sold in Charleston."

Edward stood another moment, then slowly turned and walked back to the ship.

As Edward walked away, Ben added, "That includes you as well," but Edward did not answer.

Damn! What does he suspect?

The wind was blowing away from land and dawn was barely on the eastern horizon when Ben woke the crew with orders, "Make ready to leave Solomons."

When it was light enough to cast off, they hoisted the sails and allowed the wind to push them back into the mouth of the river. The sails were tightened to drive the *Raven* forward while Ben spun the wheel to point the bow southward again. He looked back at the little dock, seeing the Overseer with a pistol stuck in his belt watching him leave, standing between two other armed men. They stood still, silent without expression, just watching him leave.

Adam stood next to Ben. "Are you really going to sell those men down in the hold, Benjamin?"

Ben looked ahead beyond the bowsprit. "It is my obligation to regain my Farm, Adam. You already know that."

"Yes, I do, and it's a heavy price to pay." He walked away to help coil the loose lines from the sails.

Ben turned the wheel again, bringing the bow toward the west to pass Cedar Point and return the *Raven* onto the Chesapeake Bay. The wind was steady and the Bay pushed low rolling swells that slipped under the hull, gently rocking the ship from bow to stern, like the prolonged gait of a giant thoroughbred. As the sun rose over the distant eastern shore, the crew swung the main sail booms to the other side of the ship to better catch the wind. Ben turned the bow farther south, for their long run toward Hampton Roads at the mouth of the Bay.

As the *Raven* made its turn, gun fire erupted from the shoreline just below the mouth of the Patuxent. Men on shore were shooting at a rowboat, pushing hard out into the Bay. After several more shots, a figure in the rowboat fell to the bottom, but the figure at the oars continued to push against the water, driving them farther away from the shore. Another volley of fire streaked out from shore and the figure at the oars, slumped forward, even as the next bullets splashed into the water several feet short of reaching the boat.

Ben and most of the crew watched the escape and kept their eyes on the fallen figures in the rowboat as it continued to drift across the path of the *Raven*.

"Looks like nigras in that boat," Jarrod said. "They almost made it, too."

Ben steered the ship to pass between the rowboat and the shore. "One of you grab the grappling hook and snatch that rowboat as we pass."

"Yeah," Jarrod yelled as he dashed for the hook at the

244

railing. "That one rowing is probably worth a reward, if he's still alive." He turned to look back at Ben. "Shares, right Cap'n?" he said with a smile.

"Shares," Ben answered.

Edward and Harry traded glances, but said nothing.

Jarrod leaned over the railing as he hooked onto the Rowboat. "Shit, Cap'n, they're both still alive! Playing possum 'til they got out of rifle range."

Edward and Harry ran to the railing to help the people up onto the deck. The two forms climbed ungainly on deck, both escapees were drenched. They looked wide eyed around the deck. One was a smallish black woman with smooth mulatto skin. The other was a tall muscular man, with nearly true black skin and the physique of a warrior. Jarrod patted them both on their backs.

"We taking them back for reward, Cap'n?," Jarrod asked, patting the black man again. "This one ought to be worth a lot."

Ben stared at the two people, locking eyes with the black man, standing in silence a long moment. "No. They are salvage. We took them unattended in open waters. They are ours, and so is the boat." Ben eyed his crew. "Jarrod, put them in the hold with the other slaves. We're taking them to Charleston."

Jarrod danced a quick little jig and whistled at his good fortune. "Aye, Aye, Cap'n," he sung as he pushed the couple to the steps near the bow.

"Harry," Ben called. "Tie the rowboat off the stern."

Edward stared at Ben for a moment then turned away.

In the captain's cabin, Lydia was already seasick from the rocking motion that flung the cabin up and down. She was on her hands and knees, hovering over the chamber pot, emptying her stomach.

"Oh God, Oh God," Lydia moaned. "What are they doing now? The maniacs are going to tip us over!"

Sonja stood over Lydia with her hands on her hips chuckling above Lydia. "They are just tacking the ship, Lydia. When you change directions of the ship, you have to change the setting of the sails to catch the wind again. It's called tacking. I've heard sailors call it wearing ship, too."

"I don't give a damn what it's called," she yelled into her chamber pot. "Tell them to stop it, immediately."

Sonja patted her on her sweat soaked back and smiled. "Lydia, they can't stop it. This will go on for days."

"Oh God, Oh God. Send Junie in to help me."

Sonja closed the cabin door behind her as she stepped down from the landing into the hold and made her way to Junie's compartment. Junie was down before her own chamber pot, praying to her Lord, wedged between her cot and the tied bundle of Lydia's luggage.

Cephus spoke from behind her in the passageway. "She'll be all right soon. I done emptied her pot twice, and ain't nothing left to come out. Soon as all de land food be out, and she take some coffee, she'll get better."

"You have fixed coffee?" she asked turning to face him.

"Oh yes ma'am. Dis ship gotta special stove top that clamps on pots and a heavy iron plate on top to open for feeding in more coal to cook. Nothing comes out from where it's supposed to be unless it's a real storm! Can't fry nothin, but I be boiling some eggs for breakfast, now."

"You are a magician, Cephus! Please help me pour a couple cups of coffee for me and Ben."

Sonja leaned against a nearby support beam, wrapping an arm around it as the ship's motion began to include rolls to the side in addition to the bow to stern rocking. She placed her other hand against her stomach and swallowed hard. Cephus handed her the coffee mugs with closed tops, turning them so she could grasp both handles with one hand.

Cephus smiled kindly, looking into her face. "Miz Sonja, you lookin a little pea-ked, yoself."

"No I'm not," she said, then straightened her stance and made her way to the steps.

On deck, Sonja shuffled wide legged, like a child learning to walk, edging toward the windward wheel where Ben stood. Ben took his coffee and savored his first few sips. Slightly forward of the tandem wheels, the ship's compass stood centered on top of a massive wood

246

pedestal almost chest high. A brass band wrapped the post just below the compass, and below that a wooden shelf circled the post with holes the size of the mugs cut on each side. Ben set his mug in the nearest hole and looked closely at Sonja's face. He smiled and gently took the mug from her hand and set it in the other hole.

Sonja readily released the mug and gripped the compass post with both hands. She responded to Ben's examination of her face, "Oh, shut up!"

Then she lunged toward the railing. Ben quickly slipped a knotted loop over the top wheel handle, then dashed after Sonja. He guided her down the tilted deck to the other side of the ship. He held her tightly as she leaned over the railing and retched.

He handed her a cloth to wipe her mouth. "You always want to do this away from the wind, dear."

She nodded in understanding and retched again.

"How are the other ladies doing," He asked.

"Worse," she said, wiping her mouth.

Ben and Sonja stepped back to the wheels. Ben slipped the loop off the handle and resumed steering. Sonja stood behind the other wheel gripping a spoke for security and sipping her coffee.

Cephus came on deck and emptied two buckets over the lee railing where Sonja had stood. He looked back at Ben. "Most of the men from Grayrocks ain't never been on a ship, before. They sick."

"Let's start bringing them up, a couple at a time, so they can get some fresh air. Hold on to them so they don't fall overboard," Ben said and then glanced around the deck to find Edward. "Edward, have Jarrod help Cephus take care of the 'Cargo'. He needs to earn his share!"

Edward gave a grim smile and sent Jarrod from the bow back down into the hold.

Ben watched Jarrod carefully when he came back up on deck with Cephus and four slaves. Both Cephus and Jarrod had ropes tied around their waists, each linking themselves to two slaves. The wind increased, driving the *Raven* faster and tilting the deck so far that waves rushed over the lee edge and splashed along the deck several feet.

The windward side of the ship raised another foot as the mast titled away from the wind.

"Ben," Edward called, "Shall we shorten sail?"

Ben inspected the sails and the lay of the ship. "Not yet. Let her run! I'm eager to be away from Solomons."

Edward grinned like a school boy and motioned for Harry. "Toss the plank over the stern. Let's see what our speed is."

Moments later, Cephus and Jarrod returned to the railing with another four slaves, standing barefoot in the December water, emptying their stomachs into the Bay. A burst of wind slammed into the sails, tilting the masts and deck farther to lee, and one of the slaves slid overboard. Cephus and Jarrod pulled together on the waist rope, joined by the other slaves and Edward. They brought the drenched and terrified man back over the railing and set him on the deck as he coughed out salty water.

"Get them down below and dry them off," ordered Edward.

"I better get my full share of the four hundred dollars for this one," Jarrod sputtered to Edward.

Edward gave him a toothy grin. "Your share of six hundred dollars, not four," he said.

Jarrod smiled, "Not to mention the price that new one will fetch," he said and pushed his charges back across the deck and down the steps to the hold. Harry made his way from the stern coiling the knotted line around the small wooden plank, water droplets from the rope flying away in the wind.

Harry gave a wild eyed grin to Ben. "Eight and a half knots," he yelled.

Ben blew out his breath and spoke to Harry and Edward " Shift the mainsail booms away from the wind, and spill some of it out. She's had an amazing run, but I won't risk her."

As the masts raised back up into the wind and the slope of the deck moderated slightly back toward level, Sonja made her way to the steps down into the cabin. Even coming down the steps she could hear Lydia screaming.

"You're going to kill us, you bastards! We're going to die, God damn you all!"

Lydia was crawling around on her hands and knees still in her night clothes, splotched with vomit, and her wig saturated on the floor. Sonja left the door open and returned to the deck, greatly satisfied with the milder slope and the gentler rock of the ship. She took up a bucket with a rope tied to its handle and dropped it overboard to fill it with Bay water. Then she carried the bucket down the steps and into the cabin, and dumped it all on Lydia with a splash. Lydia squealed and gasped for breath under the icy water.

"God damn you," Lydia screamed.

"Dry yourself off and put on some clothes, Lydia. It's time to be an adult," Sonja said and then closed the door behind her. She returned to the wheel beside Ben, sipped her cold coffee and then gripped the wheel handles. Ben watched her take the wheel and loosened his grip partially to let her take the bite of the rudder.

"How is Lydia doing in the cabin," Ben asked her.

Sonja looked at Ben over her shoulder with a wide smile. "Getting better by the moment, Ben," she said, "Getting better by the moment."

Minutes later, they neared Tangier Island off to the east. Ben helped Sonja turn the wheel, taking them true south on the last course toward Hampton Roads.

"We picked up some new passengers before you came on deck." Ben told her.

"Who? When? We've been flying since...Oh those shots..."

Ben opened his mouth to say more, but Edward and Harry stepped up to him.

"What is it," Ben asked.

Harry and Edward exchanged glances, neither saying a word. Harry bit his lip and looked at Sonja.

"What is it Edward? Do you two want to talk about shares, like Jarrod. You will get them. Just as I promised."

"I'm sure I would, Ben. I'm sure you are a man of your word, but..."

"But what? What else do you want?"

"What's the matter," Sonja asked.

Edward and Harry ignored her question and kept their attention focused on Ben.

"Ben," Harry said. "You never told us you were shipping slaves."

"Selling slaves," added Edward.

"No," Ben said. "At that time I had not yet..."

"We want off the ship, Cap'n," Harry said.

"We want to be put off the ship in Norfolk or Newport News, Ben," Edward said. "We didn't sign on to sail on a slaver. We want off this ship." Harry nodded in agreement.

Sonja stared at the two men, then focused her attention on Ben. "What is happening?"

"I wanted to believe what you told Cephus, last night," Edward said. "I even believed it when you bantered with Jarrod about slave shares. But when you brought those others on board..."

"What others," Sonja asked.

"You took them as salvage, when you could have just let them escape," Edward said. "You could have simply done nothing, and even Jarrod would have understood."

"I don't want to be a part of this," Harry added.

"Who did you bring on Board, Ben," Sonja asked.

"Runaway slaves," Harry said.

"Runways slaves that had made it safely away from Southern Maryland," Edward said.

Ben looked around the deck, seeing that Jarrod had not yet returned.

Ben looked at Harry and Edward, and then at Sonja.

"You captured runaway slaves," Sonja asked.

"No, I rescued... a friend," Ben said.

"Who," demanded Sonja.

"Simon Bond."

27

Sonja stared into Ben's face, her mouth open and her eyes wide. "Simon?"

Edward and Harry exchanged glances. "Who?" Edward asked.

I thought you were happily adjusted to selling slaves, Edward." Ben said. "You talked so strongly for it when you came on board..."

Edward blew out his breath. "I didn't know you well enough then. I wasn't sure what your thoughts were. And then you agreed to ferry slaves to Havre de Grace from St. Michaels..."

Ben stepped closer to them and lowered his voice. "Finding Simon was a surprise, and I will tell you my secrets soon, but say nothing about this in front of Jarrod or Mrs. Binterfield."

Harry showed the glimmer of a smile. "So you are not selling..."

Ben cast his eyes around the deck. "No, but please, all of you, say nothing about this to those two people, probably not to Junie, either. We are at risk if you do."

Ben reached out and grabbed the forearms of Edward and Harry. "I need you. Please stay with me. I promise, you will not betray your scruples."

"Betray what scruples," Jarrod said with a laugh as he climbed the forward steps from the hold. "They don't have any scruples, Cap'n." Then he laughed again, but kept his eyes on Edward.

Ben leaned close to Edward and spoke in a whisper. "I

will inform Jarrod as we near Newport News, that I am putting him off."

"That could be dangerous, Ben."

"He said he was from there, didn't he? I will find a way to make it acceptable to him."

Jarrod tightened the sail lines to belaying pins along the bow railing, watching Ben and Edward over his shoulder when he thought they weren't looking.

As the ship settled on the new course, Edward sent Harry and Jarrod to adjust the jib sail lines. Jarrod stepped next to Harry as he pulled down on a line.

"What's going on with the Captain, Harry?"

"We, uh...thought he maybe should have taken those escaping slaves back to their owners in Solomons..."

"Ah, there's your scruples, then. But you heard the Captain say they were salvage. Any sailor knows about salvage. He took them fair and square."

"I suppose so, but since you were asking him about them, he asked us what we thought."

Jarrod pushed his lips together and frowned. "Well, as long as we get our shares, I don't care what he does."

"So you trust him?"

Jarrod shook his head. "Hell no! Don't trust him. Don't like him. He's a pompous ass. All I want is my share of the cargo, then I'm finding another berth."

Sonja went up and down the steps between the deck and the captain's cabin, and after several useless trips, she found Ben alone at the wheel and stood next to him.

"Ben, I just took more food to the slaves in the hold. Simon looked at me like I was a stranger and said nothing."

"You didn't call him by name, did you Sonja," Ben asked

"Ben, I'm not stupid. I just expected him to give me some kind of sign."

"Sonja, those men in the hold are not his friends. They don't know him and he doesn't know them, nor do we."

"We can show them kindness..."

"Only as far as slave owners show kindness to their slaves. We don't dare do anything else until Lydia, Junie and Jarrod are off this ship."

"Did you know Simon was out there, Ben? Was that some kind of plan..."

"No. Honestly, it was a complete surprise to me, but as soon as I saw him, I knew what I must do with Jarrod. I can't trust Jarrod. His desire is to be on a slaver – a real one."

Sonja looked over the length of the deck and out beyond the bow in silence for a long moment. Then she took in a deep breath and blew it out. "I will go down to see if Lydia can eat anything yet. Cephus told me he managed to get Junie to sip some broth."

Sonja walked with more control as she crossed the deck to the aft stairway.

"Getting her sea legs, I believe," Jarrod said.

Ben spun around to find Jarrod standing only a few feet away, looping a hemp line into a bundle. "Pay attention to the ship, Jarrod, not to my wife!"

Jarrod suppressed a smirk and walked back to the railing and hung the bundle over a belaying pin.

The sun was low in the sky as Ben sent the crew to shorten sails as he spun the wheel to take them near Point Comfort near the mouth of the James River. The speed of the *Raven* dropped noticeably and they glided slowly past Fort Monroe. Bugle notes drifted out over the water from the fort as the large American flag was lowered for the evening inside the granite walls. Beyond the point Ben turned the ship into the protected cove and ordered the anchor to be dropped.

As the crew pulled down the sails and wrapped them for the night, Ben went down into the captain's cabin. Lydia sat in a chair on her side of the cabin, still pale, but reading a book. Sonja sat in her chair on the other side of the blanket curtain and smiled as Ben entered. He held his finger to his lips.

"I need a map from my chest," Ben said.

He opened the chest of drawers bolted to the wall

beam, and pulled out a leather pouch and withdrew a fist full of coins and paper dollars. He transferred the money to a small canvas bag and slipped it in his pocket as Sonja watched in silence with a frown.

"Jarrod has asked to be put off the ship," he said openly. "He has family nearby."

Sonja frowned at his back as he left the cabin.

On deck Ben called Jarrod to him. "Jarrod, you are a fine seaman..."

"Thank you, Cap'n.."

"But we don't get along..."

"What?"

"So, I am putting you off the ship here. You can take the rowboat we took off Solomons..."

"What? You're putting me off? But my share..."

"You're getting your share, Jarrod."

Jarrod stood red-faced, glaring at Ben. "You lied to me!"

"Jarrod, I do not care for your behavior on this ship, nor the attention you pay my wife..."

"You son of a bitch, I..."

"Shut up, Jarrod, or you will go into the water with nothing. As a deck hand with no shares, you could expect to make twenty five dollars when we return to Havre De Grace. If I let you stay on the ship and we get a good price for the slaves in Charleston, your share could be as much as two hundred dollars..."

"You're damned right, and you're cheating me..."

"I cheat no one. I am going to give you that two hundred dollars, and the rowboat tied to the stern to get you to shore."

Jarrod sputtered and dropped disconnected obscenities. Ben and Jarrod were joined by Edward.

"Take the money and the rowboat, Jarrod," Edward said. "You can likely get twenty more for the row boat. Take it and get off the ship."

"But, I'm..."

"But nothing, Jarrod. You're a pain in the ass, and not worth the generosity Captain Pulaski is offering you. Take the money and the rowboat, or swim with nothing."

Ben handed Jarrod the small canvas bag and Jarrod hefted it in his hand. Listening to the jingle of gold and silver coins.

"Well, I haven't seen my brother in years. Maybe he knows about another ship. Maybe a slaver." He glared at Ben. "A slaver with a worthwhile captain."

"Light's fading, Jarrod," said Harry, who stood behind Edward with Cephus. Cephus handed Jarrod his seabag containing his belongings.

Jarrod shoved the money into his pocket and snatched the seabag from Cephus. "You better not have touched any of my things, Cephus."

"Every one of'em," Cephus said.

Jarrod stepped to the stern rail and pulled up the bow line tied to the rowboat, dropping his seabag down then stepping over the railing down into the boat. Edward held the bow line and Harry used the boat hook to keep the rowboat steady while Jarrod settled onto the center bench. Then Jarrod pulled out his knife and sliced away the bow line.

"Fuck all of you," Jarrod said. He set the oars in the oarlocks and began pulling toward shore.

"Did you really give him his share, Ben," Edward asked.

"Yes. I don't want him having anything that could draw suspicion to this ship. Putting him off is my legal right as a captain. Giving him a share confirms my intention as a slaver and adds to my reputation."

"Well, Cap'n," Harry said, "I'll be content with my twenty five dollars just for watching you put that asshole off the ship."

Ben turned to face Harry and the rest of the crew. "You will all get the same share I gave Jarrod. I promise."

They stood there open mouthed. "Me too," asked Cephus.

Edward turned to Cephus. "You're crew aren't you, Cephus. And you just heard your Captain?"

"Jesus, Lord," Cephus whispered.

"Gentlemen," said Edward, "We are at anchor in a safe

harbor, and the sails are tied properly. Get out the rum!"

Cephus went down to the galley to begin cooking supper, humming to himself and occasionally whispering, "Two hunnit dollas, Lord, Lord."

Ben and Sonja joined the crew at the table for supper, while Lydia had Junie serve her in the cabin. After the ship's lanterns were lit, Lydia came up on deck formally dressed with perfectly coiffured black hair. She lingered at mid ship, away from the crew at the bow and from Ben and Sonja at the stern.

"That's a sad picture," Ben said to Sonja.

"That's a she-wolf tasting the air for the scent of blood," Sonja answered in a whisper.

Ben put his arm around her waist pulled her close. "Did you really dump a bucket of cold bay water on her today?"

"Just helping her bathe," she said batting her eyelashes.

Ben chuckled and began fishing out his pipe and pouch. "I need to talk to Simon, but I need Lydia out of hearing distance." He patted Sonja's hip and walked toward the bow. "Edward, let's begin bringing up the slaves for some air."

He paused by Lydia as he lit his pipe, "Lydia, the deck will be full of field slaves in a moment, you might want to go back down to the cabin. And please remember, whenever you come up on deck, stay clear of the crewmen so they can do their jobs."

Then he added, "Also, when the weather is mild, you are welcome to walk the deck between the two ladder ways, and around the center cargo hatch, but stay away from the wheels and the narrow walkways at the bow and stern. Those stubby compartments there are actually the tops of the sleeping cabins."

Without answering, Lydia turned and walked to the stern calling for Junie. A small group of slaves was brought up on deck at the bow. Ben allowed Lydia a moment to go ahead of him and then stepped down into the hold to inspect the slave partition. Even with four men on deck, the makeshift cabin was crowded. Small crates and buckets had been improvised for seating, with blankets folded on them for padding. Fresh straw had been spread on the deck, and a few hammocks had been hung.

As Ben entered the area Simon stood up with a smile, offering his hand. The handshake turned into a manly hug and slaps on shoulders. Ben opened his mouth to speak but Simon spoke first, indicating the small woman seated next to him.

"Ben, this is my wife, Leticia."

Ben kneeled beside her and offered his hand, but she did not take it. "I am pleased to meet you, Mrs. Bond."

She only looked at him with wide eyes.

"She has been treated terribly by her masters Ben. She has no experience with white kindness."

Ben bowed his head a moment then stood. "What amazing luck that you came out as I sailed by."

"Ben, Lettie is from Grayrocks. She knows most of the young men you picked up. One of them is her brother. They have all known for days that a ship was coming from the upper Bay to take them to Georgetown, and the Overseer mentioned the ship was named the *Raven*. I have been expecting you. You were late!"

"You were expecting me?"

"We waited in the woods on that marshy point three days, just eating dried meat and apples – the only things we could get from the root cellars and smoke house."

"Well," said Ben, "I need to tell you what the real plans are for these people and for you."

Ben went silent. The first four slaves were returned from the deck, who went for their blankets as four others were taken out.

Simon chuckled. "Benjamin, you white people still think we just sit like mute dogs when you are not around, thinking no more about what is next and never discussing what we hear."

Ben looked at Simon with a puzzled expression.

"Cephus told us while he was bringing us food, so we wouldn't worry."

"You already know?"

"All of us do, except what you have planned for me. I just hoped you were still captain of the *Raven* and would take us away, maybe north."

"We will go north, but first we have to go south, all the way to Charleston, and I need you to help me crew the ship, since I just kicked one crewman off."

"Jarrod?"

"Yes. You already know the crew's name?"

Simon smiled. "Just the asses."

Ben stepped into the passage way. "Edward! Harry! Bring them back down, I need to talk to all of you. Cephus! Come on in here, too." He turned back into the partitioned space, Let's all move into the cargo space on the other side of the passageway, I think there is more room there, if we shift the supplies around."

When they had all gathered, with sixteen faces staring at him to learn the details of their fate, he hesitated a moment then drew in a deep breath.

"Some of you know parts of what I am going to tell you, but I want you all to know what I can tell you. First, the man and woman we brought aboard off Solomons, is my good friend Simon Bond and his wife Leticia. Simon and I have been friends for over twenty years. We served together in the Georgia swamps, sailed together to China and were imprisoned together there when the Chinese rose up against the British opium trade. During the two years my family in Maryland thought I was dead, Simon was my only family. He taught me to read and write. He also shared the risk with me taking escaping slaves across the Mason-Dixon line when I was shot in the head and thought dead a second time, and he brought me home."

The crew and the slaves traded glances, sharing raised eyebrows and low murmurs.

Ben looked directly at Edward and Harry. "I am asking Simon to join our crew and help sail this ship."

Edward and Harry nodded in agreement.

"Simon is a better sailor and a better human being than Jarrod, by miles," Ben said.

Ben turned back toward Edward. "Edward please go to the captain's cabin and quietly ask Sonja to insure Lydia and Junie stay there. Tell her I will explain everything later. While you are gone, I will be telling what you already heard me say to Cephus."

Ben gathered his thoughts before speaking again.

"You men who came on board in Solomons, we will take you to a safe place on the Eastern shore of Maryland, where others will help you go north. But it will not happen soon. I must pretend to sell you in Charleston, and have the correct records of that sale, so this ship will not be burned and I can use her again to help others escape."

Murmurs swept among the men.

"How we don't know you gonna sell us anyway, down Charleston way" one of the slaves asked.

"Because he said what he will do. I would stake my life on it," Simon responded.

"How long that gonna be," the man asked.

"Two or three weeks," Ben told him.

"We gonna be down here the whole time," he asked. Other faces among the group nodded to his question

"What is your name?" Ben asked.

The man drew back and looked around among the other slaves, who were now looking down.

"What is your name?"

"Joseph," he mumbled. Then he stood up and said it clearly, "Joseph!"

Ben and Simon both smiled at his stance.

"Joseph," Ben said, "You are now the representative of the Solomons men."

"We be Grayrocks slaves, not Solomons," Joseph said.

"You came on board at Solomons, as men, not slaves. You are Solomons men."

Ben looked at each of the other faces. "If any of you have a question or a grievance, and you don't want to tell me or Edward, you take it to Joseph. He will bring it to me, Simon or Edward."

Joseph scanned among the faces looking up at him, nodding in agreement. He looked toward Simon for reassurance, then took in a deep breath and faced Ben again. "So we staying down here the whole time?"

Edward returned from the stern and listened intently to the conversation.

"No, Joseph. Those who can help work the ship will be directed by Edward, the others will help Cephus cook or help clean your quarters. But! You must not attract the attention of Mrs. Binterfield, or discuss what I have told you in any place where she might hear you! Do you understand?"

All faces showed understanding and agreement.

Edward stepped forward. "Cap'n, I think we might rearrange partitions to spread out the Solomons men on both sides of the passageway, and also give Mr. and Mrs. Bond some privacy.

Ben smiled. "See to it, First Mate."

28

January 1, 1844. Winyah Bay, South Carolina.

After an uneventful passage from Hampton Roads, the *Raven* tacked north into Winyah Bay under a falling sun, and sailed north along the inner coast toward the North Island Lighthouse. Anchored before the lighthouse they discovered a single-mast workboat. The *Raven* came within hailing distance as the crew lowered sails.

"Ahoy there," Ben yelled through a speaking trumpet. "Are you the Pilot Boat?"

"Aye! Are you the *Raven*," the captain asked, and when Ben confirmed, he added, "Your tow will be here tomorrow. She's been coming the last two days looking for you. You just missed her."

While they waited, Sonja contrived with Cephus to bake a sweetbread cake to celebrate Ben's forty fourth birthday. They served it to Ben in the mess area, with the rest of the crew and the Solomons men gathered together. Lydia and Junie stayed on the deck watching the shoreline and enjoying an afternoon of placid water after three days on the open Atlantic Ocean.

The following day, just before noon, a thirty foot steam boat, approached the *Raven* spewing a long thick black cloud in the air behind it. The null and pilot house were painted in gleaming white. Just behind the pilot house stood a ruby red smoke stack. Standing rigid on the deck at the rear were six black men in red shirts wearing white pants. Leaning out of the pilot house, a white man wearing a similar uniform as the men but displaying the gold piping of an officer, waved his hand. As the steam boat came along side the *Raven*, the polished teak wood trim and decks were immaculate.

The officer scrambled up the side ladder, promptly saluted toward the bow, and then at Ben, saying, "Ensign Cuttingham, Captain. Welcome to Georgetown." His accent was noticeably British upper class.

"Ben Pulaski," Ben said, taking his hand. "Are you British?"

His tanned face produced a white toothed smile, wrinkling his eyes. "Once upon a time, Captain. I am proud to call myself an American now, in the service of Master Jeremiah Williamson of Palmetto Haven. So, if you will kindly raise your anchor, it will be my honor to tow you upriver to the plantation."

Cuttingham noticed Lydia sitting on a cabin chair perched on the deck before the ship's wheel, holding a frilled umbrella over her against the sun, although the temperature was in the forties. The crew had reduced clothing to heavy shirts or light jackets. Sonja was leaning against the waist-high roof of the captain's cabin, with her arms folded, scowling at Lydia's back.

"If I may," Cuttingham said to Ben as he walked toward Lydia, where he removed his cap and bowed slightly, "Miss Lydia, I presume?"

Ben could not hear the rest of the conversation.

Cuttingham hurried back to Ben. "Please have your crew toss a bow line to the steamer, Captain. There is sufficient channel, if you know where it is, and there are sand bars everywhere. This is not a problem for the steamer, but the sand bars could definitely be a problem for your ship." He started to walk off the ship, then stopped and turned. "Oh, there is a small lagoon near the entrance canal to the plantation, approximately twelve miles upriver from here. You will anchor there, and we will ferry you up to the mansion to meet the master."

The officer returned to the steamer while the *Raven*'s crew raised the anchor. They were quickly under way, moving far faster than the push of the wind, a coal cloud from the steamer's smoke stack rushing through the rigging. They travelled north up Winyah Bay, and into a wide river. Ben was content to have Cuttingham tow the ship while he and the others watched the steamer charge ahead and the vast marshland slip past, hundreds of yards away from both sides of the ship. Ben noticed fresh gold lettering was recently applied to the stern of the steamer, proclaiming her the *Lydia*. Huge live oak trees grew along the shores with thick twisted limbs draped in shawls of Spanish moss. The surface of the water was dark and glass smooth, except for the meager lines created by the barge and the *Raven*.

Ben stepped next to Sonja, who leaned toward him and whispered, "She beat Junie."

Ben sighed and shook his head. "I am sorry for her. I wish we could do something."

Barely an hour later they came to a sharp eastern bend in the river. On the western shore, a tree lined lagoon marked the greater shoulder of the bend. There was a long sturdy pier extending from the edge of a well tended canal. The steamer continued toward the northern edge of the lagoon where it slowed. Ensign Cuttingham stepped out of the pilot house and yelled through a speaking trumpet.

"Kindly steer your ship to the pier, please Captain. You should have sufficient headway to make the turn. If not we will gladly provide a gentle nudge."

Ben stepped to the wheel as Edward spun it all the way to the left bringing the ship almost against the southern side of the pier. The river current overcame their headway, keeping the ship from closing completely with the pier, but several black men dressed in the same uniform as the steamer's crewmen, ran out of a dock house and held their hands out for ropes from the *Raven*. Simon, Harry and Cephus had already positioned themselves along that side of the ship and tossed mooring ropes to the pier. The docking crew pulled the *Raven* against the pier and secured her lines, while the steamer tied up on the other side of the pier, letting the barge crew run to help the docking crew.

Ben leaned on the railing and touched the brim of his hat to Cuttingham. "Nicely done, Ensign!"

The Ensign smiled as another man stepped from the pilot house and blew a boson's whistle. Both sets of crewmen lined up in two perfectly straight lines on the dock, standing at attention.

"At ease," Cuttingham said, and the crewmen stamped their bare feet apart and snapped their hands together behind their backs.

Cuttingham walked up the gangplank to the *Raven* just as Simon and Cephus slid it out. He touched his cap to Ben and then to Lydia. "If you will kindly show me where the Lady's luggage is stowed, we will transfer it to the steamer."

Like a line of ants, the Palmetto Haven crewmen marched down into the hold and carried bags, trunks, and crates to the steamer. Within minutes Lydia had vacated the *Raven*, and stood primly near the pilot house, while Junie sat on a nearby trunk. The steamer churned quickly into the canal and out of sight.

Two hours later, the steamer had still not returned. Ben gave the crew and the Solomons men permission to lounge on the deck of the *Raven*. He walked down the pier to the dock house. As he opened the door and stepped in, the Boson snapped to attention, and stamped his bare feet, British style.

"At ease," Ben managed to say.

"Help you, sir," the Boson asked.

The rest of the men in the dock house were arranged on chairs or boxes at the far side of the building near an iron stove crackling with burning wood. Some of the men relaxed on the floor nearby.

"You have food and water in here, Boson?"

"You need food on your ship, sir?"

"Oh no, I was just inquiring about you and your men."

"We are taken care of sir, no need to bother yourself about us."

Ben looked around the building. "What is this building for?"

"Shipping, sir. In and out," he answered, but remained uncomfortably silent, looking around the room from the corners of his eyes.

"Thank you," Ben said, and returned to the *Raven*.

Minutes later, the steamer returned. Ensign Cuttingham walked briskly across the pier and saluted Ben, as his eyes flickered across the *Raven*'s deck to where Sonja lounged in the chair brought up earlier for Lydia. She was still wearing her canvas breeches and a light sweater.

"I understand your wife has accompanied you, Captain?" Ben only nodded yes. "You and you wife are invited to join the master and his niece for dinner at the mansion. I am sure you will want time to...refreshen, and...dress for the occasion. I will return at 5 o'clock to carry you into the plantation."

The Ensign returned to the steamer and disappeared back up the canal beyond a cloud of black smoke hanging low over the surface. Ben asked Harry and Cephus to boil some river water as he went below deck to fish out his folding canvas bathing tub, and took it to the cabin. At five o'clock Sonja and Ben stepped onto the deck in the new clothes they had purchased in St. Michaels, just as the steamer returned to the pier.

"Are we impressed, Ben?" Sonja asked.

"Absolutely," Ben answered with a smirk. "And I believe there is much more show to come this evening."

After a journey of over a mile, along manicured grounds bordering the canal, and each side displaying carved marble statuettes every hundred yards, the steamer *Lydia* docked at the white painted plantation pier. Colorful striped overhead awnings spread over dozens of wicker chairs and settees, sitting empty in the chill. Several white serving tables were spaced among the seating, with a white uniformed slave standing straight by each table. From the pier, they walked along a brick walkway to the main house. They passed among six twenty foot marble columns and reached massive ten foot teakwood doors at the center of a the three story mansion. Servants opened the doors and bowed. Cuttingham escorted them to the receiving room, and quickly departed.

Jeremiah Williamson looked to be nearing sixty as he met them in the receiving room of Palmetto Haven. He was tall, silver haired and straight-backed, dressed in a dark blue silk suit, high white collar, and light blue neckcloth. The shine on his black shoes reflected the candlelight from the pair of crystal chandeliers overhead. Servants came and went, wearing pressed black uniforms and white gloves, carrying glasses or decanters on silver trays. Introductions complete, Jeremiah launched his speech noting all his accomplishments and his successes with Palmetto Haven, his British style navy, as he called it, the thousands of acres he held in growing rice, and the expertise of his Gullah slaves in producing the very best.

"Carolina Gold, we call it, and so do our customers around the world," he said.

They moved into the dining room, while Jeremiah continued without pause, except to sip on his wine. Lydia sat at the gargantuan table with Junie standing behind her, although there were a dozen servants lining the walls to serve the four diners. No condiments were set on the table. Salt, pepper, butter, bread, and prepared foods rested on silver platters held by the servants.

Finally, at the end of dinner, the women were banished to the receiving room to sip wine in cold silence, while Ben was invited into the den for cigars and brandy. Ben waved away the cigar tray, and withdrew his pipe and pouch while a servant set the brandy glasses nearby and another filled them, then both returned to their stations along the wall, where they stood straight, staring at the ceiling.

"Pity you couldn't have come yesterday, Mr. Pulaski. We had a wonderful New Years Day gathering. Must have been a hundred people here. Several stayed over and just left this morning. Lovely time," he said, examining his cigar. He held it up for Ben to see. "You should try one, Mr. Pulaski. They are from Cuba. Best in the world."

Jeremiah cleared his throat, and examined his cigar again. "My nephew sent word that he placed ten slaves on your ship for delivery down here."

Ben puffed lightly on his pipe, letting the blue smoke drift up into the cigar's cloud. "James placed ten slaves on my ship as consignment for me to sell at best profit, Mr. Williamson."

Jeremiah smiled, but it did not go to his eyes. "Of course, Mr. Pulaski. As you know, we can always use fresh slaves down here, between expanding rice fields and usually losing a few every year to fever, there is always a need."

"These are tobacco field hands, Mr. Williamson. I don't know how much value you will get from them for cultivating rice."

"What they need to do is bend over and shove the seedlings into the mud, one every six inches over six thousand acres, then bend over and care for the mud, then bend over and harvest the rice. My Gullahs do all the skilled work."

Ben released another trail of smoke into the air and watched it rise. "What do you offer, Mr. Williamson."

"Four hundred dollars a man."

Ben smiled into his smoke, knowing James expected his uncle to offer six, and was quiet a moment. "I have a far better offer from Charleston. The cotton fields have a huge demand, and the market there is brisk."

"Five hundred," Jeremiah said.

"These slaves are in excellent condition. Some have skills. They will draw bids of a thousand a piece in Charleston, if not more," Ben said.

"You know damned well, that is not what the sellers will pay you. They are brokers."

"As am I, sir," Ben said.

Jeremiahs face grew red. "Six hundred. That is an excellent price, and I know damned well that my nephew will more than double his investment, since they were bred at Grayrocks."

Ben sat in silence, then smiled. "I am sorry, Mr. Williamson, but..."

"Six hundred and fifty, and that's my final offer. These are from my own family, God damn it! What is James

267

doing?"

"He directed me to get the best price I could. From you preferably. If not, then where I could. I share the profits with him."

Jeremiah crushed his cigar in the ashtray. "What the hell do you require to deny a sale to your broker in Charleston?"

"Eight Hundred a piece, Sir," Ben said.

"Jesus Christ Almighty," Jeremiah said under his breath. He snapped his fingers for another brandy, and sipped it in silence. When the glass was drained, he snapped his fingers again saying. "Jason, escort these people down to the steamer, so Cuttingham can take them back to their ship." He stood and walked out of the room, speaking over his shoulder, "Good night, Pulaski."

Cuttingham said very little as they rode down the canal to the lagoon. Ben and Sonja arrived back at their ship shortly after 9 o'clock that night. The *Raven*'s lanterns were lit, Harry was playing a harmonica near the bow, and one of the uniformed slaves was patrolling the pier.

"I will return tomorrow to tow you down river," Cuttingham said from the pilot house, then spun the steamer back into the plantation canal.

In the mansion, a servant knocked on the door to Lydia's room. Junie answered it, but the servant would not speak with her. Moments later, Lydia came to the door showing a frown under her black curls. "Master says you to sleep in his room tonight," the servant said.

It was not until after three o'clock the afternoon of the next day, when Cuttingham returned to the pier with the steamer. He was polite but curt, as his crew tied *Raven*'s bow line to the stern of the *Lydia*.

"Master said to take you back down to North Island, to help you on your way."

"I still need to make my way to Buck Lumber Mill and Mansfield Plantation piers to acquire my cargo," Ben said

"I am sorry sir, but that is not my concern, nor my duty. I am to deliver your ship at North Island. I might encourage you to attempt to make your way north up the

Waccamaw on your own and spend the winter stranded on a sand bar, but my master has ordered me to see you to North Island. "

"Kindly tie on to our bow, Ensign," Ben said through gritted teeth.

The sun was low in the sky and sinking over the marsh when the tow line from the Steamer was tossed into the waters before the North Island Lighthouse. It was too late to attempt sailing out of Winyah Bay, and the wind blew inland from the sea, so they dropped anchor and spent another night off Rabbit Island.

At sunrise the following day, the tide was rising into the Bay, but the wind was a brisk land breeze , blowing out to sea. The Solomons men were once again free to move about the ship and assist the crew with the sails. The ship leaned well away from the wind and sailed swiftly down the channel from the North Island Lighthouse, beyond Cape Romain and out into the Atlantic. The *Raven*'s bow heaved up as she took the first of the Atlantic rollers, then turned south toward Charleston.

Sonja came up on deck carrying some soiled night clothes Lydia had worn, and threw them overboard, letting the wind carry them away. Then she stepped next to Ben. "I want to steer," she said.

Ben watched Lydia's night clothes swallowed by the waves. "That family has a smell about it," he said. Then he signaled for Sonja to take his windward wheel, while he reached the other and shared the steering with her. Simon and Harry adjusted the jib sails and then joined with Edward to help tighten the main sail boom. Joseph and some of the other Solomons men sat on the deck near the bow, enjoying the ride. Finished with his sail duty, Edward stepped between Ben and Sonja.

"What about the cargo, Ben? Are we not taking it on," Edward asked.

Ben continued to carry a scowl. "We will return to Georgetown after we leave Charleston."

"How long until Charleston?" Sonja asked, looking at Ben over Edward's shoulder.

"If this wind stays steady, this evening," Ben said

"Sooner in, sooner out," she said.
"Sooner in, sooner out," Ben answered.

29

The wind was little more than a light breeze in a cloudless sky, the surface of the water was a lazy scene of undulating wavelets, and the temperature was mild. Passing between Fort Sumter to the west and Fort Moultrie to the east, the *Raven* moved inland toward a lesser fort known as Castle Pinckney, sitting on an island named Shutes Folly, according to Ben's charts. Beyond that, Charleston Harbor was a shifting maze of ships and boats of all sizes, moving in and out of the harbor entrance, in and out of the docking area, and all steering around anchored vessels. Some were anchored a mile out and others were pulled in too close to the docks, all waiting for their turn. Both the Annapolis and Baltimore harbors had been far more controlled in Ben's mind, than the uncoordinated free-for-all he was witnessing in Charleston.

"There must be hundreds of ships bringing and taking cargo. The pace of business there must be incredible," Ben said.

Ben scanned the harbor looking for any approach that would allow him a margin of safety, but still provide access to the docks. Finally, he decided to anchor between the island and the harbor, but still a quarter mile from the docks, and use the *Raven*'s rowboat to get to shore.

They anchored in a location Ben decided would allow them a safe circle of movement within the length of the anchor line and the circle they would make around it to the push of tides and current. Sonja and Edward were openly disappointed that they were required to remain on

271

the ship while he went alone into Charleston. The crew moved quickly to lift the rowboat off its chocks and lower it into the water.

"We have no cargo to offload or take on, and I will only return with one passenger," he reminded them. "I have to meet with a man to obtain my certificate of sale, and we have not met before. I only have a name and address from Anthony, and a certain expression to make when we meet. He and I will both need to be careful to have a private conversation, so I dare not bring visitors that might cause him to fear for his safety."

Ben placed his papers in a canvas bag, and that in turn, he slipped inside an oiled leather pouch, to keep them dry. The money he needed to pay the broker was stuffed into the canvas money belt snugged around his waist under his shirt. Sonja stood at the railing with him.

"I was so looking forward to seeing Charleston, perhaps when you return we can discuss going back there before we sail."

He patted her hand, and smiled at her. "Sooner in, sooner out," he reminded her, but it did not mellow her mood.

He climbed down in the rowboat, adjusted the strap of his leather pouch, and took up the oars. They watched him from the *Raven* until he rounded a four-masted cargo ship and was lost from sight. Again the Solomons men were allowed free roam of the ship. Joseph had taken it upon himself to introduce each of his fellow escapees to the crew and Sonja.

"Be sure to tell the others the skills your men have," Simon told him.

At other times some of the men had been tailors, wood workers, masons, and blacksmiths. The blacksmith, Abraham, had begun opening the individual shackles and altering them so a slave would only have to press the post with his thumb to open them. One of the woodworkers, Miles, was assisting Adam to tap in additional caulking in the seams between of the deck planking, a frequent duty of a ship's carpenter.

An hour later, Ben mounted the stone steps onto Concord Street and asked a passerby the directions to State Street. He found his way easily, and began looking for the building housing the offices of Lebeaux and Chambers, Property Brokers. Inside the office, a clerk sat at a high desk near the door. His pen stopped and he looked up without saying the question.

"I am here to see Mr. Chambers," Ben said.

"The partners are very busy this morning, Sir. If Mr. Chambers is occupied, may I escort you to Mr. Lebeaux."

"I am certain Mr. Lebeaux has the same expertise as Mr. Chambers," Ben said, remembering his lines, " but I was referred to Mr. Chambers by an ardent admirer and keen businessman, Mr. Anthony, of the Argyle Corporation."

The clerk's face was placid, but he nodded and left his desk to go upstairs. Barely a minute passed when a portly red-faced man with balding head and wispy silver hair slipping over his ears, moved awkwardly down the stairs with one leg shorter than the other. He smiled as he approached Ben.

"I am Mr. Chambers, Sir. How may I be of service?"

"I am Ben Pulaski. I am referred to you by Mr. Anthony who holds you in high esteem due to your business with the Argyle Corporation."

"Please pass along my gratitude for Mr. Anthony's kind words, Mr. Pulaski. Are you kin of the famous cavalry officer of our Revolution, Sir? General Casimir Pulaski is still highly regarded here in Charleston, even as much as in Savannah."

The clerk returned to his seat.

"I think not," Ben said.

Chambers wagged a finger in front of a smile. "Never miss an opportunity to allow Charlestonians to believe you might be a descendent of Casimir, Mr. Pulaski," he said. "It would open many doors for people who might otherwise be cold strangers." Then he turned to the clerk, "Wallace, kindly trot down to the auction house and collect the list for this afternoon ."

As Wallace closed the front door behind him,

Chambers invited Ben to enter a small office behind a glass panel door near the entrance.

Once inside, Chambers spoke quietly and quickly. "We can be out of earshot from my partner down here. Tell me what you are after."

"I need to bid on Robert Hannibal and I need you to certify a sale of ten slaves from Maryland."

"The second request is easy, the first, not so much so."

Ben opened his mouth to question Chambers, but the man held up a finger to stop him and reached for a form lying on a shelf near the desk. He snatched a steel tipped pen from the desk, opened an ink bottle and began scribbling on various lines.

"What price per man?"

"Eight Hundred per head, all males," Ben said.

"Origin?"

"Grayrocks Plantation, Saint Mary's County, Maryland."

"Original seller?"

"Mr. James Williamson, on consignment," Ben said. Chambers paused and allowed a grim expression to pass over his face, then returned to his form.

"Consignment value?"

"Three hundred per head," Ben said.

Chambers made a flurry of other entries and signed the form with a flourish. Then he snatched a candle from the desk, lit it over the office lantern, letting it drip onto the form, and pressed a seal into the soft wax. He blew on the wax seal to cool it and handed the form to Ben.

"Two hundred dollars. Cash."

As Ben counted out the money, Chambers continued to speak in staccato delivery. "As for Mr. Hannibal, the auction will be open, allowing anyone to bid, which is good for you. However, Mr. Jeremiah Williamson has let it be known that the slave is highly educated and plays a musical instrument. That will drive the bidding up, which is bad for you. His agent anticipates five thousand dollars for Hannibal. I hope you brought plenty of money." He hesitated a moment. "Is James Williamson in any way connected to Jeremiah?"

"James is his nephew. There is not a strong family bond between them," Ben said.

Chambers shrugged his shoulders and rolled his eyes. He reached into his vest pocket and withdrew a folded paper. "This is your introduction to the auction house. You must understand, if you win the bid, you must pay the total bid before leaving the auction house."

The front door opened and Wallace entered with a sheaf of papers. He noticed Chambers in the little office, tapped on the door then opened it and placed the papers on the desk.

"Excellent. Thank you, Wallace. Couldn't get along without you." While Wallace smiled primly, Chambers spoke to Ben in front of him, as if he had been in mid-sentence. "So, Mr. Pulaski, here are the auction times today and the offerings on the block. I wish you well, and please give my regards to Mr. Anthony. I so enjoy working with him on the Argyle issues." He stood and offered his hand to Ben in farewell, heading awkwardly back toward the stairs.

Ben left the office and found his way to the Auction house. The auction offering Robert Hannibal was less than an hour away. Ben entered the building and noticed another clerk at a high desk sitting near the far door. Ben presented his introduction to the clerk, who looked up with a smile.

"Are you related to Casimir Pulaski?"

Ben hesitated. "...Yes," Ben said and swallowed, "a grand nephew, or second cousin," he flipped his hand. "Father was never clear enough on that. Still, there was an old cavalry sword hung over our fireplace, below the painting father always said was of Casimir."

The clerk went wide eyed, and stepped down next to Ben. "Please sir, allow me to escort you to the bidding chamber."

With his chest full, the clerk opened the nearby door and lead the way in. There were a dozen well-dressed men standing in a loose group near the stone block, chatting and sipping wine and brandy.

"Gentlemen," the clerk called with his chin up. "It is my honor to present to you the grandnephew of Casimir Pulaski, Mr. Benjamin Pulaski."

Most of the little crowd dissolved and reformed around Ben. Ben drew heavily from his recollections of the John Paul Jones painting his father had at their house in Baltimore, when Ben was young. He filled his imagination for the spew of lies he showered upon the bidders. When one of the bidders mentioned the musical skill in the piano held by the next slave, Ben was quick to spin a lie of his father playing compositions that were known "in the family" to be Casimir's favorites.

"I do hope this fellow can play that kind of music. I long to hear it again, as does my son who hopes to enter West Point next year."

"Another Pulaski in the cavalry," offered one of the men in warm appreciation of the thought.

The crowd hushed as the auctioneer stood near the block. A modest sized black man with slender physique stepped upon it, wearing a loose wool slave shirt and canvas breeches. There were obvious bruises on his face, his lip and left eye were partially swollen.

"We shall start the bidding at five hundred dollars," said the auctioneer. Ben immediately bid one thousand dollars. A second voice bid fifteen hundred dollars, but the majority of the men in the crowd gave him sour looks, and he stepped back away from the block, looking from the corners of his eyes at his peers.

"Two Thousand," Ben bid, and held his breath. Even as the auctioneer called again and again for additional bids, the room remained silent until he announced, "Sold to uh..."

A gentleman close by pulled the auctioneer down by his sleeve and whispered into his ear.

"Oh well, I see," the auctioneer said quietly, then in a louder voice, he announced, "Sold to Mr. Benjamin Pulaski for two thousand dollars."

The group clapped and offered Ben more brandy.

"I can easily see why Casimir gave his heart and his life

to the men of this city," Ben said to them. "Your kindness is overwhelming to a passing stranger," he said.

"No Pulaski is ever a stranger in Charleston," said the man who had bid against him.

Ben reached out and shook his hand. After paying his bid and informing the clerk he would send "his man" to pick up the slave later, Ben lingered in a poorly kept tavern down the street. He sat by the window sipping coffee until the rest of the auction had completed and the Gentlemen he bid against had ample time to file out of the building. He paid for his coffee and then walked back to the auction house, where the clerk was surprised to see him picking up the slave himself.

"I am so excited," Ben told him."I found a music shop not far from here, thinking I would order a new piano for my home, and the thought came to me, 'I must bring my musical slave here at once to see how well he plays!' Do have him on a leash or whatever holds him and let me lead him there. He does behave, does he not? "

The clerk brought Robert to Ben with a new piece of rope tied to the iron collar locked around his neck. The clerk happily volunteered to help walk the slave to the music shop, but Ben convinced him he wanted to walk his new property and asked for the key.

Ben leaned forward to nudge his slave forward and whispered in his ear. "Anthony Renowitz sends his regards, Robert."

Among the documents Anthony had provided Ben, was a passenger ticket for a ship docked in Charleston Harbor, bound for Philadelphia. The ticket was issued for "One Negro Freeman." On the way to the dock, Ben released the collar and dropped it in an alley, and then gave Robert his coat. At the gangplank, Robert grasped Ben's hand tightly. Both knew that too dramatic a parting would gather unwanted attention. They turned away without further words.

Two hours later, long after Ben had expected to return, he rowed toward the *Raven* and faced several anxious faces.

"Where the hell have you been," Sonja asked him as

soon as his feet touched the deck. "The sun is going down. You've been gone all day!"

"I bought you something, Sonja," Ben said. "I bought you a slave."

She frowned and folded her arms in front of her chest. "You made me worry."

Still at anchor and free of Lydia, they all sat around the mess table for supper as the sun sank over the city of Charleston. The men and women of the *Raven* had seen great success in fishing the water and there were platters of fish and biscuits.

Leticia, reached her hand to Ben, saying "I am pleased to meet you Benjamin."

And I am pleased to meet you Mrs. Bond," he said.

"Call me Lettie."

"Call me Ben."

"And call me for rum," said Adam.

And the rum flowed generously that night.

At dawn, *Raven*'s anchor was hauled up and the sails unfurled to a strong land breeze that carried them out of the harbor and out into the Atlantic within the hour. The sky above the rising sun was red, and the clouds were dark and heavy.

Simon and Edward watched the skyline intently, speaking in low tones.

30

The Atlantic rollers beyond Charleston harbor and Fort Moultrie had a meanness to their character, hitting the side of the hull with a slap, forcing the *Raven* to steer into them and venture off course, farther out in the ocean. The waves increased to 5 to 8 feet, punching the bow as the *Raven* hit them and driving water sprays into the air over the bow and delivering almost constant rain onto the forward deck. The wind warmed slightly and increased its push against the sails, causing Ben to reduce sails a second time. The crew was sent skittering around the ship tightening all hatches and doorways against the spray. Additional tie downs were thrown across the rowboat. Adam and Miles exercised the pump and made some adjustments to ensure it would be available if the weather worsened. The clouds to the south roiled in the sky, trading lightning bolts between charcoal colored masses moving ponderously toward the *Raven*.

Sonja was at the wheel next to Ben, struggling to add her weight to the rudder.

"This is going to get worse, Sonja," he said. "If you have to go below deck to ride it out, go to midships. Anything you might need from the cabin, go get it now and take it down into the passageway in the hold."

The wind increased, still driving the *Raven* farther out to sea. Even before Ben gave the order to Edward he was already preparing to reduce sail further. The mainsails were reefed, allowing only half of the sail to take the wind. The waves increased and brought cross currents that kicked the hull in the stern and then slapped it on the side, creating a gyrating motion. The dark clouds behind them looked like mountains about to fall on them.

The storm hit with shrieking winds and taller seas pushing waves ten to fifteen feet. The *Raven* slammed into the surface with her bow as she crested the waves, only to be punched in the side in the trough between them. Rogue waves twenty feet high shoved the hull into the air as it ran underneath. Ben turned the wheel again trying to meet the waves head on, but the sea was confused, and the waves seemed to come from two directions, and he struggled to pick the stronger of the two.

Adam made his way to the wheel. "This storm is going to kick our ass, Benjamin." No sooner had he spoken than a bizarre wave hit the stern quarter of the ship and spun it around.

"We need to get control of this thing," Ben yelled over the wind. "Edward, Harry and Simon joined them at the wheel. "We need to reef all sails except for a storm jib, and throw sea anchors out. That will keep the bow pointing down wind and the stern pointing upwind. I don't want to run any farther out to sea than I have to!"

Water crashed over the bow, taking the forward deck under a wave, and pushing the bow into the water. The bow stayed under as another wave twenty feet tall ran over the entire deck of the ship. Men held on tightly to anything they could, holding their breath as the *Raven* submerged. The weight of the water on her decks kept her down. The bow did not rise. The men struggled to hold their breath. The wave passed and begrudgedly allowed the men to push their heads into the air and gasp for breath. Slowly, the hull started to rise as the mountain of water continued to slide off the deck.

The back slope of the wave created a trough behind it, allowing the bowsprit to punch through the other side. The bow emerged from the wave, exposing a full third of the hull and then rode down the backside of the wave into a deadly dive into a deep trough toward the base of the next wave. Adam released the jib sails to flap loosely, releasing the pressure of the wind. Harry and Edward tugged on the remaining exposed edge of the main sail and tied it to the boom. Simon came up from the hold and tossed a heavy line into the sea with the ends of a trysail clamped to its end. He managed to pay out all the sea anchor line from the stern as the ship headed down into the water again.

"Hold on!" Edward yelled. The bow slammed into the next wave, pushed by the storm winds. Again the bow dove deep into the water, driven by its own speed before the wind. The entire ship was swallowed by the ocean. Men on deck held their breath again, until colored spots flashed in their closed eyes. Their lungs burned. And still they had to wait. Ben was ready to release the air bursting his lungs, when the peak of the wave passed, allowing only his head above water. The ship spun in the water again, but did not yet rise. Sluggishly, the hull rose, and slowly the water slid from her deck. At last the bow emerged from the water, the railings became visible again. The roof to the captain's cabin rose from the sea. The warm water swirled around Ben's waist and shuffled overboard, letting him see the deck again.

We are in the *Gulf stream*, he thought. *How far out?*

He looked around the deck. Edward was lashing the last of the main sails to the booms, Simon and Harry had grabbed the lines to the jib and staysails, and brought them down, leaving only a small storm sail where the forward jib had been. Except for the storm sale the masts were bare. The sea anchor had paid out to the end of the stern line. The gyrations of the ship had reduced. The hull rode the waves, pushed over them by the greatly diminished wind captured by storm sail, slowing their speed and giving the buoyancy of the hull time to mount each wave, rather than dive into it. Steering was useless. The rudder had no bite in the waves rolling under the hull. Only the storm sail and the sea anchor controlled the lie of the ship. Ben released the wheel and headed for the captain's cabin. The deck still pitched and rolled, but still gave sailors a deck to perch on. Hand holds were still necessary. Simon spun around looking over the deck.

"Where's Adam?" Simon Yelled.

Ben did not hear Simon. He stepped down into the cabin, but Sonja was not there. Water had worked its way around the window shutters and drained along the floor toward the hold. He dashed to the passageway, but did not find Sonja.

"Sonja," he yelled.

"In here," she said. He found her in one of the new partitions, rocking the handles of the pump with Miles. Ben then noticed the ankle deep water in the hold that had not yet reached up to the passageway.

"I'll get you help," Ben told them.

"We have help, Ben," Sonja said. "We're pumping as hard as we can. We are changing people every ten to fifteen minutes."

Joseph stood in the corner of the cabin holding a pocket watch. He nodded to Ben and said " five more minutes," to Sonja. "Abraham and Matthew," he yelled toward the canvas partition wall, "You are next."

Ben smiled and let them continue their work. He went back up on deck and carefully leaned over the railing with a lantern to check the outflow port for the bilge pump seeing quart sized spurts of water jumping back into the ocean. As he stood up, Simon approached him.

"Ben, we lost Adam. He was washed overboard."

"No!" He bit his lip and took in a raw breath, still coughing up sea water. "Please look for him again, Simon."

The waves continued at 8 to 10 feet, rocking the ship forcefully bow to stern, and slamming the bow on the back side as it crested. The ship vibrated from the continual impact, taking a beating, he knew, eventually the seams between the hull planking would begin to open.

"Edward, please go pull up the loose planking under the passageway and check for leaks in the hull. Get Miles to tamp in caulking."

Ben looked out over the menacing waves. "Damn it, Adam."

As the night wore on, the storm pushed them ever farther to the east. The clank of the pump was unending, and the pounding to drive caulking back into the seams incessant. People slept for minutes at a time, taking turns at the pumps, or the caulking, or pulling wet blankets from standing water, or watching the level of the water creep slowly higher inside the hull.

Ben went on deck to check the rigging and the storm sail. He stood by the useless wheel, holding onto the compass pedestal and showing the lantern light over the compass that seemed to perpetually point east, over the bow. He looked out into the black sea, knowing they were drifting north even as the storm pushed them east. He looked out beyond the stern.

"Damn it, Adam," he muttered.

The waves remained high, hiding in the darkness until the instant they charged into the meager light of the ship's lantern, then they dove under the ship, tossing the *Raven* into the air. The bow slammed down hard, sending vibrations and anxieties rippling through the ship. The water that sloshed in the bilge reached over the top of the passageway planks. Small waves ran bow to stern inside the hull as the ship rocked end-to-end in the angry sea. The pumps continued, only stopping for seconds as arms and hands were forced to reach for other hand holds when the hull slammed into another wave. The water inside the hull was rising.

Everyone took turns at the pump handles, giving it all the energy they had to send the water covering their ankles back into the sea. Even blessed with more than two dozen shoulders and arms, the sea was winning the contest inch by inch. Each cycle brought rested arms that had less to give than their last turn. The seams between hull planking, once so minimal it took a heavy mallet to drive in the caulking, now wept sea water at a rate that made the pump's efforts paltry.

Ben, Simon, Edward and Harry took turns quickly visiting the upper deck during rest periods, to discover which line had given way or what else had been lost overboard. The rowboat was gone, torn from its chocks and ripped through the railing on its way into the sea. More hands were needed to contain the damage topside, stealing away shoulders and arms to drive the pump. A monster wave charged into the hull from the side and rolled the *Raven* almost completely over, putting out lanterns and throwing everyone into darkness. The ship lingered on her side and seemed to surrender. They held their breath, waiting through agonizing seconds for her to roll back. There was a ragged murmur of relief as the *Raven* rolled sickly onto to her belly again, to once again swim as best she could.

Ben panicked on deck, having joined with Simon and Edward as the ship righted, but unable to find Harry. Each man tied to one of the masts, and leaned near the railing, calling out into the angry darkness. Harry heard the calls and slipped down from the mainsail boom where he had grabbed a knotted line among the sail folds when the ship rolled over. They grabbed him and slapped his back in the heavy wind and rain, joyful of finding him alive.

The wind was blowing stronger, but Ben was reluctant to shorten the storm sail any more for fear it would not keep them before the wind, and risk the ship to broaching waves coming over the stern. The ship continued to gallop over angry waves, hitting her hull hard at the bow on the far side of them, as the wind shrieked through the rigging like a thousand banshees, hiding the sound of the damage.

How long can she take this before she ruptures?

There was no sense of time. The storm and the pumping seemed endless, as if there had never been anything else and it would go on forever. Shoulders and arms burned within muscles losing their strength to pain and exhaustion. At the pumps the water was half way to the knees of the pumpers. The weight of the water was holding the ship lower, pulling her down from the surface, fighting her intention to rise above each wave, and spilling more seawater across her deck. Water dripped down onto their heads from the overhead deck where those seams there losing their fight to hold the water out.

The pump jammed. The handles locked into their last

position. Edward stumbled down from the upper deck, found a wrench, and worked by the feel of his fingers, kneeling waist deep in the water, to dismantle the pump from the hull. As he raised it up into the lantern light, he smiled.

"Thank God it's one I know about," Edward said.

Abraham held a plank under the pump as a work table as Edward opened the mechanism under the lamp. Others stood next to them, keeping them upright as the hull slammed into the sea again, and trying to ignore the sluggishness of the hull rising back up. Ben and Sonja stood nearby, the water up to Sonja's knees. All of the partitions in the hold were pulled down by the sloshing water, laying limp and useless, slender pieces of wood framing were broken like frail bones, as the ship rocked to onslaught of the waves.

Edward looked up and smiled again, "Slipped cotter pin! Just need to bend it back. Need some grease.

Cephus dashed from the doorway back to the galley, and returned with a hand full of jelled cooking grease, gouged from its pot.

"Excellent," Edward said.

He scooped fingers full of grease and smeared it on components of the pump. Moments later he worked the retaining screws back into place on top of the keel beam and reset the intake at the bottom of the hull. After a few practice pushes to confirm the pump was fixed he stood away from the pump.

"Next!"

Joseph and Miles took positions at the pump handles and returned to the mechanical exertion of pumping the water out. Outside, the wind reduced unnoticed and the wave caps rose no farther than ten feet. Ben committed himself and the crew to shares of the pumping, letting the sounds outside alert him to any need to go on deck. The hours drifted on as unbroken cycles of burning arms followed by uncomfortable rest periods letting them drift loosely in the water at their sides. They sat almost chest deep in the water, their clothing saturated, no longer avoiding it, just grateful to sit awhile.

Outside, the charcoal clouds begrudgedly allowed a sliver of dawn at the distant horizon. Sonja took her turn opposite Cephus, noticing the water was half way between her knee and her ankle.

"We are pumping it out!" she yelled.

In the blur of hellish exhaustion, no one else had noticed. Half smiles and hopeful mumbles moved among the prisoners of the hull, serving the pumps. Ben dragged himself to his feet and climbed the steps to the deck, pushing aside the hatch. On deck he could see the dawn beyond the bow. The waves had reduced to six feet, and the wind blew briskly, but no longer with the ominous shrieking that had raged all night. He heard a bird in the distance, calling, but could not identify it, and paid it no further attention. Simon made his way toward the stern, his back bent in exhaustion, grabbing at lines or surfaces to help him stay on his feet. Harry and Edward stumbled toward the bow looking for new damage. The strange bird called again, but Ben's mind only partially paid it heed.

It almost sounds like a word. Must be injured. Maybe not a bird. Porpoise?

"Ben," Simon yelled, grabbing the line to one of the sea anchors, pulling at it. "Ben," he yelled again.

Ben sighed and moved slowly toward the stern.

What now?

31

Simon hauled on the line, grinning like a madman. He said nothing, pulling with renewed strength, stopping for only a second to point frantically at the far end of the line. A hundred yards behind the *Raven*, among the knotted ends of the trysail tied together in haste as a sea anchor to save the ship, Ben saw a bald ruddy face crowned at the edges with white frosty hair.

"Adam," he screamed.

A minute later, with Edward and Harry also pulling on the line, they hauled Adam out of the ocean and onto the deck, letting him slide gently down onto the deck, coughing out seawater and cussing as he exhaled.

"It took you long enough, God damn it!"

Sonja heard them and moved stiffly from the hatch, kneeling beside Adam, kissing him on his cheeks, and stroking his sparse hair along the side of his head.

"Oh quit," he said.

"You're in trouble, Adam," Ben said. "You hid all night just to keep from having your turn at the pump. You ought to be lashed, sailor."

Adam looked around the deck, and smiled up at Ben. "Kiss my ass, young'un." Then he added, "We lose anybody else?"

Ben stopped smiling. "No, Adam. Our only loss was you...and it was almost more than my heart could take."

"Oh bullshit," Adam said, looking away.

Ben turned to Edward and Harry. "Please get him to his bed in the crew's quarters."

As they lifted him to his feet, Harry said. "Come on, slacker. Maybe we'll get a full day's work out of you tomorrow, after you lollygagging all night ."

"You can kiss my ass, too, Harry Rodgers," Adam said, as he put his arms around their shoulders.

Ben inspected the condition of the deck with Sonja and Simon, then joined Harry and Edward as they emerged from the crew's quarters.

"I think it wise, just to keep the storm sail and sea anchors just as they are, and help bring the water down in the hold."

After pumping two more hours, Ben stopped the pumping and watched the water level for another hour, while Miles tapped grease covered hemp lines into the larger seams. The water had risen only two inches, so the pumping resumed for another hour as Abraham took over packing other seams. At the end of the next rest hour, the water level did not rise. Men laid wherever they could, still not being bothered by wet surfaces, and napped. Sonja went to the captain's cabin.

When they thought it was near noon, Edward and Ben fished out the sextant from its storage chest, in hopes of finding a view of the sun between the clouds, so they could determine their position. Seas were still rough, but within reason, so Harry was sent up the mainmast to watch for other ships or land masses.

The cloud cover broke in some places, offering sporadic glimpses of blue sky, but they were quickly hidden by lower clouds scudding across. The ship's clock had run down during the worst of the storm, and had not been rewound, making it useless in determining longitude. Their position east or west could only be a guess. Still, if they could get a midday sighting at the sun, they could determine their north/south latitude. The sun peeked through an opening Ben and Edward guessed to be late morning, and they managed to get complimentary sightings with the sextant.

"A least we have a sense of how far north or south we are from Charleston, Ben," Harry said.

Ben nodded and inspected the ship's compass. "Yes. We have latitude, and it's almost perfectly aligned with Georgetown, perhaps slightly south. We must have been driven farther southward before we entered the Gulf Stream, but I fear our Longitude is far far to the east. I think we could be closer to Bermuda than to South Carolina."

They both examined the charts again and discussed the condition of the ship.

"Those greased line caulks are only temporary. I don't think this ship could take another storm and stay afloat," Ben said.

"I agree, Ben. She needs to be beached, so we can get to the seams from the outside with caulking made with good oak shavings and pitch. We have both on board in barrels. And we could probably get more shavings anywhere we land."

Ben pulled out a chart that had more details of Bermuda. "If our readings are correct we are near or on a line that would take us directly east to Bermuda. It might be today or tomorrow or the next day, but I still believe that is our closest harbor."

Edward put his finger on Bermuda. "I have been to this part. It called Saint George's Island. There is a wide well protected beach with a gentle slope, in a small lagoon-like bay called Tobacco Beach."

"Land, ho," yelled Harry.

Ben and Edward exchanged smiles. "Surely not," said Edward.

Ben cupped his hands around his mouth, "Where away," he yelled.

There was a moment's pause. No horizon nor sun's reference was available to Harry. "Wherever the bow is pointed," he answered.

Edward grinned to Ben. "Land sighted to the East, Captain."

Ben smiled. "Bermuda. It must be. There is nothing else that far out. Let's put some sails up and draw in our sea anchors."

Three hours later they moved cautiously between

house-sized boulders of volcanic rock at the mouth of Tobacco Bay. The water was a beautiful translucent teal under a brilliant blue cloudless sky swept by a balmy breeze. The bay was three times the length of the *Raven*, with only barely enough room to turn around. While Ben steered the ship with Sonja nearby on the other wheel, Edward studied the tidal lines on the rocks and the ocean water swirls around them.

"We're receiving additional luck, Ben. We appear to be arriving on a rising tide. I suggest we let her slip onto the sand across the bay before the tide peaks."

The hull of the *Raven* gave out a long hiss as she slid onto the white sand in the shallow water. Within minutes, Miles started a fire on the beach to melt the pitch as Abraham showed some of the other Solomons men how to hammer caulking into the seams. Local inhabitants began to drift to the beach to share or sell food to the new arrivals. The first day, most attention was paid to allowing everyone rest and dry out. Ben ordered shifts be arranged, so someone could keep safe vigil over the ship and the sleepers.

One local who appeared to be of Spanish origin and called himself Roberto, appeared very willing to help wherever he could, and refused any offer of payment.

"It is my Christian duty to help you, Capitan, as I was helped when I first came to this beautiful island," he told Ben. "And perhaps tomorrow or the next day, you could give me passage to the main Island when you leave. I have been offered a very nice job there with my brother, working for the Royal Navy. I would be happy to introduce you to the quarter master there. I have a cousin who works for him."

At low tide, the expanded crew swarmed over the exposed side of the hull, repairing the seams. With all the men available, the work was complete and there was time to rest before high tide. As the tide changed, the *Raven* was gently pulled onto her repaired side, allowing access to the other. Night fell on the next rising tide with a bright full moon. Heavier stowed items were removed to the

290

beach to lighten the ship. Roberto coordinated with several fishermen to take lines from the stern of the ship once she floated and pull her into the center of the little bay.

"I am amazed at how much work we accomplished in such a short time," Ben told Sonja.

"Roberto has been so helpful," she said, "and the Solomons men are amazingly skilled craftsmen. They will do well in the north and have good lives for their families."

Ben smiled and sighed. "Soon we will be fully repaired and on our way back."

"Back to the Chesapeake," Sonja added.

Ben opened his mouth to say more, but hesitated, enjoying the moment with her.

Ben asked Edward to set the anchors, and then open a rum barrel for the men. He was becoming reluctant to differentiate between the crew and the Solomons men, imagining them all as a single crew, even though he knew otherwise. The days were long and the sun rejuvenating. The local food was fresh, abundant and inexpensive. He could see in the faces of everyone the resurgence of strength and will.

Night was falling. Ben stepped into the cabin with Sonja. The air was warm and fresh. The wood in the cabin was dry. The cotton sheets on the bed felt luxurious as he stretched his muscles and nuzzled next to Sonja. His intent for more sensual time with Sonja slipped out of the window, as they held hands and both drifted off to uneventful restorative sleep to the sound of tropical surf.

The sun was up over the horizon when Ben and Sonja awoke and made their way on deck to the smell of coffee from the galley and coconut from the island. Many of the men were still sound asleep, some dozing on the upper deck, others in their cots or hammocks down below. All the hatches were open to the air. Canvas funnels were erected to capture the breeze and send it below. They had given so much for everyone's survival, and now they deserved some pampering. Ben and Sonja ambled down to the galley to get coffee.

Cephus was humming in the galley frying huge steaks

of white fish and local chicken eggs, acquired with Ben's permission and filling a few local jugs with rum. Ben took up chairs from the captain's cabin so he and Sonja could enjoy their breakfast on deck in the morning breeze.

"Ahoy, *Raven*," Roberto called up from his rowboat as he grabbed onto the ladder. "May I come on board, por favor?"

"Come ahead, Roberto", Ben yelled from his chair.

Sonja smiled at him as he came on to the deck. "Good morning, Roberto," she said.

"It was a wonderful morning, Senora," he said, bowing slightly to Sonja and flashing a wink to Ben. "I am bringing a cousin or two from the village to see this beautiful ship, *Raven*, Capitan," he said to Ben, "With your permission, por favor?"

"Of course," Ben said, "Bring them up and introduce them to me."

Roberto turned and signaled his cousins to come up. A smiling face rose over the edge of the deck on the ladder, followed by another, and then another, all quietly smiling and all standing very close behind Roberto.

Ben began to move in their direction with his hand out, while the cousins continued to smile blankly. Then he frowned and turned his head toward Sonja, opening his mouth to speak as he did, "Sonja…"

"I am so sorry, Capitan Ben " Roberto announced, " but my cousins and my friends wish to have this beautiful ship, and we ask that you remove yourself and the lady to the beach." He continued to hold the smile indicating to the men behind him, and four more climbing aboard ship from the other side, each now displaying a pistol or rifle. As they assembled in front of Ben and Sonja, pointing their weapons at their faces, a sleeping form on the deck jumped up and ran toward the aft hatchway. Before the man could drop down out of sight, one of Roberto's men shot him in the back, blowing a cloud of blood spray before him and driving him face down onto the deck. His body twitched and his legs trembled for a few seconds and then he stopped moving.

"Such a shame," Roberto said. "He would have been worth two hundred pesos in Cuba, our next port of call for our beautiful new *El Cuervo*." He pointed his pistol at Sonja while he looked at Ben, his smile fading under a growing frown. "Now, Capitan, you will call up your crew and tell them to behave, and none of them will be harmed."

Ben looked at the dead man, watching the pool of blood spreading on the deck, and stared at Roberto. "I have seen too many blood stains on the ship," he said.

"We only want your ship, and the Negros you have below, not more blood. I'm sure the Royal Navy will be happy to get you home to America."

One of the men standing closest to Roberto whispered into his ear. He huffed out his breath toward Ben and shook his head. "I know where they are Capitan," he said to Ben. With a flip of his hand, Roberto pointed toward the bow at the door to the crews quarters and gave an order in Spanish.

Two of the men behind Roberto raised their rifles and moved toward the bow. They stopped a few feet before the door and called out, "Come out amigos. All is well. Your Capitan wants you to come out."

Adam's sickly voice made its way to the boarders. "The door is stuck. We were just in a storm and it is warped. Help us get out!"

The man rolled his eyes and grabbed at the door with his empty hand The other man lowered his rifle and looked back toward Roberto laughing. Adam sprang out, stabbing the closest man in his chest, and bringing his pistol to the face of the other man, blowing the back of his head onto the deck. As the man's body crumpled to the deck, Simon charged out with a pistol and another knife. He shot one of the men standing near Roberto, and charged toward them with Adam at his side. Harry and Edward came out behind them and joined the charge, carrying knives before them and yelling as loud as they could. Roberto spun around and shot. Adam grabbed his throat and crashed to the deck. Roberto's men turned to face the charge, bringing their rifles up to shoot.

From the ladder way near Ben and Sonja, the Solomons men scrambled onto the deck with knives and belaying pins, attacking the boarders in a frenzy. The charge from the forward hatch shocked Roberto's men and in the moment of confusion over which group to fire on, the crew and the Solomons men were on them. Those not shot or stabbed dropped their guns and raised their hands.

While the *Raven*'s men bound the boarders and threw the dead overboard, Ben ran to Adam and the fallen Solomon's man. Adam lay on his back struggling to breathe. The bullet had destroyed his throat and blown out the back of his neck. He looked at Ben from the deck and smiled, his mouth forming words with no breath to speak them aloud. Still grinning, the lights left his eyes and his breathing stopped.

"God damn it!" he yelled.

He stepped to the other man and rolled him onto his back. He was breathless and already growing cold. It was Joseph. "Oh God damn it to Hell," he screamed.

Ben reached over and pulled Adam's knife from the chest of the first man Adam had killed. He stood up and marched to the boarders, pushed tightly together by the crew, hands tied behind their backs. He pointed the knife at Roberto.

"Lay him down," he ordered.

Harry and Abraham grabbed Roberto's arms and slammed him onto his back. Ben straddled Roberto's waist. The blood rushed through Ben's head, pounding in is ears. Dark red pooled at the edges of his vision and drifted inward, like a dark circular curtain being pulled closed toward the center.

"No, Ben!" Sonja screamed.

Ben placed the knife point over Roberto's heart.

Roberto cried out, "No, Capitan, No! I wanted no bloodshed. I said 'no blood'."

"You killed my dearest friend," Ben said between gritted teeth. "I knew him since my childhood. He was all the family I had left from the days of my father."

"No! Jesus! No," Roberto cried.

Ben brought the palm of his other hand over the knife handle and began to push the knife in.

"No! No Ben!" Sonja yelled

Roberto began to pray. Ben slowly pushed the knife down farther.

"You don't get to pray, you bastard. You're not going to heaven on an apology. I'm sending you to Hell."

Ben placed one hand over Roberto's mouth. Roberto began to scream under Ben's palm. Ben leaned forward with his chest over the knife and pushed the blade steadily through Roberto's heart, down into and through his spine, and impaling its tip in Roberto's hands behind him. Blood poured from Roberto's chest, bathing Ben's hands and forearms with his blood, saturating Ben's pants at his knees. Roberto struggled and twitched, his last words a bloody stifled scream bubbling up between Ben's fingers. His shoulders and legs trembled briefly, then he was still.

Sonja ran down into the cabin. Ben stood, blood dripping from his hands, the blood on his pants seeping down through the fabric toward his feet. He sniffed and rubbed his nose with the back of his hand, smearing his cheek with blood. He turned to face the *Raven*'s men.

"Throw this piece of garbage overboard," he said.

Two men grabbed the body and heaved it into the bay. A ruby colored flower spread over the teal surface, like a budding poppy. Ben walked back to Adam's body, kneeled beside it, folding Adam's hands across his chest, and bowed his head crying.

"What about the rest of these men?" Edward asked.

Ben did not raise his head to answer. "Cut their throats and throw them overboard."

Roberto's men wailed for mercy. Simon and Edward stood back in silence without expression, as others quickly carried out the order. Each penitent's voice was replaced with the sound of gurgling blood, until no voice remained.

Sonja locked herself within the cabin. Ben remained on the deck, sitting beside Adam, drinking himself into a stupor,. During the night some of the *Raven*'s men gently lifted Ben's hand off Adam's chest. They sewed Adam and

Joseph into canvas bags, laying them side by side for burial the next day. Lettie brought a wet cloth to wash the blood from Ben's face and arms.

Just before sunrise, Sonja stepped quietly on to the upper deck and found Ben asleep on his face, laying next to the spot where Adam died. Ben's his knife and a dirty scrub brush lay next to him. The two stains where the men died had been scrubbed, but they would remain there forever. Within each stain, the deck had been cut and gouged. In the middle of one stain Ben had carved the name 'Joseph'. In the middle of the other, it read 'Adam Tuttle'. Sonja kneeled beside Ben and placed her hand on his back, then bowed her head over him and wept.

32

Three days following the death of Adam, the *Raven* sailed west from Bermuda. They reduced sail over deep water, and buried Adam and Joseph. The Solomons men sang a mournful African song learned from their mothers, and sung for years over too many slaves. Afterwards, they raised sails and let the wind take them away.

The ship dried inside as they ran across a strong friendly wind over mild ocean waves. Above them, a soft blue sky was spotted with cotton ball clouds meandering toward the north. Warm sunshine mellowed by the breeze bathed them. The stress of the fight with Roberto's pirates, and the loss of Joseph and Adam weighed heavily on everyone. Sonja and the *Raven* men were still disappointed that Ben's course would take them back to Georgetown. Harry stood at the windward wheel, while the expanded crew took care of the sails under Edward's watchful eyes, or worked for Cephus.

Ben and Sonja stood together near the bow, watching the nearby porpoise race the ship. Ben's murder of Roberto and the execution of the others remained a dark cave that no one wished to enter. Sonja had been silent to Ben until the sailing routine returned at sea. The day had begun with unimportant small talk between them, but kept circling back to Georgetown, like their course.

"I still don't see why we need to risk going back there, Ben," she said.

Ben blew his breath out at the ocean. "I can only say again what I've already said. We need to make a profit for the *Raven*. The society only provides funds for rescue purchases, but I need to show a profit for the ledgers, and more importantly so we can afford to sail this ship. My commitment to Anthony...my commitment to this...endeavor...is an additional duty, beyond the business of this ship. Without profit we cannot afford supplies and we cannot afford to pay a crew, and we will not sail."

"But Ben..."

He spun around to face her, and grasped her shoulders. "Why else did we spend six months on the damned ship to claim her, if we don't work her? This was our dream."

"And what is Jeremiah Williamson's dream, Ben? Does it include learning that we still have the ten slaves on board that you told him you were selling in Charleston? The slaves he expected to buy, but then threw us out when you refused to sell them to him? He is a powerful man. Do you really want to risk that?"

"He is twelve miles up a river from Georgetown, Sonja. There is little risk."

She sighed and folded her arms. She closed her eyes to the disagreement and tried to push the tension out of her chest and in the silence between them opened her eyes and forced herself to examine the rigging and the sails. Her eyes floated from one article to another, searching for something else to focus her mind. Her eyes drifted toward the deck, but she abruptly spun around to face the sea, leaning heavily on the rail. Ben instinctively grabbed her waist to ensure she did not slip overboard, but immediately realized he was overreacting and dropped his hands.

"I cannot look at the deck here," she said. "my heart can't take it."

Ben looked out toward the far horizon in silence.

"Ben," Sonja said, placing her hand on Ben's forearm. "I saw Adam try to speak to you as he died. Could you tell what he was trying to say?"

Ben did not look at her, but spoke to the ocean. "Yes."

"What were his words, Ben?"

Ben chuckled softly, to Sonja's surprised. "He said 'Kiss my ass'."

Sonja bit her lip gently and shook her head, unable to withhold the smile. "That is so much like our Adam."

Ben nodded to the ocean. "This world will not see another man like Adam Tuttle in my lifetime."

A tear slipped down Sonja's cheek. She moved her hand to his. "You are a man like Adam Tuttle, Benjamin." She let her hand slip away and turned to face toward the stern. "But you have a demon inside you that can terrify me." Then she walked back toward the stern.

Close by Ben, the door opened from the crews quarters and Simon emerged.

Ben frowned at him. "Thought you were staying down in your cabin with Lettie?"

Simon shook his head. "Adam left a few things behind. I was bundling them up. I thought perhaps Hattie might like them. She was the closest he had to family."

Ben appeared surprised. "I guess when you worked for him, you learned more about him than I ever did."

"Not much more, I don't think. But Hattie saw through his bluster and doted on him like a sister. He once showed me the French gold coin he found on Spesutie Island. The one he wore on a string around his neck?"

Ben nodded his head, smiling at the image.

Simon patted the small canvas bag in his arms. "He said it was from Lafayette's gold, stolen from the man himself during the Revolutionary war."

"Yeah, I heard that from him as well," Ben said.

"Well there were three gold coins in his seabag, and only one had a hole in it..."

"You giving those to Hattie, too?"

"Of course, Ben. I'll bet they're worth sixty dollars. Probably more money than she has ever seen at any one time."

Ben smiled and nodded his head, then took in a deep breath. "So tell me some about what happened in Saint Mary's County, and how you wound up in a row boat off Solomons, in front of the *Raven*."

Simon leaned on the edge of the roof of the crew's

quarters and took in a deep breath. "You remember when I came to Havre de Grace in '41? Told you I had killed a man in Saint Mary's county."

"Not a thing I could forget, Simon."

"That was at Grayrocks."

Ben raised his eyebrows. "Oh..."

"When I left you on Spesutie Island, that's where I went. Lettie was there, and I went to get her. The ones you call the Solomons men are all from Grayrocks. Some of them helped her escape. The master and his brother had already decided to sell off some of their slaves. I think they suspected Joseph and Arthur had something to do with it, so they added them to be sold."

"Lettie told you all this?"

Simon chuckled and shook his head. "Ben it continues to amaze me how unaware white people are about communication between their slaves. It's better than the telegraph."

Ben stared at Simon with a wide-eyed smile.

"That surprises you, Ben?"

"No. I wasn't even thinking about that. Sometimes I forget that you were classically schooled by your owner at Sotterley Plantation, especially when you use words that sound like a professor."

Simon frowned. "Pay attention, Ben, if you want to know what happened."

Ben flipped up his palm toward Simon. "Pray continue, Professor."

"Lettie and I were hiding on an island in Saint Mary's River called Tippity Wichity. Friends brought us food. I heard that the slaves were to be sold, and they would be taken across the Patuxent to Solomons. Lettie and I walked two days through the woods to get to the Patuxent, then I stole a boat to get across to Solomons."

"And then I came along," Ben asked.

"No. First I heard a ship was going to pick up the slaves from Grayrocks at Solomons. Then I heard the ship was named *Raven*. That's when I knew it would be you, but we had to wait three more days in the swamp until you finally came. No game or snakes in a winter time swamp. We had gone two days without food."

"How is Lettie feeling today?"

"She got a fever in that swamp, and it's still with her some, but she is getting stronger."

Simon looked back toward the stern and watched Lettie talking with Sonja. "That helps too," he said.

Ben followed his eyes and smiled "You told me earlier that one of the Solomons men was her brother. Which one."

"Miles. He is a woodcarver, a carpenter like his Jesus," he said with a smile.

At noon, Ben and Edward brought out the sextant to take readings and consulted the ship's clock. They estimated a week more before returning to Winyah Bay. The wind remained steady, and the sky remained relatively clear both night and day, as if it was apologizing for the hatefulness of the storm. After discussing it with Edward, Simon and Harry, Ben decided to keep the sails up at night, since they were in the open ocean with a cooperating wind. The daily routine of the ship went unchanged and predictable. With fresh fruits and vegetables picked up on St. Georges Island before the attack, and the remaining stock already aboard, there was plenty of food. Two of the Solomons men, Bartrum and Michael, were discovered to have excellent cooking skills and began rotating with Cephus, who happily spent his working hours on deck.

Edward assigned the men among three crews, keeping an experienced seaman on each crew, and allowing a scheduled rest time for all of them. No sooner had he established the shifts, than a brief storm blew in and all were called to duty. The storm was a minor one and blew it itself out within several hours, causing no damage to the ship. Passing beyond the storm also brought them farther from the tepid air of Bermuda and closer to the cooler air of wintering America. Over the next days they shifted through the seasons of summer and autumn, and then into mild winter.

On the seventh day, they crossed the Gulf Stream and

adjusted their course slightly southward to counter the Stream's gentle current to the north. That sundown, Ben required the sails to be shortened until daylight, out of concern for nearing land or coastal shipping. During the night another ship was sighted by its stern lantern, but Ben and Edward estimated it was more than a mile off. The following morning, Ben sent men up the main mast in shifts to watch for land. That evening as the crew were shortening sail again, the man up the mainmast spotted the sliver of land under the setting sun and yelled out, "Land Ho!" Ben ordered sails shortened again to hold the ship in deep water until morning, and several hours later Edward watched the pinpoint of light from the North Island Lighthouse dancing across the lens in his telescope.

As the sun rose on the following day, the *Raven* sailed into a cold Winyah Bay with the intent to anchor off North Island, but spotted the pilot boat waiting near the lighthouse. Ben steered toward the pilot boat as the *Raven* crew lowered most of her sails to allow the ships to meet nearby.

Ben grabbed his speaking trumpet and yelled to the Pilot ship. "Ahoy Pilot Boat, is your pilot on board?"

The pilot came to the side railing with the trumpet in his hand. "Ahoy *Raven*! Welcome back, Sir. Are you ready for me to come aboard, or will Palmetto Haven send it's steamer again? I've heard nothing about that."

"No steamer to welcome us this time, Sir. If you will kindly come aboard," Ben yelled.

A dingy tied to the Pilot Boat was pulled close while the Pilot climbed down into it, and rowed to the *Raven*. The Pilot brought up the bowline as he came up on deck and handed it to Edward to tie onto the stern of the *Raven*. He looked around at the few faces on deck, not seeing the other two crews already sent below deck.

"Mr. Conner, at your service," the Pilot said as he shook hands with Ben. "How was your trip to Charleston, Sir?"

"Eventful," Ben answered.

Mr. Conner stepped to the closest wheel and laid his

hands on the handles, turning the wheel slightly in each direction to feel the resistance. "She has a firm rudder, sir. You must enjoy sailing her."

"I do," said Sonja, standing close by with her hands on her hips.

Ben suppressed a smile while Conner smiled openly at her and tilted his head in acknowledgement. Then he returned his attention to Ben. "If you would raise sufficient sails, Captain, I will be happy to steer you to the mouth of the Sampit."

An hour later they sailed past Rabbit Island and anchored near the steam tug *Hannah* waiting for fares at the mouth of the Sampit River. Ben signed Mr. Conner's ledger and thanked him for his assistance, and then escorted him to the side ladder so he could return to his dingy. The Pilot Boat nuzzled up close to the *Raven*, allowing Mr. Conner to get on board with the least amount of rowing. As the Pilot Boat sheered away and sailed south, the harbor steamer *Hannah* belched black smoke from her stack and moved close.

"May we tow you in, *Raven*?" The *Hannah's* captain called.

"Yes, If you would be so kind," Ben answered through the trumpet.

The *Hannah* moved closely before the *Raven* and received the tow line tossed by Harry. The water briefly churned beneath the side wheels as the *Hannah* took the weight of the *Raven* and pulled her up the river to the city docks. As they neared the southern end of the docks *Hannah* slowed almost to a stop and a member of its crew pointed emphatically at the dock, where stacks of lumber were pushed up against dozens of barrels, with only the barest minimum of space between all the material and the edge of the dock. The Hannah dropped the tow rope into the water, steered away from the direction of the *Raven* and put her paddle wheels in reverse. That allowed the *Raven* to slip forward between the *Hannah* and the docks. The captain of the *Hannah* stood outside his pilot house with speaking trumpet.

"You must moor there, *Raven*," he yelled.

Edward had the rest of the men come on deck to help with lines. Ben sent the crew scrambling to toss out mooring lines around the nearing posts to check the motion of the ship and draw her near the docks. As the *Raven* midships came beside the *Hannah*, the steam tug nudged her against the dock, twisting and pinching the canvas fenders the *Raven* crew had hurriedly tossed over the railings on port side. The *Raven* rocked slightly stern to bow as the lines held. From the deck, the view of the dock was completely blocked by the mass of lumber and barrels. Beyond the *Raven*, the *Hannah* made a tight circle for her return to the mouth of the river, passing close to the *Raven* again. Hannah's captain leaned out the pilot house door with his speaking trumpet.

"You must see the Harbor Master at once, *Raven*," he yelled "At once! He is waiting on you!"

Ben and Edward traded glances and both shrugged their shoulders. Ben suggested to Sonja and a few of the crew members to take advantage of the time so near shops, to buy what they needed. He advanced each crewman ten dollars, and apologized to the Solomons men that they must stay on the ship and go below decks if any one came on board.

Across the narrow river channel from the docks, Ensign Cuttingham stood on the little deck of the *Lydia* watching intently as the *Raven* docked. He was lower than the *Raven*'s deck, but saw the heads of all those on her deck. He snapped his fingers and ordered his crew to throw more wood into the firebox and the Boson to steer away. They were developing more steam as the Lydia sailed unnoticed beyond the *Raven*.

"I think Master Williamson will be happy to hear our man Pulaski has so soon returned," Cuttingham said to himself.

As soon as Ben entered the Harbor Master's office and introduced himself, the master stood red-faced.

"Pulaski! Pulaski of the *Raven*? Is that you," he asked.
"Yes, sir."

The Harbor Master slapped his hand on his desk. "You

and your company have the damndest nerve! Just like Yankees!"

"We are Marylanders, sir."

"Well, your company is Yankee and pushy, and you Captain, are damned, rude!"

"I don't understand."

"You and your damned 'Argyle Corporation' have hogged a damned empty berthing space for fifteen days! How can I keep an orderly harbor when absentee ships and Yankee companies block the damned docks?"

"Sir I am here to purchase rice and lumber. I was told I would need to engage a tug to take my ship up the Waccamaw river to the Mansfield Plantation and Buck's Mill. I never needed a berth here in Georgetown to do that."

The Harbor Master snatched several papers from his desk and shook them at Ben. "You people need to talk to each other and by God, talk to me! I'm the damned Harbor Master!"

At the lagoon-like bend in the Waccamaw River, where the Palmetto Haven canal kissed the river, the private steam tug *Lydia* leaned in its turn and dashed into the canal at full speed.

"Sir," Ben said. "You obviously know much more than I do. Please let me know what has happened that pertains to me or the *Raven*, and I give you my word that I will do the right and honorable thing for your office."

The Harbor Master took in a deep breath, then slowly let it out. He took his seat and indicated the chair in front of his desk for Ben. He spread the crumpled papers he held on the desk top and flattened them out with the palm of his hand.

"Number one, you have rented a berth on this dock for fifteen days. There are fees due for that." He laid the paper in front of Ben. " Number two, your company, through a local agent, contracted with Mr. Buck's Lumber Mill for several thousand board feet of two inch thick long leaf pine lumber, which was delivered to my docks, for which

305

I have received the invoice, and which should have been acted upon days ago." He laid the second paper in front of Ben. "Number three, your company, contracted with Mansfield Plantation for two dozen barrels of milled rice, which was delivered to my docks, for which I have received the invoice, and which should have been acted upon days ago." He laid down the next paper.

He glared at Ben over the growing stack.

"Number four, you have illegally occupied a berth at dockside for fifteen days, without advanced reservation or arrangements with this office, for which there is a fine to be paid forthwith." He laid down another paper. "Number five, your company has illegally stored merchandise on my docks for ten days without permit, for which there is a fine to be paid forthwith." He laid down yet another paper.

He spoke louder. "Number six, you were brought here using a Pilot under the pay of Georgetown, and a steam tug operating directly under the orders of this office, for which there are the customary fees, which are due immediately." He laid down the last paper and leaned back in his chair crossing his arms and scowling at Ben.

The front door to the Williamson mansion burst open and Cuttingham dashed through the halls to the den. Jeremiah Williamson stood from his desk with fire in his eyes.

"What is the meaning of this intrusion," Jeremiah demanded.

"Pulaski! Pulaski is back in Georgetown. I thought you would want to know, sir."

"Pulaski! God damned the man. Wouldn't sell me slaves from my own kin and hoodwinked gentlemen in Charleston to buy my slave off the block for a pittance!" Jeremiah started to turn, but stopped. "Get men who can shoot. Make sure they have guns and put them on the steamer. I will be there in a moment."

Cuttingham dashed to the Overseer's cottage.

Ben examined the papers in front of him. "The invoices

306

from the plantation and the lumber mill, for delivery here for my loading, as ordered by the Argyle Corporation, have payment due within 60 days." Ben looked directly into the Harbor Master's eyes. "I assure you sir, this obligation will not in any way involve you or your office."

Ben read the other documents, nodding his head in agreement as he read each. When he finished, he asked for a pencil, then totaled the fees and fines on the back of one of the papers. "These are all completely justified, of course, and the amounts are reasonable." Ben reached to his waist, opened his shirt and pulled up the canvas flap of his money belt. After quickly glancing around the office to ensure it was empty, he pulled out the necessary money, and counted it out in front of the harbor Master.

"I also offer my sincerest apologies for any ill will generated by the Argyle Corporation, and my humble apologies for any rudeness my ship or my presence has created for you, Harbor Master."

The Harbor Master counted the money, nodding to Ben during the apologies. "Well, seeing as you have so quickly resolved my issues with your vessel, I believe I have no need to detain you further."

Ben stood and shook hands with the Harbor Master, holding on to his hand he spoke further. "As a gesture of good will for the *Raven* and between us, since I intend to conduct more business in this beautiful harbor, I wish to offer a small barrel of fine Jamaican Rum for you to distribute as you see fit among your employees."

The Harbor Master stood and bowed. "Your gift will be happily received, Captain Pulaski."

As Ben walked out of the office, the Harbor Master muttered under his breath, "Pompous Ass."

As Ben walked out of the office, he muttered under his breath, "Pompous Ass."

Minutes later, Ben stood on the deck of the *Raven*, explaining the cargo on the dock to the extended crew. "We have to knock down all of the partitions to open up the hold. I don't know where we will sleep, but we have to make room for the cargo. Harry, I need you to go down to the hold and bring up a barrel of rum. Take it to the

Harbor Master's office, down the dock. Simon, let's move Lettie in with Sonja. That is going to be the one place women can have privacy for the next voyage." As the men scattered to follow their instructions, Ben went into town looking for Sonja and Edward.

The Steamer *Lydia* shoved her bow through the dark water of the Waccamaw, leaving a foot-high wake along the shore as she flew down the river. Jeremiah stood on the fore deck with ice in his eyes, gritting his teeth and fingering the handles of his new Aston percussion pistols. Behind the small pilot house stood Cuttingham and five men, each armed with pistols, rifles and fighting knives.

Jeremiah turned back toward the stern. "Kill anyone standing with Pulaski, but leave that bastard for me!"

The boson reduced throttle and made the turn into the Sampit River. Cuttingham pointed out the *Raven* to Jeremiah as they neared it.

"Pass it." Jeremiah said "Dock in front of the Harbor Master's office. He needs to know I am confronting a thief in his harbor. Might get him to impound that ship as well. Could use another."

Ben found Edward in a tavern not far from the ship, and joined him at the bar to share drink.

"Why don't you join me and Sonja for a warm meal, Edward."

"Oh, I don't want to intrude Ben..."

"Nonsense. I want you closer to me and my family, Edward. I want us to step back and meet each other anew."

Moments later the two men found Sonja in a millinery shop on front street. While Ben spoke privately with Sonja, Edward tried on a couple of the ladies' hats to the enjoyment of the mistress owner. Sonja selected the hat she wanted, an indigo felt with wide brim and a lavender ribbon around the cap. The three walked leisurely up the street to a well decorated tavern on the corner, where a lady and gentlemen had just come out. They were seated

308

right away and given hand written menus for their
selection.

Jeremiah stormed up the stairs to the Harbor Master's
office, bumping into Harry on his way down.

"Look where you're going, there," Jeremiah barked.
He turned back to his men. "Stay by the boat. Remember,
not Pulaski. Do what you want with any others, but
Pulaski is mine!"

Harry moved away quickly, but stopped behind the
next corner to peek back at the men. He noticed
Cuttingham in his uniform, and the heavily armed men
standing around him. He dashed up the alley way to Front
Street and ran down the street toward the ship. As he
passed the new Tavern he saw Edward sitting next to the
window, and ran inside.

"Edward," he called out as he zigzagged between the
tables, to the stares of the patrons. He spotted Ben and
Sonja with Edward as he neared. "We must go!"

"Why," Ben and Sonja spoke as one.

"There is a tall hateful man at the Harbor Master's
office with gunmen and a uniformed man waiting for him
at the dock." Harry said, then looked at Ben. "I think he
means you harm. He told his men to 'leave Pulaski to
him'."

Ben turned to Sonja. "Jeremiah Williamson was the
man who kidnapped Robert and put him on the block. He
must have discovered that I bought him under value."

"Would he kill for that" Sonja asked.

"Oh yes," Ben said as he stood. "We need to get back to
the ship and keep him off it."

When Ben returned to the ship, the dock was empty.
The *Raven*'s deck was crammed with lumber. They
trotted up the gangplank to find the men breathing
heavily and resting on the deck.

"It's all loaded, Ben," Simon told him. "We just
finished."

"Already?"

"We had eleven men and a woman, Benjamin! All with
good reason to be away from this place," Simon said.

"Excellent," Ben said. "Hateful men are coming here, and we cannot stay a moment longer!"

Ben looked at the sky, then glanced at the American flag flying over the Harbor Master's office down the dock. "The wind is right, Simon." Recognizing the Lydia moored nearby, Ben smiled. "Then let us be away," Ben said. "We have a westerly wind. Simon, Get everyone on deck. Harry, untie the mooring line at the bow and midships, but leave the stern tied for now. And raise the jibs, just the jibs. Edward, we are going to sail out of here!"

"Without a pilot or a steamer?"

"We'll have a steamer," Ben said.

He ran to the captain's cabin, ignoring Lettie's shriek as he charged in while she stood naked, washing. He grabbed his pistol, and stuck it in his waist, then ran out of the cabin and off the ship. He ran back up to Front Street and turned north.

In the Harbor Master's office, both Jeremiah and the Harbor Master were yelling at each other.

" God damn it!" Jeremiah bellowed. "He stole from me, and I want his ship impounded right now!"

"I don't have a warrant or orders from the proper authority Mr. Williamson. I will not allow this office to be subverted for your private deeds!"

"You will not be the God damned Harbor Master long!" Jeremiah bellowed. He kicked over the chair, burst out of the office and returned to the Lydia. He signaled the gunmen. "You come with me. Cuttingham, you stay here and keep steam up in this thing."

Jeremiah peered down the dock, locating the masts of the Raven near the end, and walked toward it. The gunmen followed close behind.

Jeremiah spoke over his shoulder. "Do not fire until I tell you."

Ben watched him walk away from the corner of the building, then dashed across the dock behind them. He bounded onto the Lydia while Cuttingham watched the boson toss logs into the fire box. Cuttingham turned as Ben's boot heel struck the deck and at the same moment

310

Ben shoved him hard in the chest, propelling him off the deck and into the river. Ben snatched his pistol from his waist and placed the barrel against the temple of the Boson.

"We are going for a little ride, Mister."

"Yes sir. Just say where."

"Back down the dock toward the ship that is starting to swing out."

There was very little room between the bow of the *Raven* and the opposite shore as the *Lydia* approached them. Ben pulled the rope to the steam whistle giving it two blasts.

Jeremiah turned to see the Lydia flash past, and stopped to stare. What the hell? Where is Cuttingham going?" then he heard Cuttingham's screams from back up the dock

Edward was on the bow of the *Raven* watching it swing slowly away from the dock when the *Lydia's* whistle blew.

"Throw me your bow line," Ben yelled to Edward.

Edward grabbed the coiled line and threw it to the *Lydia*. Ben grabbed it and tied it to the cleat at the stern of the steamer.

"We gonna have a hell of a jolt when we get to the end of that line, mistah," the Boson warned.

"Not if we do it right," Ben said with a mirthless grin. "Open the throttle all the way."

The Boson shook his head and pulled back on the throttle until it hit its limit.

"Cut the stern mooring," Ben yelled at the *Raven*, but Edward was already gone from the bow, and Ben could hear chopping from up on the deck. Someone on deck loosened the mainmast boom and swung it out over the river as the main sail was pulled up." The gentle breeze pushed the stern farther out into the river.

"Yes" screamed Ben, "Swing her ass around!"

Ben heard a gunshot and the planking near his boot exploded in ripped splinters where the bullet gashed the deck. He dashed around to the far side of the pilot house, and peeked back at the dock through the *Lydia's* windows. The Boson ducked down as two more gunshots

311

and splashes erupted on the nearby river surface.

"Keep your eyes on the river, Mister," Ben said.

The boson dropped to his knees, leaning his head out of the pilot house on the other side and reaching back in with his left hand to steer the boat.

The *Lydia* dashed ahead of the *Raven*'s bow and began snaking the bow line down river. The *Raven*'s jib sails were adjusted to give her headway as the stern swung out into the channel. As the *Lydia* became completely hidden from the gunmen, three more shots echoed off the marsh, followed by two thuds into the mud, and a final gash erupting on the stern.

Ben poked the boson with the barrel of his pistol. "Steer back closer to the dock side. Meet the tow line at an angle"

The boson smiled and nodded his head. "This won't be so bad after all, suh. We're just gonna dance her down the river."

As the *Raven* drifted toward the opposite shore, and her stern swung out, her bow and the steamer were moving in the same direction, only a few angles different. There was only a slight jolt of resistance as the steamer came to the end of the bowline, helping the *Raven* move faster from a rotation into a straight line. The steamer slowed as she took the weight of the *Raven*, and smoke form the stack thickened.

With the steamer out of sight from the dock and the *Raven* moving down the river, Jeremiah ordered his men to fire at the *Raven*, but no damage could be seen.

"What's your name, Boson?" Ben asked.

"Achilles, suh."

"How would you like to go up north, Achilles?"

Achilles smiled. "Oh yes suh. I would like that so much. Yes, suh!"

Ben lowered the pistol, uncocked the hammer, and slid it into his belt. "Then take us down Winyah Bay until we run out of steam."

Achilles released a broad grin as he stood up. He tossed more wood into the fire box with one hand and steered into the deep channel with the other. The *Raven* obediently followed behind, like a mother hound being pulled by her pup.

On board the *Raven*, those still on deck hid at the bow, behind thousands of linear feet of cured lumber between them and Jeremiah's gunmen. The only damage to the ship was to the windows of the empty captain's cabin, while Sonja and Lettie sat safely forward of the brick stove in the galley.

On the Georgetown docks, Jeremiah fired his pistols into the air, knowing the bullets would go nowhere near the ship. In a rage he threw his empty pistols toward the ship where they fell into the dark waters of the Sampit River.

"God damn you, Pulaski!" he screamed, stamping his feet. "God damn you!"

Bibliography

Raven's Risk is an historical novel, and writers of novels take liberties with dates and incidents to blend them into the story. We are known to fold the actions of multiple historic incidents and people into a single character for continuity. Although no academic work is actually cited in this book, I would be neglecting due homage to my interesting sources of historical information, without sharing a bibliography with the reader. At least here, I can identify the original truths I 'massaged' in writing this story. I also offer my humble apologies to the historic researchers I so crudely burglarized.

First, a confession of a blatant lie: The historic A.P. McCombs House in Havre de Grace, Maryland, was actually built in 1880. I was compelled to pro-create it in 1843 and litter it with iron stoves, spittoons and a couple extra rooms, as a setting for the larger-than-life Mamie Stewart.

Cautionary Notes: (1) Please note: Do not dig in the garden for gold French coins. They are not there, and you might be shot. (2) Spesutie Island is real, but belongs to the U.S. Army and may only be visited by aerial software on computers.

Anbinder, Tyler , *Nativism & Slavery, The Northern Know Nothings & Politics of the 1850s,* New York, Oxford University Press, 1992.

Bates, Bill, *Images of America, Havre de Grace,* Charleston: Arcadia Publishing, 2006.

Boyle, Christopher C., *Mansfield Plantation – A Legacy on the Black River,* History Press, Charleston, 2014

Brewington, M.V. , *Chesapeake Bay Sailing Craft,* The Calvert Marine Museum *and* The Chesapeake Bay Maritime Museum, Printed by the Anthoensen Press, Portland, 1986.

Carey, George G., *Maryland Folklore,* Centerville, Tidewater Publishers, 1989.

Clifford, J. Candace and Clifford, Mary Louise, *Nineteenth-Century Lights, Historic Images of American Lighthouses,* Cypress Communications, 2000.

Cumbo-Floyd, Andrea, *The Slaves Have Names,* Amazon Digital Services LLC, 2013

Dwyer, Eddie, *A Trip Into Yesteryear and a Tale of Granpa's Life Aboard a Canal Boat,* The Havre De Grace Record.

Glatfelter, Heidi L., *Havre de Grace in the War of 1812 'Fire on the Chesapeake',* History Press, Charleston, 2013.

Goodwin, Floyd Alister, *Survival of an Old Rice Plantation – Belle Isle, Georgetown, SC,* Publish America, 2009

Harford Historical Bulletin, Number 58, *The Tidewater Canal: Harford County's Contribution to 'The Canal Era'*, The Historical Society of Harford County ,Fall 1993.

Jay, Peter A., Editor, *Havre De Grace - An Informal History*, Havre De Grace, Sparrowhawk Press, 1994.

Kopczewski, Jan Stanislaw, *Kosciuszko and Pulaski*, Warsaw, Interpress Publishers, 1976.

Levine, Bruce , *Half Slave and Half Free - The Roots of the Civil War*, New York, Hill and Wang, Noonday Press, 1992.

Linder, Suzanne Cameron and Thacker, Marta Leslie, *Historical Atlas of the Rice Plantations of Georgetown County and the Santee River*, South Carolina Department of Archives and History, 2001

McAlister, Robert, *Wooden Ships on Winyah Bay*, *Charleston, History Press, 2011*

McAlister, Robert, *Life and Times of Georgetown Sea Captain Abram Jones Slocum, 1861-1914, Charleston, History Press, 2012*

McAlister, Robert, *The Lumber Boom of Coastal South Carolina, Charleston, History Press, 2013*

McAlister, Robert, *Georgetown's North Island, Charleston, History Press, 2015*

National Park Service Publication, *Underground Railroad,* 1998

Phillips, Christopher, *Freedom's Port - The African American Community of Baltimore, 1790-1860,* Chicago, University of Illinois Press, 1997.

Shaw, Ronald E., *Canals for a Nation - The Canal Era in the United States 1790-1860,* Lexington, The University Press of Kentucky, 1990.

Stranahan, Susan Q., *Susquehanna – River of Dreams,* Baltimore, Johns Hopkins University Press, 1993.

Sydnor, Charles S., *The Development of Southern Sectionalism 1819-1848,* Louisiana State University Press, 1948.

Waugh, John C., *The Class of 1846, From West Point to Appomattox: Stonewall Jackson, George McClellan and their Brothers,* Ballantine Books, New York, 1994

OTHER GENEROUS SOURCES OF INFORMATION:

The Susquehanna Museum at the Lockhouse, Havre de Grace, Maryland.

The Havre de Grace Maritime Museum, Havre de Grace, Maryland.

The Chesapeake Bay Maritime Museum, St. Michaels, Maryland.

The Saint Michaels Museum, St. Michaels, Maryland

The South Carolina Maritime Museum, Georgetown, South Carolina.

The Georgetown County Museum, Georgetown, South Carolina.

The Rice Museum, Georgetown, South Carolina.

Capt'n Rod's Lowcountry Tours, Georgetown, South Carolina. Well worth the reasonable cost of his narrated boat ride along the Pee Dee and Waccamaw Rivers, among the ghosts and descendants of past plantations.

ROBERT F. LACKEY lived in Havre de Grace, Maryland, for 23 years, spending many afternoons exploring the remnants of the Susquehanna and Tidewater Canal. He was a member of the Susquehanna Museum at the Lock House, and served a period as publisher for its newsletter. After moving to Havre de Grace from North Carolina in 1993, he fell in love with the little town sitting at the mouth of the Susquehanna River and head of the Chesapeake Bay. The area is rich in history and watershed culture reaching back to the beginning of the country. Among the many historic themes coexisting within the nearby sites and lanes, the Canal Era drew the author's attention first. Stepping outside technical writing to complete his first novel, *Pulaski's Canal,* Robert began a family story that has blossomed into a family saga. The series is planned to follow the Pulaski family from 1841 (Pulaski's Canal) to 1872 (Pulaski's Redemption).

"I wandered the trails and historic marker sites along the old Susquehanna and Tidewater Canal route, and it was easy for me to picture families centering their lives around the canal, the way community centers spring up along the interstates today. Of course I was drawn to the simpler times, barges only moved at three miles an hour, but my research identified not only the hard demands and historical challenges of that simpler life, but the richness of the world the people lived in then. Having access to the original gateway Lockhouse, still maintained by the local historical society, was an absolute thrill and it gave me my first backdrop.

Once the core characters of the story tumbled out of my imagination and onto the computer screen in front of me, they almost took on their own life. They frequently went in directions I had not planned in the earlier part of the day, but evolved as the story evolved. Ben and Sonja, and their sons Isaac and Aaron, ARE the 19th century. Ben was born on the first second of January 1, 1800, Sonja in 1805. The Pulaski experience encompasses the national experiences of that century, but from the eyes of a Maryland family on the canals. Much as today's national news is perceived from the living rooms and household budgets of American families.

Now they are dear friends, and I look forward to keeping their story going through the years after 1844. We will experience the changes that occurred in our country over the next two or three decades through them."

Robert is a member of the Historical Society of Harford County, Susquehanna Museum at the Lockhouse, Past President of the South Carolina Writer's Association, and a member of the Surfside Writer's group.

Robert currently lives with his patient wife, Sandi, in Murrells Inlet, South Carolina.

Coming Pulaski Saga Adventures

Bloody Ground, Shallow Graves

(Due out Summer 2020)

Brutal Peace

(Due out Winter 2020)

Pulaski's Redemption

(Due out Summer 2021)

Please visit Robert's website and Facebook(TM) page to learn about his current and future projects:

www.rflackeybooks.com

https://www.facebook.com/RFLackey.author

Books by Robert F. Lackey available at his website, and through Amazon.com, BarnesandNoble.com, Booksamillion.com, and other internet book sellers. Kindle versions are available through Amazon.com.

Share your thoughts about this novel. You can email Robert at

Rflackey.author@gmail.com